The Fifty and One

A BADGER BLISS BOOK

By

Karen D. Badger

DEDICATION

The meaning of family has never been clearer to Barb and me, having recently lost both our mothers, just a week apart. Being the oldest surviving sibling, I find myself stepping into the role of matriarch that my mother held for most of her eighty-six years. Those are some pretty big shoes to fill but I am proud to do it—especially for such exceptional brothers and sisters. All my love goes to Todd Dusablon and his wife Deb, Penny Tanner and her husband Jeff, Robert (Bobby) Dusablon, Jr., and my older brother in heaven, Steven Dusablon. Last, but certainly not least, to my mom, Eleanor Atherton, also in heaven, who was my number one fan. They have accepted me and supported me unconditionally, regardless of who I am or who I love. They are what family is all about.

I've been fortunate enough to have the full love and support of my biological family for all of my life, but just as important is the family of choice Barb and I have built around ourselves during the years. They include Darci Deo, Brenda Gomez and Sadie Deo-Gomez, Brenda Cadieux, Aretta Saunders, Cheyne Curry and Brenda Barton, Sheri Barnett and Kathey Durbin, Donna Brown, Carol Poynor, Natty Burns and Chris Jimenez, Kay and Sharon Carney, Nina Knapp, Lynn Ames and Cheryl Pletcher as well as hundreds of wonderful friends we have made who are too numerous to name, yet no less important to us. Thank you for your unwavering love and support!

ALSO WRITTEN BY KAREN D. BADGER AND AVAILABLE FROM BADGER BLISS BOOKS

ON A WING AND A PRAYER
YESTERDAY ONCE MORE (*Award Winner!*)
THE BLUE FEATHER
ALL MY TOMORROWS
1140 RUE ROYALE (*Award Winner!*)
OVER THE CRESCENT MOON (*2X Award Winner!*)
LOVE IN THE SHADOW

The Billie/Cat Commitment Series:
  IN A FAMILY WAY
  UNCHAINED MEMORIES
  HAPPY CAMPERS
  COLLECTIVE IDENTITY
  SWEET ANGEL
  RELATIVE-LY SPEAKING
  TAILSPIN
  FLASHPOINT
  IN THE BLINK OF AN EYE (*YA - Award Finalist!*)
  UDDER NONSENSE

www.badgerblissbooks.com

This is a work of fiction. All characters, locales, and events are either products of the author's imagination or are used fictitiously.

THE FIFTY AND ONE

Cover image: by Alina Vilchenko with attribution from Pexels
Cover design: by Karen D. Badger

A Badger Bliss Book
Published by Badger Bliss Books
Georgia, VT 05468

www.badgerblissbooks.com

Print book ISBN 13: 978-1-945761-36-2
Ebook ISBN 13: 978-1-945761-37-9

First Edition, August, 2021

Printed in the United States of America and in the United Kingdom

ACKNOWLEDGMENTS

I want to recognize those who worked to find my typos and fix my literary errors. A mere thank you is not enough to acknowledge the contribution of these wonderful women.

My literary squad includes Carol 'Chief Eagle Eye' Poynor, Aretta Saunders, 'Downtown' Donna Brown, Darci Deo, Callum Hancock, Nina Knapp, Mercedes Lewis and last but not least, Barb Sawyer, AKA, 'Bliss', my better half and keeper of my soul, and the most amazing plot doctor and sounding board an author could ask for.

A special thank you to Nat Burns, amazing editor and sister from another mother, who worked tirelessly to make this story the best that it could be.

One additional acknowledgement for Carol Poynor, who insisted on proofreading this book, even while struggling with chemo treatments, and despite my constant lectures about how her health was more important than any damned book! You are one of my heroes, Chief! Love you to the moon and back!

NOTE TO READERS

This book picks up two months after the events that occurred in my award-winning paranormal book, *1140 Rue Royale*. There are several references in this book to events that occurred in *1140 Rue Royale*, which could be considered spoilers if you have not yet read that book. Although this novel was written to be a stand-alone story, in my humble opinion, your reading enjoyment will substantially be increased if you are already familiar with the backstory of the characters who appear in both books.

1140 Rue Royale
First edition published by Badger Bliss Books, Sept, 2016
ISBN 13: 978-1-945761-00-3, ISBN 10: 1-945761-00-8
2017 Golden Crown Literary Society Award – Paranormal Fiction

Prologue

"Man, this place is like a maze!" the man said as he navigated his way through the St. Louis Cemetery No.1.

"Chuck, Look! There's another one piled with stuff," his companion, Curtis, said.

Both men ran to the aboveground tomb and sorted through the mound of offerings and mementoes left by visitors.

"I wonder if there's any jewelry in this one," Chuck said.

"There's only one way to find out."

The first man shoved his crowbar into a small opening on the front of the tomb and pushed as hard as he could until the panel moved.

Chuck stepped closer. "Hold on, Curtis. Let me get my hands in there and I'll pull while you pry," he said.

With much effort they managed to pry the vertical cement cover away from the tomb and allowed it to fall onto the ground where it shattered into several pieces.

"Oops!" Curtis chuckled.

It didn't take long for the two men to rummage through the bones, confiscating a necklace and a ring from the remains.

Curtis shoved them into his pocket. "That's all there is in this one. Let's move on."

For the next hour, the men desecrated five additional graves before they came to a tomb decorated with graffiti. Liquor bottles, bricks, flowers, food, pieces of clothing, letters, incense, and general rubble littered the front of the tomb. Several loose bricks also rested on top of the tomb. The front of the tomb looked as though it had been stuccoed at some point, but some of the plaster had fallen off to reveal the bricks beneath it.

"Wow, this one is a mess," Chuck said.

Chuck looked around on top of the tomb while Curtis sorted through the offerings stacked in front.

(Photo: Karen D. Badger, 2016)

"Nothing but a bunch of loose bricks up here," Chuck said. He grabbed one of the bricks and looked at it closely. "That's odd. This one is covered in wax."

"Forget that shit and come help me pry this open," Curtis said.

Chuck dropped the brick on the ground at his feet and assisted with the removal of the front panel. The nauseating odor of rotting flesh immediately wafted from the tomb.

"Jesus Christ!" Curtis exclaimed. "That's some nasty smelling shit."

"Let's rummage through this quickly and get the hell out of here," Chuck said.

Curtis reached into the tomb and immediately screamed. "Ahh! Let go of me!" he yelled.

Chuck watched in horror as he saw Curtis pulled into the tomb by some unseen force. His first instinct was to turn and run, and in doing so, he stepped on the wax-covered brick he had dropped to the ground and twisted his ankle. The impact of his foot on the brick effectively dislodged the wax. Chuck dropped to the ground and grabbed his foot just as a dark shadow ascended from the ground and engulfed him.

Chapter 1

1140 Royal Street, New Orleans, LA
(Photo: Karen D. Badger, 2016)

Elliot Walker pulled her car into the parking space in front of eleven forty Royal Street and turned off the ignition. She grabbed her briefcase and climbed out of the car. As soon as the car door opened, a heavy wall of humid air hit her square in the face.

Jesus, the humidity is enough to take your breath away, she thought. She was tempted to climb back into the comfort of her air-conditioned car.

Instead, she quickly closed and locked the car and hurried to the gated front entrance of the mansion she and her wife, Lia, had purchased six months earlier when work transferred them from New York City to New Orleans.

Elliot hurriedly unlocked the gate and let herself into the vestibule. The vestibule provided shade but did little to help Elliot escape the overwhelming humidity. She secured the gate and turned to unlock the intricately carved door leading into the lower level of her home. She stepped inside the ornate foyer and immediately basked in the coolness of central air conditioning.

"Damn, that feels good," she exclaimed to herself.

Elliot paused and remembered the first time she and Lia had stepped foot in this home. Lia made it no more than three feet into the foyer before she fainted away into Elliot's arms. When she came to, she spoke in a strange voice, which they later determined was that of a young slave girl. A young girl who had died in that house at the hands of her savage mistress, during a time when slaves were little more than disposable property.

They had almost passed on buying the house because of the horrid events that had taken place there in the eighteen hundreds. The aristocratic doctor and his wife, who owned the property at that time, had reportedly tortured and murdered many of their slaves in the fourth story attic. Lia, being a woman of color, struggled with the thought of living in a place where her people had been so mistreated, but after a time, she convinced herself that it would be a matter of honor and poetic justice to own the home where at one time, people like herself were considered subhuman.

Lia and Elliot experienced odd events soon after they moved in. Lia, in particular, saw images of the young girl appearing at various places within the house, only to vanish without a trace.

The most disturbing for Elliot was when the spirit of a slave woman named Celeste possessed Lia. It was through Celeste, that Lia experienced firsthand some of the horrific treatment that had befallen the slaves who lived there more than one hundred and eighty years earlier. It was also through Celeste that they had ultimately discovered the reason the Royal Street house was reportedly the most haunted property in New Orleans.

"Elliot, is that you?"

Elliot's reverie was interrupted by a voice calling to her from the floor above. It was Lia's voice. Lia, the love of her life and the one person she cherished more than life itself.

Elliot walked to the foot of the marble staircase that extended from the entry level directly to the third story. She looked up and saw Lia standing on the second-floor landing where the living area, dining room and kitchen were.

"Yes. I just got home."

"Before you come up, can you see if there's any mail in the box?" Lia asked. "Marissa and Julie are still waiting for the letter from the bank about their mortgage loan."

"Sure. Let me take a look."

Elliot sighed and mentally kicked herself for not checking the mailbox while she was still outside. Now, she had to go back into that oppressive heat and humidity again.

***

Elliot ascended the staircase and was met halfway by their cat, Miss Thing. Their feline friend had found her way into the house when they first purchased it and had refused to leave. The reason for her stubbornness became clear as events of their first few months in the home unraveled, but even with all that drama out of the way, the cat still staked her claim in their home and in their hearts.

Elliot stopped to scratch the cat under her jowls. "Hey there, Miss Thing. How was your day?"

"Elliot, are you coming up?"

At the sound of Lia's voice, the cat immediately turned tail and ran back up the stairs.

"Traitor," Elliot mumbled under her breath. "Yep! On my way," she called.

Elliot put her briefcase down on the second-floor landing so she could embrace her wife. She took Lia into her arms and kissed her passionately. Lia's arms easily found their way around Elliot's neck and her fingers threaded into the back of her boy-cut blond hair.

"Wow! That was some kiss!" Lia said.

"I missed you today," Elliot said. "It's Friday and I'm looking forward to spending the next two days making love to you."

Lia grinned. "That would be amazing, but are you forgetting we have house guests?"

"Marissa and Julie can entertain themselves," Elliot said.

"Well, depending on whether their letter is in today's mail, we might have the place to ourselves while they go house hunting."

Elliot grinned. "I'm going to miss them when they move."

"Me, too. I'm so glad they were here when everything happened last spring," Lia said.

Elliot touched her forehead to Lia's. "I know. If they hadn't been here, things might not have turned out so well. I still can't forgive myself."

Lia pulled her head back and placed her palm on the side of Elliot's cheek. "El, how many times do I have to say this? What happened was not your fault. You have to move past this. Okay?"

Elliot sighed and nodded.

Lia stepped out of Elliot's embrace and reached for the stack of envelopes that Elliot had retrieved from the mailbox. Lia shuffled through them. "Hopefully, their letter is in here."

Elliot picked her briefcase up from the landing and placed a quick kiss on Lia's cheek. "I'm going upstairs to get out of this monkey suit. I'll be right back."

"Okay, love. We'll be in the kitchen when you come down."

***

Julie looked up from chopping onions and saw Lia enter the kitchen, waving an envelope back and forth. She immediately put the knife down and ran to the kitchen door that exited onto the porch.

"Mar! It's here. The letter from the bank is here!" Julie said.

"Get outta Dodge!" Marissa exclaimed. She quickly returned the grill brush to its hook on the side of the grill and wiped her hands on the towel she had slung over her shoulder.

"It's here? Really?" Marissa pulled the screen door open and stepped into the kitchen.

Lia held the envelope in front of her. "One letter from the New Orleans Federal Bank, addressed to Ms. Marissa

Thompson and Ms. Julie Barrows." Lia presented the letter to them as though it were an award.

Marissa grabbed it from Lia's hand and quickly tore it open while Julie bounced up and down on her toes.

"What does it say? What does it say?" Julie asked excitedly.

Marissa unfolded the letter and quickly scanned it. Her eyes filled with moisture as she read.

Elliot walked into the kitchen at that moment, dressed in shorts and a T-shirt. She looked around the room. "What's going on?" she asked.

"Shh," Lia said.

All eyes were on Marissa as she read the letter. Finally, she looked at Julie just as a tear escaped each eye and ran down her cheeks. "We did it, Jules! They approved the loan!"

Julie jumped into Marissa's arms and wrapped her legs around her waist. She held Marissa's face between her hands and kissed her. "We did it, babe! We're going to be owners of an actual house instead of living on top of our neighbors in a condo like we have for the past twenty years!"

"Yes, we are! It took us until nearly fifty years old to do it, but heck, better late than never." Marissa kissed Julie and then put her back onto her feet.

Elliot slipped her arm around Lia's waist and pulled her close. "Congratulations, you two," she said to her friends.

Lia wiped the tears from her own face and went to embrace her friends. "We are so happy for you!"

"This calls for a celebration!" Elliot said. She pulled a bottle of champagne from the beverage cooler under the island, and popped the cork while Lia retrieved four long-stemmed glasses from the cupboard.

"A toast!" Elliot said. She held her glass high. "Julie and Marissa, I cannot think of better friends to have than you. You were here when we needed you most, and thanks to you, Lia and I are the happiest we have ever been. We wish this happiness for the two of you for the rest of your lives, and we hope we will always be able to share the good times and the bad with the two people we love most in the world. Congratulations to both of you!"

Julie hugged first Lia, and then Elliot. "*We* should be thanking *you*. Allowing us to stay with you gave us the chance to make this happen. Heaven knows, Marissa would have committed hara-kiri if she'd had to live with my mother for two months!"

"You could have lived with us forever, and we wouldn't have minded," Lia said. "I was devastated when we left you behind in New York. The day you told us you were moving to New Orleans, was one of the best days of my life."

"Yeah. What Lia said," Elliot added.

"C'mere you!" Marissa pulled Elliot into an embrace. "We love you guys so much."

"We love you, too. And we owe you our lives. I will never forget that," Elliot said.

Marissa punched her in the shoulder. "That's all behind us now. Leave it in the past where it belongs. Okay?"

Elliot nodded. "Okay."

Lia picked up a napkin and wiped her eyes. "So, what do you say we all pitch in and celebrate with a nice meal, oh, and more champagne, of course?"

"Marissa and I will cook the steaks," Elliot volunteered.

"I've already scraped the grill, so we just need to pre-heat it while the salads are being made," Marissa said.

Julie looked at Lia. "I think that's code for, Lia and Julie, you can make the salads."

"Funny how that works!" Lia replied.

***

Julie and Lia worked together in the kitchen to boil several ears of corn and make four garden salads while Marissa and Elliot tended the grill. Julie glanced through the screen door to watch them laugh and horse around. It was obvious that they enjoyed one another's company.

"Look at them," Julie said. "It's so good to see them enjoying themselves. There was a time when I doubted things would ever be this good again."

Lia glanced at her friend. "Elliot still feels guilty about it. I was glad to hear Marissa tell her to leave it in the past."

"Maybe with us out of the way, you two can focus on one another."

Lia put her knife down and took Julie by the shoulders. "Listen here. You and Marissa are not in the way. If anything, you have stopped Elliot from dwelling on it too much. It has been such a joy having you here. Besides, it's time for all of us to focus on the two of you. We are so excited for you to find your forever home."

Julie wiped a tear from the corner of her eye. "Being here was as much for our own state of mind as it was for yours, Lia. Staying in New York, while you and Elliot were going through so much, was more than I could take. I know Mar feels the same way. I'm thrilled to be closer to my family as well. It's a win-win situation for all of us."

Julie and Lia's attention was drawn to the screen door as it opened, and Marissa poked her head in.

"How are the salads coming? The steaks are nearly done," she announced.

Julie's face lit up with a huge smile. "They're just about ready," she replied.

"You two are so cute," Lia said.

"Huh?"

"I said you're cute. The expression on your face just now when you looked at Marissa was so full of love. It makes my heart sing. And you complement one another so well."

"What do you mean?" Julie asked.

"Well, you're blonde and she's brunette. You're feminine and she's butch. You're a softie and she's a tough guy."

"Like you and Elliot, huh?" Julie pointed out.

"Busted!"

"Busted, indeed," Julie laughed.

Lia walked to the stove and lifted the cover from the pot of boiling corn. "These look ready."

"The salads are finished as well. Are we eating inside or out tonight?" Julie asked.

"Let's eat around the island. The humidity today is just a tad too high for my liking," Lia replied. "And besides, you know Marissa will want to get online to search for properties while we're eating."

Julie grinned. "You know her well, don't you?"

"She was the sister I never had while I was growing up."

***

"So, where are you thinking about buying?" Lia asked.

"I would like to be in the French Quarter, and preferably within walking distance of you two," Julie replied. "But properties this close to Bourbon Street might be out of our price range. It is one of the biggest tourist attractions after all, especially during Mardi Gras."

"We bought this place dirt cheap for the size home it is," Elliot said. "Of course, considering it was haunted, and the home of a serial killer, I guess I can understand why the owner was motivated to sell it."

"Would you have bought it if you knew what was going to happen after you moved in?" Julie asked.

Lia and Elliot exchanged uneasy glances.

"I have no regrets about buying this house," Lia said.

Elliot nodded. "I agree with Lia. I wish the situation we walked into was easier to resolve than it had been, but now that it's over, I'm happy to live here, and I think Lia is, too."

"I love it. I'm looking forward to remodeling some of the rooms," Lia responded.

"Has anything weird happened since the funeral?" Julie asked.

"Nothing of any concern," Lia replied.

Julie frowned. "So, things *have* happened then?"

Lia shrugged. "Minor things. Shadows, noises, an occasional curtain being drawn, but nothing that has felt threatening—oh, and no holes being dug in the courtyard by Miss Thing either."

"That's funny. Mar and I have been here for the past two months, and I don't remember witnessing anything odd," Julie said.

"Since you two have been here, most of it has been confined to the master suite. It's almost like they realize you are guests and they don't want to alarm you."

"They?" Marissa asked.

"Lia thinks it might be Celeste or maybe Gran coming back to visit, but as long as they mean no harm, we're okay with that," Elliot explained.

Lia touched Elliot's arm. "Mean no harm. That reminds me of Samuel."

Elliot grinned and nodded. "I wonder how he's doing. We haven't seen him since the funeral."

"Back to house hunting," Lia said. "What size house are you looking for?"

"Certainly not something as big as this behemoth!" Marissa exclaimed. She clicked on the web address of the realty company she worked for and opened her saved search results for available houses in New Orleans's French Quarter.

"I'd like at least two bedrooms," Julie said. "Marissa will need an office, seeing that she will be working remotely most of the time."

"Didn't you want a room for tarot readings as well?" Elliot asked.

"That would be a bonus, but to be honest, I'm a little nervous about inviting strangers into our home, so I've given up on that idea. Phoebe has been making noises about wanting to take me on as a partner. She's been so busy with her psychic medium sessions that she's had to turn away customers who come to her shop for a simple reading. She and I used to do tarot readings quite regularly before I moved to New York to be with Marissa," Julie said.

"Who knew ghost-busting would be such a thriving business," Marissa joked.

Julie pushed her shoulder. "Stop it. Even *you* have to admit that Phoebe was pretty damned helpful when Lia and Elliot needed her."

"Yeah, I guess. Damn! This file is taking forever to open," Marissa complained.

Lia stood and collected the empty dinner dishes. "I think I'll get dessert while we're waiting. Oh, and before I forget, the steak was amazing. Thank you for cooking."

"The whole meal was wonderful. Here. Let me help you with those," Elliot said. She stood and took half of the dinner plates from Lia and carried them to the sink.

"I'll rinse, if you'll load, El," Julie said.

"It's a deal," Elliot replied.

Lia put the dishes she was carrying into the sink. "Okay, so while you're loading the dishwasher, I'll dole out the cheesecake and wine."

Marissa looked up from the computer screen. "Can I do something to help?"

"You just focus on opening that file. We've got a house to hunt for!" Julie said.

***

Elliot removed her clothes and climbed into bed. She sat with her back against the headboard and watched Lia go through her bedtime routine of applying moisturizer to her face while sitting in front of her vanity mirror.

"You know, you don't need all that stuff to make you beautiful," Elliot said.

Lia looked at Elliot's image in the mirror. "It's *because* of all this *stuff*, as you put it, that my skin is aging so well, even at fifty years old."

"You're probably right, but I would still love you, even if you were dried up and wrinkly. Your beauty comes from the inside, although I must admit, you are amazingly sweet eye candy on the outside as well."

"You are such a guy sometimes," Lia said over her shoulder. "Or make that a prepubescent teen instead of a forty-seven-year-old woman."

"What? I'm just letting you know that you're the most attractive and beautiful woman that I've ever had the pleasure of knowing."

Lia turned around in her seat. "Get real, Walker. You can't tell me you've never met another woman more beautiful than me."

"On the surface, perhaps, but when you combine your outward appearance with your inner beauty, I can definitely say I've never known anyone more beautiful. That's my story and I'm sticking to it. Now, come to bed so I can make love to you."

Lia grinned. "You know I can't resist when you turn on the charm."

"I *do* know that. Why do you think I do it?"

Lia switched off the lamp on the edge of her vanity table and plunged the room into darkness, save for the soft glow from the night light in the adjoining bathroom. She rose and walked toward the windows that faced the Royal Street side of the house, intent on removing her robe and hanging it on the coat rack positioned between two of the windows. While doing so, she glanced out the window.

She gasped. "What the...?"

Elliot was out of the bed and by her side in an instant. "What is it?"

"Look." Lia pointed to a man that stood on the corner diagonally across the street. He appeared to be looking directly at her.

Elliot looked at the man and shrugged. "I'm sure the light turning off caught his attention. It's funny though. That's where Samuel used to stand when he was watching the house."

"My thoughts exactly," Lia said.

"I'm sure it's nothing." Elliot turned Lia toward her and slipped the robe from her shoulders. "Now, if I recall, when I got home this afternoon, I *did* say that I wanted to make love to you all weekend."

"So, take my dried up, wrinkly old ass to bed," Lia said.

Elliot slipped two fingers between Lia's soft folds.

A soft moan escaped Lia's lips.

"Hmm. You, my dear, are anything but dried up."

Chapter 2

Marissa sat at the kitchen island the next morning and made phone calls to the owners of four homes she had found for sale on her company's website. She successfully scheduled viewings for all of them for that afternoon. Julie entered the kitchen just as she finalized her final appointment.

Julie approached Marissa and gently kissed her on the lips. "Good morning, my love."

"Good morning. How did you sleep?" Marissa asked.

"Not too bad. I had to get up once to pee, but that's not unusual." Julie popped a pod into the coffee maker and pulled a cup from the cabinet above it.

Marissa handed her cup to Julie. "Would you mind making me another?" she asked.

"Not at all." Julie took the cup. "How long have you been up?" she asked.

Marissa glanced at the clock on the kitchen wall. It read nine o'clock. "About three hours. I woke up early, also to pee, and then couldn't fall back to sleep. Of course, it didn't help that Miss Thing stole my pillow while I was in the bathroom, so I came down to do a little more research on the four properties I found yesterday."

"I still haven't figured out how that little Houdini gets into our room at night, especially when we make a point of closing the door before going to bed," Julie said.

"She's obviously found some sort of secret passage," Marissa said.

Julie removed her coffee from the machine and then set the next one up to brew for Marissa. She peeked over Marissa's shoulder at the home displayed on the screen of her laptop. "That looks like an interesting home," she said.

"This one is on Treme Street, near Congo Square. I also found homes on Bernville, St. Peter and St. Ann. I was surprised to find so many reasonably priced properties this close to Bourbon Street. Thank God, we got a good price for the condo in New York. We should be able to buy something without a huge mortgage."

"The extra income from my job with Phoebe will help," Julie said.

Marissa displayed a map of the one-mile search area around Bourbon Street.

Julie leaned in for a closer look. "Wow. It looks like they're all within a half-mile of Lia and Elliot."

"What's within a half mile of Lia and Elliot?" Elliot said as she walked into the kitchen with Lia right behind her.

"Good morning!" Julie said to her friends. She put her coffee down on the island and embraced Elliot. She kissed her on the cheek and went on to repeat the affection on Lia.

"Good morning, sweat pea," Lia said.

Elliot bumped fists with Marissa.

"I was just showing Julie a map of the area where I've found four properties for sale. They are all within a half mile of here," Marissa explained.

"Within a half mile? That would be great!" Lia said.

"Yes, it would. We have appointments to look at all four this afternoon, starting at one o'clock."

"Cool!" Elliot said.

Lia walked to the counter on which the coffee maker sat. "Coffee, El?" she asked.

"Please!" Elliot responded.

Lia removed the cup of coffee that sat on the brewer and turned to face her friends. "Considering you already have a cup, Jules, I assume this one is Mar's?"

"Oh, yes! I'll take that," Julie said.

"So, where are these houses?" Elliot asked.

"The one you see here is on Treme," Marissa replied. "It's two bedrooms and about a thousand square feet." Marissa paged through the pictures of the house displayed on the website. "It's a little run down, but I'll reserve judgment until we actually see it."

Marissa displayed the houses on Bernville and St. Peter streets next and discovered that they were also in need of cosmetic work.

"It seems that the homes in the French Quarter are all a bit run down," Lia said over Marissa's shoulder.

"That's pretty typical of the older homes this close to the coastline. Keep in mind that there have been some pretty traumatic storms and hurricanes throughout its history," Julie pointed out.

"Cosmetic stuff can be fixed," Elliot said. "As long as the structure is sound, a little paint and sheetrock can go a long way toward sprucing a place up. Lia and I will lend a hand with the renovations if you'd like."

"Yes, we will," Lia added.

"We'd certainly appreciate the help," Marissa said. "So, here's the home on St. Ann's Street."

Marissa clicked on the next property and pictures of a quaint, blue cottage appeared. The home was a light gray-blue color with darker blue shutters covering the doors and windows. The fences on either side of the building were also the same dark blue. Gingerbread house trim decorated the tops of the windows, doors and rooflines.

"That's a cute home," Lia said. "It would be even cuter with all the shutters open."

Marissa paged through all of the photos available for the property.

Photograph captured from Google Maps

"It looks to be in pretty good shape. The floors need to be refinished, and I'm not sure why the fireplaces are all boarded up, but overall, it looks pretty good," Marissa said.

"Those are things we can fix," Elliot said.

"Are there any pictures of the kitchen?" Julie asked.

Marissa paged through the nearly two dozen pictures available on the website, two of which were views of the kitchen.

"The kitchen is nice," Julie said. "It's a little small, but modern enough. I could live with that."

"It looks like there's a closed-in porch on the side, and I love that the windows are so tall in the living room," Lia remarked.

"How many bedrooms?" Julie asked.

Marissa paged back to the main screen. "It says four bedrooms, four bathrooms, and roughly twenty-one hundred square feet. Apparently, it was originally two units combined into one larger house. It looks like the lot size is around thirty-three hundred square feet."

"The lot is small, but then, it means less maintenance," Elliot observed.

"I'm okay with that. It's not like we need a large yard for dogs or children to play in," Marissa said. She paged to the next picture.

"Wait! Go back one," Julie said. She watched as the picture of the street view appeared. "Can you zoom in?" Julie asked. "I want to see what that writing is on the door to the left."

Marissa zoomed in. "It's a bit fuzzy at this mag."

Julie stepped back. "Oh, my! That says ten twenty, right?"

Marissa, Lia and Elliot all leaned in.

"That's what it looks like to me," they all said, almost in unison.

Julie continued to stare at the screen. Her eyes opened wide.

Marissa glanced up at her. "Jules, what is it?"

"Ten twenty Saint Ann Street." She looked at Marissa. "This is the one, Mar. I want this house."

"But, Jules, we haven't even looked at it yet," Marissa pointed out.

"I have to have this house," Julie insisted.

"Why?" Lia asked.

Julie looked at her friends. "This is the address at which Marie Laveau was born and raised. It was called Rue Santa Ana then, but it's the same place."

"What? Wait! Marie Laveau, the voodoo queen?" Elliot asked. "Are you out of your freaking mind?"

Lia touched Julie's arm. "Is that wise, sweetie? I mean, after what we've lived through during the past six months?"

"I don't see what the problem is," Julie said. "Mar?"

Marissa crossed her arms. "You're the expert on this one, Jules. This one's all yours to explain."

Julie faced her friends. "So, help me to understand what your reservations are."

"Hello? Voodoo? Evil spirits? Black magic? Sticking pins in dolls? Isn't that enough?" Elliot asked.

"Elliot does have a point, love," Lia said with a little less acerbity.

"Marissa, tell me you have the same concerns," Elliot said.

Marissa held up her hands. "I think you should listen to what Julie has to say."

"Okay, humor us. Why shouldn't we be concerned that you are about to walk into the realm of darkness?" Elliot asked.

"Because it's not the realm of darkness," Julie replied. "What you lived through for the first several months after you moved here was the realm of darkness. Voodoo is not. No, let me correct that—what you lived through with the *mistress* was the realm of darkness. The ceremonies Celeste performed were actually voodoo."

"I don't understand," Lia said.

"I grew up here, and everyday life for those of us with an open mind was filled with stories and artifacts of voodoo. Some of us were lucky enough to be accepted into the Creole community and were able to engage in the practices of voodoo. Phoebe and I, and her sister Chloe, attended ceremonies all the time when we were young adults. Many people mistakenly think voodoo is a practice that includes dark magic, evil spells, potions and sacrifices. That is so far from the truth."

"What is it then?" Elliot asked.

"Voodoo is a religion that was first brought to New Orleans in the seventeen hundreds by West African slaves. Haitian slaves, brought here by French colonists, further enhanced it. When voodoo first came to the colony of New Orleans, the West African slaves called it *vodun*, and the Haitian slaves called it *vodou*. In the beginning, it was natural and earth based. Not too long after the slaves arrived, their ceremonies and practices merged with those of the local Catholic population to form a unique religion called *voodoo*. Voodoo is similar, yet different from vodun and vodou."

"Are you saying that voodoo is part of the Catholic religion?" Lia asked.

"No. It's more of a hybrid of Catholicism and the original beliefs of the African slaves. The fact that it blended with Catholicism is one of the reasons it is so well accepted. The hybrid nature of it provided a cover of sorts for the slaves. It protected them from the Spanish, who controlled the colony until nearly eighteen hundred, and who were intent on banning the practice of voodoo.

"You see, New Orleans voodoo follows the Catholic teaching of one God and free will, but unlike Catholicism, it believes that spirits—especially the spirits of ancestors—are actively involved in their daily lives. For them, their God was unreachable, so they worshiped lesser spirits, called loa, to petition their God for favors."

Julie continued. "I guess what makes the religion seem threatening to some is that they believe they can stay connected to these spirits through rituals, dance, music, chants and snakes."

"Snakes? Well, that's pretty creepy," Elliot said.

"I know, right?" Julie replied. "Snakes wouldn't be my pet of choice either, but they are an important part of voodoo ceremonies. Practitioners of voodoo have several religious holidays, but one of the most important ones happens around the Catholic holiday known as the Feast of St. John, the birthday of St. John the Baptist. Since voodoo aligns itself with Catholicism, on the night before the holiday, voodoo priests and priestesses hold a ceremony called St. John's Eve that involved bonfires, and ceremonies all through the night on the banks of the Bayou St. John, which is located on the shore of Lake Pontchartrain. Snakes are involved in the ritual, as well as singing and dancing. There are also rumors of sexual orgies happening at this ceremony."

"Orgies, huh? Maybe voodoo isn't so bad after all," Elliot joked.

Lia punched her on the arm. "Will you stop that?"

"What did I do?" Elliot complained.

"Go on, Julie," Lia encouraged.

"Some of the participants became so caught up in the ritual that they appeared to be in a trance-like state that some believe was caused by spirit possession. They often wore elaborate costumes, body paint and masks during the ceremonies. Even I have to admit that some of the masks look evil, but they aren't meant to be.

"For years, people have misinterpreted what voodoo is, and because of that, it has taken on sinister characteristics that it doesn't deserve. Voodoo today is all about curing anxiety, addictions, depression, loneliness, and for protection. Oh, and the followers continue Marie Laveau's work of helping the poor and the sick. Some people find their methods odd, like spiritual baths, special diets, trances and such, but it is all harmless."

"I'm surprised the Catholic Church would allow itself to be associated with some of the pagan practices of voodoo," Lia said.

"Like what?" Julie asked.

"Well, like gris-gris dolls, charms, amulets, potions and talismans," Lia replied.

"Oh, you mean instead of holy medallions, candles, crosses, rosary beads and holy water?" Julie challenged.

Lia grinned and nodded. "I see your point."

"Any way, there are aspects of voodoo that have been blended with Catholicism as time passed. For example, there is a voodoo deity named, Legba. The symbol for Legba interestingly enough, is a rainbow that represents a bridge between hearth and heaven. I'm sure you've seen or heard references to our pets crossing the rainbow bridge? Well, that has its origins in voodoo.

"Legba controls the gates to the spirit world. The Catholic counterpart for Legba is Saint Peter who holds the keys to the gates of heaven. Another example is the deity, Agonme Tonne, who is the voodoo version of St. John the Baptist. Again, aligning their spirits with Catholic saints allowed them to remain hidden from the Spanish."

"What about Marie Laveau?" Elliot asked. "I always thought she was some sort of voodoo witch."

"Not a witch. She was a voodoo queen. So many people confuse voodoo with witchcraft. They are not the same. In fact, witchcraft is also misunderstood. Neither voodoo nor witchcraft is a practice intended to harm people, but like any unorthodox religion, one bad apple can spoil the whole bunch. It didn't help that there was a popular television program that portrayed Marie Laveau as a demonic force that killed innocent people. That is so far from the truth."

"You mentioned that she helped the poor?" Lia asked.

"Yes. Marie Laveau was a free woman of color, a devout Catholic, and a highly spiritual woman. She was known as a Good Samaritan who adopted orphans and looked after the poor. She was also a healer who treated patients with natural remedies like teas and herbs, and with salves and tinctures she made herself. There was a bad outbreak of yellow fever during her time, and she successfully nursed many people back to health rather than submitting them to bloodletting and other archaic medical practices. It is rumored that people sought her help at all hours of the day and night, and that she never turned anyone away. She was so powerful in the New Orleans community that many politicians asked for her advice before making important decisions. I read an article once that said some politicians even allocated payments to Marie Laveau in their budgets for consultation fees."

"How did she become so powerful?" Elliot asked.

"Some believed it was because she was a hairdresser for the wives of rich, white aristocrats, and after she gained their trust, they spilled their guts with all the secrets about their husbands' business interests and mistresses," Julie explained.

"So, she was a pretty influential woman, then," Lia said.

"You mean she was a pretty influential blackmailer," Elliot added.

"It would appear she was a cunning businesswoman as well as the head of the voodoo community in the early eighteen hundreds. She was one of the most famous voodoo priestesses who ever lived," Julie said. "Even during a time when people of color were considered little more than property, voodoo priestesses held amazing power and influence in both the white and black communities, especially if they belonged to the class of free people of color, who were never enslaved."

"Free people of color?" Lia asked.

"Yes. Free people of color were people of mixed descent, usually African and European. Marie Laveau's mother was African and her father was Creole. Her mother was actually a slave, owned and then freed by her father. Marie herself was born free," Julie replied.

"Is there any truth in the rumors that Marie Laveau helped the mistress escape to avoid capture for what she did to her slaves?" Elliot asked.

"There is also a rumor that she helped the mistress when she returned from Paris many years later," Lia added.

"The mistress and Marie Laveau lived just a few blocks from one another, as you can see on the map Marissa printed out, and they lived at the same time, so they may have known one another, but there is no evidence that they had an intimate friendship. Given the philanthropic nature of Marie Laveau, and as a woman of color who went out of her way to help black people, I can't imagine she would have helped that demon escape after what she did to her slaves," Julie offered.

Marissa, who had been quietly listening to the exchange, piped in. "But, Jules, three months ago, the mistress sought refuge at the grave of Marie Laveau. You and I were both there with Phoebe when she met her end."

"*That*, I can't explain, Mar. *That*, I can't explain."

Chapter 3

Marissa pulled the door closed behind them as they left the Bernville property. Julie, Lia and Elliot waited for her at the bottom of the porch stairs.

"Well, what did you think?" she asked.

"I thought it was really cute," Lia said. "It was a bit run down, but I like that there's a third bedroom."

"I agree with Lia. I didn't see anything structurally wrong with it, but it does need a little TLC. That is all doable though. I would definitely keep this one on the list," Elliot added.

"Julie? What about you?" Marissa asked.

"I'm reserving judgment until we see the house on St. Ann," Julie said.

Marissa sighed. "Come on, Jules. I know you have your heart set on the Laveau house, but you need to give these other three homes some serious consideration, too."

"I'm keeping an open mind, Mar. I am. I mean, the home near Congo Square is really run down, so I think we can eliminate that one. The one on St. Peter was nice too, but it's the most expensive of the four, and it also needs some cosmetic work. This one here is definitely in better shape than the other two. If the Laveau house turns out to be horrible, I could see us living here."

"Okay. Fair enough. Let's go look at the Laveau house, then afterward, I'll treat us all to an early dinner. I'm in the mood for voodoo juice," Marissa said.

***

Marissa pulled the car to the curb in front of the Saint Ann house and turned off the ignition. All four occupants of the car stared at the building for a few moments before anyone climbed out.

"It looks to be in good shape from here," Elliot said.

"Yes, it does," Marissa agreed. "I'll take that as a good sign."

"All of the shutters are open. It's very charming. Just as I thought it would be," Lia remarked.

Julie remained silent as she pushed her door open and climbed out of the car.

Marissa headed straight for the lock box attached to the doorknob and with her realtor's combination, she punched in the code to open it and retrieve the key for the deadbolt. Lia and Elliot waited patiently on the sidewalk until Marissa opened the door.

Julie, on the other hand, walked toward the house and stopped in front of the center window while Marissa, Lia and Elliot went into the house.

A moment later, Marissa peeked her head out. "Are you coming in?" she asked.

Without looking away from the window, Julie replied. "Yes. I'll be there in a minute."

Marissa disappeared back into the house.

Julie studied the window for a few more moments. "They can't see you, can they?" she asked softly.

"Jules?"

Julie looked toward the door on her left to see Marissa poking her head out once more.

"I'm coming."

Julie climbed the three steps into the house and entered a small vestibule. Inside the vestibule, there was a window on the left, overlooking the alley, and a door on the right that opened into a large living room.

"Wow! This is a big room," Julie exclaimed.

"Yes. I'm guessing it's about thirty by fifteen." Marissa took Julie's hand. "Let's look around."

"Where are the girls?"

"They're in here somewhere. Come on."

Hand in hand, Marissa and Julie walked around the living room.

"Look, there's a powder room in the corner near the entry way," Julie said.

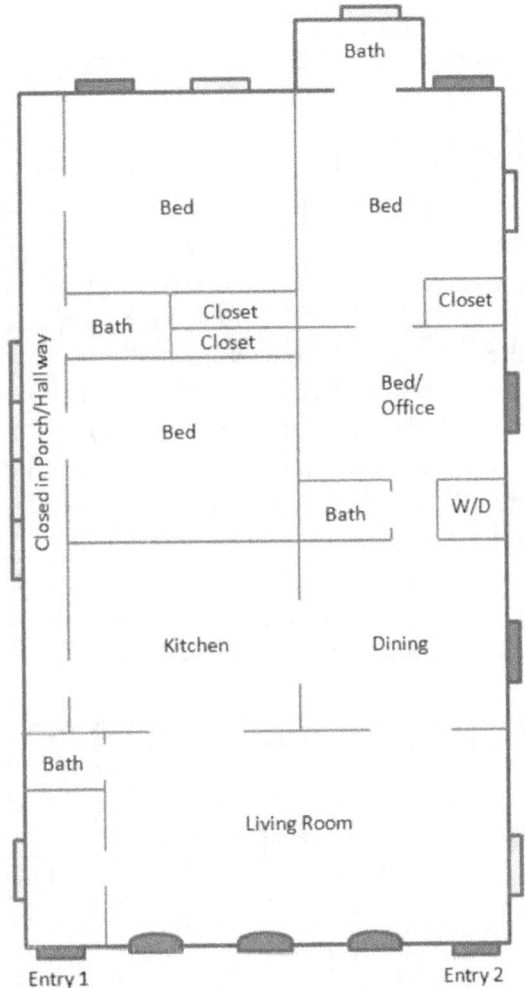

"Here's the kitchen," Marissa said. She and Julie walked into a relatively spacious area with oak cabinets and granite countertops. The floor was covered in ceramic tiles.

"It looks like we'll have to buy a stove and a refrigerator," Julie said.

Marissa pointed to a large room adjacent to the kitchen. "That must be the dining room."

"That would make sense," Julie said. She walked into the dining room and looked around. "Hey, there's a short hallway here."

"Let's check it out."

Julie walked into the hallway and noted a closet to the right. She opened it and found connections for a washer and dryer. Directly across the hall was a door leading into a small bathroom. "I found the second bathroom," she said.

"Keep going. This house goes back a ways," Marissa encouraged.

They walked into a medium-sized room with a closet in one corner that extended into the adjacent room, and an exit door into the alley on the outside wall.

"This is a strange setup. There's another room beyond this one. That would be weird if they were both bedrooms. You'd have to walk through one to get to the other," Julie said.

"I agree. Wow, this back bedroom is large, and look, it has its own bathroom. This must be the master."

"It also has a door that exits to the outside. This would make a good office for you, Mar. Your clients could come and go through that door, and you'd have a bathroom for them as well."

"We'll see. I was thinking we take this wall down between the two rooms and make a larger master suite for us."

Julie looked around and nodded. "That's not a bad idea either, but you'd still need space for an office."

"Let's go see what the other bedrooms look like. Maybe one of those will be suitable," Marissa suggested.

Julie and Marissa made their way back into the dining room, where they came face to face with Lia and Elliot.

"I like this house so far," Lia said. "It has a lot of charm."

"There's not much cosmetic work that needs to be done either," Elliot added.

"Well, I have an idea for the master that will require a wall to be taken out, but it doesn't look like a huge project. Jules and I are going to look at the other side of the house. We'll meet you back in the living room in a few minutes. Now, how to find the other bedrooms," Marissa murmured as they walked into the kitchen.

"I'm betting they're through this doorway." Julie walked through the door in the far wall of the kitchen, onto a closed-in porch that extended all the way to the back of the house. "Bingo!" she said.

They walked halfway down the hall and entered through the first door on their right.

"Bedroom number three," Marissa said.

"Nice. This will make a good guest room," Julie replied.

"Let's see what's next." Marissa stepped back into the hall and opened the next door. "Awesome! This is the last bathroom. Come look."

Julie stepped into the bathroom and looked around. "This one looks like it's been recently renovated with tile work and a walk-in shower. I really like this," Julie said.

Marissa stepped into the hall. "Okay, so we've seen three of the four bedrooms, so the door down the hall must be it."

Julie followed Marissa into the room.

"Wow! There's a door to the outside in this bedroom as well," Julie exclaimed. She reached for the handle and pulled it open. "It looks like there's a wooden fence splitting the back yard in half. Maybe if we take the fence down, your clients can use this entrance, and we can turn this bedroom into an office for you."

"I think that would work. This room is more than big enough for an office, and the bathroom is just next door. It'll be nice to have a place for clients to come and go without them having to walk through the house," Marissa said.

"Great. Why don't we meet the girls in the kitchen and see what they think?" Julie suggested.

Marissa closed and locked the back door and then swept the area in front of Julie with her arm to urge her forward. "Lead the way."

Julie stepped into the hallway and stopped short. Marissa ran right into the back of her.

"What the hell?" Marissa exclaimed.

Julie stood frozen to the spot and stared down the hallway.

"Are you all right, Jules? What are you staring at?"

"Marie Laveau. She's standing right there." Julie pointed to the end of the hall.

Marissa looked in the direction Julie was pointing. "Jules, there's nothing there." She turned Julie around and took her by the shoulders. "Are you all right?"

Julie looked back over her shoulder. The hallway was empty. "She's gone. She was there. I swear it. She was standing in the front window when we got here, too. I saw her."

***

"Oh-oh, trouble in paradise," Elliot said.

Lia and Elliot stood in the kitchen and listened to the raised voices coming from the hallway.

"That's it. There's no way we're buying this house."

"But, Mar, it's perfect for us," Julie said.

"Perfect or not, the last thing we need is another experience like we had at Lia and Elliot's," Marissa countered.

By this time, they had reached the end of the hallway near the kitchen.

"What's going on?" Elliot asked.

"Julie said she saw Marie Laveau in this hallway," Marissa said.

"You saw Marie Laveau?" Lia asked.

"Yes. At least, I think it was her," Julie replied.

"What did she look like?" Lia asked.

"She was beautiful. She was a black woman with medium colored skin. Like yours, Lia. She had on a long dress with a shawl over her shoulders and a turban-like thing on her head."

"And she was just standing there in the hallway," Elliot said.

"Yes. She was also standing in the front window when we got here. I saw her as soon as we pulled to the curb. It was obvious that none of you saw her because y'all just walked into the house without noticing her. I think I'm the only one who can see her."

"Can you believe this shit?" Marissa said.

"After what happened at our place, I'm willing to believe anything," Elliot replied. "So, Julie, why do you think you're able to see her?"

"I don't know. Maybe she knows I'm a follower of voodoo. Maybe I have some psychic abilities. Maybe she knows that I'm not frightened by paranormal events."

"So, this doesn't scare you?" Lia asked.

"Not at all. From everything I have ever heard and studied about Marie Laveau, I know that she was a good person. I had no feelings of malevolence when I saw her. This was her house for Christ's sake. I'm not surprised that she is connected to it."

"Jules, you gotta know that this was not her actual house. This structure was built after she died. It *is* on the same lot as the cottage she lived and died in, but she never lived in this actual house," Marissa said.

"I know that, Marissa. But this *is* where she lived, even if another structure was here at the time."

Marissa ran her hands through her hair and then put them on her hips. "Julie, I'm not crazy about sharing our home with a ghost."

"Mar, this house is perfect for us. It is just the right size, and there's room for your office. Believe it or not, there are ghosts and spirits in nearly every dwelling in this country. I never told you this, but we had one in our condo in New York."

"Get out! We did not!" Marissa exclaimed.

"Yes, we did. I just never told you about him. He was harmless."

"We know we have a few in our house," Elliot said.

"I'll second that. We have learned not to be afraid of them," Lia added.

Julie took Marissa's hands and placed them on her heart. "Mar, I would never ask you to live in a place that was dangerous. There is no malevolence here. I truly believe she means us no harm. I want this house, Mar. I feel like we were meant to be here."

Marissa touched her forehead to Julie's. "I sure hope I don't live to regret this," she said.

"You won't. I promise."

Marissa kissed Julie. "Okay. I'll put an offer on it first thing in the morning."

"Thank you, love."

"You're welcome. Now let's go eat. I'm starved!"

Lia and Elliot climbed into the car while Marissa secured the key to the house inside the lock box. Julie stood on the sidewalk once more and stared at the center window.

Marissa glanced at her as she closed the lockbox. "She's in the window again, isn't she?" she asked Julie.

"Yes, she is, and she's smiling."

"Well, do me a favor and tell her to be a good tenant, okay?"

Julie chuckled.

"What's so funny?" Marissa asked.

"She said, 'Watch out, Yankee, or I'll put a hex on you'."

Marissa walked down the three steps to sidewalk level and stood beside Julie. "Did she really say that?"

"She did. Jokingly, of course."

She put her arm around Julie. "This is going to be interesting!"

Chapter 4

Marissa and Julie sat on the opposite side of the table from Lia and Elliot at the restaurant. They had just placed their order for food and drink.

"So, honestly. What did you think of the Laveau house?" Marissa asked.

"I liked it," Elliot said. "I think with a few changes, it would be perfect for you. Your idea of taking the wall out between the master bedroom and that smaller room in front of it is perfect. That makes the master bedroom almost a quarter of the floor plan."

"And it eliminates the awkwardness of having to walk through one bedroom to get to another," Julie said.

"Actually, Jules, that layout is pretty common. It's called a shot-gun house," Marissa said. "If the layout was still two units and we knocked the wall out between the master bedroom and the smaller room adjacent to it, that would have turned it from a two-bedroom to a one-bedroom apartment—which would not have been a good thing relative to market value. The fact that someone combined them into one house allows us to knock that wall down without affecting the resale value of the house. Generally, eliminating bedrooms is frowned upon, but when all is said and done, we'll still have a three-bedroom house with a large master and a less awkward floor plan."

"It looks like they combined the two units by opening the wall between the kitchen and dining room, and by taking down the wall between the two living rooms," Elliot guessed.

"That's what it looks like to me, too," Lia added.

"One thing they *didn't* do was remove the partition dividing the back yard. We'll need to do that right away," Julie said.

Just then, their voodoo juices arrived, creating a lull in the conversation while the waiter transferred them from his tray to the table.

"Here you go, folks. Your meals should be out soon," the waiter said, and then he tucked the tray under his arm and walked away.

Lia took a sip of her drink. "Ooh, this is good. So, tell us how *you* feel about this house," she said to both Julie and Marissa.

"Other than the whole ghost thing, I'm feeling pretty good about it. It was in the best shape of the four we looked at today, and it was in the middle of the price range, even with the additional bedrooms," Marissa replied.

"Julie?" Lia said.

"I agree with everything Mar said, but unlike her, I'm thrilled about our houseguest."

"You're happy about a ghost living in your house?" Elliot asked.

"Yes, I am. Who better to protect us than the voodoo queen herself?"

"Did I tell you she threatened to put a hex on me?" Marissa said.

"What?" Elliot exclaimed.

"Yup. According to Jules, she was joking when she said it. Who else would be lucky enough to have a tenant who is not only a ghost, but a ghost with a sense of humor?" Marissa chuckled.

"I've had enough of humorous ghosts," Lia said. "Remember when Celeste dressed me like a bar wench and then sent me off to work?"

"That *was* kind of funny," Elliot agreed.

"Grrr," Lia replied.

"Oh, goodie! Here comes our food," Julie exclaimed.

***

It was nearly nine when the friends returned home after an enjoyable evening of good food and company. Elliot jumped out of the car and opened the gates to the inner courtyard so Marissa could pull her car inside. Unfortunately, there were limited parking spaces assigned to their property, only the one in front of the house and space for one car inside the garage. Both Lia's and Elliot's cars already occupied those spaces, so it became necessary to park Marissa and Julie's car inside the courtyard.

Elliot closed and bolted the carriage gates once the car was inside. She then pulled a ring of keys from her pocket and waited for her wife and friends to get out of the car.

Dusk was settling on the courtyard and their movements caused the motion lights to come on near the entrance to the lower level of the house.

Elliot went ahead of the group and unlocked the door that led from the courtyard. She held it open for all to pass through, and then re-locked it once they were inside. They made their way through several interconnected rooms between the courtyard and the vestibule in the front of the house where the foot of the three-story staircase was. Stored in these rooms were all of the personal belongings of Marissa and Julie that had been delivered from their condo in New York City two months earlier.

"Ugh! Just think. We have to transport all this stuff when we're ready to move into the new house," Marissa said.

"Thanks again for letting us unload all this into these rooms," Julie added. "You saved us a ton of money in storage fees."

"No problem, sweetie," Lia said. "We weren't using the rooms anyway. It didn't make sense for you to pay for storage when we've got all this space."

"Well, we do appreciate it," Marissa said.

Elliot looked over her shoulder as they made their way through the rooms. "You know, there's no rush for you to move out. I hope that the owners of the Laveau house accept your offer and then we can take whatever time we need to remodel it the way you want before you move in. That way, you do not have to live in a construction zone."

"Oh, I think we'll win the bid. One good part of being a realtor is that we'll have first-hand information about other offers that have been made on this house. We'll just outbid them, unless there's a price war that pushes it out of our range," Marissa said.

"Do you mean we could actually be outbid?" Julie's voice was tinged with concern.

"That's possible, but unlikely," Marissa replied. "Don't worry, love. I'm feeling good about our chances."

They stopped at the foot of the central staircase.

"I don't know about the rest of you, but I think I'm going to soak in a nice hot bath and then cuddle with my girl in bed. That is, if she's willing," Elliot said.

"That sounds like heaven," Lia replied. "I'll bring the wine."

"Cuddling? Is that what they call it these days?" Marissa winked.

"You two have the greatest ideas. Whaddaya say, Mar?" Julie suggested.

"I'm all in for a good *cuddle* if you are. While you run a tub for us, I'll go put the bid in on the house instead of waiting until tomorrow. I'll do it from the kitchen since my computer is already set up there," Marissa said. "And like Lia said, I'll bring the wine."

When they reached the landing for the second floor, Marissa bade Elliot a good night and kissed Julie on the cheek with a promise that she would be up soon.

Lia followed Marissa to the kitchen and retrieved two bottles of wine from the beverage cooler beneath the island. "Pinot Noir okay with you?" she asked.

"Perfect. Thanks."

Lia put the bottles of wine on the counter and then retrieved four long-stemmed glasses from the cupboard. She placed two beside Marissa's bottle of wine and then grabbed her bottle to take upstairs with her. Before leaving, she paused.

"How do you *really* feel about this house, Mar?" she asked.

Marissa stopped what she was doing to give her full attention to Lia. "I feel very good about the house. Elliot is right. It doesn't need a lot of work, and it is the right size for us."

"I hear a *but...* in there," Lia said.

Marissa nodded. "But I won't say that I'm not nervous about the whole Marie Laveau thing. Look, Julie and I have been together for more than twenty years—nearly as long as you and Elliot. I love her with all my heart, and for the most part, I've come to love all her eccentricities. This is a leap of faith for me though. I need to trust what her gut is telling her. It is almost never wrong. Am I nervous? Hell, yeah! However, my love for her outweighs any degree of nervousness I could feel. We got this. We'll make it work."

Lia wrapped her arms around her friend. "I so value the friendship we've shared since we were kids. Know that Elliot and I have your back, no matter how this turns out. We love you and Julie to the moon and back."

Marissa squeezed Lia tight. "We feel the same about you two. Now take your wine and go keep your wife company in the tub before you make me cry."

Lia grabbed her wine and walked toward the kitchen doorway. She paused. "Good night, sweetie. Oh, and ignore any odd noises you might hear tonight. Okay?"

Marissa grinned. "Only if you agree to do the same! Goodnight!"

***

Satisfied that their bid had submitted successfully, Marissa powered down her laptop, grabbed the wine and glasses and ascended the central staircase to the third story. She entered their room and found that Julie was already in the tub, covered up to her neck in bubbles.

She opened the bottle of wine and split the entire contents between the two long-stemmed glasses that she had perched on the side of the oversized tub. She then removed her clothes and prepared to step into the mound of bubbles.

"Be careful. It's a bit hot," Julie said.

Marissa stepped one foot in, and then the other and immediately felt the hot water singe the skin on her feet and shins. "Damn, baby! You weren't kidding!" she exclaimed.

"Do you want me to add some cold water?" Julie asked.

"No. No, just give me a minute." Marissa danced around from foot to foot while her skin adjusted to the temperature. Finally, she decided to brave immersion. She leaned down,

37

placed her hands on each side of the tub, and slowly squatted so that her thighs were nearly under water.

"Ah...ah...ah! Yikes that's hot! I'm burning my damned cooch!"

"Let me add some cold water," Julie said again.

"Not on your life. If you can do it, so can I."

Marissa continued to lower herself into the water. Her breath caught with each inch of immersion. Finally, she was seated, but her breath came in pants. "I...think...the skin...is peeling...off my...cooch...and...ta-tas!" she complained. She closed her eyes and forced herself to relax. It took a concerted effort to regulate her breathing back to normal. Finally, she felt her blood pressure begin to subside. "How in hell were you able to stand it?" she asked.

"I was already in the tub when it began to fill. I guess I just adapted as the water surrounded me," Julie explained.

Marissa picked up one glass of wine and handed it to Julie, and then retrieved the other for herself. They clinked their glasses together.

"A toast," Marissa said. "To new homes, boiled cooch and tender ta-tas!"

"To new homes, boiled cooch and tender ta-tas!" Julie repeated. "Don't worry , I'll kiss them and make it all better," she added.

"I'm counting on it!" Marissa replied.

Marissa and Julie spent the next forty-five minutes drinking wine and making plans to decorate their new home, all while the heat from the water enhanced the effects of the alcohol, so that by the time their glasses were empty, they were quite tipsy.

They were sitting in the tub facing one another. Marissa took Julie's glass from her and put both of them on the floor beside the empty bottle. She then reached forward and pulled Julie onto her lap. Julie went willingly and wrapped her legs around Marissa's waist.

"I love you, Julie Barrows," Marissa said.

"And I love you, too, Marissa Thompson."

Julie lowered her lips to Marissa's and kissed her passionately.

"I want to make love to you," Marissa said.

"Not until I inspect and treat your burns," Julie said.

"Oh, yeah! I forgot about that," Marissa joked. "Whaddaya say we blow this joint and go to bed, Doctor Barrows?"

Julie reached back and flipped the drain on the tub. "We should probably rinse off first, don't you think?"

"Hmmm," Marissa mumbled as she nibbled on Julie's neck.

"Or not..." Julie moaned. "Take me to bed."

Marissa pushed Julie back so that she was free to stand. Once on her feet, she stepped out of the tub onto the bathmat and extended her hand to Julie.

Julie stepped onto the mat in front of Marissa and immediately molded herself against Marissa's wet body.

Marissa took Julie by the waist and lifted her upward so that Julie could wrap her legs around her waist. She carried her into the bedroom and managed to climb onto the bed without losing her precious cargo. She lowered Julie to the bed and lay between her legs.

For the next several minutes, Marissa devoured Julie's neck and breasts while Julie moaned out her pleasure.

Suddenly they heard a loud bang. Marissa immediately lifted her head and strained to hear. "Did you hear that?" she asked Julie.

"Yes."

Another bang sounded.

"What the fuck? Maybe we should investigate," Marissa said.

"No way. I'm not walking in on whatever they're doing that's making noises like *that*," Julie said.

Marissa grinned. "Lia did tell me to ignore any noises we might hear tonight."

"My point exactly," Julie replied.

"Now where was I? Oh, yeah. I was occupying myself while waiting for my appointment."

"Appointment?"

"Yes, Doctor Barrows. My appointment."

"I see. Well then, I guess we'd better get to it."

Julie pushed Marissa onto the bed and then scurried to her knees beside her. "Hmmm. I see a little redness around your nipples. I think I need to take a closer look."

Julie bent and inhaled one of Marissa's nipples into her mouth.

Marissa moaned.

"I can see how much that affects you. Maybe I should examine the other one," Julie said.

"Oh, my God!" Marissa called out when Julie sucked and bit her other nipple.

"Sometimes the best remedy is more of the same treatment. Shall I continue?"

"God, yes!" Marissa insisted.

For the next several minutes, Julie sucked, pulled and bit on Marissa's nipples until Marissa stopped her. "I think that's enough treatment. There are other injured areas that need your attention."

"Yes, of course. Crotch flambé. I'll get on that right away."

Julie positioned herself between Marissa's legs and parted her lips. "It is a bit red down here," she said in all honesty. "Let's see if a little lubrication will help matters."

Julie ran her tongue around the tender area and then sucked Marissa's clit into her mouth. Marissa's hips immediately rose off the bed and she cried out in passion.

"Wow, that was quite some response," Julie said. "Perhaps an internal exam is in order?"

Without waiting for a response, Julie once again pulled Marissa's clit into her mouth. At the same time, she inserted two fingers deep inside and massaged the sponge-like tissue at the front of her vagina.

Marissa pressed her head deep into the pillow and the cords on her neck became pronounced as she strove to meet the rhythm of Julie's hand. Before long, her hips suspended above the bed and then her body convulsed uncontrollably for several moments before the tremors subsided and she lay limply on the bed. She placed her hand on Julie's shoulder to convey she'd had enough.

Julie removed her fingers and then climbed up to lay beside Marissa.

"Am I gonna make it, Doctor?" Marissa asked.

Julie kissed her tenderly. "You are going to be just fine. Of course, more treatments might be in order, but I think you'll make a full recovery."

Marissa rolled so that she hovered above Julie. "What do I owe you for your services?"

Julie tapped her chin with her fingertip as though she were deep in thought. "I think I'm in the mood for a little bartering."

"Bartering?" Marissa said.

"Yes. You know. I scratch your back and you scratch mine?"

Marissa's eyebrows raised on her forehead. "I see. But, what about malpractice? After all, I'm not a doctor like you are."

Julie grinned. "I'll sign a waiver. C'mere you!"

Marissa did a little doctoring of her own and after a time, they were making their own noises that were worthy of investigation.

Chapter 5

Elliot was making coffee when Marissa entered the kitchen the next morning. She stood beside Elliot and reached for a cup in the cabinet above the coffee maker. She bumped shoulders with her friend.

"You two were making some pretty loud noises last night," Marissa teased.

Elliot looked at her and frowned. "That wasn't us. We thought it was you two."

"No, it wasn't us," Marissa said. "I assumed it was you. Lia told me to ignore any sounds we might hear in the night."

"Well, it wasn't us either. Not that we weren't making noise, but *that* was definitely not us. It must have been coming from outside." Elliot removed her cup from the coffee maker. "It's all yours."

"Let me make a coffee and then maybe we can go onto the porch and look around. Whatever made that noise was pretty loud."

Elliot and Marissa stepped onto the back deck and looked over the railing into the courtyard.

"Nothing looks out of place to me," Elliot said.

They walked the entire length of the balcony that wrapped around both the Governor Nichols and Royal Street sides of the property, all while looking over the edge. Still, they saw nothing out of the ordinary.

As they were about to turn the corner from the Royal Street to the Governor Nichols side, they heard a voice calling to them. It was Lia, who had been out for a morning run.

"Hey, you two," she called.

"Good morning, beautiful lady," Elliot called over the railing.

Lia stopped just beneath them and shaded her eyes with one hand. "What are you two doing on the balcony?" she asked.

"Do you remember that noise we heard last night?" Elliot asked. "Well, it wasn't them. Mar and I were looking around to see if anything had happened outside the house."

"You're going to have a pretty rough time seeing beneath the balcony. Let me look and I'll let you know if I see anything."

"Okay," Elliot said.

Elliot and Marissa watched as Lia inspected the Royal Street side of the house.

"I don't see anything wrong here. Let me go around the corner."

Elliot rounded the corner at the same time Lia did and watched as she stopped after a few feet.

"Oh, my God, Elliot. You need to come down here," Lia said.

Elliot and Marissa ran the length of the balcony on the Governor Nichols side of the house and turned the corner toward the kitchen door. They both dropped their coffee cups on the island and turned to go back out the way they had come, just as Julie entered the kitchen.

"Hey! What's the hurry?" she said.

Marissa grabbed Julie's hand. "Come with us. Do you remember that sound last night? Well, it came from outside. Lia just called us down to look."

"But I haven't had my coffee yet!" Julie whined.

"Coffee can wait. Come on."

Marissa and Julie followed Elliot down a flight of stairs into the courtyard and directly to the carriage gates. Elliot unlocked the gates and pulled one of them open. Lia was standing on the sidewalk on the other side.

She motioned for them to come out. "Pull the gate closed," she said.

All four of them stood looking at the closed gates. There were two large splinter marks, one on each gate, as though a battering ram had hit them. However, the most striking thing was not the damage. It was the words written in white paint on the black doors. *Celeste escaped, but you never will!*

***

Elliot stood on the sidewalk in front of the open carriage gates talking to Officer Rocque from the New Orleans police department.

"Any idea who might have done this?" Officer Rocque asked.

"Not a clue," Elliot replied.

"Who is Celeste?" he asked.

"You wouldn't believe me if I told you," Elliot said.

"Try me."

"Celeste was a slave who lived in this house more than one hundred and eighty years ago."

"Oh, that's right. She's the one you had the funeral for a couple of months ago," the officer stated.

"Yes. We found her remains in the house."

Lia walked toward them through the courtyard, carrying three tall glasses of lemonade. She handed one each to Elliot and the officer and kept the third for herself.

"Many thanks, Miss Lia," the officer said.

"You're welcome, Officer Rocque. I hope you enjoy it."

Elliot looked at the officer and then at Lia. "You know, it's a little unnerving that the New Orleans police are on a first-name basis with my wife."

"That's what happens when you have a mass grave in your back yard, ma'am," the officer said.

"Don't remind me. I'd rather put that episode behind us," Elliot replied.

"So, Officer Rocque, are you finding any clues that might determine who did this?" Lia asked.

"No, ma'am. Not yet. This damage was obviously an attempt to break into your property, but at this point, I'm not even sure if the person who damaged your gates is the same one who left the message."

"Are you saying it might have been two different people?" Lia asked.

"It's possible. I need to interview several of your neighbors to see if we have any witnesses. Did you hear anything? Damage like this would have made a lot of noise."

"Actually, yes. We heard two loud bangs. I think it was around ten-thirty. Does that sound right to you, Lia?" Elliot asked.

"Yes. It was at least ten-thirty."

Officer Rocque closed his notebook and handed his empty glass back to Lia. "That's all I need for now. I'll interview the neighbors and let you know if I find anything. Thank you for the lemonade, ma'am."

Officer Rocque started to walk toward his car but stopped and turned back. "Oh, and Miss Lia, if Celeste was a slave, that means she was a woman of color. I don't want to jump to any conclusions, but I'm not ruling out this being a hate crime."

"Are you saying someone could be threatening Lia because she's a black woman?" Elliot said.

"Anything is possible, Ms. Walker. I'm just saying that I'm not ruling it out. In the meantime, I recommend you take extra precautions."

Lia slipped her arm into Elliot's. "Thank you, Officer Rocque. We'll be waiting to hear from you."

Lia pulled Elliot toward the courtyard once Officer Rocque had driven away. "Come on, let's go inside and secure the gates."

Lia and Elliot ascended the steps to the upper deck and entered the house through the kitchen. Marissa and Julie were waiting for them.

"So, did he shine any light on who may have done this?" Marissa asked.

"No. The only thing he *did* say that made any sense is that this might be a hate crime," Elliot explained.

"A hate crime? How?" Julie asked.

"It's possible that because Celeste was a black woman, that some racist asshole did that to our gates to threaten Lia. Whether they actually meant harm, or to just send a message isn't clear," Elliot explained.

"I guess that's possible," Marissa said.

"In any case, I don't want you to go anywhere alone for a while, Lia," Elliot stated.

"You can't be serious," Lia exclaimed.

"I couldn't be *more* serious," Elliot countered.

"At the risk of making you pissed at me, Lia, I agree with El," Marissa said. "If this truly *is* a hate crime, then you could be a target. Until we know more, I think you need to travel in the company of one of us."

Lia put her hands on her hips. "Well then, one of you needs to take up jogging because I refuse to give up my morning runs."

Julie raised her hand. "I'll volunteer for that. I need to get into better shape anyway, and it'll give us some girlfriend time together, too."

Lia hugged her friend. "Thank you, Julie. Girlfriend time would be awesome."

Marissa raised her hand to Elliot for a high-five. "Dodged a bullet on that one!" she exclaimed. "Okay. Now that we have that issue settled, how about you and I go fix the gates, Elliot?"

"I want to get that hateful message off the gates as soon as possible, Mar, but Officer Rocque said not to touch it until their investigation is complete. He's sending a team this afternoon to take pictures and to assess what might have been used to cause the damage," Elliot explained.

"Well, that sucks. Sign me up to help when it's time to fix it," Marissa reiterated. "Oh, whoa!" Marissa grabbed her back pocket. "My phone is vibrating."

"Vibrate, huh?" Lia teased.

Marissa pulled the phone out of her pocket. "It's my boss." She pressed the answer button and put the phone to her ear. "Good morning, Joe. What's up?" she said.

The others watched Marissa nod several times. She then looked at Julie with a wide smile on her face. "Okay. Thank you for letting me know. Yes. Please make that an official acceptance. Awesome! Thank you, Joe. I'll see you in the morning." Marissa shut her phone off and turned to Julie. "They accepted our offer! We've got the house!"

Julie screamed and ran into Marissa's arms.

Lia wrapped her arms around both of her friends. "Congratulations, you two. We are so happy for you."

"That was fast," Elliot said. "Didn't you just put that offer in yesterday?"

"Last night, in fact," Marissa replied.

"The seller must be really motivated," Elliot remarked.

"I suspect Marie has been scaring prospective buyers away," Julie said.

"What?" Marissa asked.

"I think Marie has been scaring the other buyers away, just waiting for us to come along."

"Really?"

"Yes. I think we were *pre-destined* to buy Marie Laveau's house."

Marissa frowned.

"That's not as far-fetched as it sounds, Marissa," Lia interjected. "I feel the same way about this house. I firmly believe it was not a coincidence that Elliot and I were brought to New Orleans, and specifically exposed to *this* house."

Marissa looked at Elliot. "Elliot?"

"I can't disagree. I mean, Lia is a direct descendant of the slave woman, Celeste, who died in this house. We didn't know any of that until *after* we bought the place. Something definitely brought us here."

Marissa turned back to Julie. "So, if we were destined to buy the house, who the hell is controlling the puppet strings?"

"That's a good question. Maybe it's time we have a chat with Phoebe? She might be able to help us sort this out," Julie suggested.

Chapter 6

Lia and Elliot lay in bed that evening, neither one tired enough to fall asleep. Lia's head was on Elliot's shoulder and Miss Thing lay on her chest. Lia gently stroked the cat's silky coat.

"Elliot, do you think the damage on the carriage gates was done by someone with racist intent?" Lia asked. "I mean, there is a large black population in the city and I can't imagine anyone having balls enough to bring the wrath of the community down on them."

Elliot kissed Lia on the side of her head. "I don't know what to think, love. If it *was* some racist asshole, I find it odd that they knew Celeste's name, and what in hell did they mean by *Celeste escaped*? Celeste didn't escape anything. She died right here in this house for who she was. It doesn't make sense to me."

"Me either. I was just starting to relax and enjoy our life here, and then this happens."

"Officer Rocque will get to the bottom of it. By the way, I think he's sweet on you," Elliot teased.

"He is not!"

"No, really, I think he is. Not that I blame him."

"Elliot, stop that. He's just doing his job, and besides, I must be twenty years older than him."

Lia threw back the covers, which caused Miss Thing to jump up and run off the bed. She slipped her legs over the side and stood. "Nature calls."

She made her way around the foot of the bed and into the adjoining bathroom, followed closely by the cat. A few moments later, she shut off the bathroom light and stepped into the bedroom. The cat ran ahead of her and jumped onto the windowsill. Before she could take another step, the cat growled.

Lia walked toward the window. "What is your problem, Miss Thing?"

The cats back hunched upward and she hissed.

"Something's wrong." Elliot jumped out of bed and ran in front of Lia to the window the cat was perched in. "Son of a bitch!" she cursed.

"Elliot, what is it?" Lia asked.

Elliot pushed the cat off the sill and then raised the window high. She leaned out and yelled, "You'd better have a damned good reason for being there!"

"Elliot! Get back in here. You're naked for God's sake!"

Elliot slammed the window closed and then pulled on the shorts and T-shirt she had discarded on the floor beside the bed earlier that night. "He's out there again. I'm going to get to the bottom of this."

Lia followed Elliot out of their room and into the hall. "Elliot, he has a right to be on the street."

"Yes, he does, but doesn't have the right to be stalking us. Especially after that message was left on the gates," Elliot said as she flew down the stairs.

Marissa came out of their room across the hall. "What's going on?"

"There was a man standing on the corner across the street, looking at the house. Here was there last night as well."

"Shit. She's going to get herself killed." Marissa tightened her robe and went down the stairs after Elliot.

Marissa reached the bottom of the staircase just as Elliot pushed the iron gate open to the vestibule. Marissa followed her into the street. She looked around and noted that there was no one standing on any of the four corners.

"Elliot. Come back in the house. There's no one there," Marissa said.

Elliot stood in the intersection and pointed to the corner diagonal to their house. "He was standing right there, Mar. I saw him. The coward ran away."

"Come inside, Elliot. We should call the police and report it. Considering what happened to the carriage gates, there should be no argument about putting a squad car in the area."

Elliot walked toward Marissa. "Maybe you're right."

***

Elliot paced back and forth across the kitchen while she spoke with the night shift detective on the phone. Lia joined her and made herself a cup of chamomile tea.

Elliot turned off her phone and placed it on the kitchen island. She ran a hand through her short cut blond hair. "I really thought we were through with this shit," she said.

"Are they going to send a patrol car?" Lia asked.

"Yes. The night shift officer was familiar with the report Officer Rocque filed today, so they'll have a car circle around every hour or so until they figure out who's behind this."

Lia swiveled in her chair and pulled Elliot toward her. Elliot stood between her legs and wrapped her arms around Lia.

"I don't want to lose you, Lia. I don't think I could live through another scare like we had a few months ago."

"You are not going to lose me. We'll get through this. I promise."

"Are you ready to go back to bed?" Elliot asked.

"I'll be up as soon as I finish my tea."

Elliot kissed her on the forehead. "Okay. Don't be long."

"I won't."

Lia watched Elliot leave the kitchen and then tilted her head back and closed her eyes. Suddenly, the aroma of freshly baked bread filled the room.

Lia inhaled deeply and smiled.

"Ell-ee-ot be a good woman."

Lia's eyes flew open. "Gran!"

"Old Gran thought you might needs company."

"Oh, my God, yes!" Lia exclaimed.

"You's troubled, child."

Lia looked at the cup between her hands and then back at the grandmotherly figure before her. Her eyes filled with tears. "Yes. Yes, I am."

"You's wonderin' what's a'brewin', ain't cha?"

"Gran, these past two months have been so wonderful, and now...now."

"Now you feels da evil again," Gran said.

Lia nodded. "Yes. Yes, I do."

"You needs to look inside yoself, girl. You's made of strong stuff. You's have Celeste's spirit. That girl be a sassy one, and little Lia—she be sassy too. Too headstrong to know her place, dat girl. It be da death of her."

"Tell me about Celeste, Gran."

"Celeste be born to my daughter Elzbeth in eighteen oh six. We all owned by de master in Atlanta. Da master be a fine man. Treat us good, he did, but he die and his nasty ole son sold us to da evil one when Celeste be but eighteen years. He sold us all together, 'cept Elzbeth. It be a sad day when Elzbeth be sold away to another owner. Never sees her again. Celeste's daddy be kilt on da farm when she was but a wee babe, so she have only Gran when we be sold to da evil one.

"Celeste be a beautiful woman. You looks like her. It wasn't long a'fore the master took her to his bed. Da evil one find out and she make Celeste pay for da master's sins. Near on a year after da master take her dat she become heavy wid his child. Almost lost her when Lia be born. So much blood. But Celeste be strong. Celeste be determined. She do the will of both evil masters to keep Lia safe. She learn to please both in da most awful of ways to not be kilt.

"Celeste do what she must to keep Lia safe, but she give her heart to Samuel. Dey jumped da broom not long after Lia be born. He be a good man. He love Lia like she be his. He know Celeste do what she need wid da master and da evil one, but he love her still. Da master found out and kilt him in da attic. Kilt him and made Celeste watch. She was wid child when Samuel be kilt. That child be Ethan."

Lia wrapped her hands tighter around her cup of tea. She closed her eyes and allowed the tears to escape down her cheeks as she listened to the horrors that had occurred in her home more than one hundred and eighty years earlier.

"Ethan be born not long after dat, and I sends him away. I sends him away a'fore the evil one kilt him. Celeste be broken. She be broken wid Samuel's death. She be too broken to care for Lia. Lia become wild and she be a problem for da evil one, and she kilt her, too. Dey say Lia jump to her death, but Gran know da evil one cause her to fall. Celeste was all but dead inside after dat, so I sent Ethan away."

"Tell me more about Ethan, Gran."

"Ethan be but a babe when I sends him away. I never sees him again, but I knows he's survive. He be in you, child. You have his strength, and you have Celeste's strength too. Don't you never forget dat. Ethan survive and you will, too."

Elliot was sound asleep when Lia slipped into bed behind her. She spooned herself into Elliot's back and draped her arm around her waist. "I love you, Elliot," she whispered.

Without waking, Elliot rolled onto her back and took Lia into her arms. Lia laid her head on Elliot's shoulder and once again draped her arm across her waist.

Within moments, she was fast asleep.

Chapter 7

Lia rushed into the kitchen the next morning while pulling her jacket over her blouse. "Coffee!" she exclaimed.

Elliot, who had been standing at the coffee maker, turned around and handed a travel mug to her. "I thought you might appreciate this, seeing as you're running late."

Lia kissed Elliot full on the lips and then took the mug from her. "I will love you forever," she said.

"If we leave right now, we might have time to drive through the bakery for a few beignets," Elliot suggested.

"That sounds wonderful. Sorry I overslept. I was up late. I had a visitor after you went upstairs."

"What?"

"Not to worry. I'll tell you about it in the car. Right now, we need to get moving. Those beignets are calling to me."

Elliot grabbed her mug and her briefcase. "Okay, let's hit the road."

They walked through the butler's pantry and into the open foyer near the staircase, just as Marissa and Julie came down from the third floor.

"Good morning!" Julie and Marissa said together.

"'Morning. Running late!" Lia said as she stepped into the stairwell.

Elliot looked up as she followed Lia down the stairs. "You two are signing the papers today, right?" she asked.

"Yes. We'll celebrate during dinner. Jules and I are cooking," Marissa called over the railing as her friends reached the bottom of the stairs.

"Awesome! See you tonight, loves!" Lia added.

Elliot used her key fob to unlock the car door before Lia reached for it. She turned back to lock the entry gate and then ran around the front of the car to climb into the driver's seat. Moments later, they were on their way to the bakery.

"So exactly who visited you last night?" Elliot asked.

"Gran."

"Really? I wonder what brought that on."

"You know, El, I sometimes think Gran has never left. There are times that I still smell apple pie or fresh bread cooking in the kitchen."

"I've smelled it too. I guess if we have to have a ghost, Gran is a good one to have."

"Anyway, I was sitting at the island drinking my tea and she just appeared. She said she thought I needed company. She made some odd remark about feeling the evil again, and then she told me that I had Celeste's spirit and Ethan's strength and that I would survive."

"Samuel pretty much implied that you are descended from Ethan," Elliot said. "I wonder what happened to him when Gran sent him north."

"I've been wondering about that myself, El. I've mentioned this before, but I'd like to do my genealogy. It would be good to know for sure."

"I think that's a great idea. Let's do some on-line searches tonight to find someone reputable." Elliot turned her directional on. "Here's the bakery. How many beignets do you want?"

"Get me a dozen. I'll share them with my lab mates."

Elliot pulled the car up to the window and placed two orders, one for herself and one for Lia. Soon, they were back on the road again, heading toward the Louisiana Cancer Research Center.

Ten minutes later, Elliot pulled to a stop in front of the lobby's entrance.

"Here you go, love. I'll pick you up around five. Is that okay?" Elliot asked.

"Five is great." Lia leaned toward Elliot and kissed her. "Thank you, sweetie. I hope you have a good day."

"You too! See you this afternoon."

***

Just before lunch, Marissa and Julie walked hand in hand into the office of the realtor that was representing the homeowner. The representative shook both their hands and seated them in two chairs opposite his desk. A nameplate with the words *Mr. Jonathan Richmond* faced them.

"Congratulations on the homeowner accepting your offer," Mr. Richmond said.

"Actually, I'm surprised they did. Our offer was two-hundred thousand dollars lower than the price they originally wanted for it when it went on the market two years ago," Marissa said.

"It appears you've done your homework," Richmond replied.

"I work for the realtor I'm purchasing the house through, so I was privy to the market analysis and selling history of the property. It looks like it has changed hands twice in the past two years, and each time, it sold for significantly less. Any idea why?"

The smile left his face. "I'm sorry, but you don't look familiar, Miss..." Richmond picked up the paperwork in front of him. "Miss Barrows?"

"No, that would be, Julie. I'm Marissa Thompson."

"My apologies, Miss Thompson. The realty community in New Orleans is tight. I'm surprised I haven't heard of you before now."

"We just moved to the area two months ago. We've been staying with friends," Marissa replied.

"I see. So, before we continue, your questions lead me to wonder if you are still interested in purchasing my client's property."

"Yes. We are still interested, but I do wonder why prime property this close to Bourbon Street is selling for such a low price."

"My client has been offering it as a vacation rental, and since they do not live in the great state of Louisiana, they found remote property management to be difficult."

"Are you sure that's why?" Marissa asked.

"I don't understand what you mean," Mr. Richmond said.

"Could it be because it sits on the original site of Marie Laveau's home? You know—Marie Laveau, the voodoo queen?" Julie added.

Richmond looked back and forth between the two women. "You truly have done your homework," he said.

"This *is* New Orleans, after all, Mr. Richmond. The friends we are staying with purchased a property on Royal Street several months ago and let's just say their lives were quite unsettled for a while," Marissa said.

Mr. Richmond rested his elbows on the arms of his chair and made a teepee with his fingers. "I assure you, my client's property is *nothing* like the one on Royal Street."

Marissa sat back in her chair and allowed an uneasy silence to fall between them.

After a few moments, Mr. Richmond leaned forward. "If you'll give me a moment, I will contact my clients to relay your concerns."

"Please do," Marissa said.

Julie turned to Marissa after he left the room. "Mar! What are you doing? I don't want to lose this house!"

Marissa reached for Julie's hand. "Trust me," she said.

Mr. Richmond returned five minutes later and sat behind his desk. "My client is prepared to reduce the price by an additional fifty-thousand dollars and will offer to cover the closing costs if you are still interested in purchasing the property."

Marissa raised her eyebrows. "That was not our intended outcome today, Mr. Richmond, but since your client is feeling so generous, we accept."

"Wonderful! If you would be so kind as to give me a few more minutes, I will have my secretary update the purchase price on this contract and then we can sign the papers."

"Take all the time you need, Mr. Richmond," Marissa replied.

Mr. Richmond left the room and returned less than two minutes later with two full copies of the contract that Marissa and Julie both signed, followed by his signature as his client's representative. He slipped one copy into a large manila envelope and handed it to Marissa.

"We should be able to close on the property within a week," Mr. Richmond said.

"A week?" Marissa asked. "That's pretty fast. Most closings take nearly a month."

"My client is motivated to offload the property quickly and has already taken care of the title search requirements. Like I said, they are finding remote property management to be a chore and they want to get out from under it as soon as they can."

Marissa stood and offered her hand. "I understand, Mr. Richmond."

She dug a business card out of her wallet and handed it to him. "I can be reached at this number or email address as soon as you have a date, time and location for the closing." She took Julie's hand. "It has been a pleasure working with you."

***

"Marissa Thompson, you are such a snake!" Julie exclaimed over the roof of the car as she reached for the door handle and climbed in.

Marissa settled into the driver's seat and secured her seatbelt. "What?" she said.

"You knew they would come down another fifty thousand dollars, didn't you?"

"No, I expected them to cover the closing costs, but to come down fifty thousand on top of that was a bonus. Oh, and did you notice that he was gone from the room for less than two minutes after we agreed to the new price? No secretary on the face of the earth could make several changes to a thirty-page document and print out two new copies in that amount of time. He had that offer ready in the event we threatened to back out."

"But, how did you know that?" Julie asked.

"This is not my first rodeo, sweetheart. I've seen so many deals go down in the twenty years I have been selling homes, it would make your head spin."

"I'm speechless," Julie said. "I totally didn't expect that. Not that I mind!"

"What do you say we take a ride by the house before going home?"

Julie grinned. "I'd love to."

***

Photograph captured from Google Maps
Karen D. Badger, 7/14/2021

Julie became animated and threw the door open as soon as they pulled to the curb in front of ten twenty Saint Ann Street.

"She's in the window, Mar!"

She walked across the sidewalk and stood in front of the center window. "We signed the papers today," Julie said. "In about a week, we'll be the proud owners of your home."

Marissa joined her in front of the window. "Did she say anything?" Marissa asked.

"She said she's been waiting for a long time for us to come."

"That's odd. How could she possibly know we would be moving here from New York?" Marissa asked.

Julie looked at the window and then at Marissa. "She said the cards told her."

"The cards specifically told her we would be moving here from New York and that we would buy this house? Did she have our names in advance as well?" Marissa asked sarcastically.

Again, Julie looked at the window. "Marie, this would be easier if you allowed Marissa to see and hear you."

Marissa looked at the window and then took several steps backward. "Holy shit!" she exclaimed.

Julie turned to Marissa, who now stood nearly on the curb. "I guess you can see her now."

"Yeah. She was just *there*. I can see *through* her, but she's definitely visible," Marissa exclaimed.

Julie extended her hand. "Come here. She means us no harm."

Marissa slowly approached and took Julie's hand. Julie pulled her closer to the window. Marissa simply stood there with her mouth open.

"Mar?" Julie said.

"She's beautiful," Marissa whispered.

"Yes, she is very beautiful." Julie looked at the image in the window. "Marie, please tell us what the cards said."

"You know de cards speak truth, girl. Six of Pentacles, Tower reversed, Chariot. Chaos is at our door. My home, it be disturbed. Da evil has returned. We must fight, girl! We must fight wid all dat be in us. You know de way. We know de way together."

A moment later, the apparition faded way.

"What the hell did *that* mean?" Marissa said.

Julie frowned. "I'm not sure. I need time to think."

Marissa looked at her watch. "You'll have to do that later tonight. It's nearly three. If we're going to make dinner for the girls, we'd better hit the grocery store and then head home."

"Do we have time to take a quick look inside first?" Julie asked.

'I think so, but we can't stay long."

Marissa pulled the combination to the lock box out of her wallet and retrieved the key to the deadbolt. A moment later, they were inside the living room.

"I just want to walk around to get some ideas for curtains," Julie said.

"While you're doing that, I'm going to take another look at the master to see if it makes sense to take that wall to the adjoining room down. I'll meet you back in the living room in about ten minutes."

"That should be enough time."

Marissa took several pictures of the wall she wanted to take down as well as the closet that was in the corner of the room. She walked back into the master and while she imagined where they might place their furniture once the room was larger, she was distracted by the sound of drumming and chanting. She stopped and strained to hear where the sound might be coming from.

Marissa walked to the door at the very back of the room and opened it. She stepped onto the landing and listened. Oddly, the drumming stopped.

"Well, that was weird," she said under her breath.

Marissa went back into the house and relocked the door. No sooner had she turned to walk through the room and the drumming resumed. She opened the door again and stepped outside. All was quiet.

It wasn't until she entered the house a second time that she realized the sound was coming from the living room. Marissa secured the back door once again and made her way toward the front of the house.

"Julie!" Marissa called as she moved through the second bedroom and dining room.

"I'm coming," Julie called back.

"Do you hear that?" Marissa called out.

"Hear what?"

"Drumming."

Marissa and Julie stepped into the living room at the same time, Julie from the kitchen, and Marissa from the dining room.

The drumming stopped.

"It stopped," Marissa said.

"What stopped?"

"The drumming and chanting. You didn't hear that?"

"No. No, I didn't," Julie said.

Marissa put her hands on her hips. "Well, I did. It started when I was in the master. I went outside to see if it was coming from out there, but it wasn't. It sounded like it was here in the living room."

Julie looked around the empty living room. "Well, obviously there's no one in here."

Marissa's attention was drawn to the floor directly in front of the center window—the exact window Marie's Laveau's apparition had stood earlier. "What's that?"

Julie crossed the room and picked up a single, pristine feather. She turned to Marissa, wide-eyed.

Marissa frowned. "What is it, Jules?"

"A single pristine feather was known to be Marie Laveau's trademark. In voodoo, it is a symbol of great luck for those who receive it. I need to show this to Phoebe."

"I don't remember that feather being there yesterday when we looked at the place," Marissa said.

"That's because it wasn't there yesterday," Julie explained. "Marie left it for us today."

"If she's wishing us good luck in buying this house, I'm not sure that's a good thing."

"Maybe it's not for buying the house. Maybe it's for something else."

Marissa crossed her arms. "Why do I think I'm not going to like this?"

Chapter 8

"You could actually see her?" Elliot asked.

"Yes. I couldn't at first, but Julie asked her to appear to me, and she did," Marissa replied.

Elliot looked at Julie. "Who da thunk you'd have that much clout with the notorious voodoo queen of New Orleans?"

Lia rose from the table. "I'm going to help myself to more of this wonderful lasagna. Does anyone else want some?"

Elliot handed her plate to Lia. "I'll have a little more. Thank you, love."

"Jules? Marissa?" Lia asked.

"I'll get it." Julie collected Marissa's plate and hers and joined Lia at the stove while Elliot and Marissa continued their conversation.

"So, what did she look like?" Elliot asked.

"She was translucent and fluid-like, but from what I could tell, she must have been drop-dead gorgeous in her younger years. Like Lia."

Lia placed Elliot's plate in front of her and then sat in her own chair. "Stop that, Mar. I'm not drop-dead gorgeous," she said.

"I beg to differ, my love," Elliot replied. "I agree with Marissa. Oh, and thank you for the lasagna."

Lia placed a quick kiss on Elliot's lips. "You're welcome."

"Anyway, she let me see her and then she told Jules and me that she had been waiting for us for a long time."

"Get out!" Elliot exclaimed.

Julie handed Marissa's plate to her. "That's exactly what she said." Julie looked around the table. "More wine?"

"Grab a new bottle from the beverage cooler. We killed the last one," Lia said.

Marissa stood. "You sit and enjoy your dinner. I'll get the wine." She held Julie's chair for her to sit and then kissed her on the head.

"So, how did she know you were coming?" Lia asked.

"She said the cards told her," Julie replied.

"Cards? You mean tarot cards?" Lia added.

"Yes. Tarot cards are a huge part of voodoo. They're used in the Wiccan religion as well. Anyway, she mentioned three cards, so I assume she was doing a past, present, future reading."

"Did she give you any details?" Elliot asked.

"No, she just mentioned the cards. Six of Pentacles, The Tower and The Chariot," Julie explained.

"Didn't she say The Tower was reversed?" Marissa asked while she refilled the wine glasses.

"Yes, she did. Thank you for reminding me of that, Mar. That makes a huge difference. I need to pull those three cards from my deck and study them to understand what she was telling us. I may ask Phoebe to help me with that."

"You should do *our* cards," Lia suggested.

Julie grimaced. "Reading cards for friends is sometimes awkward."

"It's just for fun, right?" Elliot asked.

"Oh, oh!" Marissa said.

"Did you really just say that, Elliot?" Julie asked. "Reading cards is serious business. They are useful tools for helping someone plan their life, or for solving difficult problems. Can it be fun? Yes, but it can also be quite disturbing."

Elliot reached for Julie's hand. "Sorry. I didn't mean to offend you."

Julie squeezed Elliot's hand. "I'm not offended, El. Unless you're a practitioner, it's tough to understand how impactful a tarot reading can be. No sweat, sweetie."

Lia watched the interaction between Elliot and Julie with interest. Her first instinct was to come to Elliot's defense, but as much as she loved her headstrong wife, there were times that she needed a lesson in humility.

"Would you consider doing our readings if we don't hold it against you?" Lia chuckled.

"Sure. I can do that. Maybe after dinner," Julie replied.

"Awesome!"

Elliot changed the subject. "I'll bet you're anxious to move into the new house."

"We are, but there's some work to do before then," Marissa said. "We actually went into the house while we were there to take another look around."

"I have some ideas about curtains and linens," Julie said.

"I can help you with that. That sounds like a shopping trip!" Lia said gleefully.

"Ugh! Shopping!" Elliot added.

"I'm with you, El," Marissa said. "Maybe while the girls shop, we can knock that wall down."

"Count me in. Anything but shopping! We need to rent a sander for the floors as well."

Lia sat back and rubbed her stomach. "I'm stuffed. That lasagna was fabulous! Thank you, Jules."

"Mar made the sauce. I just threw it together," Julie said.

"Then, thank you both," Elliot added. "It was very good."

"We should wait a while on dessert. I don't think I could eat another bite," Marissa said.

"That's a good idea," Julie added. "Why don't y'all retire to the living room while I clean up the dishes, and then we can do tarot readings?"

Elliot stood. "Nope. You and Marissa cooked. The least Lia and I can do is clean up. Go relax."

"What Elliot said. Now scram!" Lia added.

***

The four friends sat in a circle on the living room floor. Julie placed the tarot deck in the middle of the circle. "Who wants to go first?" she asked.

"Mar, why don't you go first?" Lia suggested.

"I'm going to pass on this one. We learned a long time ago that it's not a good idea to have your wife do your cards. There's just too much bias there," Marissa replied.

"Okay then, you go first, Elliot," Lia suggested.

"Sure. I don't mind," Elliot said.

"Great. Elliot, pick the deck up and shuffle them four times," Julie instructed.

"How should I shuffle?" Elliot asked.

"Shuffle them any way that feels comfortable to you. While you're doing that, think about what question or situation you would like addressed during the reading."

Elliot handed the shuffled deck back toward Julie.

"Before you give them back to me, place them on the floor in front of you and cut them into three piles. Handle the sides of the stack loosely with your fingertips and allow them to cut where it feels natural for them. Put the pile you just cut to the left of the original deck and then cut the original deck again. Place that one to the left of the first pile you cut."

Elliot followed Julie's directions as instructed.

"Like this?" Elliot asked when she had three piles in front of her.

"Perfect. Now take the cut on your right and put it on top of the center deck, and then place the cut on the left on top of that. Now pick the deck up and hand it to me."

Julie took the deck from Elliot and held it in the same orientation as it was handed to her.

"Okay. Because we are facing one another, I need to rotate the cards one hundred and eighty degrees so the top of the cards remains consistent. If we were sitting side by side, I would not do that," Julie explained.

"Why does that matter?" Elliot asked.

"Most of the cards have a different meaning if they are reversed, so it's important to keep them at the same orientation they would have been if you were the one doing the reading instead of me."

Elliot nodded. "That makes sense."

"Okay. I think we are ready. I'll do a simple four card spread."

Julie put the deck on the floor to her right. She took the first card off the top and placed it face down, some distance away, to her left. She then took the second card and placed it to the right of the first card, followed in that same order by the third and fourth cards.

She pointed to the first card on her left. "This card represents your past. It could be as recent as yesterday, or it could be years ago. We'll know more when I flip it."

Elliot nodded.

Julie turned the card. "Interesting," she said. "It's the Ten of Pentacles, reversed."

"What does it mean?" Elliot asked.

"A reversed Ten of Pentacles indicates that in the past, you had been in a state of emotional poverty and guilt, brought on by some oppositional or violent force."

"That seems appropriate," Marissa exclaimed. "You have been holding on to the guilt of what happened to Lia a few months ago."

Lia reached for Elliot's hand. "I agree. I've been telling you for a while now to let it go."

"This second card represents the present." Julie turned it. "Wow, two reversed cards in a row. This one is the Ace of Pentacles, and reversed, it indicates that an unwelcome change is coming."

"That sounds foreboding," Elliot remarked.

"Keep in mind that we don't know what that change is. It could be something major, or it could simply indicate a minor annoyance."

"Okay. I'll keep an open mind. Please go on."

"This third card represents the future. Again, like the first card, we don't know when that future will be. It could be later today, or it could be years from now. Let's take a look at it." Julie flipped the third card and smiled. "The Lovers."

"Whoo hoo!" Elliot shouted. "It's not upside down. What does it mean?"

"It means the end of isolation and the formation of a bond based on love, honor and trust."

Elliot frowned. "But I have that now. Why is it the future card?"

"Remember, we don't know how far into the future this card represents," Julie explained.

"Are you implying that I will be forming a bond of love with someone other than Lia?"

"It means the cards see a strong bond of love, honor and trust in your future. Who that is with is not indicated. Remember, Elliot, the cards don't *predict* the future. They simply give you the tools and the information to help guide you through it."

Elliot crossed her arms and sulked.

"This last card represents the final outcome if everything remains on its current path."

Julie turned the card. "The Three of Pentacles. This is a very positive card in an upright position, but since it's reversed, it means the final outcome will include disillusionment."

"What?" Elliot exclaimed. "What the hell does that mean?"

"Elliot, calm down," Lia scolded.

Photograph taken by
Karen D. Badger, 7/14/2021

Julie collected all of the cards and returned them to the deck. "Elliot, the final outcome card is an indication of what is to come *if* things continue down the current path, and *if* nothing is done to change the direction. Keep in mind that we all have control of the future. Again, the cards give you the tools to guide you through the future. Use this information to change the outcome."

Elliot ran her hands through her short-cropped hair. "You're right, Jules. I'm sorry I lost my cool."

"Apology accepted." Julie turned to Lia. "Do you still want to do this?" she asked.

"Yes, please." Lia took the cards from Julie and shuffled them four times. She then cut and restacked the deck in the same manner as Elliot and handed the deck back to Julie, who again, reversed the orientation.

As before, Julie laid out four cards and then turned the first card.

Lia gasped when The Devil card was displayed in the reverse position.

"Jesus Christ! What does that mean?" Elliot exclaimed.

"So, this card is in the past position. Reversed, it indicates that evil and sinister forces have weakened you. Considering what you lived through when you moved to New Orleans, I'd say this card is spot on," Julie explained.

Lia stared intently at the spread of cards without speaking.

"Let's move on to the present card," Julie turned the next card. "Judgment. Lia, this card indicates that you are curious about your role in the greater scheme of things and that you want to understand how the things around you interrelate."

"That's true." Lia said. "I mentioned to Elliot just this morning that I want to have a genealogy done. I need to understand why I feel such empathy for the poor souls who died here."

"That would make sense," Marissa added. "Didn't Samuel say you're a descendent of Celeste?"

"Yes, he did. And Phoebe also said the family connection is why Celeste was able to control me as easily as she did," Lia added.

Elliot chuckled. "Lia, do you remember when we first bought this place? We were firm believers that everything could be explained by science. Sheesh! How naive were we?"

"Well, we certainly have had our eyes—and our minds—opened since then, haven't we?" Lia replied.

"Indeed!"

"I, for one, have always believed in the spirit world," Julie said. "I'm just glad you no longer think I was just some sort of flake."

Lia reached for Julie's hand. "Sweetheart, we never thought you were a flake, but if we made you feel that way, I'm sorry."

"Me, too," Elliot added.

"Okay, enough of the mushy stuff. Let's get this reading over with. Dessert is calling to me," Marissa said.

Julie reached for the card in the future position and flipped it. She stopped short and stared at the card. "Oh, my," she said.

"What is it?" Lia asked.

Julie looked at Lia. "This is not a good card."

"What do you mean it's not a good card?" Elliot asked.

"The Five of Swords reversed means something will be disarmed and exposed. There is a lot of regret associated with this card in the reverse position. It could even mean death."

"Get the fuck out! Are you saying that Lia is going to die?" Elliot exclaimed.

"This is exactly why I hesitate to do readings for you!" Julie said loudly. "Could it mean that Lia might die? Yes, but it could mean so many other things as well. It's all about interpretation and applying the cards' meaning to your own situation."

"Ah, maybe we should stop right here," Marissa suggested.

"No. Julie, please read the final card," Lia urged.

"Are you sure, Lia?" Julie asked.

"Yes. Please read it."

Julie flipped the last card. It was The Tower card. She lowered her chin to her chest and inhaled deeply. "Okay, before I read this card, let's all remember that this fourth position is the likely outcome *if* nothing is done to alter current events. Do you all understand that?"

Lia and Elliot both nodded.

"Jules, I think we need to stop right here," Marissa repeated.

"No, Mar. We need to finish this." Julie turned to Lia. "The Tower card indicates the road you are currently travelling will come to an abrupt end. It signifies a sudden change is on the horizon, and Elliot, before you fly off the handle again, it does not necessarily mean death, although that is one interpretation.

What is important to repeat here is that this is the likely outcome if you do *nothing* to change it."

"So, what *is* this likely outcome, and what do we need to do to change it?" Elliot asked.

Julie shook her head. "I don't know."

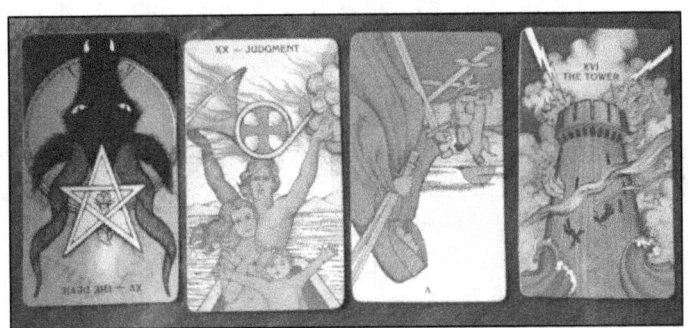

Photograph taken by
Karen D. Badger, 7/14/2021

***

Elliot paced back and forth across the bedroom while Lia sat on the bed with her laptop on her thighs.

"El, please stop pacing and come help me find a genealogist."

Elliot paused at the foot of the bed and looked at Lia. Incredulity was evident on her face. "Aren't you the least bit worried about the tarot reading?" Elliot asked.

Lia looked up from the screen. "I won't deny that I found it disturbing."

"Disturbing? Well, I found it terrifying."

"The cards certainly nailed the past and present circumstances."

"*That's* what I'm worried about, Lia. If the past and present readings were off-the-wall, I wouldn't be so concerned. But they were spot-on, leading me to believe that the future and final outcome readings are probably accurate as well."

Lia tilted her head. "They are accurate only if I allow them to be, El. Like Julie said, we have the power to change the future."

"But what if we don't recognize what needs to be changed until it's too late to change it?"

"Elliot, I'm not going to allow the tarot reading to turn me into a basket case. I refuse to live my life looking over my shoulder. Julie was right. The cards don't predict the future, and besides, there are so many ways to interpret them that we have no idea exactly what is going to happen. You're going to make yourself sick worrying about it."

Elliot climbed onto the bed beside Lia and sat close to her. She put her head on Lia's shoulder and reached for her hand, which she held close to her heart.

"I'm sorry, but I can't help worrying about you, Lia. We have been through so much during the past six months. I almost lost you. I don't ever want to go through that again."

Lia leaned her head against Elliot's. "Sweetheart, the odds are that we won't pass at the same time. Sooner or later, one of us will have to face losing the other."

"Your parents were lucky enough to go together," Elliot said.

"My parents were killed in a car accident, Elliot. I wouldn't wish that fate on either of us—even if it meant we could die together. They were way too young to die, and I was only twenty-eight. Surely you remember that?"

Elliot nodded. "We had only been together for a few months when it happened. You were devastated."

"I was an only child and had no one else to share my grief with. I'm so glad you were there for me, love."

"I have been here ever since, and I will continue to be here for as long as I have breath in my body. I just hope that's for many more decades to come."

"I agree. We need to do our level best to be sure that happens. Julie's reading encourages me to be more cautious, but I refuse to allow it to paralyze me. That's no way to live, El."

Elliot lifted her head from Lia's shoulder and kissed her tenderly. "Okay. I'll try not to worry about it."

"Good. So, help me find a genealogist. As the cards said, I have an itch to understand where I fit in here."

Elliot grinned and wiggled her eyebrows up and down. "I have an itch you can scratch."

Lia bumped Elliot's shoulder and nearly knocked her off the bed. "You are such a guy sometimes!" she exclaimed.

Elliot chuckled and righted herself. "Okay, I'll behave!"

***

Julie climbed into bed and snuggled against Marissa. She put her head on Marissa's shoulder and felt her wife's arms wrap around her. "This feels so good," she said.

"Yes, it does. The tarot reading was intense. Time to relax," Marissa replied.

"It *was* intense."

Silence fell for the next few minutes. Finally, Marissa spoke.

"Is Lia really in danger, Jules?"

"I don't know for sure, Mar. The reversed Five of Swords and The Tower right next to each other in the reading casts a dark shadow on things. They both fell into future positions, so it's hard to know exactly what will happen. So much can happen on a day-to-day basis to change the future."

"Well, if nothing else, maybe it will encourage them to be more cautious," Marissa suggested.

"Hmm."

Another few moments of silence descended upon them. This time, Julie broke the solitude.

"I'm excited about shopping for curtains."

"Well, you can have at it."

Julie lifted her head to look at her wife. "Are you sure? I'd love to have your input."

"Sweetheart, if it saves me from having to go shopping, I wouldn't care if you decorated the whole house like a circus."

"A circus?"

Marissa grinned and wiggled her eyebrows up and down. "As long as you turn our bedroom into a girlie-show venue."

Julie slapped Marissa on the stomach. "You are such a guy sometimes!" she exclaimed.

"Okay, okay, I'll behave!"

Chapter 9

"Good morning, ladies," Elliot said when she walked into the kitchen the next morning.

Julie stood at the stove and stirred a large pan of scrambled eggs while Marissa put two more slices of bread in the toaster. A tall pile of crispy bacon sat on a paper towel in a dish beside the stove.

The door between the butler's pantry and kitchen suddenly swung open. "Bacon! I could smell it all the way upstairs!" Lia exclaimed. She went directly to Julie and hugged her. "Thank you so much for cooking. I've decided I'm not going to let you move into your new house. I need you here to make breakfast for me every morning."

"Hey! I thought that was *my* job!" Elliot complained.

"No worries, El," Marissa interrupted. "If Julie is going to be chained to anyone's stove, it's going to be mine."

Julie threw a potholder at Marissa. "Like hell I am!"

Lia turned to Elliot. "Your choice, love—make coffee or set the table?"

"I'll set the table," she said.

"Okay. I'm on coffee duty."

Lia opened the cabinet to the right of the stove and handed four plates to Elliot, and then pulled coffee cups from the shelf. She moved the sugar bowl and the creamer to the center of the island, as well as the plate of bacon and a bowl of fruit, all while the first cup brewed.

Julie carried the pan of eggs to the island and dished out portions in each plate just as the coffee finished and the last pair of toast popped up. Soon, the four friends were enjoying a hearty breakfast to start their day.

"I'm meeting with Phoebe today to arrange a space in her shop for my office," Julie said.

"That's right. You're starting your tarot reading job with her soon," Lia said.

"Next week. On Monday, to be exact. She's giving me some space in the back of the shop where we can set up a private alcove. Some customers prefer not to have their cards read in public."

"That makes sense. Especially if the cards indicate a less than favorable result," Lia added.

"Like your cards last night," Elliot said.

"El, I told you not to dwell on it," Lia replied. "The reading gave me a lot to think about, but we can't spend the rest of our lives worrying about it."

"I know, I know," Elliot added reluctantly.

"While you're at the shop, you should discuss the cards Marie Laveau mentioned," Marissa suggested.

"Yes. I plan to do that, right after I tell her we're buying Marie Laveau's house. She's going to freak!"

Lia covered Julie's hand with her own. "Darlin', these eggs are to die for! Thank you for cooking."

"I'll second that," Elliot added.

"So, it looks like we may be closing on the house in about a week," Marissa said.

"Wow, that's fast. It took much longer than that to close on this place," Elliot said.

"Julie thinks the owner is in a hurry because Marie has been scaring away prospective buyers and they want to close quickly before we change our minds."

"What do *you* think, Mar?" Lia asked.

"I'm not sure what to think, but the sooner we can get into the place and begin remodeling, the better," Marissa replied.

"You know, there's no hurry for you to go," Elliot pointed out. "This is your home for as long as you want to stay."

"And we love you both for making that so, but it will be nice to have our own place. Oh, and before I forget to say it, we want both of you to feel as welcome in our home as you have made us feel in yours," Marissa said.

"Remember when we were kids, Mar, and we were so close we breathed one another's air? Remember we used to come and go in one another's homes without even knocking—almost like we lived there?" Lia asked.

"I do remember that," Marissa replied.

"I want us to be like that. I want us to always welcome and *be* welcomed and to always be able to find refuge in one another. All of us. I have no family left but Elliot and you two. You are my family." Lia took Elliot's hand. "You are *our* family."

"Damn it, Purvis! We need to change the subject before you make me cry," Marissa said.

"Too late!" Julie picked up her napkin and wiped her eyes.

***

The four friends worked together to clean up the breakfast dishes and then collected their respective briefcases in preparation for heading to work.

Marissa caught Elliot just before she followed Lia down the staircase. "El," she whispered.

Elliot looked at her with raised eyebrows.

Marissa motioned toward Lia with her eyes and a nod of her head.

"Lia," Elliot said.

Lia stopped her descent and turned to look up at Elliot. "I'm going to grab a bottle of water. Catch."

Elliot tossed the car keys to Lia, who caught them effortlessly.

"Grab one for me as well, would you?" Lia asked before she continued her descent.

Elliot returned to the kitchen with Marissa right behind her. She opened the refrigerator, retrieved two bottles of water and put them on the island. "So, what's up?" she asked.

"Lia's birthday is in a few weeks, right?" Marissa asked.

Elliot's eyes flew open. "Jesus! I forgot all about it. *That* would have been a disaster! Thank you for reminding me."

"You're welcome. I just wanted to plant the seed about doing something nice for her. I'm not sure what, but with you and Julie and me working on it, I'm sure we'll come up with something she will enjoy."

Elliot nodded and grabbed the water bottles. "Okay. Let's put our heads together in the next few days. Thank you again for reminding me. I'll see you after work."

Elliot ran back down the stairs and let herself out through the front entryway. As she stepped into the gated vestibule, she saw a man about to open the driver's door of their car. Lia was sitting in the passenger seat with her head against the headrest, and her eyes closed.

Elliot pushed the gate open so hard that it slammed into the brick wall.

"Get the fuck away from my car!" Elliot screamed.

The man stopped short and then turned tail and ran down Governor Nichols Street.

Elliot ran after him, but by the time she cleared the traffic in the intersection, he was gone. When she returned to the car, Lia met her on the sidewalk. She immediately went into Elliot's arms.

"Are you okay?" Elliot asked. "Didn't you see him coming?"

Lia nodded. "I was preoccupied thinking about the day, so no, I didn't see him, El. I would have locked the car doors if I had."

"I know." Elliot took Lia's arm and led her back to the car. She held the door open for her to climb in and then she returned to the vestibule to close and lock the gate, and to retrieve the water bottles she had dropped to the ground. Lia had composed herself by the time Elliot climbed into the driver's seat.

"Are you sure you're okay?" Elliot asked again.

Lia nodded. "I'm fine."

"I'm going to pay a visit to Officer Rocque after I drop you off at work. I think we need more than an occasional drive-by."

***

"Good morning, Phoebe!" Julie let herself into the shop and greeted her friend with a warm hug.

Not for the first time, Julie was mesmerized by the unique style of her childhood friend. She realized that some of it was intentional to fit her character as a psychic medium, but in truth, Phoebe had always been a bit of a nonconformist, even as a child.

Phoebe was of medium height with graying-black hair pulled loosely into a bun on top of her head, and with ringlets hanging at her temples. She wore her standard uniform of high-waisted, tailored slacks with low-heeled shoes, a white blouse, and an ever-present silk scarf around her neck. She also wore an assortment of bangle bracelets on her right arm. Julie wondered how many scarves her friend owned, for each day, a new one appeared. The woman's makeup was extreme. Dark eye shadow adorned her lids, and extended to her eyebrows, to be outdone only by very long false eyelashes and dark crimson lipstick. Perhaps the most striking feature of all, was the crystal blue of her eyes, so light in color, they appeared nearly transparent.

Phoebe pulled out of the hug and held Julie at arm's length. "It seems like forever since I've seen you. I'm so glad you agreed to accept my offer. I have so hated turning clients away, but I simply don't have the time for readings as well as my medium sessions."

"I should be thanking you, Phoebe. It'll be nice to have a reason to get out every day, and besides, the extra income will help with the new house," Julie said.

"New house?"

"Yes. Marissa and I just signed the papers yesterday. The best part is that it's within walking distance of the shop. It's just around the corner, as a matter of fact."

Phoebe's brow knit in thought. "I sense there is something you are not telling me, Julie."

Julie grinned ear to ear. "You *were* always able to read me like a book. Okay, I'll tell. We bought the house at the same location where Marie Laveau lived and died."

Phoebe grabbed a nearby cabinet to steady herself. "You bought the Laveau property?" she gasped.

"We did."

"Oh, my. You *do* know that it is haunted?"

"Yes! It is haunted by Marie Laveau herself. We've seen her. Both Mar and I have. I've talked to her as well."

"You've talked to her?"

"Yes. In fact, I wanted to talk to you about what she said."

Phoebe held her hand up. "Wait." She walked toward the door to the shop, locked it and turned the open sign around to closed. She turned back to Julie and took her hand. "Come with me."

Phoebe led Julie to a door in the far back corner of the store. She pushed the door open, reached for a light switch on the wall inside the door, and motioned for Julie to follow her down a steep set of stairs into the basement. When they reached the bottom of the stairs, Phoebe flicked another switch and bathed a very charmingly decorated one-room efficiency apartment in soft white light.

"Wow. I didn't know this was down here," Julie said.

"It's relatively new. I have been spending some very late nights in the shop and sometimes, it's easier to just sleep here than to walk home in the dark. Only three people know of its existence—you, me, and the man I hired to remodel it. Come sit on the couch. I'll make us tea."

Julie sat on the couch and waited while Phoebe filled an electric teapot with water and plugged it in. Phoebe turned and leaned her backside against the counter. "Now tell me about Marie Laveau appearing to you."

"Well, the first time Marissa and I went to see the house, she was standing in the front window, plain as day—at least to me. No one else saw her."

"Who is no one else?"

"Marissa, Lia and Elliot."

"So, she chose to appear just to you."

"In the beginning, yes. She made herself visible to Mar later, after I asked her to. She said she had been waiting for a long time for us to come."

Phoebe narrowed her eyes. "She knew you were coming?"

"Yes, she said the cards told her."

"Did she say *which* cards?" Phoebe asked.

"Six of Pentacles, The Tower reversed and The Chariot. I think she was doing a past, present, future spread. Phoebe, I need you to help me with a deep dive into these cards."

"Tower reversed," Phoebe whispered.

"Yes. As Marie put it, *chaos is at our door*."

The whistling sound of the teapot interrupted their conversation. Phoebe prepared two cups and carried them to the coffee table in front of the couch Julie was sitting on. She sat next to her.

"Here you go, love. Two sugars and a splash of cream, right?" Phoebe handed the cup to Julie.

"Perfect! You know me so well!" Julie replied.

"Of course. You are my sister from another mother, as the kids like to say." Phoebe chuckled. "Now, let's take a look at those cards."

Julie reached into her backpack and extracted her tarot cards. She quickly sorted through the deck and found the Six of Pentacles, The Tower and The Chariot, which she placed face up in front of them, with the Six of Pentacles on the left, The Tower in the middle and The Chariot on the right in their respective past, present and future positions. Before they began, she turned The Tower card upside down in the reverse position.

Phoebe leaned forward and rested her forearms on her thighs. She studied the cards for a long time before she looked at Julie. "I'm trying to find something positive here, but with The Tower reversed, that is somewhat difficult."

"I know. I came to the same conclusion," Julie replied.

"Did Marie say anything to you about the cards?"

"If I remember right, she said the truth is in the cards and that chaos is at our door. She also said that we would have to fight with everything we had, and that together we would know the way."

"That's a bit cryptic," Phoebe said.

"What *isn't* cryptic when it comes to the cards?" Julie joked.

"True enough. Okay, let's break each card down to see if what she said makes sense."

Phoebe closed her eyes and ran her fingertip around the periphery of the Six of Pentacles card for several minutes. She then opened her eyes and stared at the card.

Photograph taken by
Karen D. Badger, 7/14/2021

"This card is in the past position. There is a figure dressed in golden robes, indicating he is a man of wealth and status. I believe this figure represents Marie Laveau."

"That's exactly what I concluded," Julie said. "It would make sense, since the figure on the card is giving money to the beggars, and Marie Laveau was known for her philanthropy and good will to the poor."

"Again, this card is in the past position, so it represents what has already happened."

"Phoebe, before we go much farther, I struggled with the reading because I'm not sure if it applies only to Marie, or to us directly, versus to society as a whole. I mean, she did say that *we* would have to fight together to be victorious against whatever chaos is pending."

"Those are good questions. We will keep that in mind as we go through the cards."

Phoebe picked up the Six of Pentacles card and studied it carefully. "Because this card is in the past position, it could also represent a desire to return to what once was. It implies that something has changed, or is soon to change, and not for the better. This is further supported by the fact that The Tower in the reversed position is right next to it."

Photograph taken by
Karen D. Badger, 7/14/2021

"The Tower card scared me when I was first learning tarot," Julie admitted.

Phoebe smiled at her friend. "I remember."

"I mean, look at it," Julie said. Lightning, fire, people jumping out of windows to escape the chaos." Julie looked at Phoebe with tears in her eyes. "I can't help but compare it to those poor souls who jumped from the twin towers on nine eleven. It breaks my heart."

Phoebe rubbed Julie's back. "You are a sensitive soul, my friend. This is exactly why I'm so excited for you to work with me. You have an empathy that cannot be learned. That will come through in your readings."

Julie wiped her eyes. "I'm just a big baby when it comes to human suffering."

"As big as your heart is, when it becomes overfull with emotion, it has to come out somewhere. For you, it is through your eyes. They are the windows to your beautiful soul."

Julie shoulder-bumped her friend. "You're making me blush. We should probably get back to reading these cards."

"You are right, of course."

Julie and Phoebe studied The Tower card.

"I believe this card represents the chaos that Marie said was at our door—especially in the present position. The first question I have is...what chaos? The second question is to whom is this chaos supposed to happen? Do you see what I mean, Phoebe? I can't tell if this reading is directed at a particular person, or at society as a whole."

"Regardless of how far-reaching this message may be, Marie meant for *you* to have it, so I believe we need to assume it applies directly to you, or to your circle. Once we know what the chaos is, we will be better equipped to decide how widespread it may be," Phoebe suggested.

"Are you implying that Marissa and I could be in danger?"

"Perhaps. I'm not sure it actually involves danger, but that is a possibility."

"Jesus, Phoebe!"

"I doubt that Jesus has anything to do with this," Phoebe joked. "Anyway, this card implies that there is some crisis looming on the horizon that has, or is, about to topple the peaceful status quo indicated by the Six of Pentacles card. Again, it could apply to you personally, or to a wider group."

Phoebe watched Julie intently as a play of emotions crossed her face. "Are you all right, Julie? Are things okay with you and Marissa?" she asked.

Julie was taken aback. "Of course we're all right. Why would you ask that?"

"The Tower in reversed position could also mean there is a breakdown coming, and as difficult as it might be to live through, it's a way to work through something that was built on a false foundation. When the chaos is gone, there is generally peace and a renewed sense of self-reliance."

Julie stood and walked to the opposite side of the room. She turned to face Phoebe. "I can assure you that Marissa and I are solid. There is nothing false about our love for one another. Besides, why would Marie Laveau step in to be our marriage counselor? That doesn't make sense to me."

"Come back here and sit beside me. I didn't mean to offend you, Julie. You know we have always been honest and direct with one another. I believe the love you have with Marissa is strong and true, but there is no doubt in my mind that whatever this looming chaos is, it will stress every relationship you enjoy. It will have that effect on anyone who is involved in this crisis."

"This crisis? What the hell *is* this crisis?" Julie demanded.

"I suspect it will be revealed to us in time. For now, we need to steel ourselves and be as open minded as we can to any possibility. Now come and sit. We have one more card to read."

Photograph taken by
Karen D. Badger, 7/14/2021

Phoebe picked up The Chariot card and handed it to Julie. "What does this card mean to you?" she asked.

"I see this as a very positive card, Phoebe, especially in the future position. It implies that whatever this chaos is we are about to face, that we will come out victorious in the end."

Phoebe took the card back from Julie. "That is certainly one interpretation, but it comes with caveats."

"What do you mean?" Julie asked.

"Look at the picture. The charioteer is struggling to maintain control of the black and white steeds pulling the chariot. Imagine trying to guide a chariot down a narrow path with a mountain on one side and a steep cliff on the other, while the two beasts pulling the vehicle are working against one another in the opposite directions. Not only will you make no progress toward your goal, but also, you put yourself and everyone else in the chariot with you, in danger of plunging to your deaths. Success in overcoming this chaos is not guaranteed unless all of the forces involved work together toward a common goal. It will require focus and willpower as well as confidence and determination. There will be many turns and detours along the way that will try to force you over the cliff."

"So, in the bigger scheme of things, we will need to work together with a common plan," Julie said.

"That is correct. Moreover, you will need to approach whatever this situation is, with a boldness and aggression you don't realize you possess. You may see things in those around you that you never expected to see. Some of it might scare you, and some of it might forever change how you see someone close to you. But in the end, that aggression and determination must be tempered with common sense and restraint in order to achieve your goal."

Julie sighed. "The hard part will be controlling the passion in the heat of the moment and not go so far as to create an irreconcilable situation in the end."

"That is indeed the biggest challenge, unless of course, the net gain from being successful outweighs the net loss due to irreconcilable differences."

"Are you saying those involved in this crisis may not survive this intact?" Julie asked.

"That is certainly a possibility."

Chapter 10

"Good afternoon, Mr. Harden. My name is Lia Purvis and my wife and I recently purchased a home on Royal Street. It turns out I may be related to someone who lived in that home in the eighteen-hundreds."

"Did you say, Royal Street?" Mr. Harden asked.

Lia paused for a moment. Mr. Harden's high alto voice unexpectedly caught her off guard. "Ah, yes. We purchased it about six months ago."

"Exactly *where* on Royal Street?"

Lia sighed. "I suppose that piece of information is important, but it's always met with a bit of disgust or dismay," she said.

"Don't tell me. It's eleven forty, right?" Mr. Harden asked.

"Yes."

"I knew it!" Mr. Harden exclaimed. "Fantastic! I've been hoping for an opportunity to research that place."

"Wow! I'm not used to that kind of response," Lia said.

"So, before I get too excited, I guess I should ask exactly what you're looking for."

Although she knew stereotyping people was not always wise, Lia decided that Mr. Harden was of African American descent, simply by the tone and cadence of his voice.

"I will tell you, Mr. Harden, that when my wife and I first moved in, we lived under rather tenuous circumstances for the first few months. Things that happened to me in that house have convinced us both that my roots are there, but being a scientist, I need proof."

"You're a scientist?"

"Yes."

"Impressive! Do you mind telling me what your ethnicity is?"

"I'm a woman of color. African American," Lia replied.

"I thought as much when you said your roots are in that house. For that to be so, you are either related to the bitch who owned it, or to the poor souls who fell victim to her madness. I apologize for my language, Ms. Purvis, but knowing what she did to our people makes my blood boil."

Lia smiled. *I knew it!*

"Mr. Harden, I would like to set up a meeting with you to discuss you doing my genealogy. Is that possible?"

"Absolutely. When are you free to come in?"

"I work until five every day. Is five-thirty too late for you?"

"Five-thirty is fine. Would you like to come in today?"

"Actually, let's make it for tomorrow. I'd like my wife to come with me and I need to give her time to clear her schedule."

"Tomorrow at five-thirty then. I'm looking forward to it. Do you have my address?"

"Is it the same one that's on your website?"

"Yes, it is."

"I have it then. We'll see you tomorrow."

***

Lia climbed into the car and leaned to accept a kiss from Elliot. "Hey, my love. How was your day?" she asked.

"It was most excellent. I was asked to join a research project in kinesiology today," Elliot said.

"That's awesome, Elliot!"

"Yes, it is. It will be nice to get back into the research side of things for a while. I love teaching, but I miss the hands-on part of developing new technology."

"Will you be able to use your computer programming skills?"

"Yes. This project is an offshoot of work started at the Spinal Institute of Vermont by Dr. Jordan Lewis. Do you remember me telling you about her? She is a paraplegic who developed a spinal implant that promotes the regeneration of nerve synapses through a computer interface. We will be using a similar approach to develop our own interface between the muscles and a new prosthetic the research department is designing. I've got a chance to make a difference on this one, Lia."

"Well, congratulations. I knew it was only a matter of time before the University realized what a gem they have in you."

"You are giving me way too much credit," Elliot said humbly.

"No, I'm not, and you know it. They are lucky to have you."

Elliot looked both ways before she pulled into traffic. "So, how was your day?" she asked Lia.

"Not as exciting as yours, but good just the same. I had a few minutes at the end of my day to call some genealogy firms. I found one that might work for me. We have a meeting with them after work tomorrow."

"*We* have a meeting with them?" Elliot asked.

"Yes. I want you there with me. After all, you have more direct experience with Celeste than I do."

"True."

"Did you stop to see Officer Rocque this morning?"

"I did, and I told him all about the guy that attempted to accost you," Elliot replied.

"He didn't really accost me, Elliot."

"No, but he could have. We have no idea what his intentions were. Anyway, he's going to stop by this evening on his way home."

"I wish I knew what he wanted. He's been lurking around the corner for what—nearly a week now?" Lia said.

"I don't care what he wants. I just want him to stop stalking us. We have a right to feel safe in our home and so far, we're batting close to zero since buying this house."

"Did Officer Rocque say what time he'd be by?" Lia asked.

"I think he works the seven-to-seven shift, so I'm guessing it will be around seven-thirty."

"Why don't we invite him to have dinner with us? That's only two hours from now. I'll make a nice casserole and a salad. It should be ready about that time."

"That's a good idea. I'll call the station and invite him as soon as we get home."

Elliot pulled into the parking space in front of the house on Royal Street. She quickly climbed out of the car and ran around to the passenger side to open the door for Lia.

Lia climbed out and kissed her tenderly. "I love you for doing it, but you don't have to open the door for me."

Elliot kissed her back. "Come on. Let me be chivalrous once in a while," she said.

"In that case, fair knight, lead the way."

Lia offered her hand to Elliot, who held it daintily and led her to the iron entry gate. She unlocked it and allowed Lia to enter the vestibule ahead of her before securing the gate once more. She then turned her attention to the main entry door, which again, she opened and allowed Lia to enter first.

Elliot bowed at the waist. "My sword is in your service, M'Lady," she said in a mock medieval accent.

Lia stepped into Elliot's personal space. "You can put your sword in my service any time, fair knight. In fact, I'll take you up on that offer later tonight."

"M'Lady had better enter the castle immediately, or I may be forced to dishonor both our reputations right here in the vestibule," Elliot threatened.

Lia's gaze never left Elliot's eyes. "That is a very tempting threat, fair knight."

The sound of a door closing drew their attention to the second story.

"It sounds like the girls are home. We can continue this jousting later if you are willing."

"Oh, I'm willing. I'm definitely willing."

"Lia? Elliot? I saw your car out front. Are you home?"

"Julie! Lower your voice. Maybe they're—you know— otherwise engaged," Marissa said hoarsely.

Elliot walked to the bottom of the stairs while Lia closed and locked the front door. "Actually, that's pretty close to the truth," Elliot called up the stairs.

"Oh! You *are* home," Julie quipped.

"And not otherwise engaged," Marissa added.

Lia joined Elliot at the bottom of the stairs and slipped her hand into Elliot's arm. "Not yet, anyway," she added.

"Should we start dinner?" Marissa asked.

Lia and Elliot ascended the stairs together, hand in hand. "Actually, I plan to make a casserole. Elliot is supposed to invite Officer Rocque to join us, considering he's coming tonight anyway."

"Officer Rocque is coming over tonight?" Julie asked.

"Yes. Oh, you don't know, do you?" Lia said as they reached the landing.

"Know what?" Marissa asked.

"That jerk who has been watching the house nearly got to Lia this morning," Elliot explained.

"What?" Marissa and Julie said at the same time.

"Yes. Lia went to the car before me this morning and by the time I got out there, he had his hand on the handle, ready to open the door."

"Holy shit!" Marissa exclaimed.

"He ran as soon as he saw me and thanks to the traffic, I was unable to see where he went. I stopped at the station after dropping Lia at work and had a chat with Officer Rocque. He's coming tonight to take a report."

"So, as long as he's coming anyway, we are inviting him to have dinner with us," Lia added.

"Great! What can I do to help?" Julie asked.

***

"Wow! I haven't had homemade chicken and andouille casserole this good since my mom passed away four years ago. This is amazing," Officer Rocque exclaimed.

"I'm glad you like it. It's actually Julie's recipe. Did you know she grew up here?" Lia said.

"You grew up here?" Officer Rocque asked. "Whereabouts?"

"My family owns property in the Garden District, although I hung out mostly in the French Quarter. That's where most of my friends lived," Julie replied.

"Nice. I grew up not too far from here, near Congo Square. Small world. When did you leave NOLA?"

"I left a little more than twenty years ago, when I met this one." Julie reached for Marissa's hand and kissed her knuckles. "She was in town at a realtor's convention, and we ran into one another in the voodoo museum while she was sight-seeing. It was love at first sight for me."

"For me as well," Marissa added.

"Anyway, we've lived for the past twenty years in New York City, but when Lia and Elliot left to move here, we missed them so much that Marissa asked to be transferred to NOLA, and here we are."

"How did the four of you meet?" Officer Rocque asked.

"Marissa and I grew up together," Lia replied.

"You two moved here for your jobs, right?" he asked.

"Yes. Lia won a grant at the Louisiana Cancer Research Center, and I was offered a job in the kinesiology department at Tulane. The offers were too good to refuse, so we left everything we knew and loved in New York and moved to New Orleans. Unfortunately, that included Julie and Marissa."

Lia reached for Marissa's hand. "Thank God you decided to follow us here," she said.

"It sounds like a win-win for everyone," Officer Rocque said.

"It was. So, Officer Rocque, you mentioned your mother has passed. Do you have any other family in the area?" Lia asked.

"I think it's time you call me by my first name. It's Randy. Please call me Randy."

"Randy, it is," Lia said.

"So, yes, I have other family in the area. My dad passed when I was young, and like I said, my mom passed four years ago. I was only twenty-eight at the time. I'm here to tell you, that was rough."

"I was twenty-eight when both my parents died in a car accident," Lia said. "I understand how you must have felt."

"They died together? That must have been hard."

"It was. My dad was only fifty-four, and my mom was fifty-one. They were way too young to die. I don't have siblings, so I was on my own after that—except for Elliot. She was my knight in shining armor."

Elliot and Lia exchanged knowing glances, reminiscent of their conversation upon arriving home that afternoon.

"Luckily for me, I have an older brother and sister. I was already on the police force by then, so I was on my own financially, but I needed them for a long time for emotional support."

"So, is there a Mrs. Randy?" Julie asked.

Randy blushed. "There's someone I'm interested in. She's the daytime dispatcher at the station."

"Does *she* know you're interested?" Elliot asked.

"Well…" Randy said.

"Wells are for water," Marissa pointed out. "You need to get on that, dude, if you want to get anywhere with her."

"You ladies are making me blush," Randy said.

"Okay, you two. You're making our guest uncomfortable. Chill," Lia scolded. "How about some dessert, Randy?"

***

Marissa and Julie agreed to take care of the dinner dishes so the others could congregate on the sidewalk in front of the entryway to discuss the morning's encounter.

"Which direction did he come from?" Randy asked.

"I didn't see him until he was about to open the car door. Lia was inside the car with her head against the headrest and her eyes closed," Elliot said. "But the few times we've caught him watching the house, he was standing on that corner, diagonally across the intersection."

"This isn't your first encounter with him?"

"This is the first time he was bold enough to come so close, but we can clearly see that corner from our bedroom window, and we've seen him standing there watching our house at least twice," Lia explained.

"When was the first time he appeared?"

"Right after the damage to the carriage gates," Lia said.

"What does he look like?"

"I'd say he's nearly six-foot and maybe in his forties. He's a white man. Dark hair, unshaven, and dirty looking," Elliot said.

"Our cat freaks out every time he's out there. She's pretty much been our alarm every time he comes around," Lia explained.

"Your cat?" Randy questioned.

Elliot and Lia exchanged uneasy glances. "We have reason to believe our cat has some psychic ability. Let's just say there's a history there," Elliot said.

Randy scribbled a few notes in his pad and then shoved it back into his breast pocket. "I think that's all I need for now. I'll submit my report tomorrow morning. Oh, before I forget, let's take a look at your carriage doors. I have some feedback from the forensics team I want to share with you."

Lia, Elliot and Randy walked toward the corner of Royal Street and Governor Nichols.

Elliot stopped on the corner and looked down each street. "Where's your squad car?" she asked.

"I don't drive my squad car home. It makes my neighbors nervous. I have my own vehicle. It's parked behind your car."

"Oh. Okay. So, let's go look at the gates," Elliot said.

By this time, darkness had fallen, and the only illumination provided was from the streetlamps. The trio walked down the Governor Nichols side of the property and stopped in front of the carriage gates. Randy removed his cell phone from his pocket and turned the flashlight on. He held it up so that it illuminated the damaged parts of the gate.

"See this part right here where it looks like something rammed the doors?"

Elliot pulled her phone out and added her flashlight to the fray. "Yeah, I see it."

"Take a closer look. Does anything look odd to you?" Randy asked.

Lia's head snapped back. "I see it. It looks burned."

"Yes. It looks burned," Randy said. "This is going to sound crazy, but the forensics team thinks this damage was caused by some sort of explosive device rather than a battering ram. With a battering ram, the bare wood beneath the paint would have been exposed. This damage here is black, and the exposed wood was burned."

"Damn!" Elliot exclaimed. "Are you saying someone was trying to burn down the gates?"

"No, I think someone was trying to blow them open. You can go ahead and repair the damage anytime you'd like, but I recommend you keep the locking hardware because in this case, that was all that protected you during this attack."

Randy and Elliot shut their flashlights off, and they walked to the front of the property in darkness. As they neared the corner, Lia reached out and grabbed both their arms.

"Wha...?" Elliot began to say.

"Shhh! He's there. On the corner," Lia whispered.

Like a shot, Randy took off running in the direction of the man and tackled him before he was able to run thirty feet. He flipped the man onto his stomach and quickly cuffed his hands behind him. By this time, Elliot had run across the road to the corner the man had been standing on. Lia opted to stay on the corner by their home.

Randy pulled the man to his feet and pushed him in the direction of his car. Elliot followed.

"You have the right to remain silent. Anything you say can and will be used against you in a court of law. You have the right to an attorney. If you cannot afford an attorney, one will be provided to you, free of charge. Do you understand the rights I have just read to you?"

The man refused to answer.

Randy slammed him up against his car. "I said, do you understand the rights I have just read to you?"

"Fuck you," the man spat.

Randy opened his car door and shoved the man into the back seat.

The man righted himself and cast a venomous stare at Lia who stood just a few feet away on the sidewalk with Elliot.

Randy walked around to the driver's side of the car and reached for his door handle. "I'm glad I didn't have the squad car. He might not have shown his face otherwise. I'll be in touch tomorrow," he said. "Thank you for dinner."

Chapter 11

Elliot climbed into bed and gathered Lia into her arms. "Are you okay, Lia?" she asked.

"Did you see his face when he looked at me, Elliot? There was such hatred there. I could feel evil radiating from him. Even his eyes looked red to me."

"I saw the way he looked at you, but I don't understand why. We don't even know him. Let's hope Randy can keep him locked up for a while."

Lia propped herself on one elbow and looked at Elliot. "Are you saying there's a chance he might be let go?"

"I hate to admit it, but they don't have anything on him."

"Elliot, he tried to get into our car this morning. Considering the expression on his face when he looked at me tonight, heaven knows what he would have done to me if he had been successful."

"I know, but if he denies it, it's his word against ours."

"So, they could just let him go and he could go right back to stalking us?"

"Yes. That could happen."

Lia lay back down and wrapped herself tighter around Elliot. "Sometimes I wish we'd never moved here."

"Do you really mean that, Lia?"

"Yes. No. Well, sometimes. El, we haven't had a moment's peace since we bought this house."

"Lia, I'm considering buying a gun."

Lia sprang into a sitting position. "Are you out of your mind, Elliot?"

"I think you should carry as well."

"I'm not going to carry a gun! Is it even legal here?"

"I did some research. Open carry of firearms is allowed without a permit as long as you are at least eighteen and are not restricted in some way, like having a criminal record. Concealed carry, on the other hand, requires a permit. Oh, and Louisiana is a stand your ground state, meaning, you are allowed to protect yourself, your loved ones or your property if threatened."

"Listen to yourself, Elliot. Are you really considering carrying a gun everywhere you go?"

"I will do whatever it takes to protect you, Lia. If that bastard had actually gotten into the car with you, I would not have hesitated to shoot him to keep you safe."

"I can't believe you are saying this! I don't want a gun in this house."

"Neither do I, but we may not have a choice if they release him and he continues to stalk us."

Lia lay down again and rolled to her side, facing away from Elliot.

"Lia. Lia, sweetie, I'm sorry if this upsets you. I only want to keep you safe."

Lia rolled onto her back to look at Elliot. "I know that, El, but all this talk of guns scares me. There's got to be a better way."

"I won't compromise your safety."

"I know, and I love you for that."

Elliot leaned over Lia. "I don't know what I'd do if I lost you. I think I would want to die right along with you."

Lia traced the side of Elliot's face with her finger. "Don't say that, love."

"It's true. If you died, there'd be no reason for me to go on."

A tear escaped the corner of Lia's eye. "How did I get so lucky as to have found you twenty-two years ago?"

"I'm the lucky one. And to think I nearly threw it all away with my indifference. Thank you for giving me the chance to start again, love."

"Uprooting our lives and moving straight into a nightmare was a pretty tough way to start again," Lia joked.

"I don't think we would have survived it if we didn't love one another as much as we do," Elliot reasoned.

Lia placed butterfly kisses along the line of Elliot's jaw toward her ear. "Make love to me, El," she whispered softly.

Elliot rolled to lie on top of Lia and grinned. "With pleasure, M'Lady. After all, I did promise my sword in your service tonight."

Lia fell into character. "And how long is your sword, fair knight?"

"Long enough to make you scream your passions into the night, M'Lady."

"Pray tell, how shall you accomplish that?"

"I shall lay my sword at your altar and thrust deeply while I steal the kisses from your lips."

Lia wrapped her arms around Elliot's waist and pulled her close. "Thrust away, my lord. My altar awaits," she said huskily.

"Damn!' Elliot growled and then devoured Lia's mouth with her own. "God, what you do to me, woman!"

Elliot sat up and straddled Lia. She reached for Lia's T-shirt and pulled it off over her head. It soon found itself on the floor against the far wall. With that obstruction out of the way, Elliot's mouth explored Lia's neck and collarbones while Lia moaned beneath her.

Before she could continue her explorations, Lia grabbed the back of Elliot's shirt and pulled. "Take this off," she demanded.

Elliot's shirt soon joined Lia's against the wall.

"C'mere," Lia said, and she pulled Elliot toward her so that Elliot's nipples were within reach of her eager mouth.

"Ahh!" Elliot placed her hands against the headboard for support while Lia drove her to madness with her mouth. "Lia...ah...Oh, my God!"

Lia slipped her hands into the back of Elliot's panties and pushed them downward.

Elliot looked down at her. "I'm supposed to be making love to you," she said.

"I'm the queen and I'm pulling rank. Now, off with these, and then come here."

Elliot sat back, removed her panties, and then eagerly straddled her queen once more.

"Oh, no. Higher," Lia said.

A spasm ripped through Elliot's abdomen as her mind registered Lia's intent. She moved higher onto the bed until she hovered directly above Lia's mouth.

Lia dug her fingertips into Elliot's buttocks and pulled her forward. Elliot held tight to the headboard and rasped out her passion as Lia's tongue explored and feasted on her most vulnerable parts.

Before long, Elliot fell into rhythm with Lia's tongue, until finally, and beyond her will, her body stiffened and then plunged into near unconsciousness as spasms passed through her in what felt like endless waves.

Finally, with barely enough strength to hold herself upright, Elliot climbed off Lia and lay beside her. Lia rolled onto her side to face her.

"That was freaking incredible," Elliot said. "But I was supposed to be making love to you."

Lia smiled. "The night is young, my love. My altar is more than ready to accept your sword. As soon as you have recovered enough to wield it, that is."

Elliot reached down and slipped her hand into Lia's panties. Two fingers easily found Lia's folds. Another spasm ripped through her when she realized how ready Lia was.

"You are so wet," Elliot whispered.

"This won't take long, love. I had all I could do to hold it back while you came," Lia said.

Elliot pushed Lia's panties off and cupped her womanhood in her palm while she eagerly feasted on Lia's breasts.

"Elliot, please. I wasn't kidding. I need you inside me." Lia pushed on Elliot's shoulders to clearly convey her need for Elliot to move south.

Elliot immediately moved between Lia's legs and drove two fingers deep inside her while inhaling her clit into her mouth.

Lia's head pressed into the pillow as a low, guttural moan rose from deep within her chest.

As predicted, Lia came almost immediately. She grabbed Elliot's head between her hands and held it firmly in place while her pelvis bucked against Elliot's mouth and spasms ripped through her abdomen.

Finally, Elliot crawled back up to lie beside Lia. She took her into her arms and wrapped her in a cocoon of love. Within moments, they were both fast asleep.

***

The Purvis/Walker household was chaotic the next morning as everyone rushed to get out the door on time. Julie played short order cook and prepared bagel and egg sandwiches, which she handed out, along with a travel mug of coffee, to Elliot, Lia and Marissa—in that order.

Marissa accepted her breakfast and then enveloped Julie in a big hug. "Thank you so much, Jules. You take such good care of us. I love you to the moon and back. See you tonight!"

"I love you, too!" Julie called to Marissa's retreating back. "Have a great day!"

Julie followed Marissa onto the back porch and watched her swing the gates open to pull the car out of the courtyard. She immediately ran down the steps and waved Marissa out of the yard. "I'll get the gates," she called.

Julie returned to the kitchen to make her own breakfast and to clean up the debris from the morning rush. Finally, she had a moment to sit down and enjoy a cup of coffee. She stood at the counter, facing the coffee maker while it brewed. When it was finished, she removed the cup and took a sip of the rich dark liquid while she spun around to sit at the island.

"Oh!" she said, startled to see an older, African American woman standing beside her.

"Don't be scared, child," the old woman said.

Julie took a step back. Her forehead crinkled as she looked intently at the old woman. "Gran?" she asked.

"I's seen you cookin' for dem. Rushin' around, takin' care of dem all. Reminds me of me in da younger days. Course, it not be my choice back den, mind you."

"Gran?" Julie asked again.

"Yes, child. I's be Gran."

Julie put her coffee on the island and sat on one of the stools. "Please. Sit with me," she said.

"Gran only here fo a minute. I's has someting to tells you. I's sees you's da one wid sight. You's da one who believes in da spirits."

"I do," Julie admitted.

"You needs to speak to da queen. She gots someting important to tells you."

"The queen? Do you mean Marie Laveau?" Julie asked.

"You needs to speak to da queen. Go today. You needs to speak to her."

"Gran, please tell me what this is all about."

"Not mine to tell."

"Did Marie send you to me?"

"She be here wid me. Celeste be here, too. Da queen be needin' yo help. Her home be disturbed. She be needin' yo help child. Lia and El-ee-ot be needin' yo help, too."

Julie's frown deepened. "Gran, you're talking in riddles. Why do they need my help? What's going to happen?"

"Go to her, child. Gran needs to go now. Beware da Tower."

"Gran, please stay. There's so much more I want to know!"

"Go to her, child."

"Gran? Gran?"

The woman suddenly vanished.

***

Julie pushed the door to the shop open and rushed in. She stopped short and forced herself to calm down while she waited for Phoebe to take care of a customer. She caught Phoebe's eye when she looked at her over the customer's shoulder.

Phoebe directed her attention back to her patron and then ushered the customer out of the shop as soon as the transaction was complete. She closed the door behind them and swung around to face Julie.

"What is it, Jules? I can see panic on your face."

Julie grabbed Phoebe's shoulders. "You are not going to believe this Phoebs, but Gran appeared to me about an hour ago."

"Gran? Who is Gran?" Phoebe asked.

"She's the ghost of the slave woman who labored as a cook in Lia and Elliot's house in the eighteen-thirties. She's Celeste's grandmother."

"She appeared to you?"

"She not only appeared to me, but I had a conversation with her. Phoebe, she told me the *queen* needed my help. She's got to be talking about Marie Laveau," Julie said excitedly.

"Okay, calm down. What else did she say?"

Julie frowned and tried to recall the conversation. "She said that the queen's house has been disturbed."

Julie looked away as a thought came to her and she quickly looked back at Phoebe. "And if I remember right, Marie said the same thing to Marissa and me when we were at the house. Oh, and she said to be wary of The Tower. I wonder what it all means?"

"Maybe we should go to the house to have a look around," Phoebe suggested.

Julie looked directly into Phoebe's eyes and nodded. "Maybe we should."

Julie pulled her cell phone out of her back pocket. "I need to get the combination to the lock box from Mar, otherwise, we won't be able to get in," she said.

Julie dialed Marissa's number and waited for her to answer.

"Hey, love! What's up?" Marissa asked.

"Mar, I need the combo to the lock box on the house," Julie said.

"Why? Is everything all right?"

"I don't know. That's why I need the combination. Gran appeared to me this morning after everyone left. She told me the queen's home has been disturbed. Phoebe and I are going to walk there to check it out."

"Gran appeared to you? Holy shit! Wait! Didn't Marie say the same thing to us?" Marissa asked.

"Yes."

"I'm going with you. I'll meet you there in ten minutes."

Julie hung up the phone and shoved it back into her pocket. "Mar is meeting us in ten minutes."

"That's about how long it will take us to walk there," Phoebe said. "Let me close the shop and we'll be on our way."

***

Marissa had not yet arrived when Julie and Phoebe approached ten twenty Saint Ann Street. Julie pointed to the center window as they drew near. "She's in the window, Phoebe. Do you see her?"

"No, I don't," Phoebe replied.

Julie walked directly to the window. "Marie, this is my friend Phoebe. She is a medium and a practitioner of voodoo. She is a life-long friend of mine. I trust her and you should as well. She is here to help."

Phoebe's eyes opened wide when Marie appeared to her.

"I see da depth of your soul through your crystal eyes," Marie said. "Da pureness of your heart shine through dem."

"It is my pleasure to meet you. I'm humbled," Phoebe said.

Their attention was suddenly drawn to the car that pulled up to the curb behind them. Marissa climbed out of the driver's seat and walked toward them. "I got here as fast as I could. Is everyone okay?"

"Phoebe and I just got here ourselves. I was just introducing Phoebe to Marie."

Marissa looked at the apparition in the window. "Marie, are you all right?"

"I be in no danger, girl," Marie said.

"But Gran told Julie your house was disturbed. You also said that to us a few days ago, although, truthfully, I don't think it registered with us," Marissa said.

"Marissa is right, Marie. Neither of us thought any more about it—not until Gran said the same thing to me this morning," Julie confirmed.

"Yes, my home be disturbed. It be violated. Evil be unleashed."

"Mar, unlock the door. We need to have a look around," Julie insisted.

"Hold on a sec." Marissa went to the car and returned with a baseball bat.

"What the hell, Mar?" Julie exclaimed.

"What? I keep it handy in case I have to look at houses in less than reputable neighborhoods. Look, if someone has figured out how to get in, they might still be here. I'm not taking any chances." Marissa made short work of the lock box and opened the door. She motioned for Julie and Phoebe to follow her in. "We need to stick together," she said.

The trio moved from room to room, each time finding nothing out of place. An inspection of the yard behind the house also yielded nothing of concern. They ended their inspection where it started—in the living room.

"I love your new home," Phoebe said.

"Phoebs, I'm thinking we might want to smudge the house before we move in, with Marie's approval, of course. There are a few updates we plan to make, so maybe after new paint, we can cleanse the property," Julie suggested.

"We can certainly do that." Phoebe looked around the living room and her gaze settled on the center window where Marie Laveau had appeared earlier. She walked to the window and looked out. Suddenly, she turned around.

"Da Tower be in motion. Da cards don't lie."

Marissa took a step toward Phoebe. "What the fuck?"

Julie grabbed Marissa's arm. "Marie?" she asked.

"I be here."

"What did you do with Phoebe?" Marissa demanded.

"Relax, girl. Phoebe be here wid me. She be fine."

"Marie, tell me about the cards. What is the chaos you spoke of?" Julie asked.

"Da chaos be evil. It be released. It will kill da fifty and one. It always kills da fifty and one."

"I...I don't understand," Julie said.

"My home be disturbed. Da evil is free. We need all come togetter. We must stop it before da fifty and one. Togetter, we's know da way."

Chapter 12

Elliot and Lia pulled up in front of an office building in the business district of New Orleans. They were lucky enough to find a parking place in front of the building.

"Thank God it's time for most people to go home. Otherwise, we may not have found a parking spot for blocks," Elliot said.

"I'll take that as a good sign," Lia remarked.

They both climbed out of the car and met on the sidewalk.

"What's this guy's name?" Elliot asked.

"Harden. I didn't get a first name," Lia said.

They opened the door to the address Lia had obtained from the website and walked into a small lobby. On the wall was a sign with a list of businesses located within that building.

"Let's see. Harden Genealogy Services. Third floor," Elliot read.

Lia looked around. "I don't see an elevator, so I guess we hoof it up the stairs."

Five minutes later, and sweaty from the two-story climb in the heat of the day, Elliot and Lia emerged on the third floor, at the end of a long hallway. They found Harden Genealogy Services about halfway down the hall on the left. Elliot opened the door and motioned for Lia to enter before her. A bell sounded as they stepped onto a mat immediately inside the door. Before Elliot could close the door behind her, a door on the other side of the room opened and a man crossed the room to greet them. His appearance immediately left them speechless.

Mr. Harden was a man of color, and a cross between Rhett Butler and a riverboat gambler. He sported slicked-back black hair and a thin mustache that graced just the edge of his lip. He was of medium height and slight build and wore a burgundy jacket with black velveteen lapels over pinstriped, pleated slacks, white shirt with tuxedo collar and ruffled cuffs, a paisley vest, and ascot tie, and shiny black dress shoes. A chain graced the front of the vest and led to a watch pocket just out of view behind the jacket. The only things missing were a cane and a wool fedora with side feather flourish.

Mr. Harden crossed the room with his hand extended toward them. "You must be Lia Purvis," he said in the same unexpected alto voice he had presented to Lia on the phone the day before.

"Yes. Yes, I am," Lia stammered, not yet recovered from the man's appearance.

"It's nice to meet you. And you are?" Mr. Harden asked Elliot.

All Elliot could do was stare. Lia jabbed her in the ribs.

"Ah! Oh, yes. I'm Elliot Walker. Lia's wife."

"Of course! Please, come into my office."

They followed Mr. Harden across the room and entered the office in front of him.

"Please, sit down. Can I get you anything? Water, coffee, perhaps a cold glass of sweet tea?"

"No, thank you, I'm fine," Lia said.

"I'm good, too," Elliot reached for Lia's hand.

Mr. Harden circled around his desk and sat facing them. "All right then." He looked at Lia. "During our conversation yesterday, you said you believed you have a connection to the slaves who resided at your property. Is that correct?"

"It is more than just a belief, Mr. Harden," Lia began.

"Leslie. Please call me Leslie. Conveniently, it is an androgynous name," Mr. Harden said.

Lia looked at Elliot and then back at the man in front of them. "All right then, Leslie it is. I'm almost certain that I have blood ties to the slaves that worked in our home in the eighteen-thirties."

"On what do you base this certainty?" he asked.

"As I told you on the phone yesterday, we purchased the property at eleven forty Royal Street about six months ago. We did extensive research on the home before we purchased it. In fact, once we learned about what happened to the slaves who lived there, we almost didn't buy it."

"What changed your mind?" Leslie asked.

"On my second walk-through of the home, the realtor left me alone for a few moments in the kitchen and I had a vision," Lia explained.

"A vision?"

Lia nodded. "Yes. I had a vision of an elderly cook preparing a meal for the slaves. She was chained to the stove and the slaves were engaged in a discussion about how the stable boy had been whipped by the mistress. Partway through the conversation, the old woman went to the door and called for a young girl to come in for supper. She called the little girl, Lia. I felt almost as though she was calling to me. I felt compelled to buy the house after that."

"Have you had any other encounters, or found additional information that would make you believe there is a connection?" Leslie asked.

Elliot leaned forward. "In fact, we have."

"Pray tell," Leslie said.

"We discovered that a young woman named Celeste lived and eventually died in the house. The elderly cook Lia mentioned, has appeared to her several times. She told Lia that Celeste had a son named Ethan with one of the slave men and that the old woman sent him north because she feared the mistress would kill him. She also told Lia that she was descended from Ethan."

"Why on earth would the mistress want to kill a child? Especially a boy child. He would have been free labor as he matured," Leslie said.

"This is where it gets complicated. Celeste also had given birth to a daughter, Lia, eight years earlier and the master of the house is reportedly the little girl's father, so the old woman feared the mistress would have killed Ethan to extract revenge on him and Celeste," Lia explained. "Even though I'm sure Celeste had no choice but to submit to repeated rapes by that son of a bitch."

"And this child is the same girl, Lia, you saw in your vision?" he asked Lia.

"Yes," Lia replied.

Leslie sat back in his seat. "I see. After our call yesterday, Miss Purvis, I did some research into your home. Your mistress is quite notorious. Have you ever seen her spirit there?"

Lia exchanged a knowing glance with Elliot. "She was there when we bought the house, but she no longer haunts us, nor does she have control of our home anymore."

"So, if I understand this correctly, your belief that you are somehow related to this Celeste person comes from feelings and ghostly appearances. Is that correct?"

"Lia, tell him about Samuel," Elliot encouraged.

"Samuel?" Leslie asked. He wrote Samuel's name down as Lia spoke.

"Yes. Samuel McGinty. He is a local resident who is a multi-generational descendant of the old cook I told you about," Lia said. "Not too long after we bought the house, he came by to introduce himself and to encourage us to save the souls of the slaves who were killed there."

"Jesus, Mary and Joseph!" Leslie exclaimed. "I think I would have packed my bags and moved out immediately," he said.

"That thought crossed my mind, too," Elliot admitted.

"So, Samuel said you had a familial relationship to Celeste," Leslie said.

"Yes. Oh, and our friend, Phoebe also said there were blood ties," Lia added.

"Phoebe? As in, Phoebe Frost?" Leslie said.

"Yes. Do you know her?" Elliot asked.

"Not personally, but I know *of* her. She has a very good reputation in the voodoo community," Leslie explained.

"We had her to the house and she did a séance, during which both Samuel and Celeste appeared," Elliot said. "That pretty much confirmed that Ethan was a real person that the old woman had sent him away as a baby."

"I don't remember the séance, considering that Celeste appeared through me," Lia added.

"Are you telling me that Celeste possessed you during this séance?" Leslie asked.

"She did."

"I can confirm that, since I saw it happen—not to mention the other times Celeste appeared and possessed Lia. Some at rather inappropriate times," Elliot said.

Leslie's eyes opened wide. "No! She didn't appear when you were..."

"Making love? Yes, she did," Elliot said.

"That's a story for another time," Lia interrupted.

"Damn! You should write a book about that!" Leslie quipped.

"Anyway, Mr. Harden, does this sound like something you would be willing to take on?" Lia asked.

"I would be a fool to say no. I cannot possibly guarantee a confirmed lineage since Ethan was reportedly sent away rather than sold, but from what you have told me, I think it is worth a try. We will need to start with you, and go backward, Lia, so I will need as much information as you can give me on your own family tree. That is, of course, if you choose to hire my services."

Lia felt Elliot squeeze her hand. She looked directly into Elliot's face and saw the affirmation she needed to make her decision. "I believe I *will* hire you, Mr. Harden."

"Fantastic!" Mr. Harden stood and retrieved a packet of papers from his file cabinet, slipped them into a manila envelope and handed it to Lia. "I will need you to fill these forms out as completely as you can. I will begin my search once you return them. My fees are explained on the first page of the packet. If you don't mind returning the retainer fee with the rest of the information, it would be most appreciated."

"I think I can manage that," Lia said.

Lia and Elliot rose, and both offered their hands to the genealogist.

"Thank you, Mr. Harden. I will return these forms as soon as I can," Lia said.

"It was nice meeting you," Elliot said. Elliot grasped Mr. Harden's hand and shook it firmly.

"The pleasure is all mine. I hope to hear from you soon."

Mr. Harden followed them to the door and bade them a good afternoon.

Elliot followed Lia down the two flights of stairs to the sidewalk and reached for the car handle to usher her in. She then walked around the front of the car and climbed into the driver's side. Once inside, she and Lia looked at one another, and almost on cue, they spoke the same words at the same time.

"Mr. Harden is trans. How cool is that?"

***

Officer Rocque was waiting for them when Lia and Elliot parked their car in front of eleven forty Royal Street that evening. They met him on the sidewalk in front of the entrance gate.

"Hey, Randy. What brings you here this evening?" Lia asked while Elliot unlocked the gate.

"I have some news about your stalker," Randy said.

Elliot opened the gate. "Do you want to come in and tell us about it?" she asked.

"I can't stay. I asked Susan to dinner tonight," he said.

Elliot grinned. "Dispatcher Susan?" she asked.

"Yeah. I took your advice and asked her out. I was surprised when she said yes."

"I'm not surprised at all," Lia said. "You're a great guy."

"So, what about the stalker?" Elliot asked.

"We came close to releasing him last night. We really didn't have anything on him, but I convinced the chief to let him cool his jets overnight," Randy explained.

"Please tell me he's not out on the streets," Lia said.

"No, we still have him, but like I said, we couldn't hold him for stalking. He was uncooperative when we locked him up. He pretty much refused to say anything at all. It was almost as though he was in some sort of trance. Funny thing is this morning he was like a different person."

"Different, how?" Lia asked.

"Like I said, last night he just refused to cooperate. You saw how he was when I read him his rights. This morning, he was all polite and talkative. I don't know if he had a come-to-

Jesus moment, or if he was just happy to get away from his cellmate this morning."

"You locked him up with someone else?" Elliot asked.

"Yeah. His cellmate was picked up on a drunk and disorderly and he was thrown into the tank to sober up. Our guy was put in with him. Apparently, the cellmate was verbally abusive to him all night. Come morning, the other dude was released with a fine, and your stalker was booked."

"On what charges?" Elliot asked.

"Standard procedure before locking someone up is to confiscate their personal possessions. What we found on him gave us the evidence we needed to hold him longer."

"Did he have drugs or something?" Elliot asked.

"No. He had estate jewelry on him. Some pretty old pieces at that."

"So, he broke into someone's house," Lia said.

"We are more inclined to believe he got it through grave robbing."

"What? Who in their right mind robs graves?" Elliot asked.

"You'd be surprised what some people will do for drugs or money. There's been a rash of robberies in several of the cemeteries lately. The fact that the graves here are mostly above ground makes them relatively easy to break into. He might be one of the culprits. In any case, I wanted you to know that he's still incarcerated—at least until a public defender can get him released."

"So, he denied stalking us," Lia surmised.

"He didn't exactly deny it. He claims he doesn't remember stalking you."

"Really? I'm here to tell you, counting last night, he stood on that corner right there and watched our house on at least three separate occasions," Elliot said. "And he absolutely tried to get into the car with Lia."

Randy held up his hands. "You don't need to convince me. I believe you."

"Randy, did you check to see if he had evidence of any incendiary devices on him, or maybe residue on his clothing?" Elliot asked. "I mean, it's possible that he had something to do with the damage on the carriage gates."

"Wow! I never thought of that. I'll call into the station before I pick Susan up and ask them to swab his clothes. I can't believe I didn't think of that, myself. Thanks, Elliot."

"What are the chances he'll stalk us again when he's released?" Lia asked.

"If they let him out, it will probably be under house arrest, so he'll have to wear an ankle bracelet and we'll be able to tell where he is. Is there a chance he'll stalk you again? Yes, but it isn't likely. I wouldn't worry too much about it."

Randy glanced at his watch. "I gotta go. I don't want to be late picking Susan up. I'll be in touch if anything changes."

"Thanks for stopping by, Randy, and enjoy your dinner," Elliot said.

Chapter 13

"Gran actually appeared to you yesterday?" Lia asked.

"Yes. She told me Marie's house has been disturbed and I needed to help her," Julie explained.

"Wow. She hasn't even appeared to Elliot yet."

"Somehow, she must have known we bought Marie's house. She knew we were in contact with her."

"What did you do?" Lia asked.

Marissa placed a large plate of French toast and sausage in the middle of the island. "Jules, Phoebe and I went to the house to see if there was any damage," she said.

"And did you find any?" Elliot asked. "Damage, I mean?" She carried two cups of coffee to the island and went back for the other two.

"No. We checked every room and even the back yard, and we didn't find anything out of the ordinary," Julie said.

"El, will you grab the maple syrup from the refrigerator?" Lia asked. "Why would Gran say Marie's house had been damaged if nothing was wrong?"

"I don't know," Julie replied.

The four friends settled in around the island to enjoy their breakfast. "The weirdest thing is what happened when Marie took control of Phoebe," Marissa said.

"What? Is Phoebe okay?" Lia asked.

"She's totally okay. Through Phoebe, Marie told us that some evil had been released and that we all had to stop it."

"We *all* have to stop it? Like all of *us*?" Elliot asked.

"To be truthful, I don't know who she was talking about," Julie admitted.

"She said some weird stuff," Marissa said. "Like it was going to kill the fifty and one, whatever the hell that means."

"Fifty and one what? People?" Lia asked.

"Damned if I know," Julie said. "What I *do* know is that there is a feeling building inside me that makes me uneasy. Call it intuition if you'd like, but something is not right."

"Maybe Phoebe can help," Lia suggested.

"We plan to put our heads together today to try to make sense of this," Julie said. "We had planned to spend the day at the new house so we could involve Marie, but it seems the inspectors will be there for most of the day for a final look before we sign the papers tomorrow."

"You're signing papers tomorrow?" Elliot asked.

"Yes. Sorry, I thought I told you about it. I got a call at work yesterday from the owner's lawyers. They are ready to do the closing tomorrow instead of next week," Marissa explained.

"That's actually a good thing," Elliot said. "Maybe we can start ripping that wall out this weekend."

"My thought exactly," Marissa said. "I'll call the contractor my firm uses to determine if that wall is load bearing. If it isn't we might be able to take it down ourselves."

Lia placed her hand on Julie's arm. "I see shopping in our future this weekend!"

Julie raised her hand for a high-five. "I'm right there with you, sistah!"

"Hey, I have a fun idea!" Marissa said. "What if we celebrate by having a sleepover pajama party in the new house tomorrow night?"

"I love it!" Julie exclaimed. "We could bring air mattresses and a cooler for drinks."

"But you don't have a stove yet. How would we cook dinner and breakfast?" Lia asked.

"We could get Chinese takeout for dinner," Elliot suggested.

"And it's a short walk to the bakery for donuts and coffee the next morning," Julie pointed out.

"This is beginning to sound like fun. Should we invite Phoebe?" Lia suggested.

"Absolutely!" Julie exclaimed. "I'll talk to her about it today."

"Maybe together, we can make sense of the riddles Marie Laveau spewed yesterday," Marissa suggested.

"Maybe we can even get Marie to participate," Julie said.

"*That* would be worth sleeping on the floor for!" Elliot replied.

***

Julie and Lia stood on the sidewalk on the Royal Street side of the house and waited for Elliot to lock the entry gate. When she finished, she pointed the remote key fob at the car and unlocked the doors.

"Considering Marissa had to leave so early this morning, can we offer you a ride to work, Julie?" Elliot asked.

"No, I think I'll walk. It's only a few blocks away, and besides, it's great exercise on such a beautiful morning," Julie replied."

"Jules, you and I ran five miles this morning. Isn't that enough exercise?" Lia asked.

Julie hugged Lia and then moved on to Elliot. "It'll be a nice walk. I'm good, but thanks for offering. Have a great day!"

***

A man stood, partially concealed in a doorway across Governor Nichols Street, and watched the affectionate scene between the three women. He reached up to rub his forehead.

This body is so much better than the last, but this interminable headache is tiring, not to mention it smells like alcohol and stale cigarettes. I'm glad they let him out of jail yesterday.

He watched two of the women climb into a car and drive away, while the other walked down the street.

She is one of them.

The man stepped out of the shadows and walked in the same direction as the woman. He tried to keep a respectable distance to avoid revealing himself too soon to her.

The woman stopped in front of a bakery and hesitated for a moment before going inside. The man ducked into another doorway and tried to appear innocuous while he waited for her to come out. While he waited, he noted that his hands were shaking.

What is wrong with him? This will not do.

His attention was suddenly drawn to the woman who reemerged from the bakery carrying a bag. She stopped and looked around. A frown formed on her brow. Finally, she continued down the street. He slipped out of his alcove and continued to follow her.

He followed her across the street and then stopped suddenly.

What is happening? Why did he stop? She is getting away!

The man stood in front of the plate glass window and looked at the array of liquor bottles. His hands shook violently as he retrieved his wallet from his back pocket and entered the store.

No! What is he doing? She is getting away!

The man selected a bottle of whiskey and walked to the checkout counter. His hands shook so violently, he dropped the bills he had pulled from his wallet.

Luckily, a young man with shocking red hair stood beside him. He quickly stooped and picked up the bills. He handed the money back to the man and then placed his hand on the man's shoulder.

"Here you go, sir. Are you all right?"

The man quickly grasped the countertop to prevent himself from falling. The young man by his side caught him and leaned against the counter as well, to stabilize them both.

"I'm okay. Thank you." The man paid for his bottle and waited for it to be bagged. Moments later, he shuffled out of the store.

The cashier looked at the younger man. "Poor guy. He'll feel better once he opens that bottle."

"I'm glad I never got into the hard stuff," the young man said. "This is about it for me." He placed a six-pack of hard cider on the counter and paid for his purchase. Soon, he was on his way out of the store.

This one feels so much better. Now, where did that woman go?

***

"Good morning, Phoebs. I brought beignets! I almost didn't stop, but they looked so good from the window." She held up the bag she was carrying for Phoebe to see.

"Good morning, Jules." Phoebe hugged her friend. "I'm going to gain a hundred pounds if you keep feeding me like this! I'll make coffee to go with those treats. How are you today?"

"I'm good, although I had the oddest sensation when I came out of the bakery this morning—almost like I was being watched," Julie said.

"Did you see anything suspicious?" Phoebe asked.

"Not really. It was just a feeling. So, how are you this morning?" Julie asked.

"I didn't sleep well. I found myself thinking about Marie Laveau."

"What about her?"

"It was odd being on the inside, looking out yesterday when she took control of my body. It was as if I was seeing things from both her perspectives and mine at the same time. Something bothered me about what she said," Phoebe explained.

"She said a lot of confusing things. Which one are you talking about?"

"When she said her home had been disturbed, I don't think she meant your new house."

"What else could she have meant?" Julie asked.

"The word *home* might be a metaphor for something else. Maybe she was talking about the tenets of voodoo. Maybe she was referring to her own legacy. I just don't think she was talking about a physical house. I think that was confirmed by the fact that you found nothing when you went through each room on Saint Ann Street."

"You might be right."

"I'll have to give it more thought."

"I was confused about her fifty and one comments. I have no idea what she meant by that," Julie said.

"I struggle with what she meant as well. I hope it does not mean fifty-one people will die."

"Jesus, Phoebe. That would be horrible."

"Indeed."

"What do you think about her statement that we all had to come together to stop the evil?" Julie asked.

"It could mean anything. I think it all depends on what the evil is. It might be something small enough for our group to deal with, or it might be something large enough to involve the entire voodoo community. We need to know what we're up against before we can figure out how to fight it."

"Ahh! This is so frustrating! We have more questions than answers," Julie complained.

"There is power in numbers, Jules. We should meet soon as a group to discuss this."

"That's a perfect segue into something I want to ask you," Julie said.

"And that is?"

"How would you like to sleep on the floor tomorrow night?"

***

Elliot surveyed the pile of coolers, air mattresses, sleeping bags, pillows and miscellaneous camping equipment piled on the floor of the first-floor entryway.

"Okay, I think we have everything we need for our slumber party tomorrow."

Marissa entered the vestibule from one of the rooms that held their possessions. She carried two propane lanterns. "We might need these. The power isn't scheduled to be turned on until Saturday." She placed the lanterns with the rest of the supplies.

"I hope we have power on Saturday," Elliot said. I'm looking forward to knocking that wall down and we'll need our power tools for some of it."

"I'm right there with you. At least the water will still be on. We should grab some paper towels, toilet paper and hand soap while we're thinking about it," Marissa said. "Oh, and a trash bag or two."

Lia joined them via the staircase from the second story. "We might also need these." She placed a cardboard box filled with various candles on the pile. "They might come in handy if we want to do any tarot readings."

"I found them!"

Lia, Elliot and Marissa looked toward the storage room where Julie emerged carrying a bag.

"I found the incense, gris-gris bags and talismans. I'm sure Phoebe will bring some as well, but you can never have too many," Julie said.

"This is going to be a slumber party like no other I've ever attended!" Elliot exclaimed.

"It'll be fun," Julie said.

Marissa pulled her cellphone out of her back pocket. "Can anyone think of anything else we'll need? I'll make a list in my reminders."

"We need a lighter for the candles," Lia said.

"Lighters, toilet paper, paper towels, hand soap," Marissa said as she typed them into her phone. "Anything else?"

"Ice for the cooler, and of course a few bottles of wine, oh, and paper cups," Julie added.

"Mar, text me that list. Jules and I can go shopping for what we need," Lia said. "And maybe we can pick up pizza for tonight's dinner instead of cooking."

"Pizza sounds awesome. Please add some wings to that," Elliot said.

"And beer. Definitely beer," Marissa added.

"All right. Let me grab Elliot's car keys and we can get going," Lia replied.

Chapter 14

Elliot pulled up to the front door of the Louisiana Cancer Research Center the next morning. She leaned and accepted a kiss from Lia. "Have a great day, sweetheart," she said. "I'll be here at five to pick you up."

"Don't forget to drop the genealogy forms off to Leslie between classes this morning," Lia reminded her.

"I won't forget."

"Thank you, love."

"Do you want to pick up Chinese before or after we get to Mar and Julie's new place tonight?"

"We might want to wait until after we all settle in. There's no way to reheat anything there right now, so we shouldn't order until just before we're ready to eat," Lia reasoned.

"That makes sense. So, the plan is for Marissa and Julie to bring all our gear sometime this afternoon?" Elliot asked.

"Yes. Their schedules are more flexible than ours are, so they volunteered to take care of that. We only need to head to their new house directly from work."

"That sounds like a plan. Oh, I should text Julie and ask her to feed Miss Thing before they go."

Lia smiled and cupped the side of Elliot's face with her palm. "She's grown on you, hasn't she?"

"Guilty as charged!" Elliot exclaimed.

Lia looked toward the front door of her workplace. "I'd better get going. I'll see you at five. Love you!"

"I love you, too. Have a good day," Elliot replied.

***

"Good morning, Mr. Richmond." Marissa shook hands with the realtor selling the property at Saint Ann Street.

"Good morning, ladies. Follow me," Mr. Richmond said. "The lawyers representing the property owner are waiting for us in the conference room."

"The owner is not here?" Marissa asked.

"No. As I've said previously, they do not live in the state of Louisiana."

"I see. Okay, lead the way."

A half-hour later, Marissa and Julie left the realtor's office as the proud owners of ten twenty Saint Ann Street. Mr. Richmond offered to go to the house and remove the lock box, but Marissa assured him that she would do that and deliver the box to his office the following Monday. Mr. Richmond also handed them a ring containing the keys to the other five external doors of the house.

Marissa and Julie climbed back into their car and looked at one another.

"I can't believe we did it, Mar. We bought Marie Laveau's house," Julie said.

"I know. I'm kind of numb right now." Marissa handed the key ring to Julie. I guess we should get some copies made of these keys, as well as four copies of the key currently in the lock box."

"Why so many?" Julie asked.

"One each for you, Lia, Elliot and Phoebe," Marissa replied. "After all, we each have a key to Lia and Elliot's home."

"And I have a key to Phoebe's shop, although I need one since I work there," Julie said. "Speaking of which, I have a client booked at one o'clock for a reading. I'll ride with Phoebe to the house after we close the shop."

Marissa looked at her watch. "Awesome. It's only eleven-thirty. That means I have time to take my best girl out for a celebratory lunch."

"Best girl? I'd better be your *only* girl," Julie joked.

"Yes, dear!"

***

Elliot wasn't so lucky on her second visit to Harden Genealogy Services. The closest parking space she could find was two blocks away. By the time she walked two blocks and then climbed two flights of stairs to Harden's offices in the typically high humidity conditions in New Orleans, she was damp with sweat. She was thankful she had opted for the more casual polo and dress slacks that morning instead of her normal suit coat.

Once again, a bell rang when Elliot opened the door to Harden's waiting room and stepped on the welcome mat. It didn't take long for Leslie Harden to emerge from his office once Elliot was inside the door. He was dressed in a manner similar to the day before, but in shades of blue rather than maroon.

"Hey, Leslie. Just dropping off Lia's paperwork," Elliot said.

Leslie approached Elliot with his hand extended. "Nice to see you again, Elliot. Have you got a moment to talk?"

"I have a class to teach in an hour, but sure, I can talk for a few minutes."

"What do you teach?"

"This particular class is on the integration of computer code into artificial prosthetics."

"Wow, that's a mouthful!" Leslie exclaimed.

"More simply put, it's about adapting prosthetics to accept a computer interface between an artificial limb and human tissue."

"That sounds like fascinating work."

"It is. This particular class is for students who have already earned a degree in computer programming, so it starts out at a pretty advanced level."

"Well, I won't keep you long. I just wanted to chat with you a bit about Lia's genealogy. I sometimes find it helpful to interview the significant others of my clients for a different perspective before I begin my search."

"What would you like to know?" Elliot asked.

"For starters, how well do you know Lia's family?"

"I hate to make your job harder, Leslie, but Lia doesn't have any family left—except me, that is."

"She has no one at all?"

"Not that we know of. She was an only child. We believe her relationship to Ethan comes from her mother's side, and I think her mother was an only child as well. Unfortunately, her parents died in a car accident when she was only twenty-eight. I'd only known her for a few months by then, so I had met them, but I didn't know them well."

"Where were they living at the time of this accident?" Leslie asked.

"Lia grew up just outside of New York City. I think she included that information in the forms," Elliot said.

"Yes, of course. All right then, I will let you go. I'm sure you need time to prepare for your class. Thank you for dropping the forms off, Elliot. I appreciate it."

"You're welcome." Elliot turned to go but stopped before she reached the door. "Oh, any idea how long it'll be before you have something to share with us?"

"It could be weeks, or even months. As I said when we met earlier, because Ethan was sent away, rather than sold, there may not even be any record of his existence. Lia's information will give me a starting point. Hopefully, there will be a good enough paper trail leading from Lia back to the eighteen thirties, to determine if there is a familial connection there."

"Okay. I guess we can't ask for anything more than your best effort. We appreciate it," Elliot said.

Leslie rose and shook Elliot's hand. "I'll be in touch as soon as I have something to share."

***

Lia and Elliot pulled their car to the curb in front of the Saint Ann Street house at five-thirty that afternoon, right behind Marissa's car that sat at the curb with the trunk lid open. Marissa came out of the house just as Lia and Elliot pushed their car doors open.

Lia climbed out of their car and ran into Marissa's arms. "Congratulations, sweetie! We are so happy for you and Julie."

"It is the most amazing feeling!" Marissa exclaimed just as Elliot made it around the front of the car and joined in the hug.

"We'll give you a hand bringing stuff in," Elliot said.

They managed to unload all the camping gear after three more trips between the car and house. Lia looked at the mountain of equipment in the middle of the living room.

"This won't look so bad once all the bedding is moved to the bedrooms. Speaking of which, I'm calling dibs on the back room," Lia said.

"I don't think Phoebe will mind the first bedroom, and of course, Jules and I will take the master," Marissa added.

"Where *are* Julie and Phoebe?" Elliot asked.

"They're still at the shop. They should be here soon," Marissa said.

As though on cue, they heard a car horn sound from in front of the house. Mar looked out through one of the tall front windows. "Speak of the devil, they're here!" she said.

"Awesome. I'll help bring in their stuff," Lia said.

"I will, too," Elliot added.

"While you're doing that, I'll start lugging some of this pile to the bedrooms before we run out of daylight," Marissa said.

"Hey, you two!" Lia called out as she approached Phoebe's car. She accepted a very excited Julie into her arms.

"I'm so glad we're doing this, Lia," Julie said. "This will be so much fun."

"It will indeed. Congratulations, love. El and I couldn't be happier for you and Mar. So, are we still on for shopping this weekend?"

"You bet! I can't imagine what could be more important than that!" Julie replied.

"Shopping?" Phoebe interjected.

Lia turned to hug Phoebe. "Oh yes. We're planning to shop for curtains and accessories while Elliot and Mar do the guy thing and rip down a wall," Lia explained.

"Got room for a third? I love to shop," Phoebe asked.

"Absolutely! We'll make a day of it!"

"Well, you can have it," Elliot said as she waited her turn for hugs. "I'd rather be getting dirty and sweaty than crawling through the mall."

"Where's Mar?" Julie asked.

"She's trying to distribute the mountain of gear from the living room to the bedrooms. El and I volunteered to help you bring your stuff in while she's doing that," Lia explained.

"Well, there's not much. Just an air mattress, sleeping bag, pillow and a duffle with pajamas and a change of clothes. Oh, and my tools," Phoebe said. "I don't go anywhere without them."

"Well then, we should be able to get it all in one trip," Elliot remarked. "Let's go!"

As predicted, all of the gear was transported into the house in one trip and brought directly to the first bedroom beyond the kitchen. The five women spent the next half-hour arranging their sleeping quarters for the night, after which they met in the living room.

Lia looked at her watch. "It's almost six-thirty. Who's hungry?"

A unanimous show of hands set the agenda for the next few minutes.

"Someone suggested Chinese yesterday," Julie said.

"That would be me," Elliot replied.

"There's a Chinese takeout place on the next block that makes pretty good food. I think their menu is online," Julie added. "We didn't bring plates or utensils, so we'll have to order the individual combo meals."

Five cell phones suddenly appeared and within minutes, they had assembled an order that Marissa volunteered to call in. She slipped her phone back into her pocket once the order was placed. "It'll be ready in about twenty minutes."

"This one is our treat," Elliot said. "Lia and I can go pick it up. Is that okay with you, love?"

"Sure. It's a beautiful evening. We can walk if you'd like and avoid having to find a parking place," Lia suggested.

"Sounds good to me!"

A short time later, Lia and Elliot returned with two large bags. While they were gone, Marissa, Julie and Phoebe had retrieved everyone's pillows and arranged them in a circle in the middle of the living room, along with one large candle at each setting.

"What's all this?" Elliot asked when they entered the house with the food.

"We forgot to bring lawn chairs, so our pillows will have to do to sit on. I thought we could take this opportunity to dig into some of the cryptic messages we have been receiving from Marie, and to have a group discussion, and maybe some tarot readings after dinner," Phoebe suggested.

"That's a great idea!" Lia said. "But I think we need to slip into something more comfortable before we do that. This *is* a pajama party, after all."

Elliot put the bags of food in the center of the circle and then followed Lia to their room as the rest of the gang dispersed to their respective bedrooms. They returned to the living room, one by one, wearing their pajamas.

"God, it feels good to get out of that bra!" Lia exclaimed.

"I'm right there with you," Julie agreed.

"You need to wear a sports bra like me and Mar," Elliot said. "They're much more comfortable than the frilly things you wear."

"Maybe so, but they also mash you down. You don't mind looking like a guy, but I do. I like my curves," Lia said.

Elliot grinned. "I like your curves, too!" Elliot reached forward and cupped Lia's breasts.

Lia slapped her hands away. "Stop that! Are you forgetting we're not alone here?"

"Hey, you can't fault a girl for trying!" Elliot exclaimed.

Elliot, Lia, Marissa and Julie all sat down on their pillows and retrieved their dinners from the bags. Lia pulled Phoebe's dinner out as well and placed it on the floor in front of her pillow. She looked at the others in the circle. "Where's Phoebe?" she asked.

"I saw her go into the bathroom on my way back to the living room," Elliot said.

"I'm coming!"

Everyone's attention was drawn to the voice coming from the kitchen.

"Phoebe?" Marissa said.

Phoebe stepped into the light provided by the candles.

"Wow! You are beautiful!" Elliot instinctively said. "Not that you aren't beautiful with your makeup on, but, damn, woman, you are stunning!"

Phoebe wore boxer shorts and a T-shirt. Her thick, black and gray-streaked hair hung loosely about her shoulders in gentle waves, and she had removed the false eyelashes and washed away all of the severe makeup she normally wore. A smattering of freckles graced the tops of her cheeks, and a healthy glow radiated from her face. Her lips were full and pouty. The almost translucent appearance of her eyes made it difficult to look away from her.

"Wow, Phoebs. I just had a flashback from our teenage years," Julie said. "I've always said you were beautiful and you never believed me. Judging by Elliot's reaction, I hope you can see now that I wasn't lying."

"You're too kind," Phoebe said. She sat down on her pillow and completed the circle.

"I hope everyone is okay with chopsticks, since we didn't bring utensils with us," Lia said.

"We'll make do." Marissa climbed to her feet and pulled the large cooler toward them. "Anyone for drinks?"

***

The sun had fully set by the time they finished their dinners and cleared away the debris from their meal.

"I'm so stuffed! That was a great dinner with awesome company," Marissa said.

"I'm stuffed, too," Elliot agreed. "This was a great idea. I'm enjoying myself."

"I'm so glad you all agreed to come," Julie said. "I wouldn't want to share the first night in our new home with anyone else. We love you all so much."

"Ditto on what Jules said. Oh, and before I forget..." Marissa stood and ran toward the back of the house.

"Where did she go?" Lia asked.

Before Julie could answer, Marissa returned with a small manila envelope. She sat down again on her pillow.

"Julie and I have something for each of you." She opened her left palm and emptied the contents of the envelope into it—three keys. She gave one each to Lia, Elliot and Phoebe. "This is the key to the front door. We want each of you to feel like this is your home too. You have our complete permission—and encouragement—to come and go at will."

Lia immediately crawled across the circle and wrapped her arms around both Julie and Marissa. It wasn't long before Elliot joined the fray.

"Oh, what the heck!" Phoebe said as she too joined the pile of bodies on the other side of the circle, which by that time more closely resembled a football pile than a group hug.

"All right! All right! You're squishing us here!" Marissa called out. "I love you guys, but you weigh a ton!"

Lia was the first to climb to her feet. "Elliot, give me your key. I'll run them to our bedroom and when I get back, maybe we can start making sense of these messages Marie keeps sending."

Elliot handed her key to Lia, but remained where she was, lying crosswise on both Julie and Marissa. "I'm comfortable right where I am," she said.

"Like hell you are!" Marissa exclaimed. She pushed Elliot off them and then pounced on her with a tickle attack.

Phoebe reached her hand toward Lia. "Give me a hand up. I'll put my key away, too and get my tarot cards while I'm at it."

Lia pulled Phoebe to her feet and together, they walked toward the long hallway that led to the bedrooms they were using.

"You and Elliot have been together for a while, haven't you?" Phoebe asked as they walked toward the bedrooms.

They stopped at Phoebe's door.

"Twenty-two years and counting," Lia replied.

"Twenty-two years is a long time. It's obvious how much you love one another."

"She's a little over-protective sometimes, but I know she means well," Lia said.

A silence fell between them.

"Is there someone special in your life, Phoebe?"

"There was—many years ago," Phoebe replied. "But that is a topic for another time. Right now, I'm going to grab my tarot cards."

Lia took the hint and stopped pressing. "Okay. Let me drop these keys into my purse and I'll be right back."

When Lia and Phoebe returned to the living room, they found both Julie and Marissa sitting on top of Elliot, who was face-down on the floor.

"I take it, the petulant child was out of control?" Lia asked.

"We had to give her a timeout," Julie said.

Lia got on her hands and knees so she could talk to Elliot face-to-face. "I suggest you tap-out," she said.

"No fair! They tag-teamed me!" Elliot complained.

Lia lowered her face to Elliot's and whispered something in her ear.

Elliot's eyes opened wide. "Promise?" she said.

Lia smiled and nodded.

Elliot slapped the floor three times with her hand. "Okay. I tap-out!" she announced.

Julie and Marissa released Elliot and Marissa helped her to her feet.

"Let's get this party started," Elliot said. "Anyone ready for another drink?"

Julie raised her eyebrows at Lia.

"I had to offer her a private wrestling match later," Lia said under her breath.

Chapter 15

"All right. Before we begin, let's review what Marie has already told us," Phoebe said.

"Let's see. She said her home has been disturbed. She said chaos is at our door and she said that evil has been released," Julie said.

"Gran told you Marie's house had been disturbed as well," Marissa reminded them.

"Yes. That's right," Julie replied. "Gran also said that evil has been released and that Marie needed our help. Oh, she also said Elliot and Lia needed our help."

"What? Gran said that?" Lia asked.

"She did," Julie confirmed.

"Wow. When Gran appeared to me about a week or so ago, she asked me if I was feeling the evil again," Lia said.

"Let's not forget that someone tried to blow up our carriage gates, too," Elliot pointed out.

Phoebe leaned forward. "Someone tried to blow up your gates? This is new information for me. I assume you reported this to the police?"

"Yes. There are two marks on the gates that are burned, and if I recall the night it happened, it made some loud noises. Oh, and someone left a message in white paint that said something like, *Celeste escaped but you never will*. Whoever did it left no clue as to who they are. Part of me wonders if there is some cause rooted in voodoo or something along those lines," Elliot said.

"Voodoo is almost never used toward destructive ends, Elliot, but that doesn't mean whoever did it didn't use voodoo as a cover," Phoebe commented.

Phoebe took the tarot deck out of its box and shuffled the cards. She looked around once more before she dealt them. "Is there anything else before we begin?" she asked.

"Wait! Yes. What about the fifty and one comments Marie made?" Julie asked.

"That's right! Marie said something about the evil killing the fifty and one. Does that make sense to anyone?" Phoebe asked.

The women all looked at one another and shook their heads.

"All right then. I will assume that we will be dealing with some unnamed chaos on the horizon. In an attempt to figure out what that means, I will use the conflict resolution spread," Phoebe explained. "For those who are unfamiliar with it, there are five cards involved, laid out in a cross configuration. The card in the west position, to the left, represents the current situation. To the north, is a card with our desired outcome. The card in the east position, to the right, will represent what others want for an outcome, and the card in the south position will represent what is realistic, given the current situation. Finally, the card in the center represents the actions we may need to take to influence the outcome toward our desired result. Are there any questions before I begin?"

Phoebe continued as no response came. "Good. I will review the purpose of the cards again as we expose each one. Let's begin."

Phoebe turned the first card and placed it face up to the left. It was The Tower reversed. "Damn," she said softly. She looked at the trepidation of the faces of the others. "This card represents the current situation. We've seen this card before. In the reversed position, as it is now, it means that some crisis is looming. This is exactly what Marie said to you, Julie, the first time she appeared."

"Yes, it is," Julie said. "But what is the crisis?"

"Based on other things Marie has said, it must have something to do with this evil she has referred to. Once we determine what that is, we'll know better how to deal with it. In the meantime, The Tower implies there is a process we need to go through to find peace."

Phoebe drew the next card and placed it in the north position.

"This card represents our desired outcome. The Star is a major Arcana card and in the upright position, it has a very positive meaning. It represents renewed power and strength to make it through a difficult time, especially when it follows The Tower. It is an indication that we need courage and determination to make it through the crisis that lies ahead of us. It also means that we have been through adversity in the past and made it through without losing hope. We just need to realize that we have the strength to face anything—especially if we face it together."

"So, this is the outcome we *want*, correct?" Elliot asked.

"Yes. This is the desired result after the conflict has been resolved," Julie explained.

"Okay. I'd say that card is spot on," Elliot added.

"All right. The next card represents what others want for the outcome," Phoebe said. She flipped the card and placed it to the right, in the east position. "Hmm, this card is not so positive."

"So, before you read this card, Phoebe, who exactly, are the *others* who want this outcome?" Lia asked.

"Well, since this is a conflict spread, the *others* would be whoever is responsible for the crisis we are about to face."

"But we don't know who they are, correct?" Lia added.

"That is correct," Phoebe replied. "As I mentioned to Julie earlier, we won't know how to attack this problem until we know who is behind it, and what the problem is. I suspect determining those two factors will be the biggest challenges we'll face here."

"So, you've turned the Five of Swords card, and it's reversed. What does that mean?" Marissa asked.

"Normally, the Five of Swords in the reversed position means one is resigned to the outcome of a conflict, regardless of if they come out the winner or loser, but in a conflict spread, this card in the east position represents our adversary's point of view. It is more likely to represent the manifestation of a situation that will be very upsetting to us, and that ultimately, we will be the losers in this battle."

"Are you saying this card is predicting that we'll lose whatever this fight is?" Elliot asked.

Julie put her hand on Elliot's arm. "El, this card represents what out adversary *wants* the outcome to be—not what it might *actually* be. We may have the power to influence that."

"Sheesh! This is confusing," Elliot said.

"For those who don't practice tarot on a regular basis, yes, I agree with you, Elliot," Phoebe said. "So, let's look at the next card. This one will be placed in the south position, and it will represent the likely outcome if nothing is done to influence it."

Phoebe flipped the Ace of Swords card and placed it south of the other cards. It was reversed.

"It makes me nervous when cards appear upside down," Lia said.

"Not all reversed cards have negative meanings, Lia. But in this case, I have to agree," Phoebe said. "In the reversed position, this card implies that the chances of failure are pretty high."

"Jesus Christ!" Elliot exclaimed.

"Let me finish. The chances of failure are high if we do nothing to influence the outcome. It also implies that our approach to solving this crisis needs to be methodical and well thought out."

"How the hell are we going to do that if we don't even know what the problem is we're trying to solve?" Marissa asked.

"Yeah—what Marissa said," Elliot added.

"We may need to seek advice from those who know more than we do," Phoebe replied.

"So, if we do nothing, and pretend that this crisis doesn't exist, we will fail," Elliot said.

"That is what the cards imply," Phoebe replied.

"So, what exactly does failing mean, and how to we prevent it?" Lia asked.

"Lia, we won't know what failing means until we figure out what the problem is," Julie said. "It could be something big, or it could be some minor annoyance. I, for one, tend to believe it's big. Otherwise, why would Marie, and Gran for that matter, appear to us several times to point it out? I don't want to think about what the consequences of failure might be—especially if it could mean losing someone I love."

"Phoebe, what does the final card say?" Marissa asked.

"The final card will represent the action that we need to take to influence the final outcome," Phoebe said.

"So, this is the card that will tell us how we can beat this thing?" Elliot asked.

"In a manner of speaking, yes."

Phoebe pulled the final card from the top of the deck and placed it in the center of the spread. It was the Ace of Rods in the upright position.

Photograph taken by
Karen D. Badger, 7/14/2021

"The Ace of Rods. This card is associated with using our vision and creativity in a cosmic way. It implies that we should face this problem in a bold and direct manner, and it encourages us to follow our instincts and not to hold back. Whatever this thing is that we are facing, we need to do it with courage and determination. In this way, we will be able to confront the chaos, and increase our chances of winning."

"Reckless abandonment. Hopefully that approach won't get us all killed," Elliot deadpanned.

The five friends stared at the cards for several minutes. Finally, Phoebe reached forward to pick them up.

"Wait!" Julie shouted. She put her hand out to stop Phoebe.

"What is it, Jules?" Marissa asked.

Julie pointed to the Five of Swords and Ace of Swords cards. "Look—a five and a one. I wonder if that has anything to do with the fifty and one Marie talked about."

"Are you suggesting that if our adversary gets their desired outcome that it will result in the death of fifty and one?" Phoebe asked.

"I...I don't know. I guess that's one way of thinking about it. I mean, the five *is* in the desired outcome position for the adversary, and the ace, or one, is in the likely outcome slot if we do nothing to influence it. It could be just a coincidence that these two cards fell the way they did...or, there just might be something to it. It's something to think about," Julie said.

"It is indeed," Phoebe agreed.

Elliot climbed to her feet and paced across the room.

"El, are you okay?" Lia asked.

She stopped and held her hands out to the sides. "This is all fine and good, but we still don't know what this crisis is, and until we do, we will not be able to fight it."

Phoebe collected the cards from the middle of the circle and tucked them back into the deck. "You are right, Elliot. You will recall me saying we need to ask for help from someone who knows better than we do."

"And who would that be?" Elliot asked.

"Marie Laveau."

Chapter 16

Phoebe reached her hand toward Elliot. "Elliot, give me a hand up."

Elliot pulled her to her feet.

"Thanks." She turned to the others. "Rearrange the pillows so that we can sit close enough in a circle to hold hands. I'll be right back."

Julie watched Phoebe walk toward the kitchen. "Where are you going, Phoebs?"

"To get my tools. We need some answers and I intend to get them."

Phoebe returned a moment later with a canvas bag in hand. While she was gone, the others had arranged the pillows in a circle with an approximate diameter of five feet.

Julie immediately dropped to her knees to help Phoebe arrange her implements while Marissa, Elliot and Lia stood by.

"We're having a séance, aren't we?" Lia asked.

"Yes," Phoebe said over her shoulder.

"Great!" Elliot exclaimed. "The last time we did this, Lia, Samuel and I passed out and I ended up locked in the room above the library."

"These are different circumstances, Elliot," Julie pointed out. "For starters, we're here instead of at your house, and secondly, we are not trying to exorcise any evil spirits."

Lia placed her hand on Elliot's arm. "Give it a chance, love. If it's relatively harmless and helps us to find some answers, then I'm all for it."

"Key words—relatively harmless," Elliot quipped.

The others watched while Phoebe and Julie positioned six candles—one in front of each pillow and the sixth one in the middle of the circle. Phoebe also pulled from her bag several crystals, a black-handled athame, incense, dried herbs, a small black kettle, a lighter and a bowl, into which she poured a small mound of salt. She arranged these around her in front of her pillow, and then sat cross-legged, facing the center of the circle.

Phoebe looked at her friends. "Please join me."

Julie and Marissa sat on either side of Phoebe, with Lia and Elliot sitting directly across from her. She placed the herbs and the incense inside the kettle and lit them on fire. The dried petals and leaves burned rapidly and when the flames subsided, a slow tower of smoke rose continuously from the residue inside the kettle, filling the air with the aroma of cinnamon and lemongrass incense.

"Please turn off your phones until the ceremony is done," Phoebe said. She waited while everyone did as instructed. "Now, join hands. It is important that we do not break the circle while we communicate with the spirits, or we will risk losing contact with them."

"But Phoebe, Marie has appeared to you without prompting. Why do we have to go through all of this when you can just ask her to appear?" Elliot said.

"You are correct, Elliot, but there are others that may require a safe environment to communicate with us." Phoebe looked around the circle. "I understand if any of you are uncomfortable with this. If that is the case, the spirits will sense it, and it would be better for you not to participate, however, if you are all committed to this ceremony, then we will begin."

"I'm in," Marissa said.

"Me, too," Lia added.

"If Lia is doing this, then I am, too," Elliot said.

"I'm a given," Julie replied. "Let's begin, Phoebe."

The circle of friends all joined hands and waited for the next instruction.

Phoebe looked around the circle. "Please close your eyes and focus on the problem at hand. We need to understand what this crisis is that we are about to face so that we can determine how to confront it. Prepare, in your mind, questions you'd like to ask to whoever chooses to communicate with us."

For several moments, the friends sat in total silence. Finally, Phoebe spoke.

"Spirits of the night, we beseech thee. Find favor with us as we beg thee to grace us with your presence. Speak of things that need to be spoken. From this moment on, we invoke thy power to guide us in things that need to be done."

Lia's head suddenly dropped back onto her shoulders and a gasp escaped her lips.

"Lia!" Elliot's eyes flew open.

"Be still, Elliot. Don't break the circle," Phoebe said. "She is not in danger."

Without warning, Phoebe's head also fell back.

By this time, Elliot, Marissa and Julie were all sitting ramrod straight with their eyes open."

"What's happening?" Marissa whispered.

"Shh," Julie said.

Lia's head slowly rose and she opened her eyes. Her lids narrowed and her lips upturned into a seductive smile. She tilted her head to one side and looked at her wife.

"El-ee-ot."

"Oh, my fucking God!" Elliot exclaimed. "Celeste?"

Phoebe suddenly sat forward. "Celeste, yo te rele nou isit la pou ede, pa sedwi medam sa yo. (Celeste, we were summoned here to help, not to seduce these ladies.)"

All eyes swung suddenly toward Phoebe.

"Marie?" Julie whispered.

"It be me, child," Marie replied.

"Ou ap pèdi tout plezi mwen. (You are ruining all my fun)," Celeste said.

"Pral gen tan pou plezi pita. Kounye a, yo bezwen èd nou. Ou ta dwe konprann ke plis pase pifò. (There will be time for fun later. Right now, they need our help. You should understand that more than most)," Marie scolded.

"What have you done with Lia?" Elliot demanded of Celeste.

Celeste turned her seductive gaze on Elliot. "Lia hear. Lia see. Lia not be afraid. She be here wid us."

"Let me talk to her," Elliot insisted.

"As you wish."

Celeste closed her eyes and dropped her head back. A moment later, Lia reappeared.

"Elliot, I'm okay. Please don't worry," Lia said. "Celeste is willing to help us. Listen to her."

Lia's head dropped back once more, and Celeste returned. "You's be happy now, El-ee-ot? She be my blood. I's not be hurting her. You's needs to relax, El-ee-ot."

"I be watching you wid da cards," Marie said. "You know dat evil be released. You be wanting to know how to fight da evil."

"Marie. What *is* the evil? We can't fight what we don't know," Julie said.

"El-ee-ot know da evil," Celeste said.

"Elliot?" Marissa said. "How could Elliot know what the evil is?"

"Da mistress is da evil one. She be free. She be doing harm. She be wanting to kill Lia dead. Da mistress be da evil one wid a dark heart."

Julie's eyes opened wide. "Celeste, are you saying that the mistress has been released? How can that be? We imprisoned her in the brick."

"My home be disturbed, child," Marie said. "I be telling you dat many times. My home be disturbed and the evil be released."

"Your home?" Marissa said. "Oh, my God, you mean your grave, don't you?"

"Holy shit!" Elliot exclaimed.

"What is it, El?" Julie asked.

Elliot turned to Celeste. "Celeste, I need to talk to Lia."

"I make dat be so," Celeste said and a moment later, Lia appeared.

Elliot squeezed her hand. "Did you hear what Marie said, Lia? Her grave has been desecrated."

Lia eyes opened wide. "Elliot! Our stalker!"

"Yes. He must have somehow broken the seal on the brick. The mistress must have jumped into him."

"We need to contact Randy," Lia said. "If it was him who tried to blow up the carriage gates, that means the mistress is trying to get back into the house."

"Da evil one not be easy to defeat," Marie said. "Da evil in her heart give her great power. She be driven by revenge. I try to redeem her when she come back to New Orleans after she kill da slaves. I try, but da evil be too great."

Celeste once again came forward. "Her heart be black, my queen. They be no saving dat one soul. She kilt my Samuel. She kilt my Lia. She kilt me and hid da bones. She be da reason my Ethan be sent away. She need to burn in hell," Celeste spat out.

"What can we do to stop her?" Julie asked.

"We needs to work together," Marie said. "We needs to stop her before she do more harm. We needs to stop her before she do da fifty and one."

"Marie, what is the fifty and one?" Marissa asked.

"She kill da fifty and one. She always kill da fifty and one. She do it for revenge."

"Marie, we don't understand what you mean," Elliot said.

"We must stop her before da fifty and one."

"What the hell does that mean?" Elliot shouted loudly.

Lia abruptly returned to herself. "Celeste is gone," she said.

"Marie is gone, too," Phoebe added.

The friends fell silent for a few moments and thought about what they had heard. Finally, Phoebe rose to her feet, walked to the large window at the front of the house and looked out into the darkness.

"The mistress is free. *She* is the chaos. *She* is the crisis we must face. At first light, I need to go to the cemetery to see for myself."

"I'm going with you, Phoebe," Julie said.

"You're not going without me," Marissa added.

"We'll all go," Lia said. "We all have a stake in this. After all, it was Julie, Marissa and Phoebe who imprisoned her, and I'll be damned if I'm going to stand by if there is something I can do to help."

"I agree with Lia," Elliot said. "We will all go at first light."

"We will ward your house before we go to the cemetery," Phoebe said. "We cannot allow the mistress to get back in."

"We need to do this house as well," Elliot said. "Like Lia pointed out, Marissa and Julie helped to imprison her. If the mistress finds out they purchased this place, she'll be all over it like white on rice."

"I'm not sure she could hold her own against Marie," Phoebe said. "The priority needs to be your place. We'll take care of this house and my place after the cemetery."

"I agree with Phoebe," Marissa said. "There is nothing here for her. Your place, on the other hand, is a goldmine to the mistress. I know the emotional pull is no longer there, but who knows what else might be in your house that she could attach herself to? She *did* own the place at one time."

"We need to get a good night's sleep if we're getting up early tomorrow," Julie said.

"I might be gone when you get up in the morning," Phoebe said. "I need to go to the shop for a few things. I'll meet you at Lia and Elliot's house."

"All right. I guess we'll see you all in the morning," Julie said.

***

Phoebe met her friends in the gated entryway of the Royal Street hose the next morning. She handed half the supplies to Julie.

"Jules, take Elliot with you and do the protection spell at the door that opens to the courtyard. Lia and I will do the same spell here in the vestibule. Marissa, you can choose to participate with either."

"I'll go give Julie and Elliot a hand," Marissa said.

"All right then. We can meet in the kitchen when we're finished," Phoebe said.

"What can I do to help?" Lia asked.

"Carve a pentacle into this candle while I tie the rosemary and sage sprigs together. Be sure to draw a circle around it and be careful. The knife is sharp."

"I can do that," Lia said.

Lia handed the candle back to Phoebe when she was finished.

"That looks great. Okay, we need to sit on the floor facing the door."

Once both were seated, Phoebe placed two bowls in front of them. She put the candle in one bowl and the herbs in the other.

"Okay, close your eyes and take five deep breaths. It is important that we are calm, relaxed and focused for this part."

Phoebe lit the contents of both bowls. "Lia, while the smoke rises from the herbs, imagine your home filled with cleansing and protective energy."

"The burning herbs smell amazing," Lia whispered.

"Yes, they do. Now, focus on the candle flame. Imagine the flame is converting all the negative energy in your home to good energy and positive thoughts while the smoke and aroma of rosemary and sage chase away any lingering negativity and fill your home with a protective glow. Let me know when you feel focused, calm and clear."

"I'm good," Lia said.

"All right then. Repeat each sentence after me. I will pause to give you time to chant before I continue to the next sentence."

"Okay."

"Sage and rosemary, I call on you to fill me with your protective energy…Cleanse my home and all those we welcome across this threshold and allow me to capture your protective spirits…May this candle flame transform all the negativity to joy, love and light…May it bring us love and laughter through each day and night."

Phoebe waited for Lia to repeat the last sentence. "Now, open the door and release the smoke. As it flows away, imagine all the negative energy flowing out with it."

Lia did as she was told, and then turned to Phoebe. "Is that it?" she asked.

"For now. We'll need to put the candle in a safe place and allow it to burn down until it goes out on its own. Once that happens, you will need to dispose of it away from the house."

"That sound easy enough," Lia said. "What do we do with the sage and rosemary?"

Phoebe picked up the bowl containing the still-smoldering herbs and handed it to Lia. "Walk around each room on the upper two floors for additional cleansing and protection. I'll check on the others while you're doing that. They can use their herbs to cleanse this level, the courtyard and garage, and other outbuildings. After that, the house should be protected and only *invited* entities will be able to enter your home."

Lia met the rest of the crew in the kitchen once she finished cleansing the second and third stories, including the library and the remote apartment above it. She placed the bowl of slightly warm ashes on the island next to the one Elliot carried into the kitchen. "El, we need to remember to dispose of the candles and ashes after they burn down."

"I'll dispose of them in a dumpster at the university," Elliot said. That should be far enough away from the house."

"All right then. I guess we should head to the cemetery," Phoebe said.

"Let's take two cars," Elliot suggested. "After the cemetery, some of us can help Phoebe with the protection spell on her shop, and the rest of us can go clean up the mess on Saint Ann Street and pack up the camping gear."

"That's a good idea," Julie said. "I'll go help Phoebe and then we'll meet you at the house."

Chapter 17

St. Louis Cemetery No. 1 - New Orleans, LA

Elliot took her phone from her pocket as she climbed out of her car. "Do I need to pull up a map of the graveyard so we can find Marie's tomb?"

"We don't need a map. I know exactly where it is," Phoebe said. "Unfortunately, the only parking to be had was on the Treme Street side, so it's a bit of a hike. It's also a maze so follow closely."

Phoebe led the procession of women on a winding path from the Treme gate, to where Marie Laveau's tomb was located on the Basin Street side of the cemetery. When they arrived, they found a circle of yellow crime-scene tape with a diameter of about twenty-five feet, where Marie Laveau's tomb, as well as several other tombs, was contained. They were able to get close enough to see that the front panels had been pulled away from several of the tombs and that there was general debris on the ground around them.

"Who the hell would do something like this?" Elliot said.

"Someone either really desperate or really stupid," Marissa replied.

"I vote for stupid," Julie added. "Not only is this illegal, but it's dangerous."

"How are we going to get close enough to see if the brick has been disturbed?" Lia asked.

"We're going to duck under the tape," Marissa replied. "And since I'm the one who put the brick on top of the tomb, I'll go. I know what I'm looking for."

"Wait," Phoebe said. She reached into the canvas bag she carried on her shoulder and pulled out a small pouch. "Take this gris-gris bag. It will help protect you."

"If I remember right, when we originally encased her in that brick, the mistress was able to pick you, Julie and me all up at the same time and throw us several feet away. I'm not sure a gris-gris bag is going to give me much protection," Marissa pointed out.

"It won't hurt to take it, Mar," Julie said.

"Okay, okay." Marissa took the bag and shoved it into her pocket. "All right, here I go."

Marissa ducked under the crime scene tape and approached Marie Laveau's desecrated tomb. "Phew! There is a foul odor coming out of this tomb," she complained. Marissa reached the side of the tomb and felt around on top. "There are several loose bricks up here. I'll need to climb up to see if any of them have wax on them."

Marissa stepped on the decorative molding around the base of the tomb and hefted herself high enough to see over the top of it. She moved several bricks out of the way and then looked back at the others who remained outside the circle of tape.

"I don't see anything. The brick is gone."

"Damn," Phoebe said under her breath.

"I'm coming in to help you look, Mar," Julie called out. She slipped under the tape and searched the ground around the base of the tomb while Marissa continued to scan the debris on top of it.

"Wait! I think this is it!" Julie exclaimed. She reached for a brick on the ground just a few feet away from the tomb.

"Julie, don't touch it!" Phoebe called out.

Julie snatched her hand back quickly.

Phoebe ducked under the tape and joined her friends inside the barrier. By this time, Marissa had climbed off the base molding and stood beside Julie.

All three of them looked at the brick Julie had identified.

Phoebe once again opened her canvas bag. She retrieved a pouch of black salt and poured a thin circle of the substance around the brick. "This should help to contain the evil in the event any of it still resides on the brick or in the wax."

Phoebe stood and looked around. "I need a stick," she said.

"There's one right here," Elliot said. She picked up a stick that was lying nearby and handed it to Phoebe. Phoebe used it to turn the brick.

Wax was visibly present on the underside of the brick, but it was evident that large portions had been broken off and were now crushed into smaller pieces on the ground around where the brick lay.

"I don't see any evidence of the ash that was sealed under the wax," Marissa said.

"Ash?" Lia asked. "Why would you expect to see ash?"

"Part of the binding ritual requires that the name of the evil spirit be written on paper and then burned. Hot wax is then poured on top of it to seal it in," Phoebe explained. "It is obvious from the condition of this brick that someone removed it from the top of the tomb and either intentionally or accidentally destroyed the wax seal. I'm afraid the ash has been scattered to the winds, trampled into the ground, or washed away by rain."

"So, it's true then. The evil has been set free," Elliot said.

"Unfortunately, Celeste is right. The evil has been released," Phoebe confirmed.

"I hate to break up the party, but I think we should go before we're caught inside this tape line," Marissa said.

***

Marissa, Elliot and Lia returned to Saint Ann Street while Julie and Phoebe went to Phoebe's shop to execute the protection spell. When they walked into the living room, they realized the kitchen light was on.

"Awesome! We have power!" Marissa exclaimed. "I guess I should have checked that the light switches were all off before we left this morning."

Lia grabbed the trash bag and immediately collected the debris left from dinner the previous evening.

"It's too bad we got sidetracked today. We were supposed to start knocking that wall down," Elliot said.

"It's only Saturday. We can still start it today and work on it all day tomorrow," Marissa suggested.

Lia tied the trash bag and set it near the front door. "Listen to yourselves. You are talking about knocking a wall down while there's a murderous serial killer on the loose. Shouldn't we be doing something about that?" Lia asked. "I mean, shouldn't we call Randy and tell him what we know?"

Elliot ran her hands through her short hair. "I don't know what to tell him, Lia. All we know is that the spirit of the mistress seems to have been set free. The New Orleans police department already thinks we're nuts after we told them about the mass ascension of spirits in our courtyard a few months ago. I mean, you saw Randy's face when you told him that Miss Thing spazzes out when the stalker is nearby."

"I think we at least need to know if the stalker is responsible for bombing our carriage gates. If they can prove he did it, and he remains in custody, then I'll feel a lot better about things," Lia said.

"Okay. I agree we can do at least that much. I'm a little concerned that it's Saturday. He might not be working today," Elliot said.

"He gave us his personal cell phone number and told us to call him any time, day or night," Lia pointed out.

"You're right. He did." Elliot pulled her phone out of her pocket and dialed Randy's number. She put him on the speakerphone when he answered.

"Hello?"

"Randy, this is Elliot Walker. Sorry to call you on a Saturday.

"Good morning, Elliot. No problem at all. I told you to call any time."

"I appreciate that, Randy. Hey, Lia and I were wondering if you were able to detect any explosive residue on the stalker's clothing. We're feeling a little uneasy that there still might be someone out there trying to harm us."

"As a matter of fact, we did. I was going to call you with that news later today."

"That's great! So, I assume you'll be holding him a little longer, then?"

"He's been booked on attempted breaking and entering, destruction of private property, not to mention the evidence we have linking him to the grave robberies."

"Has he confessed to any of it?" Elliot asked.

"Not all of it. He claims to have no memory of the incidents leading to *any* of the charges except the grave robbing. He swears he's innocent on the B&E charges. The good news, however, is that we've identified his accomplice in the grave robberies, and our guy is turning state's witness against him. The guy has been on a bender for the past week. He says something pulled him inside Marie Laveau's grave, but he managed to escape."

"Pull him inside the grave?" Elliot asked.

"That's what he said, but he appeared no worse for wear. Oh, and some of the jewelry both he and the stalker had on them has definitely been traced back to Marie Laveau, as well as some of the other graves that were desecrated."

"That *is* good news, Randy. I feel like we can rest easier now. Sorry again for calling on a Saturday. Keep us posted on his status, okay? Especially if he's released."

"I'll do that. You have yourself a good weekend now, oh, and say hi to Miss Lia for me."

"You got it. Thanks again. Bye."

Elliot hung up the phone and looked at Lia. "If the mistress did possess our stalker, at least she's locked up for the time being."

"That makes me feel better, El, but I won't rest easy until we find a way to get rid of her once and for all," Lia said.

"That's going to take something bigger than all of us," Marissa said.

"We can discuss that with Julie and Phoebe when they get back," Lia said. "In the meantime, we need to get our stuff packed up and loaded into the car."

"I think we should leave it here for the time being," Elliot suggested. "I mean, if we're going to be tearing out walls, and painting, we might end up working late into the night and it would be great not to have to go home, just to get up early and come back."

"That's a great idea, El," Marissa said.

"But Phoebe's stuff still needs to be packed," Lia pointed out.

"I think we can take down her air mattress and fold her sleeping bag, but we need to let her pack her own personal gear. I don't want to invade her privacy," Marissa said.

"I agree. I'll go get started," Lia said.

"I can help," Marissa offered.

"We both can," Elliot added.

The three of them went into Phoebe's room and deflated the air mattress. Lia took Phoebe's sleeping bag and laid it out on the floor beside the bed in order to fold and roll it up.

"Mar, can I ask you something about Phoebe?" Lia said.

"Sure. Julie knows her better than I do but ask away."

"I was shocked to see how she looked under all that makeup. She is a beautiful woman. Her eyes are so striking, it's hard to look away from them. I can understand why she would take the makeup off at night, but she didn't reapply it this morning. I don't know why, but I expected her to," Lia said.

"It's only been recently that Julie and I have spent this much time with Phoebe, so I don't know what her routine is. My guess would be that she wears it when she's working. It's part of her psychic medium persona. As far as I know, she's not working today, so maybe that's why she didn't reapply it," Marissa reasoned.

"I don't know why, but she feels like a different person without the makeup," Lia said. "She seems more vulnerable to me. She and I had a bit of an intimate moment yesterday when I asked her if there was someone special in her life, and she got all cryptic about it."

"Yes, there is a traumatic story behind that," Marissa said.

"Is it something you can share with us? No pressure if not."

"No, I think it's okay to share. You see, Phoebe had an identical twin. I think her name was Chloe."

"*Had* an identical twin?" Elliot chimed in.

"Unfortunately, yes. When Phoebe and Chloe were in college, Phoebe had this boyfriend named, Troy. He was a good guy, and he didn't seem to mind that Chloe and Phoebe were a package deal. Chloe went nearly everywhere with them.

"From what I understand, Troy apparently had one problem—testosterone poisoning. He was pretty much a guy's guy and of course, he got all macho around his friends."

"I deal with college-aged men every day and it's been my experience that most of them are like that – especially the younger ones," Elliot said.

"I agree. Anyway, Phoebe, Chloe and Troy went bowling with a bunch of their college friends and afterward, Troy and one of his buddies got into a bit of a challenge with their cars. Unfortunately, things got out of hand during a reckless game of chicken and the cars collided. Troy's car flipped three times before it finally came to a stop on its roof. Chloe was thrown from the car and was crushed by it during one of the rollovers. Troy also died of head injuries. Phoebe survived with a broken leg, a concussion, and several broken ribs. Julie was supposed to have gone with them, but she was home sick."

"Oh, my God, how horrible!" Lia exclaimed.

"It was devastating to her. She and Chloe were what she refers to as psychic twins. They shared sensory experiences, and

Julie swears they could read one another's minds. Phoebe lost a part of herself when Chloe died, and she's had survivor's guilt ever since. Not too long after that, Phoebe immersed herself in psychic medium activities to the point that she didn't have time for relationships. Julie thinks it's a way for her to feel connected to Chloe. I for one, believe it's her way of protecting herself from further tragedy."

"I guess I can see how that might have turned Phoebe off relationships," Elliot said.

"You said they were in college. Didn't you and Julie meet around that time?" Lia asked.

"We met about a year after the accident. Julie felt guilty about moving to New York. She felt like she was deserting Phoebe, but Phoebe encouraged her to follow her heart."

"Yet, they've stayed close friends during the past twenty years," Elliot said.

"Yes. Every year Phoebe would visit New York City and Jules would visit New Orleans, so they saw one another at least twice a year—more than that when Julie visited her family here. Their bond is very strong," Marissa explained.

"My heart breaks for her," Lia said. I sense there is so much more to her behind the makeup and costumes. It feels like the makeup is a mask she hides behind. Like I said, she seems like a different person without it."

"That's a good way to put it," Marissa said.

"I would love to see her in a relationship with someone she can be authentic with," Lia said.

"Okay, Little Miss Matchmaker. Don't go poking your nose in where it might not be wanted," Elliot warned.

"Poking? Who, me?" Lia batted her eyes innocently at Elliot.

"I'm on to you, Lia," Elliot teased.

"Well, I never!" Lia said in her best Southern accent.

"Okay. I've got the mattress rolled up as small as possible. Elliot, would you mind holding the canvas bag open so I can put it in?" Marissa asked.

"The sleeping bag is ready to go as well," Lia said. She stood and looked round. "I think I'll go tidy our room while we're waiting for the girls to return."

Elliot stacked the mattress, sleeping bag and pillow in a pile. She looked at Marissa. "What time is your guy coming to check out the wall?" she asked.

Marissa looked startled. "Shit! I forgot about that." She looked at her watch. "Phew! It's only eleven. He's supposed to drop by around noon."

"Good. Maybe I have time to run home to pick up some tools," Elliot said.

"I'll go with you if you'd like. I have a few tools stored with our stuff that I can grab as well."

"An extra pair of hands would be good, Mar. I'll let Lia know we're going and see if she wants to come with us."

"Tell Lia what?"

Marissa and Elliot's attention was immediately drawn to the bedroom doorway. Lia stood there with one hand on each side of the doorframe. The sunlight behind her created the illusion that she was haloed.

Elliot approached her and took her face between her palms. "You, my love, look like an angel with the sun behind you." Elliot kissed her. "Mar and I are running to the house to pick up tools. Do you want to come with us?"

"No, I think I'll stay here and wait for the girls—unless you need my help, that is."

"I think Mar and I can handle it. I just didn't want to leave you out if you wanted to come with us."

Lia kissed Elliot. "Thank you for thinking of me, but I'll be fine here."

"Just so you know, I have a guy coming to see if that bedroom wall is load-bearing. He supposed to be here around noon, but in case he shows up before we get back, his name is Bill."

"Bill. Got it," Lia said. She stepped aside to allow Elliot and Marissa to enter the hallway to the kitchen. Lia followed them to the car.

"Okay. We'll be back soon," Elliot said as she climbed into her car.

Chapter 18

Lia waved to Elliot and Marissa as they drove away and then sat on the stoop to enjoy the warm sun. She pulled her phone from her back pocket and texted Julie.

Hey, Jules, how are things going?

Julie texted back.

We just finished the protection spell on the shop. Phoebs is gathering a few more supplies to do our home. We'll be there within a half hour.

Awesome! Mar and El just left to pick up tools at the house. I stayed behind in case the contractor arrives while they're gone. Let's see who gets here first! I'll see you soon.

Lia sat on the stoop for another ten minutes and then decided to go into the house. She stood and slipped her phone back into her pocket. Just as she turned to walk up the steps, a truck pulled to the curb. *Bill Murphy – General Contractor* was displayed on the door. She slipped her hands into her front pockets and waited for the driver to climb out.

A tall thin man walked around the front of the truck wearing a carpenter's tool belt around his hips. He approached Lia with his hand extended. "Hi, I'm Bill. Sorry if I'm a little early. Is Marissa here?" he asked.

"Marissa will be back shortly. She's gone to collect a few of her tools. My name is Lia. Lia Purvis. She told me you'd be coming."

The man narrowed his eyes at her and for a moment, he looked angry.

Lia took a step back. "Are you okay, Bill?" she asked.

Bill rubbed his forehead. "I'm sorry. I've been having these flash headaches for the past few days. They come and go with no warning. I'm sorry if I alarmed you."

"I'd offer for you to come in and sit, but there's no furniture in there yet. Would you like to sit for a while on the stoop? Like I said, Marissa should be home soon. Maybe you'll feel better by the time she gets here."

Bill nodded. "Maybe I will."

"Good. Have a seat. We have a cooler inside. I'll get a bottle of water for you."

***

Bill rubbed his forehead once more and then sat on the stairs. *What in hell is wrong with me? I hope I don't black out again.*

Bill fought a rage that he felt building inside his chest. He became nauseous and fought to remain in control of his consciousness. He dropped his head between his knees and inhaled deeply.

***

Lia stepped out of the house once more. "Here you go, Bill. I hope this helps." She handed him a bottle of water.

Bill sat upright and accepted the cold drink. "Thank you, ma'am," he said.

"You're welcome."

Lia watched him drink half the bottle in one gulp. He put the cap back on it and looked sideways at her. "I appreciate your kindness, Miss Lia," he said.

"Don't mention it. Heaven knows I've had days when I've felt under the weather. How are you feeling now?"

"Better. Much better."

"Do you want to have a look at that wall?" Lia asked.

"If you don't mind giving me a few more minutes?"

"Take all the time you need," she said.

Bill looked at her again. "I knew Marissa's other half was a woman, but I didn't expect her to be so beautiful," he said.

Lia chuckled. "Well, I thank you for the compliment, but Marissa's wife is Julie—who is also a beautiful woman I might add. My wife, Elliot, and I are Marissa and Julie's best friends. We live a few blocks away on Royal Street."

The man's brow knit once more into an angry frown.

Lia put her hand on his shoulder. "Are you sure you're okay, Bill?"

Bill squeezed his eyes closed and lowered his head again. "I'll be fine. Damned headaches."

Lia thought he looked like he was fighting some sort of internal battle.

He looked up at her again. "Maybe I should go look at that wall now. The sooner I can go home to bed, the better I think I'll feel."

"I'm sure Marissa won't mind if you reschedule," Lia suggested.

"No. I'm already here, so I might as well get the job done."

"All right then. Let's go inside."

"Give me a moment to get my ladder out of the truck."

Lia led Bill through the living room and dining room and into the bedroom beyond that. She pointed to the wall that stood between the first bedroom and the master bedroom at the back of the house. "This is the wall they want to take down," Lia said.

Bill looked at the wall. "Is there a way to get into the attic, ma'am? I'll need to see what framing was used in the construction."

Lia looked at him with a blank expression on her face. "Ah...that's a good question."

Before she could say anything more, Lia heard a voice calling from the living room.

"Bill? Where are you?"

"Saved by the bell," Lia said. "That would be Marissa. Wait right here."

Lia rushed into the living room. "Mar! Thank God you're home. Bill needs to get into the attic and I haven't faintest idea where the entrance is."

"Well, that makes two of us," Marissa said. "We're going to have to look for it."

"I'll give you a hand with that. We can unload the rest of the tools later," Elliot said, heading toward the bedroom.

Moments later, Phoebe and Julie walked in through the front door.

"I'm so glad to see you two," Lia said. "I was totally out of my element with Bill."

"Who's Bill?" Julie asked.

"Your contractor. He showed up a few minutes ago. He wanted me to show him where the attic is, but I have no freaking clue. Thank God Mar and El got home just before you two."

"We could always use your help with the cleansing." Phoebe said.

"Yes, I'd be happy to."

The three women sat on the floor facing one another.

"How did it go at the shop?" Lia asked.

"I don't think the shop is in any danger, simply because I don't think the mistress knows it exists, but it's better to be safe than sorry," Phoebe said. "The spell went without a hitch."

Lia hugged Phoebe. "Thank you for doing this, Phoebe."

"Phoebs, this house has six doors. How are we going to cover all of them in one spell?" Julie asked.

"Like we did at Lia's, we'll do the primary and secondary entrance doors. The other ones will be treated like windows would be. They will be protected when the sage and rosemary are carried from room to room at the end of the spell."

"That makes sense. I think we should wait until the contractor leaves. We'll need to split up and do both spells simultaneously again," Julie suggested. "We'll need Mar for that since at least one homeowner needs to participate in each spell."

"I agree. It would also be good not to be interrupted once the spell has begun," Phoebe added.

"He won't be here long," Lia said. "I think he's just checking to see if the roof will collapse if Elliot and Marissa take that wall down."

There was a pause in the conversation while Phoebe unpacked the bag she had brought from the shop. When she was finished, four bowls, two candles, a large cluster of sage and another of rosemary, a lighter, and two ceremonial knives lay on the floor in front of them.

Bill climbed down from the attic entrance they'd found inside the laundry closet.

"Whoever built this place used trusses in the attic. That, combined with this long wall in the middle of the structure that extends from the kitchen all the way to the back of the house, provides all the load bearing the roof needs. Knocking down this wall won't cause any structural issues at all."

"That is awesome news, Bill," Marissa said.

"Are you going to do this yourself?" Bill asked.

"Yes, we are," Elliot confirmed.

"Well, before you touch any of the electrical, find your breaker box and shut off the power. Oh, and remember to cap all the wires—even if the power stays off. You'll need an electrician to reroute the wires for you. Even if you know how to do it yourself, you'll need it checked by a certified electrician, otherwise it won't be to code."

"Are you a certified electrician?" Marissa asked.

"I am."

"All right. I'll know who to call when we get to that point."

Bill folded his ladder. "Well then, I guess I'm done here for today."

"What do I owe you?" Marissa asked.

"Why don't we deal with that when I come back to do the electrical?" Bill suggested.

Marissa shook his hand again. "We can do that. And when you come back, the beer is on me."

"I prefer hard cider," Bill said.

"That can be arranged. Thank you again, Bill."

Marissa led Bill through the house to the living room. He stopped when he saw Phoebe, Julie and Lia sitting in a circle on the floor with ritual implements laid out in the center of their circle.

Elliot nearly ran into the back of him when he came to an abrupt stop. "Whoa, there," she said.

Bill grabbed his head and squeezed his eyes closed. "Damn," he whispered.

All three women looked up at him.

Phoebe froze.

Lia immediately rose to her feet. "Oh, Bill. I'm so sorry your headache is back." She retrieved another bottle of water from the cooler and handed it to him. "I hope you feel better soon. Are you okay to drive?"

"I'll be fine. Thank you for the water, Miss Lia." He looked at Marissa. "Do you mind if I go out this other door so I can avoid maneuvering my ladder around the ladies."

"Of course you can," Marissa said. She went before him and unlocked the front entry door on the far side of the living room to let him out. A few moments later, after securing his ladder to the roof rack, he climbed into his truck and drove away.

Lia looked at Phoebe after Bill left. She had a deep frown creasing her forehead. "Are you okay, Phoebe?" she asked.

She looked at Lia and relaxed her brow. "I'm fine," she said.

Julie looked up at Marissa. "What did he say about the wall?"

"The wall is not load-bearing. That means Elliot and I can knock it down any time we'd like. I like Bill. I've worked with him before on houses my firm was selling. He's a nice guy," Marissa said.

"I've never seen a man with such shocking red hair," Julie commented.

***

Julie wrapped her arms around Phoebe and pulled her close. "Thank you for the protection spell, Phoebs. You are such a good friend."

"You are my family, Julie. At least you're the closest thing I have left to family," Phoebe replied. "I will do whatever I can to protect you."

"I'm honored to be your sister, although I could never replace Chloe. I still miss her so much."

Phoebe wiped a tear from the corner of her eye. "I do too, but she is here with me." Phoebe laid her palm over her heart.

Julie rubbed Phoebe's back.

The sound of pounding interrupted their moment.

"Ugh! We need to get out of here while they're tearing that wall down. Are you still up for shopping?" Julie asked both Lia and Phoebe.

"I'd love to go shopping, but I'm a little concerned that the mistress is out there," Phoebe said. "We should probably take extra precautions."

"Actually, the mistress is *not* out there right now," Lia said.

"But Marie and Celeste said she's been released," Julie pointed out.

"Yes, but the police have caught the guy who robbed her grave," Lia explained. "He's the same guy who was stalking us, and it turns out, he had explosive residue on his clothes, so we think he's also the one who tried to blow up the carriage gates. Right now, he's sitting in jail on breaking and entering charges, and defacing private property. *And*, they found jewelry on him from the graves he and his buddy robbed—including Marie's. I don't think he'll be out walking the streets for a while."

"What makes you think the mistress has jumped into him?" Phoebe asked.

"He's been stalking our house for the past couple of weeks, and he tried to get into the car with me one morning last week while I waited for Elliot to come out of the house. When Randy finally caught him, he looked at me with such hatred in his eyes it made my blood chill. I don't think it's a coincidence that he had jewelry on him from Marie Laveau's grave, either."

"But that still doesn't prove that the mistress has taken him," Phoebe said.

"He admitted to breaking into Marie's tomb but says he doesn't remember doing anything after that. He denies blowing up our gates despite the evidence the police got from his clothing, and he says he has no memory of stalking us, even though Randy actually caught him doing it. The same thing happened to Elliot when the mistress possessed her. She had no memory of the things she did while the mistress was in control."

Phoebe narrowed her eyes in thought. "I agree all of this gives us reason to hope, but I still think we need to be cautious. I think we need to carry the gris-gris bags with us at all times— especially when we venture out. If what you say is true, it only buys us time. We still need to deal with her on a more permanent basis."

"I agree," Lia said.

"Ditto for me," Julie said. "So, I'll go let the girls know we're going shopping and then we can head out."

"What are we shopping for today?" Lia asked.

"Curtains, bedding, towels, oh, and I'd like to look at appliances as well. As you can see, there is no stove or refrigerator in the kitchen," Julie said.

"Thank God they didn't take the dishwasher with them," Lia noted. "Julie, I don't remember—did you bring your washer and dryer with you from New York?"

"No, we didn't, so we'll need to put those on the list as well. I'll go tell the girls we're leaving."

"And I'll go fetch a few gris-gris bags from my room while she's doing that," Phoebe said. "I'll be right back."

Julie returned to the living room a few moments later carrying a piece of paper and a tape measure. "I have measurements here for the laundry closet," Julie said. "And we need to measure the space the stove and refrigerator sit in so we'll know what size to look for. I already have the window measurements."

"So, we're buying appliances today as well?" Lia asked as they walked toward the kitchen.

"I don't want to buy them without Marissa's inputs, but we'll definitely look at what options are available." Julie looked around. "Is Phoebe still in her room?"

"I'm coming!" Phoebe called from the hallway leading to the bedrooms. She met them in the kitchen. "Thank you to whoever took care of my mattress and sleeping bag," she said.

"You're welcome. We didn't feel comfortable touching your personal stuff. Elliot decided we should leave our room set up in case we're here late working on the house."

"I appreciate the gesture." Phoebe watched Lia and Julie take measurements. "Are we buying appliances today, too?"

***

Lia, Julie and Phoebe returned five hours later. They pulled their car in front of the house and immediately noticed the small dumpster sitting on the sidewalk in front of the tall windows.

Marissa came out of the house carrying a large piece of sheetrock just as they climbed out of the car.

Julie pointed to the dumpster. "Where did this come from?"

"El and I were tripping on the debris torn from the walls, so I had this dumpster delivered," Marissa explained. "I need to warn you that the house is a mess right now. There's sheetrock dust on everything. We closed the bedroom doors when we realized the dust was spreading, so hopefully, those two rooms aren't too bad."

Phoebe stood behind the car waiting for Julie to open the trunk. "Maybe we should leave your purchases in the car for now, Julie?" she suggested.

"Good idea. Let's go see what the girls have done," Julie replied.

Lia, Phoebe and Julie stepped into the living room and immediately stopped.

"Oh, my God. What a mess," Julie said.

The air mattress, bedding, clothing and other personal effects that had been in the master bedroom were piled against the far wall of the living room, and a layer of dust covered everything.

"Wait until you see the bedroom," Marissa warned.

"I'm so glad we don't have any furniture in here yet," Julie said as they walked through the dining room and into the short hallway where the bathroom and laundry space were. Dusty footprints formed a trail between the bedroom doorway and the front door where it was obvious, several trips had already been made to the dumpster.

Marissa went in front of them and pushed the door open into the smaller of the two bedrooms that would soon form the master suite.

Julie looked around with wide eyes. "I have no words," she said.

Marissa and Elliot had removed all of the wallboard on both sides of the wall separating the two bedrooms so that they could see straight through to the back wall of the house. The framing for the wall was still in place, along with all of the electrical wires and outlets. Piles of broken sheetrock, baseboard and ceiling littered the floor on both sides of the partition. Elliot stood in the middle of it. Her clothing, face and arms were nearly white with dust.

Lia burst out laughing. "My God, Elliot. You look like a kabuki girl under all that dust!"

Elliot clapped her hands together and a white cloud dispersed from them. She pulled her dust mask away and allowed it to dangle around her neck. A circle of pink flesh was exposed where the mask had been. "This is the worst part of the job," she said.

"I'm glad to see you're wearing masks," Phoebe remarked.

Julie walked around and looked back and forth between the two rooms. "I can envision how this might look when it's finished. It's going to be a huge room," she said.

"Yes, it is." Marissa walked toward Julie and put her arm around Julie's waist.

"Ewww! Mar, you're getting me all dirty!" she complained.

"Oh, my God, you're such a girl!" Marissa said.

"Be that as it may, I'm not dressed for this," Julie said in her own defense.

"Fair enough. So, I guess that means you don't want to give us a hand picking up this mess," Marissa suggested.

"Not on your life."

Marissa looked at the other two. "Lia? Phoebs?" she said.

"Ah, no. I think I'll pass," Lia said.

"Me too," Phoebe added.

"All right then, how about Mar and I take care of this debris while the three of you put your heads together and plan something for dinner. I'm starved," Elliot said.

"That, we can do," Julie replied quickly.

"Are you two finished for the day?" Lia asked.

Marissa and Elliot looked at one another. Elliot shrugged. "We are at a good stopping point, Mar," she said.

"I agree. As soon as we pick up this mess, that is," Marissa added.

"Good." Lia turned to Phoebe. "Phoebe, did you want to collect your things today, or is tomorrow soon enough?"

"Most of it can stay here tonight, but I do want to take my tools with me," Phoebe said. "I'll go get them."

Julie watched Phoebe walk toward the dining room. "What did you have in mind, Lia?" Julie asked.

"I thought we could all camp out at our place tonight and maybe plan how we are going to address the problem with the mistress. Phoebe is welcome to stay in the courtyard bedroom if she wants to."

"I'll go ask her," Julie said.

"And I'll work with our two kabuki girls here to decide what sounds good for dinner."

***

Julie traced Phoebe's dusty footprints back through the dining room, living room, kitchen and finally down the hall toward the bedrooms. As she approached Phoebe's room, she heard a conversation in progress. She slowly approached the door that had been left slightly ajar and stopped when she was close enough to hear.

"Da danger be near, girl."

Julie was sure this was Marie's voice. She moved closer and saw Phoebe pacing back and forth across the room.

"I know. I can feel it," Phoebe clearly responded.

"Da evil one be causing harm if not be stopped."

"We have taken steps to protect our homes. We have cast the appropriate spells."

"Da spells only be good if evil not be invited in."

"Yes, I'm aware of that."

"Da fifty and one be coming. Da evil one must be stopped."

Julie waited for several more moments, but no further conversation was forthcoming. She peered into the room once more and saw Phoebe collecting a few items that she shoved into her bag.

Julie quickly retreated to the kitchen and pretended to just then be on her way to Phoebe's room. Phoebe came out of the room when Julie was about halfway down the hall.

169

"Hey! I was just coming to ask if you're up for another slumber party—at Lia and Elliot's this time. Lia suggested we could all powwow about how to tackle our problem with the mistress."

Phoebe looked at Julie and then back down the hall. Her brow creased when she looked at Julie again. "You were listening, weren't you?" she said.

Julie went ashen. "How did you know?"

Phoebe pointed down the hall. "The footprints in the dust. Clearly there are more present than from my entrance and exit."

Julie sighed. "I'm sorry, Phoebs. I didn't want Marie to go away if she knew I was there. I only listened for a moment. Forgive me?"

Phoebe smiled. "This is your home. You have a right to know what is happening in it, and I understand your motives, so, of course, I forgive you, but next time, just come in. I'm sure Marie wouldn't have minded."

Julie smiled. "That was the gentlest ass-kicking I've ever received. Thank you, my friend."

"So, yes, another sleepover sounds great to me. I'm liking this girl-time we've all been enjoying during the past two days."

***

Julie and Phoebe returned to the living room where the other three were waiting for them.

"We're in!" Julie said.

"Awesome! We've decided on Indian food. Is that okay with you two?" Lia asked.

"I love Indian food," Phoebe said. "I know the perfect place to order it from."

"Works for me, too," Julie added.

Lia turned to Elliot and Marissa. "Okay. Let's call it in. I guess we'll go pick up dinner and meet you at home in...an hour, maybe?"

"That should work," Elliot said.

Lia followed Julie and Phoebe toward the door but then stopped and turned around. "Oh, and the two of you need to get out of those dusty clothes before you get into the car. Wear your pajamas home if you have to. I don't want sheetrock dust on our work clothes on Monday."

Chapter 19

Marissa sat beside Elliot in the car. "I feel foolish going home in my pajamas," she said.

"Well, it's better than facing the wrath of Lia if we get sheetrock dust on the car," Elliot pointed out.

"Trust me—I know all about the wrath of Lia. I grew up with her, remember?" Marissa chuckled.

"You know, we should teach her a lesson," Elliot suggested.

"I'm game. What did you have in mind?"

Elliot and Marissa parked the car on the Royal Street side of the house. They very quietly got out of the car, closed the doors and entered through the gate. Elliot unlocked the door to the vestibule and they slipped inside. She gently closed the door and then turned to Marissa.

"Let's get ready, and then I'll open and slam the door to announce that we're home," Elliot said softly.

Marissa nodded, a look of evil glee on her face.

It took less than a minute for the ladies to prepare their surprise.

"Are you ready?" Elliot whispered.

Marissa looked down at herself. "I can't get any more ready than this," she said.

"Okay. Here goes." Elliot opened and slammed the door and then started the countdown. "Three, two, one..."

"Elliot, is that you?" Lia called from above them.

"That's our cue!" Elliot said. "Follow my lead."

Both women raised their hands into the air and screamed as they ran up the marble staircase, buck naked!

"Elliot! Oh, my God! What are you doing?" Lia exclaimed when they reached the second-floor landing.

They ran into the kitchen where Julie was warming the Indian food in the microwave.

"Jesus, Mar. Are you out of your goddamned mind?" Julie yelled.

They ran around the island and then headed to the living room where Phoebe, who had already been alerted by the commotion, stood in the doorway. She stepped aside and let them pass and watched them run around the coffee table and out again. "Sweet Goddess, poke my eyes out! I cannot un-see this!" she said, and then laughed.

Finally, Marissa and Julie ran up to the third story where they went into their respective bedrooms to shower.

Lia, Julie and Phoebe met on the second-floor landing.

"What the hell was that?" Julie asked.

"I suspect that was in retaliation for me insisting that they don't wear their dust-covered clothes in my car," Lia said. She shook her head. "I see Elliot written all over this one."

"Mar was right there with her, Lia," Julie said.

"Do you guys always have this much fun?" Phoebe asked.

***

They all sat around the kitchen island enjoying their takeout fare.

"This is amazing Indian food," Elliot said.

"It is. It's from a restaurant Phoebe suggested," Lia replied.

"Well, this is the best I've ever had. Indian food can be hit or miss, but I'm impressed. We'll have to order from there more often."

Lia picked up the plate of naan. "Garlic naan, anyone?" she asked.

"Oh, yes," Phoebe replied. "This doesn't do much for my waistline—or my breath for that matter—but I can't resist it."

"Your waistline is perfect," Julie said. "I should be so lucky."

"I beg to differ," Marissa said. "I happen to like your waistline, thank you very much."

"Well, that makes one of us. I could stand to lose a few pounds," Julie complained.

"Keep running with me in the mornings and you'll be in shape in no time," Lia said.

"But that takes so much effort!" Julie whined. "Wouldn't it be great if there was some voodoo spell that could just transform your body overnight?"

"I could make a fortune if that were the case," Phoebe said.

"Speaking of voodoo spells, what are we going to do about the mistress?" Lia asked.

"I think the first thing we need to do is to determine where she is," Phoebe said.

"She's possessing the dude that's in jail for grave robbing and blowing up our gates," Elliot pointed out.

"I'm not sure about that."

"What do you mean, Phoebs?" Julie asked.

"I mean, I guess it's possible, but we need to determine that for ourselves," Phoebe suggested.

"And how do we do that?" Elliot asked.

"We need to get close enough to him to see how he reacts to a talisman, or holy water," Phoebe said.

"So, if he freaks out, we can be sure the mistress is inside him?" Marissa asked.

"Exactly. And if he doesn't, then we can be pretty sure she isn't," Phoebe added.

"So, how do we do that?" Lia asked.

"Maybe Randy can help," Elliot suggested.

"Maybe, but like you said, I think he's already skeptical about our sanity after the ghosts in the courtyard episode," Lia said.

"It's certainly worth a try," Elliot reasoned. "What have we got to lose by asking?"

"Absolutely nothing. You're right, Elliot. I'll call him tomorrow," Lia offered.

"How long ago were the graves desecrated?" Phoebe asked.

Elliot looked at Lia. "I think it was about a week and a half ago, wouldn't you say, Lia?"

"About that," Lia confirmed.

"So, I wonder what the mistress has been up to since then? If she's been out that long, she's been awfully quiet. Unless, of course, she really *is* trapped inside our grave robber," Phoebe reasoned.

So, assuming we can trap her somewhere, how do we get rid of her permanently? Obviously, our previous attempt was pretty temporary."

"That is a very good question, Marissa," Phoebe said. "To be honest, I don't know. I will need to consult others from the voodoo community. Maybe together, we can come up with something."

"That doesn't sound very encouraging, Phoebe," Lia said.

"I know, and I apologize for that, but from what Marie has said, the mistress is very powerful, and it could be that strength in numbers might be the best approach. But like I said, if she's been out for the past ten or so days, she's being very low key. I suppose it's possible she could have moved on and we'll never hear from her again."

"In a way, that might be good, but then how will we know that she'll stay away? I for one would feel better if we were able to permanently banish her in some way," Julie said.

"I agree with Julie," Elliot commented.

"Yes. I agree as well," Phoebe said. "But until we know where she is, it will be difficult to do anything. I suspect she will show herself in some way, so we all need to be on guard. She has reason to seek revenge on all of us, so none of us should wander off on our own. It is good that our homes are protected, but we'll be vulnerable when we are away from them."

"Phoebs, your home isn't protected. I mean, we did your shop, but not your house," Julie pointed out.

"Don't worry about my home, Julie. I renew protection spells on my home on a weekly basis. I deal with many hostile spirits daily while performing my psychic medium duties, so I make a point of doing spells on a regular basis," Phoebe explained.

"Phoebe, how do you get from your house to your shop every morning," Marissa asked.

"I generally walk. It is only three blocks away," Phoebe replied.

"Well, until we resolve this little problem we all have, Julie and I will pick you up each morning and bring you to the shop. I will have to bring Julie anyway, so it's no trouble to swing by your place first. Okay?" Marissa insisted.

"That is very kind of you, Marissa."

"Well, like you said, Julie is your family, so I guess that makes me family-in-law, and nobody fucks with my family if I can do anything to stop it."

Phoebe eyes filled with tears. Lia immediately got up and wrapped her arms around her.

"Oh, sweetie, don't cry. You are among people who love you."

Phoebe allowed her head to fall back onto Lia's shoulder. "I'm sorry for being such a baby. It's just been so long since I have felt this close to someone."

Julie added her arms to the huddle while Marissa and Elliot both reached for Phoebe's hands.

"Thank you for trusting us enough to be vulnerable around us, Sis," Julie said.

"I do trust you, and I love each and every one of you," Phoebe said.

"The feeling is mutual, Phoebe," Elliot said.

"I agree with Elliot," Marissa added.

"Me, too," Lia and Julie said in unison.

Phoebe reached up to wipe her eyes just as the grandfather clock in the second story balcony chimed. They all stood very still as they counted the gongs.

"Is it ten o'clock?" Marissa exclaimed. "Where has the time gone?"

"We didn't get home from your place until nearly eight," Elliot pointed out.

"I guess you're right."

"You know, if we're planning an early start tomorrow, we should probably get to bed," Elliot suggested.

"You go ahead upstairs, El. I'll be up as soon as I clean up the dishes," Lia said.

"I'll help with the dishes," Phoebe offered.

"That makes three of us," Julie added.

"Okay then. I'll see you in a few minutes." Elliot kissed Lia and then she turned to leave the kitchen.

"Oh, Elliot?" Lia said.

Elliot turned around. "Yes?"

"If you leave before us in the morning, remember to grab a towel, toiletries and a change of clothes. We don't need another display of your skinny ass when you get home tonight."

Elliot grabbed her chest. "Ouch!" she said. "I thought you liked my skinny ass!"

"I do, but that doesn't mean everyone else does."

"That goes for you too, Mar," Julie said to Marissa.

"Hmph! No respect! I get no respect, I tell ya!" Marissa joked.

Julie grabbed the dishtowel from the counter and rolled it up. She snapped it in the direction of Marissa's backside.

"Yikes!" Marissa said. "I'm outta here!"

Phoebe laughed as she watched Elliot and Marissa run out of the kitchen. "They are very funny together," she said.

"They're like two kids," Lia replied. Can you believe they streaked through the house earlier?"

"I can believe it," Julie said. "I wouldn't put anything past those two when they're together."

Lia began collecting the dishes from the island. "I guess I should be happy they feel comfortable enough with everyone to pull something like that."

"I know what you mean," Julie said as she took the rinsed dishes from Phoebe and loaded them into the dishwasher. "I can remember when my siblings and I were young, we would all hang out in the living room in our underwear and watch television in the evening. There's no modesty around family."

"I was an only child, so I missed out on that," Lia said.

"My sister and I used to do the same thing." Phoebe paused and stared into the sink. "I really miss her," she added in a very soft voice.

Julie took her by the shoulders. "Phoebs, I know we can never replace Chloe, and God knows, I would never try, but we are here for you."

"Yes, we are," Lia added.

Phoebe nodded and went back to rinsing dishes.

"Okay, that's the last one," Julie said. She turned around just as Lia finished wiping off the island.

"All clean for another day. Time for bed," Lia said.

***

Lia, Julie and Phoebe hugged one another goodnight at the top of the third-floor staircase and went their separate ways—Lia and Julie to join their wives in their respective bedrooms, while Phoebe retired to the third bedroom adjoining the balcony overlooking the courtyard.

Elliot was waiting for Lia when she came to bed. She sat against the headboard with the covers pulled to her waist and wearing nothing else. She put the book she was reading down on the nightstand when Lia came in and watched her remove her clothing and slip into bed beside her. Elliot opened her arms to Lia.

Lia snuggled against Elliot and placed her head on her shoulder. "El, I feel so bad for Phoebe," she said.

"Why?" Elliot asked.

"Because she has nobody but the four of us. She has no one to share her life with on a more intimate level."

"Have you thought that maybe she likes it that way?"

Lia pulled her head back to look directly into Elliot's face. "Maybe, but I suspect that after spending a day and a half with all of us, she sees there's so much more she could have."

"Did she tell you that, Lia?"

"No, but..."

"But it breaks your heart to see her alone. Sweetie, I love that you are worried about her, but she's a big girl. If there is someone out there for her, they will find one another. Like when you and I met at that Starbucks so many years ago. It was meant to be. Have faith that it will happen for Phoebe as well."

"If she *lets* it happen," Lia said.

"If it was meant to be, she won't be able to resist it. Trust me on this one."

Lia traced the side of Elliot's cheek with her fingertip. "That was cute what you and Mar did tonight. I think you shocked the hell out of Phoebe."

"Do you really think my ass is skinny?" Elliot asked.

"Compared to mine, yes, but I love it anyway."

Elliot rolled on top of Lia so they were nose to nose. "And I love how curvy *you* are. If it had been you streaking through the house instead of me, I would have tackled you and made mad passionate love to you, right there in front of everyone. I would not be able to help myself."

"Well, you've got me in tackle position right now. What are you waiting for?" Lia teased.

***

Marissa lay in bed with her hands behind her head, and watched Julie remove her clothing. She pulled back the sheet and held it open for Julie to join her. Julie lay on her side facing Marissa, with her hands folded under her cheek.

"Mar, I'm worried about Phoebe," Julie said.

Marissa rolled to face Julie and slipped her arm under her pillow. "How so?" she asked.

"This is the first time that I know of in decades that she has spent so much one-on-one time with anyone, let alone four women. I think we've overwhelmed her for the past day and a half."

"How do you know she's overwhelmed? She might just be enjoying it," Marissa said.

"Well, she did say she was enjoying our girlfriend time together, but she's been more emotional than I can ever remember seeing her since Chloe died."

"Maybe that's a good thing, Julie."

"I don't know, Mar. It's just that you and I are here together, and Lia and Elliot are no doubt doing the wild thing right now across the hall, yet Phoebe is all by herself in the courtyard room."

"We could invite her in here for a threesome," Marissa suggested.

Julie slapped Marissa on the arm. "Stop that!" she said. "I'm being serious here."

Marissa cupped the side of Julie's face with her palm. "Look, love. If Phoebe is destined to meet someone special, it will happen when she least expects it. You need to stop worrying about her and let fate take its course."

"I know you're right, but I so want her to have what we have. I want her to feel for someone what I feel for you."

"You have such a beautiful heart, Jules."

Julie lifted her upper body off the bed to kiss Marissa.

Marissa took advantage of the opportunity to pull Julie on top of her as the kiss deepened.

When the kiss ended, Marissa held Julie's face between her palms. "Tell me more about this wild thing," she said.

***

Phoebe pulled the pillow over her head to drown out the sounds of lovemaking coming from the other rooms.

It was going to be a long night.

Chapter 20

Phoebe hovered on the edge of consciousness, trying hard to ignore the nagging urge of nature calling. She opened one eye and looked at the clock on the bedside table. It read one-thirty-seven. Knowing she still had several hours of sleep ahead of her if she would just get it done, she resigned herself to getting out of bed.

She threw the covers off and slipped her legs over the side of the bed. Her feet made contact with a thick carpet, and she immediately wondered where she was. She looked around in the dark at the unfamiliar surroundings, and as her eyes adjusted to the dim lighting cast from a night light in the adjoining bathroom, she recalled that she was a guest in Lia and Elliot's home and that she was in the courtyard bedroom.

Phoebe stood and made her way toward the night light inside the bathroom. Luckily, it was bright enough that she didn't need to turn on the overhead lights to take care of business. She quickly ran her hands under the water in the nearby sink and then made her way back to the bed. She climbed in and pulled the covers up to her neck.

Thank God the sounds of lovemaking had stopped. She lay awake for hours fighting the waves of desire that had coursed through her as she imagined the melding of bodies, hearts and minds in the nearby bedrooms.

Phoebe tried to fall back to sleep, but she found herself feeling sad that she had no such relationship in her life. But then, sadness turned to anger when she recalled that the one serious relationship she had allowed herself more than twenty-five years ago had resulted in the death of her beloved sister. She vowed then that she would never again allow someone into her heart in that way.

She tossed and turned for another half hour before she gave up and got out of bed. Phoebe paced back and forth across the dimly lit room for several minutes before she finally decided to go onto the balcony adjacent to her room, in the hopes that fresh air would help to put her into a better frame of mind. She stepped onto the balcony through the door in her room and left that door open when she went outside.

Phoebe stood at the railing that overlooked the courtyard. She saw Marissa and Julie's car parked below, illuminated by the full moon that cast a nearly day-like glow across everything. The night was warm, and she found herself grateful that she had worn just a T-shirt and boxer briefs to bed that night.

She scanned the area beyond the walls of the courtyard and gasped when she saw a man standing across the street, just opposite the carriage gates. He was leaning against the building and staring at her on the balcony, a cigarette hanging from his lips. She immediately became suspicious and took a step back. He casually pulled a lighter out of his pocket, lit his cigarette and then tipped his hat to her before walking away.

Get a grip, Phoebe. Not every person passing by is possessed by an evil spirit.

She wrapped her arms around herself and closed her eyes. For the next several minutes, she listened to the sounds of Bourbon Street just a block away. Bourbon Street never slept. There were always revelers and jazz music playing into the wee hours of the morning.

Phoebe felt a sudden, slight breeze. She smiled and inhaled deeply, enjoying the feel of coolness on her skin. Still, her eyes were closed.

"Dis be da most peace ever in dis place,"

Phoebe's eyes flew open and she took a step back.

"Lia?"

"Not be Lia. Lia be sleeping."

"Celeste?" Phoebe whispered.

"Dat be me," Celeste said.

Phoebe looked at her closely. She was completely naked.

"Celeste, wait here. I'll be right back." Phoebe ran into her room and grabbed the lightweight robe she had draped on the foot of the bed. She returned to the balcony and offered it to Celeste. "Here. Let me help you put this on."

Celeste complied. "You not like Lia's body?" she asked.

"No! No, Lia has a beautiful body. We just don't get naked around one another much," Phoebe explained.

"Dat not what I see. El-ee-ot and da other one be naked. Dey be all crazy, runnin 'round da house."

Phoebe couldn't help but smile. "Yes, well, I have no explanation for that."

"Sometings best not to know," Celeste chuckled.

"Are you here all the time, Celeste?"

"Not all da time. I come when dey needs Celeste."

"And they need you now?"

"Da evil one be free. Da fifty and one be near. Da evil one must be stopped."

"Celeste. We don't know what the fifty and one means. Please tell me," Phoebe begged.

"Celeste not be tellin 'bout da fifty and one. It be for Lia to know."

"Is Lia in danger?"

"Lia be my blood and my blood be cursed by da evil one. Lia be in danger. El-ee-ot be in danger. You all be in danger."

"Celeste, tell us what to do to stop her," Phoebe said.

"Da evil one be powerful. She not be stopped by simple spells. Seek da wisdom of da queen."

"The queen? Do you mean, Marie Laveau?"

"She be da queen."

"Celeste, why are you helping us? Aren't you putting yourself at risk by doing so?" Phoebe asked.

"Da evil one do her worst to me already. She kilt my Lia. Lia be eight years old when she be kilt. I try hard to protect her. I warm dere beds, I give dem sexual pleasure, I take da beatings, but da evil one still kilt my Lia. She kilt her for she be da master's blood.

"She kilt my Samuel. She poke his eyes out and stir his brains. Da evil one kilt my heart when she kilt Samuel. She be da reason my boy Ethan be sent away. He be took from my breast when he be born and I never sees him again. Da evil one do all dis, and she make Celeste watch. Den, she kilt me and hid da bones so I be tied to dis place forever."

Phoebe waited patiently while Celeste continued.

"El-ee-ot find da bones. Dey give me and my Lia a proper-like burial. Den we be free. Miss El-ee-ot and Mis Lia set us free. Dat is why Celeste help. Dere is nothing da evil one can do to Celeste dat she ain't already done."

Phoebe wiped the tears that had fallen freely down her cheeks as she listened to Celeste tell her story. "I'm so sorry she did all of that to you. You have lost so much in your life."

"Dat be true, girlie, but dey all wid me now. Samuel, Lia and Ethan all be wid me now. Da evil one kilt our bodies, but she not kilt our love. She lose. We win."

Phoebe lowered her face into her hands and sobbed. It was several minutes before she regained control.

"Why you be sad?" Celeste asked.

Phoebe looked at the courtyard. "I've been thinking about my life. About what I've lost. I'm ashamed of myself when I see how much more you have lost. My own pain pales in comparison to yours."

"You be tinking 'bout Chloe."

Phoebe's gaze swing to Celeste. "Yes. How did you know?"

"She be here."

"She's there? With you? Right now?" Phoebe asked excitedly.

Celeste nodded. "She be wantin' to talk to you."

Phoebe covered her mouth with her hands. "Oh, my God. Yes! Yes, please."

Celeste closed her eyes for a moment and when she reopened them, she smiled.

"Phoebs? Phoebs, is that you?"

Phoebe's eyed opened wide. "Chloe?"

Chloe pulled Phoebe into a hug and held her for several long moments while Phoebe cried.

"Chloe, I miss you so much," Phoebe cried.

Chloe broke the embrace and held Phoebe at arm's length.

"Phoebs, please don't cry. I'm okay. I'm more than okay."

"I have felt you near me all these years, Chloe. You have always been in my thoughts."

"I know I have. I can feel you with me, but it breaks my heart to see the guilt you have carried for so long. Sweetie, you are not to blame for what happened to me. I've tried to get that message across to you for years. Please stop beating yourself up about it."

"It should have been me," Phoebe said.

"No! Stop that! Phoebe, you've mourned for twenty-five years. Please stop. I love you so much for grieving my loss, but I'm in a good place. It is beyond time for you to focus on your own life now."

"I will never forget you, Chloe."

"You're damned right you won't, because I won't let you. You know how strong willed I can be."

A small smile erupted from Phoebe's features.

Chloe lifted Phoebe's chin. "I was hoping to see that beautiful smile."

"You only call me beautiful because I look like you," Phoebe teased.

"And I couldn't be more proud of that fact. Look, Phoebs, I want you to be happy. Truly happy. You need to live your life to the fullest. If you want to honor my memory, open your heart to love. Promise me you will."

Phoebe wiped the tears from her face once more and nodded. "Okay. I promise."

"Good, now give me another hug. I gotta go but know that I will always be in your heart, and any time you want to see me, look in the mirror. I will be there."

Phoebe allowed herself to be embraced in the warmth of Chloe's memory for several long moments.

"She be gone."

Phoebe stepped out of Celeste's embrace. "Thank you for that gift. I will forever be grateful."

"I need get Lia back to bed. Stop da evil one Phoebe. Da queen and da others will help. I be watching. I come back if I needs to."

"Thank you, Celeste. Thank you for everything."

Celeste crossed the balcony and entered Phoebe's room. Phoebe followed her and then stood in the doorway as Celeste walked across the hall toward Lia and Elliot's bedroom. She paused before going in and blew a kiss to Phoebe. She caught it and held it close to her heart.

Phoebe returned to her own bed and lay down. Her heart swelled with emotions she hadn't felt in many years—hope and expectation. She closed her eyes and drifted off to sleep with a smile on her lips.

***

Phoebe and Julie enjoyed coffee together the next morning around the kitchen counter. Julie had risen early and assembled a quiche that was currently filling the kitchen with an enticing aroma as it baked. Phoebe's hair was a tumble and she sat there in her T-shirt and boxer shorts, enjoying her coffee.

Julie looked at her friend with interest. "You look different today, Phoebs. Is everything okay?"

Phoebe smiled. "Everything is wonderful. I have some news to share but I want to wait until everyone is here."

"Coffee!"

Julie swung around to see Marissa shuffle into the kitchen through the butler's pantry. "Coffee," she repeated.

A smile lit up Julie's face. "Good morning, my love." She crossed the room and went into Marissa's arms for a morning hug.

"I need coffee," Marissa said once more.

"Have a seat at the island and I'll make you a cup."

Marissa shuffled to the island and sat down. "'Morning, Phoebs," she said.

"You are sporting the most attractive hair style this morning, Mar," Phoebe said.

Marissa reached up and attempted to smooth several strands of hair that were sticking straight up on her head. "Do you like it?" she asked. "It's called bed head."

All attention diverted to the kitchen door as Elliot walked in, with Lia right behind her. She was carrying Phoebe's robe. She stopped just short of the kitchen island. Lia stood beside her, biting her lip.

"So, I wake up this morning and find Lia sleeping with this robe on. Anyone know how that might have happened?" Elliot asked.

Phoebe grinned. "Yes. She was in my room last night. Naked, I might add."

"Phoebe?" Julie asked incredulously.

"I agree with you, Elliot. Lia *does* have sexy curves," Phoebe added.

"What the fuck?" Marissa exclaimed.

"I...I don't remember going into your room, Phoebe," Lia said in her own defense.

"I'm not surprised you don't remember. That's because Celeste brought you there."

"Did she..." Elliot began.

"Did she use Lia to seduce me?" Phoebe asked. "No. But she did show up naked as a jaybird. I used my robe to cover her up. As beautiful as she is, it was a little uncomfortable standing there talking to Celeste with Lia's naked body on display."

Lia punched Elliot in the arm. "See? I told you there'd be a simple explanation."

"Celeste is anything but simple," Elliot said. "So, why did she appear to you?"

"That's what I wanted to tell everyone this morning. She told me all about her life in this house, and how the mistress and master treated her so poorly. She told me about all the people she loved and lost at the hands of those monsters, but she also said that they are together again in the afterlife. She said something very profound. She said that the mistress killed their bodies, but she couldn't kill their love, and so in her mind, the mistress has lost and they have won."

"Wow, that *is* profound." Julie said.

Phoebe began tear up. Her voice quivered when she spoke again. "I think what she was trying to tell me is that we all live through heartbreaking things in our lives, but in the end, we will all be together again."

Phoebe paused to regain control but lost it again the moment she resumed. She looked at each of her friends.

"Guys, she allowed Chloe to appear to me. We held one another forever. Chloe is okay, and she told me to stop feeling guilty for surviving. She said it was time I started to live my life."

By this time, Phoebe was no longer able to speak through the sobs.

Lia and Julie immediately enveloped her in a loving embrace.

Elliot looked at Marissa, and in an unspoken message, they both knew they needed to lend their love to the vulnerable woman who was their friend, so they added their arms to the tableau and held the group in a tight huddle.

"What an amazing gift you were given," Julie said as the huddle broke apart.

Phoebe wiped her eyes with her napkin. "That's what I said to Celeste after Chloe left." She took Lia's hand in hers. "Lia, thank you for allowing Celeste to be who she is."

Lia grinned. "I generally don't have any control of her, but if it results in something like this, I'm happy to oblige. It would be nice if she waited until I had clothes on, but heck, we're all among friends here."

"Did Celeste say anything else while she was here?" Elliot asked.

"She did say again that we needed to stop the mistress. She said the mistress was very powerful and that we needed to ask the queen for help," Phoebe replied.

"I assume she meant, Marie Laveau?" Julie asked.

"Maybe. There are several other modern-day voodoo queens about town. Voodoo kings as well, for that matter. I got the impression from Celeste that it will take more than just a few of us to stop her. Maybe when we go to the house to work today, we can summon Marie and talk to her about this. Oh, and she implied that we were running out of time. She said again that the fifty and one was approaching. I wish I understood what she meant by that. I asked her to explain, but she said Lia would have to find out for herself," Phoebe explained.

"I need to find out for myself? I wonder what that means. And why me?" Lia asked.

"I don't know," Phoebe replied. "I'm hoping we can get some answers out of Marie today. I recommend we head there after breakfast."

The oven timer chose that moment to sound.

"Ah, the quiche is finished, right on cue," Julie said.

"Quiche? I was wondering what that amazing aroma was," Marissa said.

"Okay. Since Julie cooked, she gets out of clean-up duty," Lia said.

"Marissa and I will do cleanup this morning since you girls did it last night," Elliot volunteered.

"Thanks, love. Phoebs, if you don't mind setting the table, I'll throw together a fruit salad to go with the quiche."

"I'd be happy to set the table. Just point me to the dishes," Phoebe said.

Chapter 21

When the friends arrived at Saint Ann Street that morning, Phoebe went directly to her room to prepare to summon Marie Laveau, while the others congregated in the master bedroom where the wall was being taken down.

"Wow! This looks so much better with the mess cleaned up," Julie said.

Marissa put her arm around Julie's shoulder and looked at the framing that was still in place. "Just imagine this wall completely gone. This room alone will be almost a quarter of the footprint of the house. I think we'll have room for our bedroom furniture as well as a sitting area. We will have to build new closets across the wall adjoining the dining room. It will make the room look a little smaller, but it will also lengthen the hallway between the dining room and master."

"I'm glad we made such a huge profit on our New York condo. That gives us a considerable amount of money for these renovations and new furniture," Julie said.

"Speaking of which, I'd like to take some time today to study the pictures you took of the appliances when you went shopping yesterday," Marissa said.

"Okay. Just let me know when you're ready to do that."

"I'm going to run out to the car to get the cleaning supplies we brought. We'll need to clean up the dust before we do anything else today. After that, I need to call Randy," Lia said.

"I'll go with you, Lia. I don't want you out there alone," Julie said.

***

Phoebe joined them in the kitchen just as Julie hefted a bucket of soapy water out of the kitchen sink and placed it on the floor.

"What can I do to help?" Phoebe asked.

"Are you all set up for the summons?" Julie said.

"Yes. I'll bring the tools out once we have a clean place to work."

"Great. Lia and I are cleaning up the dust on the left side of the living room for now. Mar and El will still need to track through the other side to carry debris to the dumpster, so we'll leave that side *and* the dining room alone until they're finished. In the meantime, if you wouldn't mind wiping down the kitchen cabinets and countertops, that would be a big help. How does your room look?"

"There's hardly any dust in there. I think the girls closed the doors before things got bad on this side of the house," Phoebe said.

"Good. Once half the living room is clean, we'll come in and mop the kitchen floor and hallway. Between the three of us, it shouldn't take more than an hour."

***

The girls worked together and managed to complete their efforts in under an hour. They worked their way from the living room, through the kitchen and down the hallway, ending up in Lia and Elliot's bedroom.

"I'm glad there's an exit door here," Julie said. "I suspect the living room floor is dry by now, so we can just go through the alley to the front."

"Yeah, but my tools are still in my bedroom, so we need to wait for the hallway to dry before I can get them," Phoebe pointed out.

"No worries. I need to call Randy anyway. That will take a few minutes," Lia said.

Lia sat on the back stoop while Julie and Phoebe walked around the small yard.

Julie grabbed the chest-high fence that divided the yard in two and shook it. "Wow, this is rickety. I bet we could knock it down with very little effort," she said. "Phoebe, if you don't mind, get on the other end of this and let's push on it."

Between the two of them, they easily flattened the fence.

"Well, that didn't take any effort at all," Phoebe said.

"I don't wonder why. Look at the bottom of the posts. They're all rotted away. This fence must have been erected decades ago," Julie said.

Julie picked up one end of the fence and dragged it away so that the whole thing sat parallel to the house instead of dissecting the yard in half.

"That really opens up the back yard," Phoebe said.

Julie went to stand beside Phoebe. They both looked at the back of the house.

"I don't think this is the same structure Marie Laveau lived in. It's too new," Phoebe said.

"You're right," Julie replied. "It isn't, but I suspect it was built on the same foundation. You can see where it's been patched and rebuilt."

"It looks like more repair work is in order," Phoebe pointed to the foundation where the fence had previously been secured to the house. "I see a break right where we tore the fence away from the building."

"I see what you mean. Let's take a look," Julie said.

Julie and Phoebe approached the house just as Lia completed her call to Randy. The stoop she sat on was right next to the area the girls planned to inspect.

"How did the call go with Randy?" Phoebe asked.

"Sheesh! I don't know what's so hard to understand here." Frustration tinted Lia's voice.

"What do you mean?" Julie asked.

"Randy just can't seem to grasp what I was telling him about the mistress. He'll be here in about a half-hour. I thought it would be better to talk to him about this as a group."

"You're probably right. It's a lot to take in," Phoebe said.

"What are you two looking at?" Lia asked.

"As you can see, we tore that god-awful fence down, but it appears to have exposed a break in the foundation. We are about to investigate if you'd like to join us," Julie said.

"Sure!" Julie walked down the steps.

Julie dropped to her knees in front of the foundation and removed some of the loose stones that lined the hole.

"Is it smart to be removing part of the foundation, Jules? I mean, what if the floor caves in?" Lia asked.

"For that to happen, we'd have to remove nearly this whole side. This foundation is thick. Almost two feet thick, in fact. I think it's safe enough to remove a few stones." Julie continued to remove stones while Phoebe and Lia watched. Suddenly, she stopped. "What's this?" she asked.

Removal of the final stone exposed a piece of wood, about six inches long by four inches wide, mortared into the foundation.

"It looks like wood," Lia said.

"It looks more like a box to me." Phoebe pointed to the object. "It looks like it has a lid."

Julie continued to remove the stones and rocks that were strategically holding it in place. More and more of the box was exposed as they removed additional stones. Several rocks later, the entire front of it was exposed. It had been mortared into the foundation vertically, and it measured approximately a foot wide by six inches deep and four inches tall.

Phoebe and Lia watched intently as Julie wiggled the box back and forth and, in the process, loosened the old mortar that had held it in place. Finally, enough of the mortar had disintegrated to allow Julie to remove the box from its prison.

Julie's brow knit with concentration as she carefully lifted the box. "Wow, it's heavy," she said. She handed it to Phoebe while she climbed back to her feet.

"Open it, open it!" Lia said excitedly.

"No! Don't," Phoebe said. "We don't know what's in it. I want to perform a cleansing first. Besides, it looks like the lid is glued shut. We'll need tools to open it."

"It's better to be safe than sorry," Julie said. "Randy should be here soon anyway. We'll see what's in it after he's gone."

***

Lia met Randy on the sidewalk in front of the Saint Ann Street house. She immediately walked into his embrace for a warm hug.

"Thanks for coming, Randy,"

"I'm sorry about giving you a hard time on the phone, but you were talking about some heavy stuff there," Randy said.

"Believe me. I totally understand just how heavy it is. All we ask is that you have an open mind."

"I'll try." Randy looked at the front of the house. "So, this is Marissa and Julie's new place?"

"Yes. It's very nice inside, although Marissa and Elliot have been tearing a wall down for two days, so it's a bit of a mess at the moment."

"They're tearing a wall down?" he asked.

"Yes. They are knocking a wall down between two bedrooms to make a larger master suite."

"Maybe I can give them a hand. I have nothing else to do today," Randy suggested.

"It's a Sunday. You could be spending time with Susan," Lia pointed out.

"Yes, except she's working today, so I'm at loose ends."

"I see. I suspect Mar and El would welcome the help. Let's go inside."

Lia led Randy through the left door, on the clean side of the living room.

"Wow! This is a big room," Randy said.

"Hi, Randy!" Julie said. She also gave him a hug. "I'll go get Mar and Elliot."

"Randy, this is our friend Phoebe," Lia said.

Randy extended his hand. "Phoebe. As in Phoebe Frost?" he asked.

"Yes. You've heard of me?"

"Who hasn't? This is New Orleans, after all, and your name is pretty big in the voodoo community...and your eyes are legendary. I can see why."

Phoebe blushed. "I get that all the time."

Their attention was diverted to voices coming from the dining room.

"Randy," Elliot said as she walked toward him with her hand extended.

"Stop right there, missy!" Lia said. "Please wipe your feet on the towel I put down before coming onto this side of the room. We spent all morning cleaning." Elliot wiped her feet and then greeted Randy with a handshake.

Randy shook her hand and then that of Marissa who entered the room right behind her.

"Thanks for coming. We need your help with something only you can do," Elliot said.

"Lia tried to explain it to me on the phone, but it was so out there that I thought it would be better to discuss it in person."

"It certainly is *out* there," Marissa agreed.

"So, what's up?" Randy asked.

"You're going to think we're nuts, so I'll just say it," Elliot said. "We're pretty sure that an evil spirit entered the grave robber when he broke into her grave, and we are hoping she is still in there."

Randy raised his eyebrows. "An evil spirit?"

"Yes," Lia added. "We think she jumped into the guy you have locked up right now. That's why he couldn't remember stalking us or blowing up our gates. He was possessed by the evil spirit at the time."

"You want me to believe that an evil spirit is responsible for blowing your gates up?"

"Yes, and she is capable of doing so much more if she's loose, so we need your help to see if she's still inside the guy in your jail," Lia said.

Randy looked at each of the five women in the room. "Do you all believe this?" he asked.

Every one of them nodded.

"You're right. I *do* think you're nuts," he said.

"Randy," Elliot said. "How do you think we knew where to look for all those bodies you exhumed from our courtyard a few months ago? They had been in there for more than a hundred and fifty years, so obviously *we* didn't put them there."

Randy put his hands on his hip. "I don't know how you knew, but I'm sure you're going to tell me."

"We were led to that location by the spirit of the child who died in our house," Elliot said.

Lia reached for Randy's arm. "Randy, Elliot and I are scientists. When we first purchased the Royal Street property, we were both convinced there was nothing that couldn't be explained through scientific means. We were wrong. We have seen the spirit world firsthand."

"Do you really expect me to..." Randy began.

"Wait!" Julie exclaimed. "Marie is here. She's by the window."

Randy looked at the window Julie was pointing to. "I don't see a damned thing."

"Phoebe, do you see her?" Julie asked.

"Yes, I do."

"I see her as well," Marissa said.

Julie approached the apparition. "Marie, please let him see you. This is important."

"Holy shit!" Randy took several steps backward. "No way!"

Marie reached her hand toward Phoebe.

Phoebe stepped forward and walked directly into the ghostly figure. Her eyes closed and her head fell back onto her shoulders. A moment later, she lifted her head and looked directly at Randy.

"Dey speak da truth, Officer Rocque."

Randy narrowed his eyes at her. "How did you know my name?"

"Da queen know many tings. I knows dey be a long line of lawmen in your history. I knowed Thomas Claybourne."

"You knew him? He was like my grandfather, five or six generations ago."

"He be a great man. He be one of da first black lawmen in New Orleans."

"Damn! How else could you know about Thomas if you weren't real?" he asked. "So what do you want of me?"

"Da evil one be free. She be doing chaos on da streets. She be killin dose who don't deserve to die. Dey needs to find her before it be too late. Lia need your help. El-ee-ot need your help."

"What do you mean that chaos will be in the streets?"

"De dead ones will walk. Dey do da bidding of da evil one. All will be lost on St. John's Eve if da evil one not be stopped."

Marie looked at Lia and Elliot. "We must seek da help from da queens and da kings. We must call on da loa for guidance. Togetter we must stop da evil one or all be lost."

Marie closed her eyes and her head fell backward onto her shoulders. A few moments later, Phoebe returned and she reached for Randy's arm to steady herself.

"Are you okay?" Randy asked.

Phoebe nodded. "I'm fine."

Randy turned around and looked at the expectant faces of his new friends. "Okay. As long as it's not illegal, I will help you."

Chapter 22

Julie, Lia and Phoebe sat on the living floor with the box they had found mortared into the foundation, in front of them. Phoebe had just completed the cleansing ceremony and they were now ready to open it.

"The box is really old. Be careful not to break the hinges. They look rusty," Lia said.

"I'll be gentle," Phoebe said. She released the clasp on the front of the box and attempted to lift the lid. As expected, it did not move.

"I'll be right back," Julie said. She got to her feet and ran into the other room where Elliot, Marissa and Randy were working. She returned with a sheetrock knife and a flathead screwdriver.

Julie handed the tools to Phoebe. "Here. Use the knife to cut the glue and then pry it open with the screwdriver."

Phoebe struggled to drag the knife through the material sealing the lid. "I think this is tar rather than glue," Phoebe said.

"Do you want me to try?" Julie asked.

"No. I'm getting it. It's just going to take me a few minutes."

It took nearly fifteen minutes of chipping away at the tar to break the seal on all four sides of the box.

Phoebe put the sheetrock knife down and picked up the screwdriver. She looked at her friends. "Here goes nothing."

Very carefully, Phoebe inserted the screwdriver into the small groove she had made around the rim of the lid, and gently twisted it. She had to repeat the process at several locations around the three non-hinged edges of the box before the lid opened enough for her to grasp its edge with her fingers. It opened slowly, despite the resistance she continued to feel from residual tar.

"Finally!" Phoebe said when the lid fully opened.

All three looked into the box.

"Wow! The box is lined with lead. No wonder it's so heavy," Julie said.

"I'm willing to bet the lead—and the tar around the lid—were intentional to keep moisture out," Lia said.

"I think you're right, Lia. If I recall correctly, this is called a sea box. Sea boxes were used to transport moisture-sensitive produce and products by sea. Otherwise, the contents could be destroyed. It would make sense to use this box for long-term storage in a place as humid as New Orleans."

"Why is it filled with dirt?" Lia asked.

"That's a good question," Phoebe said.

"There's some sort of paperwork in there," Julie said. She reached for the folded document and shook the loose dirt from it before she carefully unfolded it.

"What is it?" Lia asked.

"Oh, my. It looks like a boarding pass for the White Star Line Oceanic passenger ship. It's dated eighteen-seventy-two."

"Wasn't the Titanic part of that shipping company?" Lia said.

"Yes, I think so," Julie replied.

"What was the passenger's name?" Phoebe asked.

Julie held the document closer. "The ticket's been folded where the name is filled in, and the ink is faded, but I can make out the first few letters. D, E, L." Julie suddenly looked up. "Wow! This ticket was for the mistress!" She scanned the entire document again a little closer. "It's for passage from Paris to New Orleans in August of eighteen-seventy-two. This confirms the rumors that she came back from Paris after she escaped the law here in New Orleans for murdering her slaves."

"And because we found it under the foundation of this house, it also suggests that Marie Laveau gave her refuge," Phoebe said.

"Marie said during the séance that she tried to redeem her, but the evil was too great. I don't think Marie intentionally harbored her from the law," Lia said.

"Be careful with that document, Julie. We might need it later," Phoebe pointed out.

Julie carefully refolded the document and put it aside. "What else is in the box?" she asked.

Phoebe reached for the next item. It was another document, folded in half. She pulled it out of the box and opened it. Phoebe covered her mouth with her hand to stifle a gasp.

"What is it, Phoebe?" Lia asked.

She looked at her two friends with tears in her eyes. "This breaks my heart," she said. "It looks like a list of her slaves. Celeste, Samuel and Lia are on the list. Their names are crossed out along with the names of several others."

Lia took the list from her and studied it carefully. "She must have crossed them out as they died." Her eyes were also filled with tears when she looked back at Phoebe. "How can one human being do this to another?"

Phoebe placed her palm on the side of Lia's face. "Sweetie, you need to remember that back then, the slaves were not considered human beings. They were little more than property. I know that hurts your heart, Lia, but unfortunately, that's how it was."

Lia closed her eyes and allowed the tears to run down her cheeks. "I know. What hurts even more is that some people still feel that way about my people today."

Julie reached for Lia's hand. "Well, we certainly don't feel that way, and I for one, will take on anyone who wants to challenge me on it."

Phoebe took the list back from Lia and placed it with the boarding pass. She felt around inside the box again. "There appears to be two canvas packages in here under the dirt. They're tied with string." She lifted them out carefully. The names Lia and Ethan were written in scripted handwriting on each package.

Lia stiffened and her eyes opened wide. "What be in dose packages?" she said in a thick Creole accent.

Julie's head snapped up. "Celeste?"

"What be in dose packages?" Lia said almost at a shrill scream. "Gif dem to me!"

The hammering that had been coming nonstop from the master bedroom suddenly halted.

"Lia!" Elliot yelled. "Lia!" She ran into the living room with Marissa and Randy right behind her.

Phoebe held up her hand to stop them from advancing.

"What the hell is going on here?" Elliot demanded. "I could hear her screaming from the other room."

Julie climbed to her feet and quietly filled them in on the box and its contents, while Phoebe handed the two packages to Celeste.

Celeste laid the packages carefully on the floor in front of her and then untied the one with Lia's name on it. The package contained a small tooth. She lifted sad eyes in Phoebe's direction. She then turned her attention to the other package labeled with Ethan's name. Inside, she found a lock of dark curly hair.

Celeste covered her mouth with one hand and sobbed. "How she git dese? Dey my babies. She da reason dey be gone." She looked up at Elliot. "El-ee-ot, da evil one took my babies 'way. She took dem 'way."

Elliot moved swiftly toward Celeste and dropped to her knees behind her. She gently pulled the distraught woman into her arms and held her tight. "I know. I know, Celeste. We will get justice. I promise," Elliot said.

Randy, Marissa and Julie stood helplessly a few feet away. Marissa held Julie in her arms while her heartbroken wife cried into her shoulder.

Phoebe gently reached for the artifacts.

Celeste reached swiftly forward and grabbed Phoebe's wrists.

"No! Dey be mine!" Celeste exclaimed.

"Sweetie, I promise to treat them gently," Phoebe said. "We may need them to stop the mistress. You can have them back when the time is right."

"It's all right, Celeste. You can trust, Phoebe," Elliot said softly.

Celeste released Phoebe's wrists and allowed her to retrieve the objects.

Phoebe rewrapped them gently in their original canvas and placed them back into the box, along with the two documents that had been set aside. The moment she closed the lid, Lia returned to herself.

Lia sat up straight again and looked at Elliot. "What happened? Why were you holding me?"

"Celeste appeared," Elliot said.

"Celeste?"

"Yes," Phoebe said. "We found two packages inside the box that contained a tooth and hair clippings from Lia and Ethan. Celeste was upset when she saw them."

"Why would the mistress have things like that in her possession?" Lia asked.

"My guess is that she planned to use them in a black magic ritual," Phoebe said. "I've seen no evidence that she was a practitioner of voodoo, so chances are, she would've had to engage with the darker factions of the religion to do that."

"Where did that box come from?" Elliot asked.

"We found it," Julie replied.

"You found it?" Marissa said.

"Yes. Quite by accident, actually," Julie replied.

Marissa's forehead creased. "Where was it?"

"Mortared into the foundation."

"In the foundation? What the hell were you doing tearing apart the foundation?"

"Well, you see, Phoebs and I knocked the fence down in the back yard and we noticed that there was a hole in the foundation that the fence was concealing," Julie explained.

"There's a hole in the foundation?" Marissa asked.

"Yes. It's actually bigger now than when we found it because I had to make it larger to get the box out of it," Julie explained.

"Oh, my fucking God," Marissa said.

At this point, Elliot went to stand beside Randy while both of them struggled to hide the smiles on their faces.

"Anyway, I had to remove several stones and rocks to break it free."

"And now we have a hole to repair in the foundation," Marissa said.

"But it was so worth it, Mar," Julie said. "There's a boarding pass in here dated eighteen-seventy-two on the

Oceanic. It has the mistress' name on it. That proves she came back to New Orleans after she escaped to Paris in eighteen-thirty-four. And there's a list of her slaves with some of the names crossed off—including Celeste, Samuel and Lia. Don't you see what this means? That box had been hidden in the foundation almost one hundred and fifty years ago."

"More importantly, it gives us something that belonged to the mistress. We might be able to use it to find her, and hopefully eliminate her once and for all," Phoebe added.

***

"Can you believe they made that hole bigger?" Marissa said.

"They *did* find something that might be useful," Elliot pointed out. "I mean, if it helps resolve this mess with the mistress, it'll be worth it."

"Yeah, I guess you're right."

"So, what's the deal with this mistress?" Randy asked.

"She was the one responsible for killing all those slaves in our home. When the slaves' remains were found, their souls were released, so the mistress lost her power in our house. Their misery at being trapped is what made her powerful."

"So now she's pissed at you for taking her power away?" Randy asked.

"Yes—and for confining her spirit to Marie Laveau's grave two months ago. Unfortunately, your grave robber let her out and now we fear she may be after us again," Elliot explained. "We think that's why the guy sitting in your jail cell right now was stalking us."

"Do you know how crazy all this sounds, Elliot?" Randy asked.

"Trust me, Randy. Six months ago, both Lia and I would have considered this to be totally unbelievable. But look at us now."

"I'm trying to keep an open mind, and I did promise to help you, but this is so far out there it's almost funny."

Randy pulled the electrical wires into the outlet box and stripped the plastic coating off the end of them. "Wanna hand me the pliers and screwdriver, Marissa? Phillips head, please," Randy asked.

Marissa handed him the tools. "Sure, here you go."

"Thanks." Randy wrapped the bare wires around the terminal ends on the outlet and tightened the screws. He then shoved all of the extra wire as deep into the box as possible and centered the outlet in the box. "Okay, all I need to do is tighten these two screws and we'll be ready to have this new wiring inspected."

"I appreciate you stopping by this morning to help," Marissa said. "Not only did we finish taking the framing down, but you've moved the wiring for us as well. It was a good idea to reinstall the outlet in the space where we removed the wall."

"Well, the wall and the ceiling were already open there, so all we had to do was run the old wire through the ceiling joists and down the wall to move the outlet. Now it's a matter of sheetrock work to patch the openings and you'll be ready for paint. After that, the floors can be refinished where the wall used to be, and you can install new baseboards."

"You make it sound so easy," Elliot said.

"The fact that the wall was put up after the floors went in saved us a bunch of work," Marissa said.

"You got that right," Randy agreed.

"I guess I'll give Bill a call and set up some time with him to come inspect this before we move on to patching the sheetrock," Marissa said.

"Bill?" Randy asked.

"Yes, Bill Murphy. He does work for the realty firm I'm with," Marissa said as she dialed his number.

"I know Bill. He's also done some work at the station. Tall, red hair—right?"

"That's him!" Elliot said.

"Hello, Bill? Hi, this is Marissa Thompson. I'm sorry to bother you on a Sunday, but I'd like to set some time up for you to inspect the electrical work before we close up this wall."

Marissa looked at Elliot and Randy. Her eyebrows raised high on her forehead. "Really? You can come right now? I didn't expect you to give up your Sunday, Bill, but if that works for you, it would be great. All right, we'll see you in a few minutes then. Thanks! Bye."

Marissa disconnected the call and looked at her friends. "Cool! With this inspection out of the way, we'll be able to move forward with the renovation." She looked at her watch. "Wow, it's almost four o'clock. I vote we stop for the day once we have Bill's approval, then go home to get cleaned up. I for one would like to have a nice dinner and a relaxing evening. It's been a hectic weekend. In fact, I'd like to take everyone to dinner tonight as a thank you for all the help. What time does Susan get off work, Randy?"

"You don't need to do that, Marissa. It's not like I did a whole lot," Randy said.

"What? We are ahead of schedule because of your help today. You bet your ass you did a lot. So, what time does she get off work?"

"In about an hour. I'll call to see if she's interested in going to dinner," Randy said.

"I'm thinking maybe seven o'clock. How does that sound?" Marissa asked.

"That should give us enough time to go home and shower," Elliot said.

"Okay. I'll make a reservation for seven people then."

***

"Wow, Jules, I don't remember you buying this much stuff, yesterday," Lia said. "Each of us has made three trips to Phoebe's car."

"I'm glad you remembered all of this was still in your trunk, Phoebs," Julie said.

They looked at the pile of curtains, linens, towels and toiletry supplies on the blow-up mattress in Lia and Elliot's room where it would be safe from sheetrock dust.

"There is a lot of stuff here, but this place is bigger than the condo in New York. There has to be three times more windows. I can't wait to paint and decorate the place," Julie said.

"I'm looking forward to that too." Lia paused when she felt her back pocket vibrate. "Oh! I wonder who this is?" She pulled the phone from her pocket. "Hello? Oh, hi, Leslie. No! You're not bothering me at all. Elliot and I are helping our friends with a renovation project. What's that? I'm sure I can help to answer your questions. When would you like to meet?"

Lia looked at her watch. "Hold on a second, Leslie." She pushed the mute button on the call and addressed Julie and Phoebe. "It's my genealogist, Leslie Harden. He has some questions he needs answered before he can move forward. He wants to meet today."

Phoebe and Julie looked at one another. "I don't see why that's a problem. Go ahead," Julie replied.

"No, you don't understand. He'd like to meet with me here. Apparently, the building where his office is located is undergoing a yearly fumigation and he can't return there until Wednesday."

"Ugh, the Formosan termites are horrible at this time of year," Phoebe said. "I usually have my house bombed around this time as well."

"Tell him to come but warn him that he'll have to sit on the floor," Julie said.

"Thanks, Julie." Lia un-muted the phone. "Leslie, as long as you don't mind sitting on the floor, we can definitely meet here, you see, my friends just bought this house and they haven't moved their stuff in yet. Good. Okay. The address is ten twenty Saint Ann Street. Yes, that is exactly what I said. Ten twenty Saint Ann Street. Okay, we'll see you soon."

"The fact that you told him the address twice leads me to believe he realizes this was once Marie Laveau's home," Phoebe said.

"You are probably right. Oh, I need to warn you that Mr. Harden is just a little eccentric. The two times we saw him, he was dressed like a riverboat gambler. I don't know if that is part of his business image, or if he always dresses that way. I guess we'll find out what his weekend attire is like," Lia said. "There is also something else about him that I'd like you to take note of...something I'd like verified."

"And that is?" Julie asked.

"You'll see. Anyway, I'm excited to see what he's already found," Lia said. "I'm especially interested to know if he's found a way to connect Ethan to Celeste."

"That shouldn't be too hard," Julie said.

"It might be harder than you think. He said that since Ethan was sent away, rather than sold, it might be difficult to establish that connection because there would have been no birth certificate or bill of sale. Ugh! I can't believe I just used the phrase *bill of sale* in connection with a human being!"

"You know, Lia, the hair we found in the box might show a DNA match between you and Ethan," Phoebe suggested.

"I don't think he'll have an issue tracking *me* back to Ethan. I think the bigger problem will be tracking me and Ethan back to Celeste," Lia pointed out.

"What about the tooth?" Julie said.

"The tooth?" Lia asked.

"Yes. If the tooth belongs to Little Lia, and Celeste is her mom, then a DNA match between you and Lia's tooth would prove a connection to Celeste."

Lia grabbed Julie's face between her hands and kissed her full on the lips. "Of course! Julie, you're a genius!"

"We need to be careful here," Phoebe said. "We promised Celeste we would protect these items."

"Yes, we did." Lia said. "From the work I do with cancer research, I know that a DNA signature can be obtained from very small amounts of matter. I can order the testing myself in the lab I work in. With that level of control, I believe I can minimize any potential damage to these precious artifacts."

"We will need Celeste's permission before we proceed," Phoebe said.

"I agree with you completely, Phoebe," Lia replied.

Chapter 23

Bill Murphy pulled his truck to the curb in front of the Saint Ann house at four-fifteen. He rubbed his forehead to stave off the headache he could feel hovering behind his eyes. He had been fighting a lightheaded feeling ever since Marissa Thompson called him about a half-hour earlier. He was hoping to do a quick inspection of the wiring and then head back home to bed before the headache caused a blackout. The last time it had happened, he found himself wandering around the neighborhood near the intersection of Royal Street and Governor Nichols. He had no idea why he was there.

Bill inhaled deeply and then pushed his door open. He climbed out of his truck and walked to the front door. Before he could even knock, the door swung open and Lia Purvis stood before him. A searing pain shot through his temple and he had an overwhelming urge to grab Lia by the throat.

"Bill! It's so nice to see you again. Marissa said you were coming to inspect the wiring—on a Sunday, no less. Please, come in." Lia stepped aside and allowed Bill entry into the house.

With his fists clenched at his sides, he walked into the living room and came face to face with a woman whose eyes were so clear they appeared transparent. He was immediately on guard. For some unknown reason, he felt that he needed to avoid her at all costs.

What the hell is wrong with me? he thought.

"Phoebe, do you remember Bill?" Lia said.

Phoebe grabbed Lia's arm and pulled her away from their visitor.

"Phoebs?" Lia said.

"Bill!" Marissa came out of the dining room with her hand extended. "I can't thank you enough for coming out on a Sunday. Go ahead into the bedroom. Elliot and Randy are back there. I need to grab my checkbook so I can pay you before you leave."

Marissa watched Bill walk into the dining room and then turned to the other two ladies. "Do you know where Julie is? My checkbook is in her bag."

"In the back bedroom," Lia said. She turned to Phoebe. "Phoebe, what was that all about?"

"I don't know," Phoebe said. "The alarm bells just went off when I saw him. My intuition told me to keep you away from him."

"Well, I'm certainly not going to question your intuition. I wonder what it is about him that makes you feel that way," Lia said.

"I don't know. He has an aura about him that just didn't feel right," Phoebe said.

"What didn't feel right?" Marissa said when she returned with her checkbook.

"Bill. There was something about Bill that set off alarm bells for Phoebe," Lia said.

Marissa frowned. "That's odd. I've met him a few times since we've moved here, and I've found him to be a pretty good guy. Sometimes people just rub you the wrong way, I guess. I'd better get back there to see how the inspection is going."

Marissa walked away but stopped before reaching the dining room. "Oh, before I forget, I've made dinner reservations for seven o'clock. I'm taking all of us, as well as Randy and Susan, to dinner as a big thank you for all the help this weekend."

Phoebe turned to Lia as soon a Marissa was out of earshot. "I hope she doesn't invite Bill."

* * *

Randy shook hands with Bill. "Long time no see," he said. "The last time I saw you, was when you repainted the jail cells a few months back."

"Of course!" Bill said. "That's where I know you from. That job was a bitch. It's amazing how much damage can be done to a concrete wall."

"Well, the occupants of those cells usually go in angry and vengeful, and unfortunately the facility takes a beating. I've seen some pretty nasty stuff smeared on those walls, if you know what I mean," Randy said.

"Do me a favor and don't call me for one of those smear jobs," Bill joked.

"You and me both, bro," Randy said.

"So, what brings you here on a Sunday, dude? I don't see a uniform, so I assume you're not on duty," Bill said.

"Nope. It's my day off. Just here to help some friends," Randy replied.

Bill looked at Marissa. "It must be nice to have friends in high places."

"Actually, we met when he came to investigate vandalism at Elliot and Lia's house. It seems like some idiot tried to blow up their carriage gates," Marissa explained.

"Yep, and now he can't get rid of us, can you, Randy?" Elliot teased.

"Actually, you ladies have grown on me. I'm especially fond of Miss Lia," Randy said.

"Hey, what am I—chopped liver?" Elliot joked.

"I like you, too," Randy said.

"I'm messing with you, Randy," Elliot said. "I'm pretty fond of Lia myself."

A searing pain shot through Bill's head. He grabbed his head and moaned.

This is the one. He can get close to them. Bill shook his head.

Randy put his hand on Bill's shoulder. "Hey, are you all right?" he asked.

Bill leaned against the wall to steady himself. "I'm okay. Just a headache. They've been happening a lot lately."

"We don't have to do this today, Bill," Marissa said.

"No. No, it's all right. This will only take a few minutes."

Bill pushed himself off the wall and focused on the work that had been done to verify the wiring. "So far, so good," he said when he inspected the wiring running through the ceiling joists. He pulled his tape measure out of his tool belt and measured the height of the new electrical box relative to the floor. "Perfect," he said. He returned the tape measure to his belt and found his electrical meter. "Now for the final test."

Bill inserted the probes into the outlet and registered no flow of electricity. He verified that his meter was turned on and tried again with similar results. He looked at Marissa and grinned. "Don't tell me—you haven't turned the power back on yet, have you?"

"Sheesh! You can tell who the rookies are, here!" Marissa said.

"I'll get it." Randy went outside to the electrical box and flipped the breaker. "Try it now," he called out.

"We got power!" Bill said.

Randy came back inside and watched Bill measure the voltage and look for leaks along the length of the wire they had relocated.

Bill shut off his meter and shoved it back into his pouch. "This looks good to me," he said.

"Awesome. Now all I have to do is pay you for your time," Marissa said.

"Fifty should do it," Bill said.

"Like hell it will. You've been here twice. I'm making the check out for a hundred," Marissa insisted.

"I appreciate it, ma'am."

Get him alone.

Bill shook his head.

"Are you all right, Bill?" Marissa asked. She had been standing there holding the check for him to take.

"I'm sorry. What did you say?"

"I asked if you were okay. You zoned out on us for a minute."

"I'm sorry. Like I told Miss Lia, I've been having these headaches lately."

"Maybe you should get off your feet and take it easy for the rest of the day," Elliot suggested.

"That's good advice. I guess we're finished here so I'll head out," Bill said.

Just as Bill was about to say his goodbyes, Randy's phone rang. He pulled it out of his pocket. "It's Susan. I've got to take this." He waved at Bill. "Nice seeing you again!" He used the door at the back of the room to take his call in private.

Marissa and Elliot both shook Bill's hand.

"Thank you, Bill. If we need any other work done, I have your card. I appreciate you coming. Especially on a weekend."

Marissa walked him through the house to the front door and watched as he climbed into his truck.

As soon as he slipped behind the wheel, another bolt of pain shot through his head. He clenched his jaw and waited for the pain to subside.

I should have jumped when he had his hand on your shoulder.

***

No sooner had Bill pulled away from the curb, than another car pulled up. Elliot chose that moment to join Marissa in the living room.

"I wonder who that is?" Marissa said.

Elliot looked out one of the tall windows. "That's Leslie," she said.

"Leslie?" Marissa repeated.

"Leslie Harden. Wow, he looks different than the last time I saw him. Would you mind getting Lia?" Elliot went outside to meet Leslie on the sidewalk.

"Leslie, nice to see you again. Lia told me you were coming," Elliot said.

"Yes. I've hit a roadblock and I have a few questions for her that I hope will help me get over that hurdle."

"Come inside. I have to warn you that there's no furniture yet," Elliot said.

"Lia has already told me."

The front door opened just as Elliot and Leslie reached the bottom of the stairs.

"Leslie!" Lia said. She stopped short. "Wow! Forgive me, for saying this, but I almost didn't recognize you. You look so different."

Leslie wore faded blue jeans, black boots and a white button-down shirt, tucked in and opened at the neck, as well as a black vest and a black necktie that hung loosely below the open collar. His hair was combed back, but free of the slick styling gel that held it in place when Lia had seen him. The thin mustache was also gone, giving him a soft and sexy androgynous appearance.

"Thanks. Do you like it?" Leslie asked. "I was ready for a change."

"I love it!" Lia replied. "Do you mind if I ask you a personal question?"

"Let me guess. You want to know how I identify, right?" Leslie asked.

"You've read my mind!" Lia replied.

"Lia, maybe that's something he'd rather not share," Elliot interrupted.

"I don't mind at all. In fact, I love it when people feel comfortable enough to ask. The answer is, I don't identify at all. I consider myself gender fluid. I'm what I am at any given moment."

"That must be very freeing," Lia said.

"It is indeed. Shall we go inside?"

"Oh, I'm sorry. Where are my manners?"

Lia opened the door and stepped into the living room, followed by Leslie and then Elliot. Julie was waiting inside.

"Jules this is Leslie Harden, my genealogist. Leslie, this is one of our best friends, Julie Barrows."

As Julie shook Leslie's hand, a loud ruckus came from behind her. She glanced over her shoulder. "Ah, that would be my wife and our friend Randy."

As if on cue, they entered the living room.

"Sorry for the noise, I dropped the hammer and it echoed like crazy," Marissa said.

"And this is Julie's other half, Marissa Thompson, and our good friend, Randy Rocque." Lia said. "The two of them, and Elliot, just finished ripping a wall out of a bedroom."

"Gotta love those B&D dykes," Leslie said. "No offense intended, of course."

"What the hell are B&D dykes?" Randy asked.

"Black and Decker dykes. You know, butch women with power tools...and not the vibrating kind."

Elliot laughed out loud. "I like that. B&D dykes. I'll have to remember that."

"I hate to run, but I need to get home to shower and then pick Susan up for dinner tonight," Randy said. "We'll see you at the restaurant. Nice to meet you, Leslie."

"You too, Randy," Leslie called.

Leslie turned to Lia. "So, you have dinner plans tonight. We can do this later if you'd like."

"We've got two hours before dinner. That should be time enough to answer your questions and still get home to shower," Lia said.

"I'm going to excuse myself for a bit and go clean up the room we just tore apart," Marissa said.

"I'll give you a hand, Mar," Julie offered.

"All right then. Let's have a seat and discuss what I'm struggling with," Leslie said. "It mostly has to do with names of some of your ancestors. This shouldn't take much time at all."

***

Twenty minutes later, Leslie gathered the papers he had scattered all around them and put them back into the manila folder. "That should just about do it," he said.

"Leslie, have you had any luck with Ethan? I mean, you thought it might be difficult making the connection between him and Celeste," Lia asked.

"Unfortunately, no, I haven't. The problem is that he doesn't appear in the slave records. I found Celeste, and a little girl named Lia, but no mention of a baby boy named Ethan. I believe he is in your lineage, but so far, I have no way to connect him to Celeste."

Lia looked at Elliot and then at Leslie. "I think we may have something that will help with that problem." She turned to Elliot. "Sweetie, would you mind getting the box we found so we can show Leslie what's inside it? It's in our room on the bed."

Elliot climbed to her feet. "Sure. I'll be right back."

"You found a box?" Leslie asked.

"Yes, and I think what's inside it will help solve the Ethan mystery."

Elliot returned and handed the box to Lia. She put it on the floor in front of them and opened the lid. Lia removed the two documents and then retrieved the packages at the bottom of the box. She put them on the floor in front of Leslie.

Leslie looked at the artifacts and then back at Lia. "What is inside these packages?" he asked.

"There is a tooth in the one marked with Lia's name, and a lock of hair in the one marked with Ethan's name," she said.

"Put them away," he insisted.

"What?"

"Put them away," he said more firmly. "These are things normally used in black magic voodoo spells. They are likely cursed."

"No. They're not cursed. We had the box cleansed before we opened it," Lia explained.

Leslie visibly relaxed. "How do you think these may help?" he asked.

"Leslie, I'm a scientist and I work at the Louisiana Cancer Research Center. I have access to DNA testing facilities. We may be able to use these to establish that link."

"Given Ethan is *in* your lineage, you mean. I haven't gone that far back yet, but if he's there, you might be right about linking him to the child Lia, and through her, to Celeste."

"There's one hitch," Elliot said. "We need permission from Celeste before we do anything to these artifacts."

Leslie raised his eyebrows at Elliot. "And how to you propose to get that?" he asked.

"Let's just say we have a special connection with Celeste," Lia said.

Their attention was suddenly drawn to a door closing in the hall leading to the bedrooms.

"Elliot, would you mind giving me a hand with..." Phoebe stopped short when she saw the stranger in the living room with Lia and Elliot.

Leslie immediately climbed to his feet and straightened his vest. All he could do was stare at her.

"Phoebe," Lia said. She stood and walked to her friend. "Phoebe, this is Leslie Harden. Leslie, this is Phoebe Frost."

Phoebe and Leslie appeared to be locked in a staring contest as neither one spoke.

Elliot nudged Leslie. "Dude, your mouth is open," she whispered.

Leslie broke the stare and looked briefly at Elliot. "I, ah. I'm sorry. I'm Leslie Harden. I'm doing some genealogy work for Lia." He took two steps toward Phoebe who still hadn't looked away.

Lia rubbed Phoebe's back and gently snapped her bra strap to subtly get her attention.

Phoebe's gaze shifted toward Lia.

Lia simply raised her eyebrows and tilted her head in Leslie's direction.

"Oh! Ah, I'm Phoebe Frost," she said while she offered her hand. "I'm sorry. I knew you were coming, but..."

"But you didn't realize I'd be so charming and handsome," Leslie answered for her.

Phoebe smiled and nodded. "Yes, that's it exactly," she said.

"You have the most remarkable eyes," Leslie said.

"I knew you were going to say that," Phoebe replied.

"You were about to ask Elliot for help with something. May I be of some assistance?"

"I was just going to carry my camping gear to my car."

"I think I can manage that." He handed his manila envelope to Lia. "Lia, would you mind keeping an eye on this while I help this beautiful lady with her things?"

"Of course not. Oh, Phoebs, we'll need to be at the restaurant in about an hour, so we'll all have to get out of here in the next few minutes if we want to freshen up first," Lia suggested.

"Oh, that's right. I'll run home to shower and then meet you at the restaurant," Phoebe said.

Marissa and Julie had walked into the living room in the middle of this conversation. They were carrying brooms and dustpans.

"Phoebs, I'd rather you weren't out alone—especially at night," Julie said. "And especially with a certain evil one on the loose. Mar and I will pick you up."

"If I could be so bold as to invite myself to join you, I'd be happy to pick Phoebe up," Leslie said. He looked at Phoebe. "That is, if you're willing, of course."

Phoebe looked at her friends. "Is that okay with you?" she asked.

"As long as you're okay with it," Elliot said.

"Ditto," Lia added. "I think El and I can vouch for Leslie."

"I agree with El and Lia. You need to be comfortable with this," Julie said.

"I am," Phoebe said.

"Okay then. Let's get the ball rolling. Randy and Susan will meet us there, so I don't want to keep them waiting," Marissa said.

While Marissa, Elliot and Leslie carried Phoebe's belongings to the car, Phoebe, Lia and Julie went through the house and secured all the windows and doors and turned out what few lights had been turned on as the sunlight faded.

Finally, Marissa locked the front door and the friends headed toward their cars. Marissa held Leslie back.

Leslie looked directly at Marissa as she spoke.

"Phoebe is very important to us. She has been through hell and back and we don't want to see her hurt in any way. Do you understand what I'm saying?" Marissa asked.

Leslie smiled. "She is a lucky woman to have so many people love her like the four of you do. You have my word that I will not intentionally do anything to harm her, and I will certainly not push her into any situation she doesn't want to be in."

"I see honor in your eyes, Leslie. Please don't make me regret trusting you."

"I understand that trust is earned, Marissa. I won't deny that something magical happened when I first saw her, but if this goes anywhere, I promise you, it will be on her terms."

"I can't ask for any more than that." Marissa extended her hand to Leslie. "We'll see you and Phoebe at the restaurant."

Chapter 24

Elliot stood and raised her glass. "A toast! To Julie and Marissa. May you live a long and happy—and hex free—life in your new home. Congratulations, my friends. We love you to the moon and back!"

Everyone seated at the round table clinked their glasses with those within reach and then clapped for the new homeowners.

"That hex free part might be difficult if Marissa and Marie butt heads too often," Julie joked.

"You'll find Marie to be a pleasant and helpful house guest if you make an effort to get along with her," Phoebe said.

"As long as she doesn't appear at inappropriate times, we'll get along just fine," Marissa replied.

"That never stopped Celeste," Lia piped in.

"Don't even go there," Elliot said. "Imagine having sex with your wife's great-great-great-great-great grandmother! I mean it was awesome when I thought it was Lia, but that takes the concept of old-lady sex to a whole new extreme!"

"Are you telling me that Celeste appeared when you and Lia were in the middle of..." Randy tried to get out.

"Actually, it wasn't in the middle. She initiated it. I never would have known if she hadn't spoken Creole to me," Elliot replied.

"Needless to say, I don't speak Creole," Lia added.

"Wait. Are you all talking about ghosts appearing to you?" Susan asked.

"Not just appearing," Julie said. "We have actually seen Lia and Phoebe being taken control of by ghosts."

"Get out!" Susan exclaimed.

Leslie placed his hand on Phoebe's. "You've had ghosts take control of you?" he asked.

"Several times. That is one aspect of what I do," Phoebe said.

"What *do* you do?" Susan asked.

"I'm a psychic medium and spiritualist," Phoebe explained.

"So, you do séances and things like that?" Susan said.

"Yes," Phoebe replied.

Susan sat back and opened her eyes wide. "Wait a minute. I didn't make the connection until now. You're Phoebe Frost, aren't you?"

"Yes, I am."

"You've done work for the department. I've seen your name on some of the cases involving voodoo."

"Yes. I have done some consulting for the New Orleans police department."

"I'm in total awe of people with gifts like yours," Susan said.

"I must admit that I was a non-believer until I actually saw a ghost enter Phoebe's body," Randy said.

"You saw it?" Susan exclaimed. "Do you know who the ghost was?"

"Marie Laveau," Phoebe said.

Leslie nearly choked on his food. "Marie Laveau? Are you freaking kidding me?" he asked.

Phoebe patted him on the back. "Are you okay?" she asked.

"I'm fine. Marie Laveau? How did that happen—no, wait, don't tell me—the house Marissa and Julie just bought is on the site of Marie Laveau's original cabin, isn't it? That's why the address Lia gave me sounded so familiar."

"It is indeed," Marissa said, "Hence, the hex joke Elliot made earlier. She threatened to put a hex on me if I didn't behave. Jokingly, of course."

"How does it feel to be inhabited by a ghost?" Randy asked.

"I'll go first," Lia said. "For the first several times Celeste took me, I was totally unaware of it. It was like losing blocks of time. The one time she allowed me to be present during a takeover was when we did a séance in the house this past weekend. For me, it felt like I was a casual observer."

"And for me," Phoebe said. "Sometimes I'm aware, and sometimes not. I have done séances where I've had to depend completely on the participants to tell me what happened. With Marie, she always allows me to participate. It's like seeing through both sets of eyes. I can feel her emotions and hear her thoughts."

"That must be an amazing experience," Leslie said.

"Leslie, what do you do for a living?" Susan asked.

"I'm a genealogist. That's how I met Lia and Elliot. I'm working on Lia's lineage right now."

"That is fascinating work. My mom had her family tree done years ago. You must discover some interesting things about people," Susan said.

"Absolutely. Sometimes it's a little shocking, like when you discover some person's ancestor is an axe murderer, but most of the time, it's pretty fulfilling work. The best part is that it allows me to explore the history behind a person's lineage. I've always been a history geek."

"There's nothing wrong with being a geek," Elliot said. "Lia and I are science geeks, although I have to say some of our beliefs have been sorely challenged since we moved to New Orleans."

"*That's* an understatement," Lia agreed.

Marissa stood and picked up her glass. She reached for Julie's hand and encouraged her to stand as well. "I'd like to say something," she said.

All eyes turned to Marissa and everyone fell silent.

"I look around this table and I see people I have known all my life, others I have known for decades, and still, some I have just met. I find myself at a point in my life when what matters the most, is surrounding myself with people I love, and those who love me. Sometimes, family is what you make it. When I look at you, I see family. Family is there for one another, as you have been there for Julie and me this weekend—and some of you, for much longer than that. I think I can speak for both Julie and me when I say thank you, from the bottom of our hearts, for being here when we needed you."

Julie wrapped her arm around Marissa's waist and looked into her eyes. "I couldn't have said it better, love."

***

It was nearly ten o'clock by the time the party of eight left the restaurant. Before they went their separate ways, Phoebe took Randy aside and gave him a small package.

"What is this?" Randy asked.

"It's for the test we need you to do with the gentleman incarcerated in your jail right now."

"Got it," Randy said. "I'll take care of that tomorrow and let you know what happens."

"Thank you."

"You are welcome, Phoebe."

Leslie came up from behind Phoebe as soon as Randy walked away and draped her shawl around her shoulders. He gathered her long dark hair and positioned it over the shawl.

She placed her hand on his and smiled at him. "Thank you, Leslie," she said.

He locked gazes with her for several seconds. "My pleasure," he said. "Are you ready to go home?"

"I am."

Leslie rested his hand lightly on her upper back and led her toward the door. To the casual observer, they looked like a handsome couple—she, with her creamy white complexion, long, dark hair and casual dress, and he, with his mocha-colored skin, sporty attire and short hair.

Leslie held the door for Phoebe to climb into the car, and when they pulled to the curb in front of her house, he hurriedly ran around the front of the car to open her door again. She slipped her hand into the crook of his elbow when he escorted her to her door.

She turned when they reached her stoop and pulled her shawl closer around her.

"Thank you for escorting me tonight, Leslie. It felt good not to be the fifth wheel."

"You're welcome. I enjoyed your company. You live such a fascinating life. Mine pales in comparison," he said.

"There are days I long for a simpler life. Things can be very crazy in the spirit world."

"Yet you continue to do what you do, and from all accounts, you're very good at it."

"It brings me joy to help people connect with loved ones they have lost. Especially when the loss is tragic."

"I would like to see you again if you are willing," Leslie said.

Phoebe tilted her head to the side and smiled. "That would be nice. It's rare to meet someone as authentic as you, Leslie. You have a golden aura about you."

"Golden aura? What does that mean?"

"A person with a golden aura is respectful, self-disciplined, understanding and mindful of others. They generally have huge hearts, and they are eager to show love. When they love, they love completely, and they give everything they have to their partners. What I admire most in a person with a golden aura, is that they don't care who is watching, and they don't care about being judged. They care only for those they love and about being true to themselves. That is what I see in you, Leslie. All of that makes me feel safe with you."

"You *are* safe with me, Phoebe. I would never do anything to hurt you nor to make you doubt me."

"I know. I felt that immediately when we first met. My psyche has never reacted to another person the way it reacted to you," Phoebe said. "I felt instinctively that I could trust you."

"When you walked into the living room at Marissa and Julie's this afternoon, it felt like someone had knocked the wind right out of me. I couldn't breathe, and I couldn't look away. I too have never had that reaction to another person. It was powerful. I wanted to drown in those magnificent eyes of yours."

"It's always about the eyes when I meet someone new," Phoebe said.

Leslie stepped in closer and placed his hand on the side of Phoebe's face. "That is because they are an open window to your soul. I get the impression you don't allow many people to see that deeply into you."

"You are right. It has been a very long time since I trusted someone enough to let them in."

"May *I* come in?" Leslie asked.

Phoebe looked directly into his eyes. "Let's just say I may be willing to open that door."

"May I kiss you?"

"Yes."

Leslie lowered his lips to Phoebe's, tentatively at first, but with increasing passion, which she returned with equal ardor. Leslie ended the kiss with a string of butterfly kisses he placed along her jaw line.

He rested his forehead against Phoebe's. "You make me feel things I've never felt before. I should go before I break your trust." He kissed her gently once more and then stepped back. "Good night, Phoebe Frost. You have changed my life forever. I will wait right here until you are safely inside."

Phoebe felt the heat rise into her cheeks, as well as in other vulnerable places on her being. She struggled to control her heartbeat when Leslie stepped back. All she wanted to do was to grab the front of his vest and pull him close in order to savor the feel of his mouth on hers again, but she understood his need to be respectful. It was a golden aura thing, and it was, after all, their first date.

Phoebe turned and walked up the few steps to her door. She turned and smiled at Leslie once more and then went into the house.

Leslie inhaled deeply and felt a strange lightness in his chest.

What feeling is this? Could I be falling in love? Is that even possible? I've only known her for a few hours.

He forced himself to abandon his position on the sidewalk and return to his car. He sat in the driver's seat for several minutes just looking at Phoebe's door.

How will she feel when she discovers the truth?

Finally, Leslie started the car and drove away.

Phoebe pulled back the curtain and watched Leslie drive away from the curb.

I am in so much trouble here, but I promised Chloe I would open my heart to love.

Phoebe gasped. *Wait! Am I falling in love? But I've only known her—I mean him—for a few hours!*

***

Marissa pulled her car to a stop in front of Phoebe's house the next morning. Phoebe came out of the house before Julie could even open her car door to let her know they were there. The woman who stepped out of the house was Phoebe the mystic advisor, complete with exaggerated makeup and big hair, but with a radiant glow that Julie had not seen on her friend's face since her sister, Chloe, died.

Julie and Marissa watched her bounce down the steps.

"Does she look different to you?" Julie asked.

"She's practically glowing," Marissa replied.

"I wonder if Leslie has anything to do with that?" Julie mused.

"Good morning, my lovelies!" Phoebe said as she climbed into the back seat.

"'Morning, Phoebs. You look happy this morning," Julie commented.

"Well, why shouldn't I be? The sun is shining, the day is new, and life is good," Phoebe responded.

"How did things go with Leslie?" Marissa asked.

"Splendidly," Phoebe said. "Leslie is a truly unique individual. I connected with him like no other I've encountered."

"I think he's sweet on you," Julie teased.

Phoebe blushed. "Well, I could certainly do worse."

Julie swung around in her seat. "Does this mean you are finally going to open your heart to possibilities?"

Phoebe grinned. "I *did* promise Chloe that I would."

Marissa looked at her in the rearview mirror. "He seems like a decent guy, but if he crosses any line that you don't want crossed, I'll kick his ass."

Phoebe laughed. "I will remember that my friend. Thank you for loving me."

"Always," Marissa said. She pulled to the curb in front of Phoebe's shop. "We're here. I hope you ladies have a good day."

Julie kissed Marissa. "You too, my love. I'll call you if I need a ride home."

"I'd like to spend some time at the new house after work," Marissa said. "The sooner we can start on the sheetrock work, the sooner we can move in. Oh, and we need to make a decision on appliances too."

"Okay. We'll talk about it tonight. I'm sure Elliot will give you a hand as well." Julie kissed her once more. "I'll see you tonight."

***

Randy arrived at work the next morning and went directly to the holding cells. They were all empty.

"Where is he?" Randy asked the desk guard.

"Where's who?"

"The guy who was locked up in cell two. He was booked on grave robbing and B&E."

"He's on his way to court. His arraignment is today," the guard said.

"Shit! I had a few questions for him."

"Don't get your panties in a wad. He should be back before noon. They're not gonna let him out that quick. Oh, and if I were you, I'd be careful about what you say to him. The last thing we need is for him to get off on a technicality."

"You let *me* worry about what I'm going to say to him, all right?" Randy said.

"Ooh, touchy this morning, aren't we? Must be you didn't get laid last night."

Randy grabbed the guard by the front of his shirt. "Watch what you say, Striker, or I'll arrange the lowest scab job possible for you."

"Jesus, Rocque. I was just kidding. Like I said, the guy you're looking for should be back before noon."

"I'll be back."

***

As much as it irked him to be reprimanded by the guard, he acknowledged that it was probably prudent to arrange for the man's lawyer to be present when he interviewed him. He just needed to figure out how to carry out the task Phoebe had given him without violating the man's rights or causing any suspicion.

Just before noon, Randy returned to the holding cells, and as predicted, the suspect had returned.

Randy approached the guard. "Jim, I want to apologize for being gruff with you earlier. It's just that I have some important questions for this dude, and it irked me to have to delay getting the information I need."

"No problem, Randy," Jim said. "Monday mornings suck for me as well. We're all entitled to a bad day now and then."

"Thanks, man. Hey, has his lawyer checked in yet?"

"Yes. He's in the waiting room," Jim replied.

"Could you have the suspect brought to the interrogation room for me?"

"Sure! No problem."

"Thanks."

Randy went to the waiting room and collected the man's lawyer and led him to the interrogation room where the guy was waiting. The lawyer sat down beside the suspect and Randy sat opposite them.

"Let's get this over with, Officer Rocque," the lawyer said. "What questions do you need to ask my client?"

The suspect coughed several times.

"Are you okay?" Randy asked.

"Let's just get on with it," the suspect said.

"Okay. There are a couple of things I'd like to know. First, you say you don't remember stalking Lia Purvis and Elliot Walker, is that correct?"

"I don't remember doing that. I don't even know where they live," he insisted. He coughed again.

"Sir, I was at the home of Ms. Purvis and Ms. Walker just a few days ago and saw you with own eyes. In fact, I ran you down and arrested you for stalking them. Do you remember that event?"

The man shook his head and coughed again. "Could I have some water?"

A small grin formed on Randy's face, and he sat back in his seat. "Sure. I'll be right back."

Randy left the room and went to the coffee station down the hall. He pulled a paper cup from the cabinet above the coffee maker and then removed the package from his pocket that Phoebe had given him the night before. He opened the container and poured the clear liquid into the cup. He returned to the room and put it down in front of the suspect.

The man reached for the cup and drank the entire contents in one gulp.

Randy sat and watched him for a few minutes. Nothing happened.

After a few more moments, the man's lawyer leaned forward. "Let's get this over with, Officer Rocque. I don't have all day."

Randy's jaw clenched. *This is not good*, he thought.

"Officer Rocque, what is the *real* reason you called me here today?" the lawyer asked.

Randy stood. "Just doing my job," he said. "I was hoping he'd confess to the stalking, but now I see that I need to prepare to be a witness for the state. I have no more questions for your client, sir."

Randy left the room. "Take him back to his cell," he told the guard as he walked by.

Chapter 25

Phoebe glanced up from her register where she was checking a customer out, to see Officer Rocque enter her shop. He busied himself by browsing the items on a nearby shelf. Phoebe handed the bagged purchase to the customer and bade them a good day. The customer eyed Randy warily and scurried out the door, even though he greeted her with a pleasant good morning.

Randy approached the counter. "I wish people weren't so afraid of the police. I mean, I understand some have had reason to be cautious, but we're not all bad," he said as he watched the customer leave.

"I know. It's a tenuous world we live in. I fear for Lia—and now for Leslie as well," Phoebe said.

"Speaking of Leslie, he seems like a nice guy," Randy said.

Phoebe's smile was radiant. "He *is* very nice. I'm looking forward to knowing him better. Susan seems very nice as well."

"I like her. She got a kick out of all of you last night with your outrageous ghost stories."

Their attention was suddenly drawn to the back of the store where a curtain was pulled back and from which two people emerged.

Julie followed her tarot card client to the front of the store and saw them out. She then turned and walked across the store and into Randy's arms for a hug. "Hey, Randy. Nice to see you," she said.

"Likewise," he said.

"So, what brings you into our fine establishment?" Phoebe asked.

"I did the test you asked me to do."

Phoebe grabbed his arm. "You did? How did it go?"

"Nothing happened. I gave him the holy water to drink. He drank the whole thing in one gulp and nothing happened."

"You gave it to him to drink?" Phoebe asked.

"Yes. I couldn't think of any other way to get it on his person," Randy said.

"Wow! If he was truly possessed, ingesting holy water might have had some intensely adverse effects," Phoebe said.

"The fact that there was no effect means the mistress is not inside him," Julie pointed out. "That's not a good thing."

"I agree," Phoebe said. "The question is—if she's not inside him, then where is she?"

"All the more reasons for you ladies to stick together when you're outside of your protected environments," Randy said.

"Elliot is not going to like this news," Julie said.

"I can't say that I blame her," Randy replied. "She's very protective of Lia."

"The spirits have not always been kind to Lia—especially the mistress. She almost died a few months ago because of her," Phoebe said.

"So, what do we do now?" Julie asked. "I mean, how can we stop her if we don't know where she is?"

"I don't know that we can. As I mentioned earlier, she's been very quiet—especially since the stalker was arrested. I don't believe there's been another incident since then," Phoebe said.

"She must have been in that guy when he was stalking Elliot and Lia, so if she isn't there now, then she must have jumped into someone else," Julie reasoned.

"Damn! I think I know who," Randy said. "Now that I think of it, it all makes sense. A guy who was arrested for drunk and disorderly was put in the same cell as him. When I first arrested the stalker, he was uncooperative and relatively nonresponsive, but after spending a night in jail with the other guy, he was singing like a songbird the next morning. The mistress must have jumped to the other guy while they were locked up together."

"Do you know where the other guy is now?" Phoebe asked.

"No, I don't. He was released the next morning after he sobered up."

"Was he charged with anything?" Julie asked. "I mean, will he have to go to court or something?"

"No, he wasn't charged. Our courts would be packed full if we charged every drunk guy we picked up in New Orleans. He was just released the next morning."

"Well, that's unfortunate," Julie said.

"There is no telling if she is even still inside the second man. In fact, if he proves to be a habitual drinker, she may have already jumped into someone else. She is not going to stay inside anyone who is not useful to her. We must all be on guard for anyone who acts suspiciously," Phoebe explained.

"Well, there's strength in numbers. Until we figure out how to find her again, we need to stick together," Julie said.

Phoebe sighed. "I'm afraid the next move will be hers. I just hope there are no dire consequences associated with it."

***

Julie filled Marissa in on the news about the mistress when she picked her and Phoebe up at the end of the workday.

'Well, that sucks!" Marissa exclaimed. "Now what do we do?"

"There is nothing we *can* do, Marissa," Phoebe replied. "We can only wait until something happens. We simply don't have enough information to predict what her next move will be."

Marissa glanced at Phoebe in her rearview mirror. "What about this fifty and one thing?"

"We still don't understand what that means, and according to what Celeste implied, it is something Lia has to find out for herself. Apparently, Celeste isn't allowed to explain it to us, and Marie is either unwilling or unable to do so either," Phoebe said.

"Well, we can't just stand by and allow her to hurt us or the people we love—or worse," Marissa insisted.

"I'm afraid we may have no choice short of putting all of us under lock and key, or under twenty-four-hour surveillance, which I'm sure even Randy couldn't pull off," Phoebe replied.

A few moments later, Marissa stopped in front of Phoebe's house and as she climbed out of the car. Julie rolled down her window.

"Phoebs, promise us you won't go anywhere alone tonight. If you need to go somewhere, call us and one of us will go with you," Julie said.

"Jules, I'll be fine," Phoebe said.

"Promise me, Phoebs," Julie insisted.

"Okay, okay. I promise I won't go anywhere alone tonight. Thank you for caring so much about me."

"You're welcome. Now get into the house. We're not leaving until you're safely inside. We'll see you in the morning."

"Nag, nag, nag!" Phoebe teased. She climbed the stairs to her house and then waved at them before stepping inside.

***

Elliot paced back and forth across the kitchen. "So, we're sitting ducks, then," she said.

"Kind of," Marissa agreed. "I mean, until we know where she is, we can only react defensively."

"Well, that's just great!"

"El, we'll just take extra precautions for now. You can't let this make you crazy," Lia said.

"I'm sorry, Lia, but knowing my wife is in danger, as well everyone else I love, makes me just a little crazy, you know?" Elliot said sarcastically.

"I don't deserve that attitude, Elliot," Lia said. "I'm just as worried as the rest of you."

Elliot stopped and put her hands on her hips. She sighed. "I'm sorry, Lia. I don't mean to be crass, but we're talking about our lives here."

"I know we are, but we can't do her job for her by giving up, either."

Julie had been leaning against the refrigerator with her arms crossed during this exchange. "I think we need to talk to Marie about this. She must know something, and even if she doesn't, maybe she can give us some advice about how to protect ourselves."

"That's not a bad idea, Jules," Marissa said. "You and I were going to the house tonight anyway, so why don't we all go and see if she can help us."

"Weren't you going to work on the sheetrock tonight?" Elliot asked.

"I think our lives are more important than sheetrock. It will be there for us when we are ready to deal with it," Marissa said.

"Okay. Let me get out of these work clothes and then we can go. Maybe we can order pizza and have it delivered so we don't have to expose ourselves," Lia suggested.

"I need to get changed as well," Elliot said.

Elliot followed Lia up the stairs to their bedroom where they both changed into clothing suitable for renovation work in the event that they had time to help Marissa and Julie after speaking with Marie. Elliot grabbed Lia's arm and pulled her close just before they left their bedroom.

Lia could feel Elliot tremble. She kissed the side of Elliot's head. "Sweetheart, it will be all right. You'll see," Lia said softly.

"I'm scared, Lia. I'm so afraid of losing you."

"You are not going to lose me, silly. In fact, you're stuck with me forever, do you understand?"

"One can only hope," Elliot said.

Lia stepped out of her embrace. "Now pull yourself together, love. You'll lose your butch card if Marissa and Julie see you crying."

Elliot smiled through her tears and wiped her eyes. "Okay. Let's go."

***

Phoebe reached for her cell phone on the table beside her chair. "Hello?"

"Hi, beautiful. This is Leslie."

A rush of heat invaded Phoebe's head. "Leslie! I was just thinking of you."

"Really? What about?"

"I was remembering what a good time we had at dinner, and about the..."

"About the kiss afterward?" Leslie finished for her.

"Yes. About the kiss afterward." Phoebe felt something unfamiliar brewing in her abdomen.

"I have been distracted by the memory of that kiss all day," he admitted. "I'm glad I had Lia's genealogy to work on or I would have gotten nothing done today."

"Are you making any progress?" Phoebe asked.

"Yes. That's why I'm calling you. I'm seeing an odd pattern in her lineage that I wanted to run by you before I show it to Lia."

"Isn't that a breach of confidentiality?"

"Normally, yes, but since she is your friend, and I suspect you will need to see this anyway, I wanted to get your thoughts on it first."

"Why would you think I would need to see it anyway?" Phoebe asked.

"I don't want to do this through a phone call, Phoebe. Can you come to my office—or can I come there?" Leslie asked.

"I promised Marissa and Julie that I wouldn't go out alone, so I guess you'll need to come here," Phoebe said.

"Okay. I can be there in ten minutes."

"All right. I'll see you then."

***

Phoebe opened her front door and stood there with her mouth open. Leslie stood before her dressed in the same riverboat gambler attire, complete with the mustache he had been wearing when he first met Lia and Elliot.

Leslie also stood there with his mouth open, until he shook himself out of his stupor. "Phoebe? You look so different."

Phoebe suddenly realized that she had not removed her makeup, nor changed her clothes since she got home an hour earlier. She reached up to touch her hair. "Sorry. I haven't changed out of my work persona yet, but I could say the same for the way you look."

Leslie grinned. "Ditto on the work persona. This is my genealogy uniform. I figured that dressing in period garb would lend credence to my role as a genealogist."

Phoebe laughed. "My thoughts exactly on the appearance matching the role. Give me a few minutes and I'll go lose the mystical makeup and big hair."

"You don't need to do that," Leslie said.

"No, I want to. Normally I do it the moment I get home, but I was a bit distracted today."

"Wanna talk about it?" Leslie asked.

"Maybe. Give me a minute and I'll be right back."

While she was gone, Leslie stood in front of the mirror that hung above Phoebe's fireplace and peeled off the fake mustache. He then removed his jacket and draped on the back of a chair. Finally, he ran his hands through his hair to loosen the hold the gel had on his curly black locks. The overall effect was more relaxed and casual compared to the more formal southern gentleman look.

Phoebe returned ten minutes later with a freshly washed face, free of makeup, and her hair flowing down her back. She had also traded the more formal clothing for a pair of sweatpants and a T-shirt.

"There," she said as she folded herself into one corner of the couch. "This is so much more comfortable. You look much less formal as well. Have a seat."

Leslie sat in a chair adjacent to the couch. "Damn, you are beautiful," he said.

Phoebe smiled. "I like what I see as well. You have such a welcoming smile and kind face."

Leslie blushed. "I want to kiss you right now, but I have something important to show you."

Phoebe unfolded her legs from beneath her and put her feet on the floor. She leaned forward. "What is it, Leslie?"

"I found something in Lia's lineage that I find to be odd, and even a little frightening." He unfolded a large sheet of paper that had been folded twice and placed it across Phoebe's lap. On it was a typical layout of a family tree beginning with Samuel and Celeste at the top of the page.

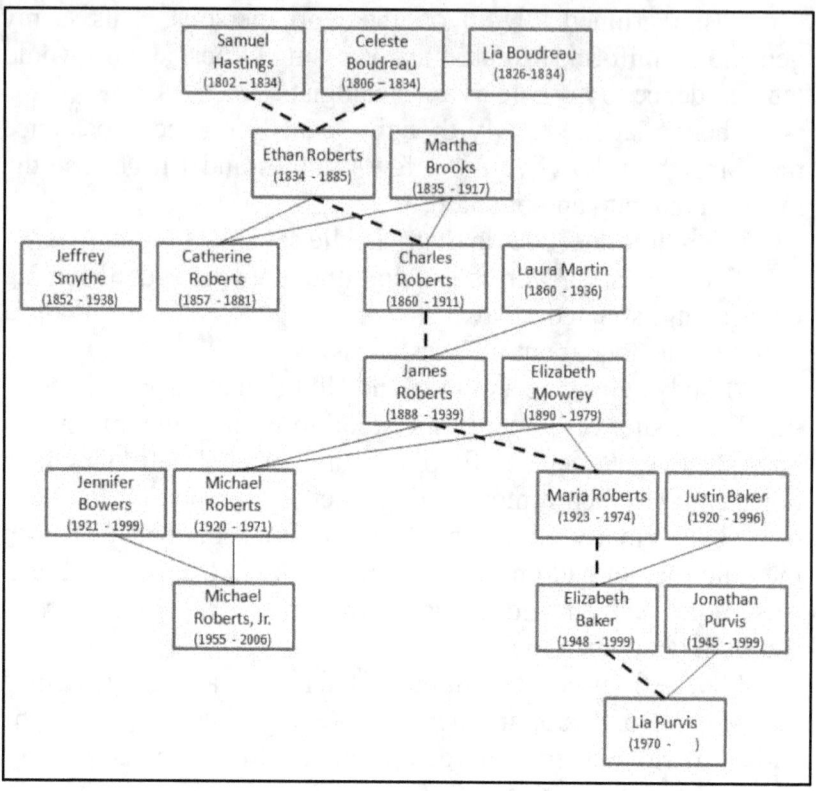

Phoebe studied the family tree. It appeared Lia was the sixth generation beyond Celeste and Samuel.

Leslie watched her face as she studied the lineage. "What do you see, Phoebe?"

Phoebe frowned. "I…I don't know."

Leslie removed the map from her lap and refolded it. He then extracted another folded sheet from the manila folder and placed it across Phoebe's lap. "Now what do you see?" he asked.

Phoebe looked at it for a few seconds and then suddenly jumped to her feet. The lineage diagram flew to the floor several feet away. She looked at Leslie in horror. "Oh, my God!" she exclaimed.

Leslie took Phoebe into his arms and held her close. "You're shaking like a leaf," he said.

Phoebe laid her head on Leslie's chest and wrapped her arms around his waist. "We need to tell her, Leslie. We need to tell her."

Leslie rubbed her back. "Yes, we do. We should call her and arrange to see her right away."

Phoebe nodded and then pulled out of Leslie's arms. She wiped the tears from her cheeks and reached for her phone. Lia answered on the second ring.

"Hey, Phoebe! How are you today?" Lia said.

"Lia, Leslie and I need to see you right away," Phoebe said.

"You and Leslie? Why?"

"He found something in your genealogy that you need to see as soon as possible," Phoebe explained.

"Why are you calling me and not Leslie?" Lia asked.

"He's here with me, at my house. He wanted to run it through me first to verify what he was seeing. He didn't want to alarm you until he was sure."

"Alarm me? Jesus Phoebe, what did he find?"

"We want to come show it to you, Lia. This isn't something that can be done on the phone," Phoebe explained.

"Well, come to Marissa and Julie's. That's where we are right now."

***

Lia and Elliot were waiting for them on the sidewalk in front of Marissa and Julie's house when they arrived. Lia stood in one place with her arms wrapped around herself, while Elliot paced back and forth.

Elliot reached for the door handle on Phoebe's side of the car as soon as the car came to a stop.

"Let's go into the house," Phoebe said as she climbed out of the car.

Lia slipped her hand into the crook of Phoebe's arm and walked with her into the house, followed by Elliot and Leslie. Marissa and Julie were waiting inside. A palpable aura of fear permeated the room as they waited for Leslie and Phoebe to speak.

Phoebe reached for Leslie's hand and pulled him down to the floor. Within seconds, all six of them were kneeling in a circle watching as Leslie pulled the folded paper out of its envelope.

He opened the paper and placed it in front of Lia.

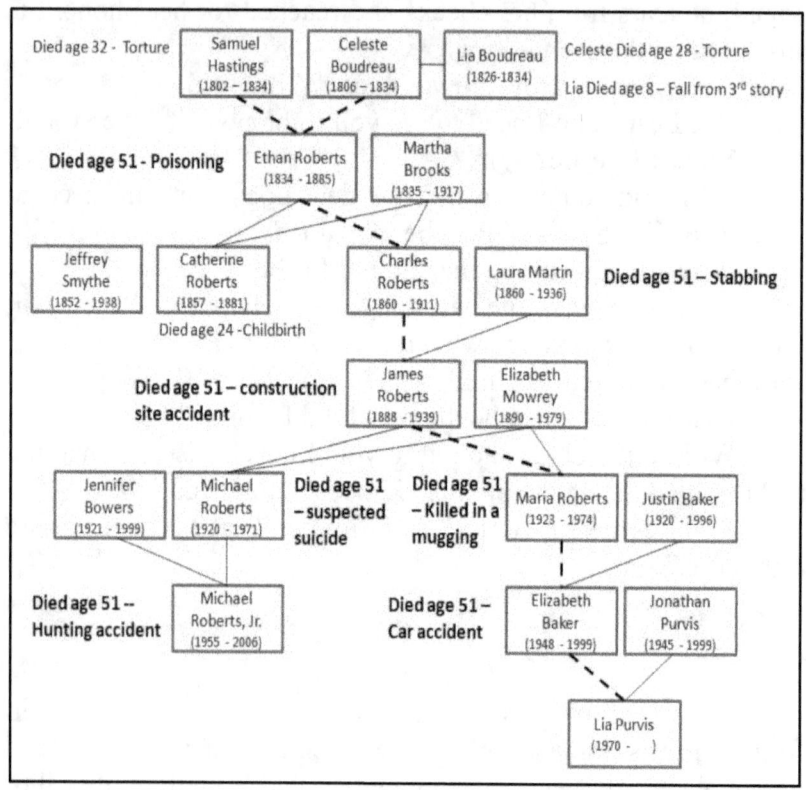

Lia's hand flew to her mouth. She saw it almost immediately. "Oh, my God! The fifty and one!"

"No! No fucking way!" Elliot cried out.

"I'm sorry, Elliot, but it's true. Every single person in the direct line between Lia and Celeste died at age fifty-one, except for Ethan's daughter who died in childbirth," Phoebe said.

"Even more bizarre is that they all died on their fifty-first birthdays," Leslie added.

Lia picked the paper up and looked at Phoebe. "I will be fifty-one next week," she said.

Chapter 26

"We need to talk to Marie," Phoebe said.

"Talking to Marie has gotten us fucking nowhere!" Elliot yelled. "That bitch is still out there."

Leslie took a step in Elliot's direction but was held back by Marissa.

"Elliot!" Lia stood and walked into her personal space. "Just this once, can you look beyond your own personal fear and do what's right for *all* of us?" she shouted. "Stop smothering me!"

Elliot stopped in her tracks and looked at her wife. Tears filled her eyes.

Lia opened her arms and Elliot went into them. She fell to her knees and wrapped her arms around Lia's waist as she cried. Lia continued to hold her close.

Phoebe took control of the situation. "We need to form a circle. Do we have candles?"

"I have some in our room," Lia said. She reached down and helped Elliot to her feet.

"I'll get them," Julie said.

Marissa approached Elliot and rubbed her back. "Are you okay?" she asked.

Elliot wiped her face. "I will be." She looked at the others. "I'm sorry for the way I acted."

"If it were Phoebe in that position, I would feel the same way," Leslie said. He offered his hand to Elliot, who shook it firmly.

"I've got the candles." Julie fell to her knees, laid them out in a five-point star formation, and lit each one.

"You know the drill. Everyone, please take a seat, join hands and close your eyes," Phoebe said. "You too, Elliot."

Phoebe waited for the circle to be complete. She closed her own eyes and spoke in a clear voice. "We call on the spirit of

Marie Laveau in this, our time of need. Our world is in danger of succumbing to the power of an evil so great that it has survived for decades. We seek your wisdom and guidance in our time of need."

Phoebe's head fell back and then slowly rose. "I be here, child."

"Marie. We know about the fifty and one," Julie said. "Please, tell us what to do."

"Now dat Lia know da fifty and one, I can say dere be a curse on da family of Celeste. All be cursed. Da evil one come to da queen and want da queen to curse da family. I say no, but da curse be done widout me."

"How do we stop her before she kills Lia?" Elliot asked.

"Da evil one not kilt da others. Da curse kilt da others. Da curse not need da evil one to kill."

"Wait. Are you saying Lia will die even if we stop the mistress? Is that what you're saying?" Marissa demanded.

"Dat what I say. Da curse be done by dose more evil den her. Stopping da evil one, will not be stopping da curse."

"That's bullshit," Elliot said vehemently.

"Elliot, please," Lia said softly. She turned to Marie. "Marie, how do we stop the curse?"

"How da curse start is how da curse be stopped."

"How did the curse start?" Julie asked.

"Da queen not know how da curse start. Da queen only know it be started when Celeste's Lia die."

"What is the significance of fifty-one, Marie?" Lia asked.

"Da master be fifty and one when he take Celeste to his bed. Dey all be kilt at the fifty and one to punish Celeste for da day Lia come to be."

Marie's head suddenly fell back onto her shoulders and a moment later, Phoebe reappeared.

Leslie squeezed her hand. "Are you all right?" he asked.

Phoebe nodded.

"Did she let you hear what was said, Phoebe?" Julie asked.

"Yes, I was aware of everything."

"So, you know that there is nothing we can do," Julie added.

"That is *not* what Marie said," Phoebe replied.

"Phoebe, she said stopping the mistress will not stop the curse and that Lia will still die. I don't think it gets any clearer than that," Elliot said bitterly.

"What she said was that the curse could be stopped the way it was started," Phoebe said.

"That's just peachy," Elliot complained. "Not only do we need to stop the mistress, but we also need to stop the damned curse she is responsible for. *And* we need to do it all before this fucking curse kills the one person who I love more than anything else in this world."

Everyone in the circle fell silent for a very long time.

Finally, Lia spoke. "I want to go home, Elliot."

Elliot rose to her feet and reached a hand down to help Lia up.

"We need to go too, Mar," Julie suggested.

"I agree. The sheetrock can wait for another day," Marissa said. "Come on you two, we'll take you home."

"I guess that's our cue to go as well," Phoebe said. "Will you all be okay?"

Lia placed her hand on Phoebe's arm. "It's a lot to take in, Phoebe, and I won't deny that I'm scared." She turned to Leslie. "Leslie, do you mind if I have this diagram of my family tree?"

"No, of course not." Leslie removed the diagram from the folder and handed it to her. "I have another copy made for our records."

"Thank you," Lia said. She slipped her hand into Elliot's. "Let's go home."

***

Lia unfolded the family tree diagram on the island in the kitchen and studied it carefully. Marissa and Julie sat on either side of her while Elliot paced the floor in front of the island. A heaviness filled the room like the air just prior to a thunderstorm.

Julie rubbed Lia's back and kissed her on the temple. "We'll figure this out, Lia. I know we will," she said. Her voice was filled with emotion.

Lia ran her fingers across the names of each of her ancestors, beginning with Ethan. "They all died so young," she said. She stopped on the name of her maternal grandmother. "I hardly remember her. I was only four when she died." When her fingertips reached the names of her parents, Lia openly wept. "Mama," she whispered through her tears. "They didn't have to die. It wasn't their time."

Julie gathered Lia in her arms and held her head to her chest. She spontaneously rocked Lia gently back and forth.

Marissa stepped away and tried to compose herself. That was when she noticed Elliot had stopped pacing and was standing with her back to them. Her shoulders were shaking.

Marissa took Elliot into her arms. "We will fight this, El. We will fight this with everything we have," she said.

"I can't lose her, Mar. I can't."

"She isn't gone yet, Elliot. There is still time to figure out how to stop this."

"Her birthday is next week."

"I know. I'm the one who reminded you about it, remember?" She held Elliot at arm's length. "Look, we can't allow our fear of something that hasn't happened yet to paralyze us into inaction."

Elliot broke out of her friend's embrace and walked to the island. She pointed to the paper spread out there. "The evidence is right here on this diagram, Mar. Every single one of them died at fifty-one, and with the exception of one, *none* of the deaths was from natural causes. They might have been made to look like accidents, but the fact that they all occurred on their fifty-first birthdays is no coincidence."

Marissa approached Elliot once more. She pointed to the diagram. "Yes, but what *we* have that *they* didn't is this history. Thanks to Leslie and Marie, we *know* that something is about to happen. These poor souls were caught totally unaware. Don't you see, El? Knowledge is our advantage."

"I think the two of you need to take some time off from work—at least until after Lia's birthday next week," Julie suggested. "For the next week, we need to do everything in our power to protect Lia, twenty-four hours a day."

"No," Lia said.

"No?" Elliot repeated. "Did you just say no?"

She turned sorrowful eyes toward Elliot. "I refuse to fall victim to this, Elliot. I'm the last one in Celeste's line. Do you think the evil behind this will allow me to slip through the cracks simply by hiding in the house for the next week? It will find a way to get to me."

"I can't lose you, Lia," Elliot said in a voice filled with fear.

Lia reached over the island and took Elliot's hand in hers. "I can't lose me either. I have so many more plans and hopes for the future—for *our* future, but there will be no free pass here. This evil will not stop until I'm dead, or until we figure out how to stop it."

"How do we do that, Lia?" Elliot said sadly.

Lia looked at Julie. "I agree that we need to take some time off from work, but not to hide." She turned back to Elliot and Marissa. "We need to fight."

***

Leslie held the door open for Phoebe and offered her a hand as she got out of the car. They faced one another on the sidewalk.

"May I come in?" Leslie asked.

"Yes, of course," Phoebe replied.

Leslie offered his arm as they walked up the steps toward the house. "Ladies first," he said when Phoebe unlocked the door.

Leslie closed the door behind him and stood facing Phoebe with his hands shoved into his pockets. She walked a few feet into the room and then turned around. The sorrow and fear on her face was painful to see. Leslie pulled his hands out of his pockets and opened his arms. Phoebe willingly walked into his embrace and wrapped her arms around his waist.

He held her for several long moments with his cheek resting on top of her head. "You're trembling," he whispered.

Her voice had been robbed by the tears falling from her eyes. All she could do was nod.

"Lia means a lot to you, doesn't she?"

"They all do. They are my family."

"Tell me about them," Leslie said.

Phoebe stepped out of his embrace.

Leslie pulled a tissue out of the box on a nearby table and handed it to her.

"Thank you." She wiped her eyes and then looked at him. "I grew up with Julie. She was the only thing that kept me going when my twin sister died in an accident twenty-five years ago. A couple of years after that, I met Marissa when she and Julie fell in love. I have only known Elliot and Lia for a few months, but it feels like I have known them forever. The four of them are the souls I have traveled with through many generations."

"I'm sorry to hear about your sister. Losing someone you love is difficult enough, but losing a twin must be devastating," Leslie said.

"It was. The boyfriend I had at the time was responsible for her death. I have pretty much closed my heart to relationships ever since."

"So, you have been with men before," Leslie said.

"Just that one. There was no one before him, and no one since," Phoebe said.

"I'm sorry to hear that," Leslie commented. "Someone out there has been missing out on your beautiful heart."

"Or maybe I have been unknowingly saving it for someone special," Phoebe replied."

"Is there hope that *I* may be that someone special?" Leslie asked.

Phoebe stepped into Leslie's personal space and looked directly into his face. "There is always hope," she whispered.

Leslie continued to look directly into her eyes. "There is so much you don't know about me," he said softly.

"I know that you are a wonderfully kind and beautifully fluid human being," Phoebe replied. "I know that I feel safe with you. I know that I need a cocoon to crawl into to feel protected and loved right now."

"Phoebe, I may not be what you expect," he said.

"The only expectation I have is that you will treat me with tenderness and respect, and I will return the favor in kind."

"I'm hoping that what you see inside my cocoon is a butterfly and not a moth," he said.

"I'll let you know once I'm inside."

"I want to kiss you," Leslie said.

"What are you waiting for?"

Leslie took Phoebe's face between his palms. Their lips touched, gently at first, but then deepened. He felt Phoebe's arms pull him closer as the kiss deepened.

Leslie's lips moved to Phoebe's jaw and then to her neck. With all his will, he stopped and rested his forehead on her shoulder. His breath came in passionate pants.

"Leslie?" Phoebe said when he stopped.

Leslie looked at Phoebe. "I'm sorry. I need to go before I do something you might regret."

"No. Please stay with me tonight. I'd rather not be alone right now," Phoebe said.

"I don't trust myself. I want you so badly. I'm afraid…"

"You are afraid that I may reject you once I discover just how fluid you are? Is that it?"

Leslie looked away, but Phoebe turned his face back to her. "Sweetie, I don't care. I want to make love to *you*—not your gender."

Leslie looked deep into Phoebe's nearly translucent, cerulean eyes and saw the truth in her words.

"Where is your bedroom?" he asked.

"Come with me." Phoebe took his hand and led him up the stairs to a large master suite, decorated in wild colors and accessories reminiscent of Phoebe the mystic rather than Phoebe the woman.

Leslie looked around and smiled.

"I know," Phoebe said. "She is more a part of me than I'd like to admit sometimes."

Leslie wrapped his arms around her waist. "I love everything about you, Phoebe."

Phoebe's eyes opened wide. "You love me?" she asked.

Leslie looked like he had disclosed a secret he hadn't intended to reveal.

"Don't look so scared," Phoebe said.

"I'm sorry. I didn't intend to say that so soon. I was afraid I'd scare you away."

"I'm still here," she replied.

Leslie smiled and pulled her closer. He touched his forehead to hers. "Yes, you are."

"Make love to me, Leslie. Teach me."

Leslie kissed her again—tenderly this time, while moving from her mouth to her jaw and neck. He slowly pulled her T-shirt over her head and trapped her arms in the material as the trail of kisses followed a line from her neck to her shoulder. Phoebe's eyes were closed, and her head leaned back, while small whimpers escaped her lips.

Phoebe's shirt slid off her arms and drifted to the floor. Leslie stood before her and admired the softness of her skin while his fingertips traced lines down her arms. "You are so beautiful," he whispered.

He reached behind Phoebe and unclasped her bra. A sigh of relief came from deep within Phoebe as the bra released its hold on her. Leslie chuckled and gently scratched Phoebe's back.

"Oh, my God," Phoebe called out. "That feels so good. Can I keep you?"

"I'm yours for as long as you want me," Leslie said.

Leslie cupped Phoebe's breasts in both hands and gently thumbed the erect nipples.

Phoebe nearly doubled as a spasm ripped through her abdomen at his touch. Phoebe's breath was choppy as she tried to control the growing passion in her breast.

The sweatpants were the next to go, and soon, Phoebe stood before him clad only in her panties. She was on fire.

Leslie took a step back, removed his vest and threw it on a nearby chair.

"No. Let me," Phoebe said. She closed the space between them and unbuttoned his shirt, pulling the tails out of his trousers to gain access to the bottom buttons. That joined the vest on the chair. Beneath the shirt, he wore a sleeveless T-shirt, which Phoebe promptly removed, revealing a thick elastic wrap.

He looked away, embarrassed when this undergarment was revealed.

"Leslie, look at me," she said.

He locked gazes with her and did not look away while she slowly removed the wrap and allowed it to fall to the floor. Another intense spasm ripped through her when moderately sized breasts were exposed. She gently ran her hands over them and kissed each nipple. Leslie visibly trembled under her touch.

Before Phoebe could proceed, Leslie placed his hands on Phoebe's shoulders, slipped his shoes off and kicked them away.

Phoebe made short work of Leslie's trousers and socks. Soon, they stood in front of one another wearing only panties and boxers.

Leslie stepped forward and took Phoebe into his arms. His hands lowered to her backside where he cupped two handfuls of flesh and pulled her toward him. "I want to taste you and to be inside of you," he growled.

Phoebe slipped her hands inside the back of his boxer shorts. "Take these off."

Both undergarments were discarded quickly.

Leslie took Phoebe's hand led her to the bed. He gently lay down beside her.

"Let me look at you," Phoebe said.

Leslie folded his arms behind his head and left himself vulnerable to Phoebe's scrutiny.

She sat back on her knees beside him and gently ran her hands across his skin. "Your skin is so soft," she said.

Leslie had all he could do not to grab Phoebe, throw her on the bed and make mad passionate love to her, but he knew he needed to go slow. He knew he needed to be gentle, so he endured her exploration.

Phoebe ran her palm over Leslie's abdomen and smiled when she felt a spasm ripple through him. Finally, she cupped the mound of black, curly pubic hair and gently squeezed. "You are so beautiful," she said.

Leslie couldn't take any more of Phoebe's torture. He sat up, grabbed her and pulled her down beside him. In one swift movement, he rolled on top of her and pinned her to the bed, flesh to flesh.

"You, my dear, are a tease," he said.

Phoebe grinned. "What do you mean?"

"You were driving me crazy with your touch."

"Well then, we're even," Phoebe said.

"And how's that?"

"Since the day we met, you've been driving me crazy every time you looked at me," Phoebe said.

"I'll show you crazy," Leslie said. He kissed her once more with such passion, Phoebe moaned. He then moved down and feasted on her breasts. Phoebe grabbed his head and held it in place, objecting when he chose to explore farther south.

"Oh, my God, Leslie. I don't remember it feeling this good," Phoebe said.

"He must have either been a clumsy clod or an inexperienced child not to make you feel the way you deserve to feel," Leslie said.

"I need more," Phoebe said.

"Your wish is my command, beautiful lady." Leslie kissed his way across Phoebe's abdomen, kissing, licking and nipping the tender skin around the inside crease of her leg.

Leslie glanced at Phoebe's face and nearly lost control of his own desire when he saw the passion on his lover's face.

"Leslie. Please. I need you," Phoebe begged.

Leslie pushed Phoebe's legs farther apart and gently sucked her clit into his mouth. Phoebe's pelvis rose off the bed while a guttural moan escaped her lips. Her hips moved in cadence with Leslie's tongue. Sensing she was close to climax, Leslie placed two fingers near her opening and plunged them deep inside her.

"Leslie!" Phoebe screamed.

Leslie froze. "Am I hurting you?" he asked.

Phoebe half rose into a seated position and grabbed his arm. "Don't stop," she said. "Please, don't stop."

Leslie resumed his thrusts while passionate cries filled the air. A short time later, Phoebe's pelvis suspended above the bed for a few seconds and then she plunged repeatedly into wave after wave of orgasmic pleasure.

Phoebe touched the top of Leslie's head when she'd had enough. Without removing his hand, he repositioned himself beside her and kissed her tenderly on the mouth.

Phoebe's eyebrows rose. "Is that what I taste like?" she asked.

"Yes. Are you all right?" he asked.

"I'm more than all right. Thank you," she said.

"I love how vocal you were. It was a major turn-on for me."

Phoebe blushed. "Who would have thought that I'd be a screamer," she said.

"Hold on a minute." Leslie gently removed his hand, causing yet another string of soft spasms to run in waves through her.

"Oh, my," Phoebe exclaimed.

"That was dessert," Leslie teased.

"I can't believe I've been missing out on this all these years."

"It's not the same with everyone," Leslie said. "True fulfillment requires the right person."

Phoebe traced the side of Leslie's face with her finger. "Then I guess I'm with the right person, because I truly feel fulfilled."

"Then my job here is done," he said.

"But mine is not. What about you?" Phoebe asked.

"You asked me to teach you, right?"

"Yes. Tell me what to do."

"Do exactly what I did to you."

***

Sometime later, Phoebe lay tucked into Leslie's shoulder as they both lay sated in bed.

"Hmm, that was amazing. You are an excellent student," Leslie said.

"A student only learns as well as a teacher teaches," Phoebe replied.

"I see more lessons in your future," Leslie joked. "I wish regular school had been this fun."

Phoebe kissed Leslie's jaw. "Thank you for being so patient with me."

"You're welcome."

"I can understand now why the girls look at one another so lovingly all the time. This level of intimacy requires an intense amount of love and trust."

"Yes, it does."

Phoebe fell silent for several minutes.

Leslie raised his head to look at her. "Are you okay? You got quiet all of the sudden."

"I was thinking about Lia."

Leslie rolled to his side and propped himself on his elbow to look directly at Phoebe. She was crying.

"Sweetie, don't cry."

"How can I not cry, Leslie? Unless we can do something to stop it, Lia will be dead within a week."

"There must be something we can do," Leslie said. "Is there anyone who can help?"

Phoebe's brow creased. "Maybe there is. Marie told us to engage the kings and queens. We need to stop this, Leslie. We can't let Lia die."

Chapter 27

Phoebe called Julie the next morning while Leslie was in the shower.

"Good morning, Phoebs. How are you today?" Julie asked when she answered the phone.

"I remember the days when you had to say hello to learn who was on the other end of the line," Phoebe said.

"Modern technology has its benefits," Julie said. "It's nice not to answer the phone when the person calling is someone you don't want to engage with."

"I'll remember that the next time you don't answer your phone," Phoebe joked.

"Very funny, Phoebs. I always pick up your calls."

"I'm just teasing you," Phoebe said. "So, I'm calling you for two reasons. First, I don't need a ride to work this morning. Leslie will drop me off. And second…"

"Leslie will drop you off? Oh, I see! Did we have a sleepover?" Julie teased.

"Remind me to talk to you about that. I have lots of questions," Phoebe said. "But more importantly, the second reason I'm calling is to ask if you want to go with me this morning to see the voodoo queen."

"The *current* voodoo queen?" Julie asked.

"Yes. I have an appointment with her at nine o'clock this morning. I want to talk to her about Lia's problem."

"Yes. Absolutely, yes. I'll go with you," Julie said.

"She works out of a shop just two blocks from mine, so we can walk there. If she can have Marissa drop you off an hour earlier than normal so we can discuss what we want to say to her."

"Okay. I'll be there promptly at eight," Julie said. "Oh, and Phoebs?"

"Yes?" Phoebe asked.

"I'm happy for you and Leslie."

***

Elliot sat up in bed. "Lia, what do you think you're doing?"

"I'm going for a run, and then I'm going to shower and go to work."

"No, you're not. It's not safe."

Lia finished tying her shoe and then turned to Elliot. "Elliot, I'm relatively safe until my birthday. Until then I'm still fifty. I'm not going to stay holed up in the house in the hopes that the mistress can't get me. That is no way to live."

Elliot got out of bed and grabbed her arm. "You're not going, Lia."

Lia looked at the hand on her arm. "Take your hand off me, Elliot," she said vehemently.

"Lia, what if she decides to do the job herself instead of letting the curse do it? I mean, you're the last one in Celeste's line. What does it matter *when* you die?"

"I'm betting she will let the curse run its course, and that she'll be right there to watch it happen. There is no way she is going to jump the gun."

"Lia, please listen to reason."

"I'm going, Elliot. Don't try to stop me."

Lia opened their bedroom door and walked into the hall. Elliot followed close behind to the top of the central staircase. "Lia, please."

"I'll be back in an hour, Elliot," Lia said. She ran down the flight of stairs and headed to the kitchen for a bottle of water. Julie had just hung up her phone and slipped it into her pocket when Lia entered.

"Hey, you. Where are you going so early?" Julie asked.

"I'm going for a run. I'll be back soon." Lia grabbed a bottle of water and headed back through the butler's pantry and toward the staircase where Elliot had just descended to the second floor. Elliot watched her run down the stairs and leave through the front door.

"What's going on?"

Elliot looked up and saw Marissa coming down from the third level.

"Lia's gone for a run—alone," Elliot said.

"I wonder why Julie didn't go with her," Marissa asked just as Julie entered the hall from the butler's pantry.

"Because I need to head to work early this morning," Julie said. "I have to be there by eight. Phoebe and I are paying a visit to the reigning voodoo queen this morning to talk about this curse."

"If something happens to her on that run, we may not need to worry about a damned curse," Elliot said.

***

Lia returned from her run just as Julie and Marissa were ready to leave. She went directly to the kitchen and retrieved another bottle of water, which she drank from thirstily while Julie made a travel mug of coffee. Marissa was in the car waiting for her.

"How was your run?" Julie asked.

"It was awesome, and as you can see, I came back in one piece."

"You know she loves you."

"Yes. I know she does. But I don't want to spend my final days on earth smothered in a cocoon—even one made of love."

Julie took Lia by the shoulders. "Lia, stop talking like that. We still have time to figure out what to do about this curse."

"And if you don't figure it out? What then?" Lia asked bitterly.

"I refuse to consider defeat," Julie said. "I won't give up on you, so damn it—don't give up on yourself!" Julie grabbed her coffee and walked to the back door. She stopped and turned around. "I love you, Lia Purvis," she said, and then she was gone before Lia could reply.

***

Bill Murphy sat in his truck by the side of the road and watched the traffic go by. He'd sat there the previous morning as well.

It will be time soon. Untie the ladder, the voice in his head said.

Bill pushed his door open and climbed onto the back of his truck. He dutifully untied his extension ladder from the cargo rack and then stood there awaiting further instruction.

Get back into the truck.

Bill did as he was told and climbed back into the cab of his truck. Once again, he kept his eyes on the side mirror as traffic flowed by.

Now!

He pressed the gas pedal to the floor and lurched out of his parking place. As expected, the extension ladder flew off the rack and landed in the middle of the road, causing the car that was about thirty feet behind him to slam on their breaks and swerve to avoid running over it. Bill immediately pulled to the side of the road.

The car came to a stop a few feet away from Bill's truck. The blue lights on the roof came on and the driver swung the door open and got out. He slammed his door and walked toward the truck. He stopped dead in his tracks when he saw the name on the door. *Bill Murphy – General Contractor.*

"Bill? Bill, is that you?" he called out.

Bill shook his head. "What the hell am I doing here?" he whispered under his breath. He looked at the person standing beside his door. It was a police officer. "Randy?"

Randy opened Bill's door. "I need to ask you to get out of your truck, Bill," Randy said.

Bill climbed out and immediately noticed his ladder on the ground in front of the police car. "What happened?" he asked.

"That was my next question for you. You pulled out of a parking place and the ladder flew off the top of your truck," Randy said.

"Fuck! I must have forgotten to tie it down," Bill said.

"That was my thought as well. Here, let me give you a hand with it."

Randy and Bill each picked up one end of the ladder and carried it back to the truck where they hefted it onto the rack. Bill climbed onto the back of the truck and securely tied it down.

He jumped off the back end and approached Randy. "I'm sorry, man. I'm usually more careful than that."

"Are you still having those headaches?" Randy asked.

"I had one again this morning, but right now my head doesn't feel too bad," Bill replied.

"Well, that's good. Maybe you should take it easy for the rest of the day and hope it doesn't come back," Randy suggested.

"I might just do that." Bill extended his hand to Randy and shook it firmly while he said his final apology. "Again, I'm sorry for being so careless. Thank you for understanding."

"No problem," Randy said.

The handshake ended and Bill went back to his truck feeling better than he had in a long time.

***

Phoebe and Julie were escorted through a shop and into the private residence of Bettina Thibodeaux, the reigning Voodoo Queen of New Orleans. The transition between the shop and her home was almost indiscernible since the decor of her shop appeared to spill into her home.

Bettina Thibodeaux began her reign as the Voodoo Queen of New Orleans nearly forty years earlier. The title was handed down to her from her aunt, who was reportedly a granddaughter in the lineage of Marie Laveau. She presided over the faction of the voodoo community that religiously followed the teachings and methods practiced by Marie Laveau herself.

Queen Thibodeaux was waiting for them in her sitting room. The room was made artificially dark by thick drapes that covered the windows. Several strategically placed candles cast a soft glow across the room.

The queen sat in a wingback chair in the center of the room. She was a woman of color and easily sixty or more years old. Stocky in stature, she wore a flowing kaftan, complete with scarf and headdress. Around her neck was an ornate tribal necklace, with tusks, shells, leather and beads. Large hoop earrings adorned her earlobes while a dozen or more beaded and metal bands graced her right forearm.

"Please come in. Sit," the queen said.

Phoebe and Julie sat in two chairs opposite the queen.

"May I offer you some tea?" the queen asked.

The women graciously accepted and watched as the queen herself poured the beverage into three teacups.

The queen picked up her tea and sipped it. "Which of you is Phoebe Frost?" the queen asked.

"I am," Phoebe said.

"You have quite a reputation in the voodoo community, Miss Frost."

"All good, I hope," Phoebe said.

"Very good indeed. I have been looking for a reputable medium, and I would be honored if you would consider lending me your services on occasion."

Phoebe's face flushed. "I'm honored by your request. I would be happy to work with you."

The queen looked at Julie. "And you are?"

"Julie Barrows. I work with Phoebe. Primarily tarot readings. I have known Phoebe nearly all my life. She is like a sister to me."

"Julie and her wife Marissa just purchased the Laveau property," Phoebe said

"Is that so? It is reported that Marie still resides there," the queen commented.

"Yes, she does. We have seen her and spoken with her. In fact, she has used Phoebe as a conduit to speak to all of us," Julie said.

The queen raised her eyebrows. "Really? When you say *all* of us, to whom are you referring?"

"Let's see," Julie said. "Phoebe and me, of course. My wife Marissa. Our friends Elliot and Lia, and Phoebe's partner, Leslie."

Phoebe blushed when Julie mentioned Leslie as being her partner."

"She must trust you to appear in front of such a large group," the queen observed.

"We hope she trusts us. She has been a great help in trying to resolve this matter we are dealing with. It is a matter of life and death, in fact," Phoebe said.

"You implied as much when we spoke on the phone this morning. Tell me more about this problem, Miss Frost."

Phoebe looked to Julie for moral support before she began.

"We are up against a great evil. It began in the eighteen-thirties in a mansion on Royal Street where several slaves were tortured and murdered in the attic."

"Eleven forty Rue Royale," the queen said bitterly.

"Yes," Phoebe said. "Our friends, Elliot and Lia moved to New Orleans and purchased that property nearly six months ago. Lia is a woman of color, and it was soon discovered that she had a kinship with some of the slaves who lived and died there."

"A kinship?" the queen asked. "Please explain."

"Through several possessions, sightings and séances, we learned that a slave woman named Celeste lived in the mansion in the early eighteen-thirties. The master of the house took a lustful fancy for her and commanded her into his bed. She bore him a child. A girl named Lia."

"The girl had the same name as your friend Lia who currently lives in the house?" the queen asked.

"Yes."

"I will tell you right now that it was not a coincidence that your Lia was summoned to New Orleans. Why—I don't know, but it was not a coincidence. Please continue."

"As you probably know, the mistress of the house was as evil as they come. She killed the child Lia when she was eight years old," Phoebe explained.

"She is the child that fell to her death from the third story," the queen said.

"Yes, that was Lia."

"Not too long after that, the old woman who served as their cook set fire to the house rather than be sent to the third floor to suffer the same fate as the others. After the fire, the mistress reportedly escaped and fled to Paris."

Phoebe paused and sipped her tea. She had become emotional during the telling of her story, and she needed a little time to compose herself. Finally, she felt that she could continue.

"Queen Thibodeaux, do you recall ripples that ran through the overworld a few months back when the souls of the tortured were released?"

"Yes, child, I do."

"We are here to seek your help in saving one of the women responsible for those ripples. She has very little time left unless we can do something to change what is predestined to happen."

"And what is that destiny?" the queen asked.

Julie touched Phoebe's arm. "Let me," she said.

Julie reached into her backpack and retrieved a large, folded piece of paper. "Lia left this on the kitchen island. I grabbed it in case we needed it."

She spread the paper out on the table before the queen.

Julie pointed to Lia's name at the bottom of the page. "This is Lia," she said. "And the dotted lines trace her lineage, directly to Celeste."

The queen looked at the chart and then at her guests. "Her family has been cursed," she said.

"Yes, and the curse was brought on by the same evil mistress who murdered and tortured the slaves on Royal Street," Phoebe pointed out.

The queen traced the dotted line on the chart. "They all died at the age of fifty-one."

"Yes. And each of the deaths occurred on their fifty-first birthdays," Julie said. "We learned from Marie that the master was fifty-one when he first took Celeste to his bed."

The queen looked at Phoebe. "You said your friend has very little time left. When is her birthday?"

"Jules?" Phoebe asked.

"Her fifty-first birthday is next week, on June twenty-third," Julie replied.

The queen's eyes flew open, and she grasped the arms of her chair. "She was born on St. John's Eve! Is she aware of her power?"

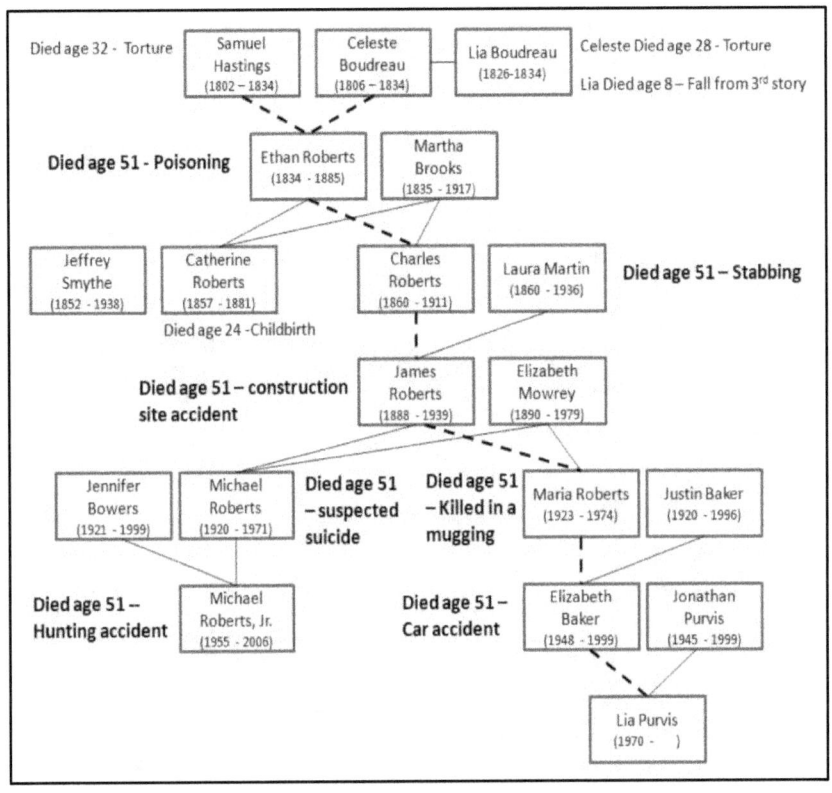

Chapter 28

"Her power?" Phoebe asked.

"Yes. Those born on St. John's Eve are thought to have special powers that allow them to reach into the minds of those around them. I'm not talking about superhuman powers like those that you see in the movies these days. I'm talking about the power of persuasion and empathy, and the ability to steer another's destiny."

"Empathy is something I can understand. Lia always seems to be acutely aware of how others are feeling, but persuasion is another thing altogether. If Lia has that kind of power, I've never seen her use it," Julie said. "And I've known her for more than twenty years."

"The power will remain dormant if the possessor is unaware. It appears when needed and then grows in strength when cultivated," the queen explained.

"So, we're talking about being able to influence the actions of others," Phoebe said.

"Something like that," the queen replied.

"Well, unless we figure out how to break this curse, there won't be time for her to cultivate anything," Julie pointed out.

"There are many different curses and many different ways to break them," Queen Thibodeaux said.

"Marie implied the curse had to be broken in the same way it was placed," Phoebe said. "That was more than one hundred and eighty years ago. It feels like an impossible task to figure out how it was placed."

"When exactly was it placed?" the queen asked.

"Marie said it was placed when Celeste's Lia died," Phoebe replied.

Julie quickly scanned the family tree diagram. "According to this record, Little Lia died in eighteen-thirty-four."

"Hmmm. The fact that Marie knows *when* the curse was placed gives me hope that she may be aware of *how* it was placed. We will need to speak with her about this," the queen said.

"I can arrange a séance with her as soon as you are available," Phoebe offered.

"Our girl has limited time, so we need to do this as soon as we can," the queen pointed out. "Tonight, at dusk, if possible."

***

Phoebe and Julie hurried back to the shop. When they arrived, Julie called Marissa while Phoebe called Elliot and Lia to fill them in on the news.

***

"Mar, we are having a séance tonight with the reigning voodoo queen, so we need to move at least the dining room furniture as soon as possible today. We can't expect the queen to sit on the floor," Julie said.

"Whoa. Stop right there," Marissa replied. "Run that by me again. We're having a séance tonight?"

"Yes. Phoebs and I met with the voodoo queen this morning to talk about Lia's predicament. Her name is Bettina Thibodeaux and she's been the reigning queen for the past forty years. Anyway, she's willing to help us, but we need to have a séance with Marie to better understand the curse that the bitch cast on Lia's family."

"Does she think she can break the curse?" Marissa asked.

"She doesn't know, but she's willing to try."

"All right. I'll see if I can line up some help this afternoon to at least move the table and chairs," Marissa said. "Do Lia and Elliot know about this yet?"

"Phoebe is calling them right now," Julie replied.

Marissa paused for several moments.

"Mar? Are you okay?" Julie asked.

Marissa's voice was choked with emotion. "I don't know what I'll do if we can't save her, Jules. I've been crying on and off all day just thinking about it."

"I know, love. Meeting with the queen this morning gives me hope, but there are still no guarantees. We need to do everything in our power to stop this, but we might fail. We need to be prepared for that."

"But there is hope, right?" Marissa asked.

"There is always hope," Julie replied.

***

"Hi, Elliot. This is Phoebe. Call me as soon as you can. I have an urgent matter I need to talk to you and Lia about. I've already left a voicemail on Lia's phone. Thanks."

No sooner had she hung up the phone, than Lia called back.

"Lia. Hi. Look, I have something important to talk to you and Elliot about. Is this a good time?"

"It's good for me, but I can't vouch for Elliot," Lia replied.

"Oh, wait a minute, Elliot is calling back. I'll put you on hold. Don't hang up," Phoebe said when Elliot's number flashed across her cellphone screen.

Phoebe pressed the hold button and answered Elliot's callback.

"Phoebe! Elliot here. Sorry I missed your call. What's the urgent issue you need to tell me about? Please tell me it's good news about Lia."

"Hi, Elliot. Actually, I have Lia on hold. Give me a minute and I'll conference her in."

"Okay."

Phoebe tied the three-way call together. "Lia? Elliot? Do I have you both?"

"Yes, I'm here," Lia said.

"Me too," Elliot replied.

"Good. So, Julie and I went to see the current voodoo queen this morning and she is willing to help us put a stop to this curse."

"What? That's awesome news!" Elliot exclaimed.

"Don't get too excited yet, Elliot," Phoebe said. "There is a lot to figure out before we can even attempt to lift the curse—and there is no guarantee that it will work—but it is definitely better than doing nothing."

"So, what do we need to do?" Elliot asked.

"For starters, she wants to talk to Marie Laveau. I told her that Marie knew *when* the curse was placed, and Queen Thibodeaux is hoping that she may also remember *how* it was placed."

"Does it really matter how it was placed as long as we can break it?" Lia asked.

"Marie specifically said it had to be lifted in the same manner it was cast, so, yes, I think it matters," Phoebe explained.

"Marie also said she wasn't there when the curse was laid down, remember? She said the mistress came to her to do it and she said no. Someone besides Marie cast that spell. How do we know what spell they used?" Lia reasoned.

"Those are all good points, Lia. I believe the queen is hoping Marie was familiar with what the typical spells were at the time. Things change with each generation, and since Marie is in the same generation as the mistress, it is possible there was a standard spell used at that time that Marie might be familiar with."

"It sounds like a long shot, Phoebe," Elliot said.

"That may be, Elliot, but it might be the only shot we'll get."

"So, we'll need another séance then," Lia said.

"Yes, and since we have limited time, the sooner the better. The queen is willing to do it tonight," Phoebe replied.

"You know, part of me wants to just look at this whole fiasco as nothing but a bunch of mumbo jumbo," Elliot said. "I mean, what if we had never come to New Orleans? What if we never had to deal with the bullshit we stepped into when we bought our house? What if we had continued living our lives in New York City without a care in the world? What then?"

"Then Lia would die next week in some freak accident in New York City," Phoebe said. "You can wish it away if you'd like, Elliot, but her family tree is based on historical fact. Do you really want to treat this like mumbo jumbo when you have her family's history staring you in the face?"

Elliot whimpered softly. "I'm sorry," she said. "I can't lose her. I just can't."

"I'm sorry, too," Phoebe said. "I shouldn't have been so harsh. Look, we have nothing to lose and everything to gain by getting Marie and the current queen in the same room. They have decades of experience between them. We have to try. I don't know what else to do."

"We will be there, Phoebe," Lia said. "Both of us. What time?"

"At dusk. The sun sets around eight. I would recommend being at Marissa and Julie's no later than seven, so we'll have time to make introductions with Queen Thibodeaux."

***

Phoebe and Julie arrived at Saint Ann Street at six that evening. As promised, Marissa had recruited help among her coworkers to transport their dining room set to the new house earlier in the day. Luckily, it was large enough to accommodate everyone who was expected to be in attendance.

Phoebe brought a tablecloth, several new candles in various colors, incense, rosemary, sage, basil, a porcelain bowl and black sea salt. She and Julie worked together to trace a pentagram on the tablecloth with the salt and to arrange a candle at each point and one in the middle. The rosemary, sage and basil were arranged in the bowl, ready to be lit to cleanse the area prior to beginning the séance. The incense was lit immediately to generate an appropriate atmosphere prior to the ceremony beginning.

They stepped back and inspected their handiwork.

"I think this will do," Phoebe said.

"I hope we can learn something useful tonight," Julie commented.

"I do as well," Phoebe said. "In all my years of doing this kind of work, nothing has been more important than this. I can't imagine losing Lia. It would be devastating to Elliot, and to all of us as well. I've lived through my share of losing the people I love. I don't want to lose another."

"Speaking of people we love, is Leslie coming to the séance?" Julie asked.

Phoebe's gaze darted to Julie. "Is it that obvious?"

"It's written on your face when you're with him," Julie said.

"I thought about asking him to attend, but I didn't know how well received it would be."

"Are you kidding me?" Julie exclaimed. "He's one of us. He became one of us when he became part of you. Of course, he would be welcome."

"There *is* strength in numbers," Phoebe mused. "I'll call him."

Julie walked away to give Phoebe privacy while she called Leslie. She stood in the front window and looked out at the street. A feeling of serenity washed across her when she realized this would be her forever home with Marissa. She was looking forward to meeting her neighbors and enjoying the feeling of the French Quarter—that is, if life ever returned to normal again. An anxious feeling suddenly invaded her consciousness when she realized she may be looking at a future without Lia.

"Okay, Leslie will be here around seven. Thank you for including him, Julie."

Julie swung around to face Phoebe. She wiped a tear from her eye. "That's awesome. I'm looking forward to knowing him better."

Phoebe rubbed her arm. "Are you okay?"

"I'm fine. I was just thinking about how much we have to look forward to in this house and hoping that Lia will be able to share it with us."

"We are all hoping for that, my friend, and if we are lucky, we'll learn something tonight that will help."

"I sure hope so." Julie abruptly changed the subject. "So, tell me about Leslie. You said you had questions."

Phoebe blushed. "We made love. It was so not what I expected."

Julie raised her eyebrows. "So, Phoebs, I gotta ask this question..."

"He is biologically female," Phoebe jumped in quickly.

"That's what I thought. That's what we all thought, in fact. So, what questions do you have?"

Phoebe placed her hands over her heart and inhaled deeply. "Like I said, the experience was so different than anything I had ever felt before. I mean, I had only been with Troy. There's been no one since him. I didn't realize I was capable of such passion. Jesus, Julie, I swear I almost lost consciousness at one point."

Julie smiled. "I know just what you mean. Marissa has brought me to that point many times. It is both terrifying and exhilarating."

"Yes! Exactly."

"It sounds like you reacted to him exactly the way you should have, so what questions do you have?"

"Well, I mean, Troy always took care of himself. He didn't have a problem reaching climax, so I never had to worry about him, but Leslie—well, Leslie has lady parts. He was a good teacher, and I was able to bring him to climax, but I felt so inadequate doing it."

"I see." Julie draped her arm around Phoebe's shoulder. "We have a few minutes before everyone arrives. Come have a seat and let me give you a few pointers for the next time."

***

Lia, Elliot, Marissa and Leslie all arrived before Queen Thibodeaux. The first thing they did when all were present was a group hug.

"We are in this together," Phoebe said directly to Lia. "And we'll do everything in our power to affect a good outcome."

"I so love every one of you. You are my family, and I trust you," Lia replied.

A knock on the door interrupted their hug-fest.

"That is most likely the queen. I'll get the door," Julie said.

Julie opened the door and welcomed Queen Thibodeaux into her home. "Please, come in. I apologize for the sparse furnishings. We haven't moved in yet."

The queen touched the side of her face. "Not to worry, child. I'm sure it will be fine."

The queen walked through the vestibule and into the living room. She stopped and observed the group of people all waiting to meet her. Her gaze scanned each of them, and then returned to focus on Lia. She walked directly up to Lia and took her hands.

"You are Lia," she said.

"How did you know?" Lia asked.

"Your aura gave you away."

"My aura? What does that mean?"

"Everyone has an aura, child. It is simply a vibrant ray of colorful energy that flows around you. It is the portal to a more mystical realm, and it provides insight into a person's personality and power. Your aura borders on indigo and violet, meaning you have great intuition and inner knowledge, as well as spiritual and psychic abilities. I sense that you are very empathetic toward others. This makes sense for those lucky enough to be born on St. John's Eve."

Lia's gaze diverted sharply to Julie.

"I told the queen your birthday is on June twenty-third," Julie said.

"Your birthday. Yes, we have some work to do before then," the queen said as she looked around the room. "We should begin the séance as soon as possible."

"All right then, let's gather around the table. Julie, would you mind lighting the candles?" Phoebe asked.

"Lia, come sit beside me," the queen said. She reached her hand forward and Lia politely took it and escorted the queen to the table.

Elliot pushed the queen's chair in for her and then sat in the chair beside Lia.

The queen leaned forward to look intently at Elliot and then at Lia. "You are life partners," she stated.

"Yes, we are," Elliot said. She reached her hand forward. "My name is Elliot Walker. Lia and I have been together for twenty-two years. I love her with everything that I am."

"Yes. I can see that in the way you look at her," the queen said. "You must be terrified to think of what might be if this curse cannot be broken."

"If Lia dies, I will have no reason to go on," Elliot said. Her voice was heavy with emotion.

"I knew of love that intense once, and was it not for my children, I would have felt the same way you do."

"I'm sorry to hear that," Lia said.

The queen squeezed her hand. "It was a long time ago, dear, but not a day goes by that I do not think of him."

The rest sat around the table with Lia and Elliot on the queen's right, followed by Julie, Marissa, Leslie and finally, Phoebe, who stood behind the chair to the left of the queen. Phoebe lit the dried herbs and carried the smoldering bowl slowly around the table.

"I summon a divine abundance of inspiration. May the truth we seek come to fruition in a form that benefits the highest good. May it be manifested into the form that expresses truth in the knowledge we seek."

She returned to her position beside the queen and gently placed the still smoking bowl of herbs on the table.

Phoebe sat and then looked at her friends. "Please join hands and close your eyes. Focus on the task before us, and please do not break the chain during the ceremony or we will risk losing our connection as we seek guidance from our guest."

Phoebe closed her eyes and spoke. "We, your humble servants, call forth the spirit of Marie Laveau. We seek your wisdom and guidance in this, our time of need. One among us is in grave danger and we seek your help to protect her before it is too late."

Silence fell upon the room for several moments.

Phoebe spoke again. "Marie, we respectfully ask..." Suddenly, Phoebe's head fell back onto her shoulders.

"I be here, my child."

All eyes opened.

Marie looked around the table, beginning with Leslie on her left. "You be da one my Phoebe be in love wid."

Leslie smiled. "I hope with all my heart that what you say is true."

Marie turned to Marissa and Julie. She grinned. "I knew you be here. You always be here."

Next, her gaze fell on Lia and Elliot. "Lia, my child. Marie do what I can to help. You be important to da world. You and El-ee-ot save da souls of my people. We must now fight to save your soul and beat da evil one."

Finally, Marie looked at Queen Thibodeaux. "Bettina, my queen. You be da powerful force to help my girls. I be helping in any way I can."

"You know who I am?" Queen Thibodeaux asked.

"I knows many tings. How it be dat Marie can help?"

Chapter 29

"Marie, it is obvious to me by looking at Lia's family tree that her lineage has been cursed. Nearly every descendant of Celeste died at the age of fifty-one," the queen said.

"Dat be truth," Marie said. "Da evil one come to me. She want Marie to do da curse. I do my best to change her heart, but it be black wid evil. Dey be no way to save her soul."

"So, I assume you didn't help her?" the queen asked.

"No. I not be helping her. She go to another. I not be knowing who," Marie said.

"Marie, we need your help. Surely you know that Lia will reach her fifty-first birthday on St. John's Eve. If this curse is allowed to run its course, she may die," Queen Thibodeaux said.

Marie sat up straight and looked directly at the queen. "I knowed she be da fifty and one soon, but on St. John's Eve? I not knowed dat." She looked at Lia. "You have da gift, Lia. You need to use da gift."

Lia looked back and forth between the queen and Marie. "Gift?" she asked.

Julie interrupted. "Lia, we will explain that later, right now we need information about the curse. Marie, we need to know what curse was used."

"Marie was not dere when da curse be placed," Marie said.

"But you said that the curse had to be lifted in the same way it was placed. That was more than one hundred and eighty years ago. How in the hell are we supposed to know how it was placed?" Julie asked. "We weren't there, but at least you lived during that time."

"Julie is correct, Marie," the queen said. "I understand you were not present when the curse was cast, but maybe you can help us to understand what types of death curses might have been used during that time."

"Dat be true. I not be dere," Marie said. "Da death curse be used to target da weakness of da victim."

"What do you mean by targeting the weakness of the victim," Elliot asked.

"When a death curse is cast, it begins by looking for a weak point and then it manipulates the person's behavior until that weakness is exploited and they die," Queen Thibodeaux explained. "For example, on Lia's family tree, I noted that her great grandfather, James Roberts, died in a fall at a construction site. It is possible he was a daredevil and careless at great heights. The curse would recognize that tendency and use it to send him to his death. Of course, if the curse fails to manipulate a person's weakness, other means become necessary to fulfill the curse. In James Robert's case, it is also possible that he was pushed—especially since this curse had a specific target date for execution."

"I wonder what Lia's weakness might be?" Marissa said.

Elliot looked at her friend. "Lia is one of the strongest people I know. I'm not sure she has a weakness that could be exploited."

"Everyone has a weakness, Elliot," the queen said.

"It be her heart. Lia be kind. Dat be her weakness." The voice came from Lia.

All eyes turned suddenly in her direction.

The queen's eyes opened wide. "And who do we have here?" she asked.

"I be Celeste. I be who da evil one hate da most. I be da reason the evil one kilt my babies, and dere babies, and dere babies, too."

Julie leaned forward. "Celeste, it is not your fault that this curse was cast. You had no choice. You were forced into the master's bed. This is not your fault."

"How be it dat one be so evil?"

Marie leaned forward. "Celeste, we not know why da mistress be so evil. We only know we mus' fight to save Lia. She be the last of your kin. We cannot be letting da mistress win."

"Da good dat be in Lia's heart must kill da hate dat be in da evil one. Lia have da power to stop da evil one," Celeste said.

"Yes, Lia has powers she isn't even aware of yet," the queen said. "But they will be useless if we cannot break the curse."

"Celeste know dat be so. Celeste be dere when da time come to defeat da evil one."

Lia's head fell back and then she returned to herself. "What happened?" she asked softly.

"Celeste made an appearance," Elliot replied. "Are you all right?"

Lia nodded. "I'm fine. Did she say anything useful?"

"She said that the goodness in your heart would be needed to defeat the blackness inside the mistress. She also implied that she would return when she was needed," Elliot explained.

"Ah, I don't want to point out the obvious, but we still don't know what curse was used—never mind how to break it," Marissa pointed out.

"You are right," the queen said. She turned to Marie. "Queen Laveau, your wisdom and experience are sorely needed here. You said the mistress approached you about placing the death curse. Did she specify which curse?"

"She did not," Marie said. "But da most common death curse dat be used need tings from da victim or tings dat represent da victim. Some attach deese tings to a poppet. It need deese tings to be buried. It need dirt from da graveyard, and it need da curse to be chanted wid hatred in da heart."

"Things from the victims," Julie said. "But there are victims spread out across more than one hundred and fifty years. How could the mistress have used things from victims that weren't even born yet?"

"Those questions will have to be answered before we can attempt a reversal," the queen said. "I will need to assemble the other queens and kings to ask their help. Phoebe, if Marie has allowed you to be aware through this visit, I would like you to attend the meeting with me."

She looked at all those seated at the table. "Maybe between all of us, and with the help of the general voodoo community, we can come close to the spell that was actually used and then figure out how to reverse it."

Queen Thibodeaux turned to Marie. "My queen, you have been a tremendous help. Thank you."

"I be dere if you need me. We must save my Lia. She be important to da world."

Queen Thibodeaux nodded. "I agree. If we fail in this effort, the evil one's power will be unstoppable—and Lia will die."

Phoebe suddenly returned to herself. She looked across the table at Lia, who was quietly crying. She broke the circle, went to Lia and wrapped her in her arms. "We will do everything in our power to stop this, Lia. I promise we will."

"I know you will," Lia said softly. She looked at everyone still seated around the table. Everyone fought back tears—including the queen. "I love you all so much," she said.

One by one, each of them rose from the table and wrapped their arms around the growing tableau of bodies. Each of them vowed their love and determination to fight the almost insurmountable task before them.

The queen was the first to break the huddle. "I must go. There is much that needs to be done. I will call a meeting with the Council of Kings and Queens tomorrow to solicit their help. If nothing else, there is strength in numbers."

Elliot helped the queen to her feet and held her hands close to her heart. "I can't thank you enough for everything you're doing to help," she said. "Lia is my life. I will do whatever it takes to save her, even if it means forfeiting my own life."

Queen Thibodeaux looked directly into Elliot's eyes. "Miss Lia is a lucky woman to have you in her life. Your love and support will be critical here. We will do everything humanly, and spiritually possible to turn this curse around, but you need to understand that we may fail."

"We can't fail," Elliot said. "We can't."

"We will see."

Marissa approached Elliot and the queen. "I'll drive you home," she said.

"I appreciate that," the queen said. "We were not formally introduced, but it is obvious to me that you are Julie's life partner."

"Yes. My name is Marissa Thompson."

The queen looked around the room. "I see so many people here who love one another. You are all truly blessed to have such an extended family."

"Sometimes the best families are chosen rather than born into," Marissa replied.

"Indeed. Please excuse me for a moment. I need to say goodbye to Phoebe."

Phoebe and Leslie met the queen halfway across the room. "I'm glad you didn't leave before I had a chance to thank you for everything you're doing," Phoebe said.

"We will talk more tomorrow after we have met with the council. In the meantime, we need to digest the information Queen Laveau provided in order to plan how to move forward."

"Yes. We will brainstorm among all of us as well," Phoebe said.

"Phoebe, if there is anything I can do from a genealogical perspective, please let me know," Leslie offered.

"Oh, I'm sorry. Queen Thibodeaux, this is Leslie Harden. He is my partner."

Leslie grinned from ear to ear in reaction to Phoebe's declaration.

The queen extended her hand and openly assessed the person before her, dressed in men's cargo pants, T-shirt and sandals. A hint of breasts and the outline of a sports bra could be seen through the material. "It is so very nice to meet you, Leslie. It warms my heart to see someone with your bravery of convictions in a world where hate is sometimes more prevalent than love. It is obvious to me how much you two care for one another."

"Thank you," Leslie said. He kissed the back of her hand. "I'm happy to have met you—and again, I have come to love these ladies very much, especially this one, and I will do anything I can to help."

"All right. I must speak with Lia before I go," the queen said.

"I'll get her for you." Leslie walked away and left Phoebe with the queen.

"Queen Thibodeaux, again, I can't thank you enough for helping us," Phoebe said. "What time will the meeting be with the kings and queen tomorrow?"

"Most of them have jobs or businesses to run, so our council meetings are normally in the evening around seven or eight. Does that work for you?"

"Shall I meet you at your shop?" Phoebe asked.

"Yes, that would be fine. We will walk to the meeting place together."

"I'm looking forward to working with you on this," Phoebe said.

"This evil must be stopped—for Lia's sake as well as for the sake of the whole community. Ah, here comes Lia."

Phoebe touched the queen's arm. "We'll be in touch."

Phoebe and Leslie walked away to give the queen an opportunity to speak to Lia before she left.

The queen opened her arms to Lia, who went into them willingly. After a long hug, she released her and held her hands. "I need you to stay strong, little one. We will do everything we can to stop this curse. I will pray to the gods that we are successful. In the meantime, know that as a child of St. John's Eve, you have special abilities at your disposal. You have very little time to become familiar with them but know that they are there if you need them."

"I don't understand. What abilities are you referring to?" Lia asked.

"You have empathy and the power of persuasion. I don't know if they will become necessary in this fight, or even if they will be useful, but know that they are there."

Lia looked down at their locked hands and then back into the queen's eyes. She couldn't stop the tears from coming. "I'm scared," she whispered.

The queen pulled Lia into her embrace once more. "I know you are, child. I am scared, too."

Chapter 30

Elliot stepped into the shower behind Lia the next morning and pulled her into her arms. Lia was nearly finished bathing but had yet to rinse the soap from her hair and body. The soap provided a slick surface that facilitated Elliot's sensual grind against Lia's backside.

Lia laid her head back and rested it on Elliot's shoulder while she savored the feel of her wife behind her. A sharp intake of breath, followed by a guttural moan escaped her throat when Elliot's hands snaked around to the front of her and gently squeezed her nipples.

"Oh, my God, that feels so good. Don't stop, El."

Elliot kissed Lia's neck and pinched Lia's soft brown nubs into hardened peaks.

Lia reached back and held Elliot's head in place as each nip on her neck sent waves of passion directly to her core.

Elliot moved around to the front of Lia and blocked the spray of water that had been hitting Lia's chest. She grabbed Lia neck just below her chin and devoured her mouth with an invasive kiss.

Lia wrapped her arms around Elliot's waist to prolong the kiss.

Elliot broke the kiss and traced the line of Lia's jaw with her tongue as she worked her way toward Lia's collarbone. She felt her head being held between Lia's hands and knew immediately where Lia wanted her to be.

Elliot lowered her face to feast on Lia's breast, inhaling one and then the other erect nipple in her mouth.

A deep growl emitted from deep within Lia. "More, Elliot. Please. I need to feel you. Make me feel alive."

Elliot paused slightly and looked into Lia's passion-filled eyes. She understood in that moment what Lia needed. She needed to block out all the heartbreaking thoughts and worries that had so dominated their lives during the past forty-eight hours.

Elliot put her hands on Lia's shoulders and roughly pushed her against the shower wall. She put one knee between Lia's legs and pressed herself against her while she grabbed Lia's face between her hands and aggressively devoured her mouth.

Taking this beautiful woman by force was not something she did often, but today the invitation was offered, and she was happy to oblige. Elliot wanted nothing more than to satisfy the primal hunger that had grown in her chest, but as a growl escaped her own throat, she realized that she could easily lose control.

Elliot pulled her face away from Lia's and looked into her eyes. She saw a collage of passion, love and trust. Her jaw clenched and she struggled with how much force to use with the one person she loved more than life itself.

Lia answered that question for her. "Fuck me," she demanded.

Lia seldom used profanity, but somehow those two little words reverberated at decibel strength in Elliot's ears. She was so turned on by Lia's boldness that if Lia had touched her in just the right way at that moment, she knew she would have no control of her own climax.

Elliot devoured Lia's mouth once more, but then rapidly moved onto her breast, nipping and biting until Lia indicated with a light touch to her face that she'd had enough.

Elliot followed her cue and dropped to her knees. She glanced once more into Lia's face and then pushed her lover's legs apart. She closed her eyes and inhaled Lia's essence before she sucked Lia's clit into her mouth and swirled the tip of her tongue around it.

Lia slammed her head into the wall of the shower and moaned loudly.

It wasn't long before Elliot realized Lia was on her toes and pressing her entire body into the shower wall. She quickly climbed to her feet and once again pressed her body against Lia's.

She looked into Lia's unfocused eyes. "We do this together," she growled.

Elliot took Lia's right hand and placed it between her own legs while she slipped her fingers into Lia's folds.

"Now!" Elliot growled and instinctively, each knew what to do.

A crescendo of passion filled the room as each woman brought the other to climax. The only thing keeping them upright was the collective weight of their bodies pressed against the wall of the shower.

Lia wept.

"Lia, I'm sorry, did I hurt you?" Elliot said, tenderly.

"No. That was so beautiful, my love."

"Why are you crying?"

"I refuse to give this up, Elliot. I refuse to give in to the blackness of her heart. I will not let her destroy what we have. I will not let her destroy me."

It was several minutes before they were recovered enough to finish their showers and get dressed for work.

***

Officer Randy Rocque checked in with the New Orleans police dispatcher after his first round of surveillance that morning. "Hey, beautiful," he said.

Susan looked around. "Randy, don't say that to me at work. What if someone hears you?" she replied in hushed tones.

"They would think I'm the luckiest guy in NOLA to have such a beautiful girlfriend," he said.

Susan grinned. "You're such a charmer!"

"Yup! You can call me Prince Charming," Randy joked.

Susan rolled her eyes. "There's no conceit in your family! You've got it all!"

Randy laughed. He leaned over the desk. "Does dispatch have anything that I need to be aware of?" he asked.

"Oh, yeah." Susan picked up the dispatch log and handed it to Randy. "This one came in at shift change. I sent Anderson out on it."

He looked at the log and then back at her with raised eyebrows. "Zombies?" he said.

Susan took the log back. "That's what the caller reported. Apparently, someone broke into their house in the wee hours of the morning and according to the caller, this person looked like they were in a trance."

"Only in New Orleans," Randy said. "St. John's Eve is just a week away. I'm sure it's just someone jumping the gun early. I've seen my share of zombie-like creatures roaming the streets after too much to drink."

"Or too many drugs," Susan added.

"That, too," Randy agreed. He stared at the log on Susan's desk for a few more minutes.

Revenants! Ask about the bokors.

"Hey, I'm wondering if we should be proactively checking out the bokors in the area—you know, to be better prepared for next week's celebrations," Randy said.

"Bokors? What are bokors?" Susan asked.

"Hold on a sec and I'll tell you." Randy pulled his phone out of his pocket and selected the internet provider logo. He typed the word *bokor* in the search bar and waited for a response.

"Okay, here it is. Bokors are associated with the creation of zombies by using a brew containing the poison extracted from puffer fish. The potion causes the drinker to appear as though they were dead. The person is alive, but they can't control what they say or do and can be easily manipulated by suggestions."

"So, bokors are zombie-like people who willingly take poison and make themselves susceptible to mind control?" Susan asked.

"Actually, the bokors are the ones who create and control the zombie. They are not zombies themselves."

"Who in their right minds would intentionally ingest poison?" Susan asked.

"Someone who wants a good high, I suspect. Anyway, with the St. John's Eve celebration coming up, I thought it might be a good idea to identify the more prominent bokors and to keep an eye on them."

"That's not a bad idea. Let me do some research for you and I'll see if I can come up with a few names," Susan said.

Randy leaned over the counter and kissed her quickly on the lips. "Thank you."

"Now, get out of here before we get caught," Susan said.

***

Randy double-parked his patrol car on the street in front of Phoebe's shop. He turned his flashers on and then climbed out of the car and approached the front door. He glanced inside the window and saw both Phoebe and Julie assisting customers.

Randy grabbed the doorknob and pushed. The door did not open. He frowned and tried again. Still the door did not open. "What the hell?" he said under his breath.

There is a protection spell on the shop. You need to be invited in. Knock on the window.

Randy leaned in close to the window and shaded his eyes with one hand. He could clearly see his friends inside. He knocked on the window and caught Julie's attention.

"Oh, wow! Randy is here," Julie said out loud. She motioned for him to come in.

Randy raised his hands to the sides and then pointed to the door.

Julie's eyebrows raised in surprise. She lifted one finger up in a silent plea for him to be patient, and then finished checking out her customer, whom she then escorted to the door.

The door opened easily for her.

"Thank you for coming," she said to her customer as Randy stepped aside to allow them to exit the store.

"Come in," Julie said.

Randy stepped over the threshold into the store. "Thanks. I don't know why the door wouldn't open for me," he said. "It must have been stuck on something."

Randy and Julie walked to the back of the store together.

"What brings you here this morning?" Julie asked.

"I have an odd request," Randy said.

"Well, you've come to the right place. What in this store *isn't* odd?" Julie joked.

"I'm actually looking for information."

"What do you need?" Julie asked.

By this time, Phoebe had finished with her customer and was drawn to the conversation between her two friends.

"I'm looking for a place where I can find tetrodotoxin and datura stramonium," he said.

Phoebe's head snapped back. "Why on earth would you need those substances?" she asked.

"What are they?" Julie said.

"They are poisons and deliriant drugs that are used in mind-control potions," Phoebe explained.

Julie looked at Randy. "Seriously? I'm with Phoebe. Why would you be looking for stuff like that?"

"Susan had an odd call on dispatch early this morning. The woman who called said there was a zombie-like person breaking into her house on Treme. The investigating officer said the person seemed high on drugs or something. Despite the zombie craze these days, I know they are not real, but a little trip down Internet Lane led me to something called bokors. I've never heard of them before. Are they a real thing?"

"Bokors are absolutely real although they're not as prevalent now as they used to be," Phoebe explained. "They lie pretty low and tend to resurface mostly at events like St. John's Eve next week. They are believed to be witches who practice both good and evil voodoo."

"The article said the bokors drug people with these substances to simulate zombie-like behavior. If I can find where these substances are sold, I should also be able to find the bokors who purchase them."

"I believe those substances are strictly controlled by the Center for Disease Control," Phoebe suggested. "A small amount of tetrodotoxin could paralyze a person's autonomic nervous system in a matter of minutes. Datura stramonium is a delirium drug that comes from the nightshade family. Both of these substances can be toxic and could lead to death. A combination of both substances in the right amounts would almost certainly be lethal. Bokors have been known to use them to create these zombie creatures, which the voodoo community calls revenants, but possessing them would most likely mean jail time. I have no idea where you might find them illegally, if that's what you're looking for. If you're looking for legal sources, I recommend going to the CDC."

Randy nodded. "That's a good idea. Thanks."

Randy turned to leave, but then stopped. "Oh, I wanted to offer my help to work on the sheetrock. I'm pretty handy with mud. Have Marissa give me a call when you're ready to do that."

"Thank you, Randy. I was going to suggest to the girls that we all get together this evening to chat about yesterday's séance. If we decide do work on the walls after that, we'll give you a call."

"Séance?" he asked.

"Yes. We got together to brainstorm about how to break this curse Lia is under."

"Lia is under a curse?" he asked.

"Her whole family has been—all the way back to Ethan. Each one of them has died on their fifty-first birthdays," Julie explained.

"Now, who would do a thing like that?" Randy asked.

"The mistress."

You must stop them!

Randy grabbed his head.

"Are you okay?" Julie asked.

"Yeah. I'll be fine. It was just a flash of pain in my temple. It's gone now." He glanced at his watch. "I need to get back to the station. I'll have my guys check out the CDC for those substances. Thanks for the advice."

"You're welcome," Phoebe said.

"Maybe I'll see you later, then."

"Bye, Randy," Julie said. She watched him walk to the front of the store and easily pull the door open. He closed the door behind him, waved to them through the window and headed back to his car.

"Well, that's odd," Julie said.

"What's that?" Phoebe asked.

"He couldn't open the door to come in but had no problem opening it to go out."

Phoebe's eyes opened wide. "He couldn't open the door to come in?"

"No. I had to open it for him."

Phoebe walked to the front of the store and opened the door. She felt no resistance. She stepped outside onto the sidewalk, closed the door behind her and inspected the sill for anything that might interfere with it opening. She found nothing, so she turned the knob and gently pushed on the door. It swung open easily. As a final check, she opened and closed the door a few times to see if the locking mechanism on the knob might have caught. Again, with each try, the door opened easily.

There's only one other reason I can think of for why he might have trouble getting in, but then, there was nothing suspicious about his behavior, she thought.

***

Marissa, Julie, Lia and Elliot met for dinner at a local steakhouse after work. They sat in a secluded booth at the back of the restaurant and placed their food and drink orders. Julie reached for Lia's hands once the waiter walked away from their table.

"How are you feeling?" Julie asked.

"I've been better. Fear of the unknown is very unsettling," Lia said.

"You got that right," Elliot added. "I don't feel like I can relax for even a moment. No matter how busy you try to keep yourself, your thoughts always come back to the curse."

"I'm worried that we'll get this wrong," Marissa said. "I mean, if what Marie said was true, we might need the exact curse, and even then, we need to figure out how to reverse it."

"So, let's talk about the curse," Julie said. "Marie said death curses cast back when the mistress was alive involved things from the victims and graveyard dirt and recitations of hatred when it was buried."

Lia removed her hands from Julie's and rubbed her face. "This feels so impossible," she said. "Julie, you were right when you pointed out the victims span more than one hundred and fifty years. For the curse to work for that amount of time, the items used would have to apply to everyone. I can't imagine how that could be when most of them didn't even exist at the time the curse was placed."

"Phoebe and Queen Thibodeaux are meeting with the Council of Kings and Queens tonight. I hope they can come up with something more than we have," Elliot said.

"Life was so much simpler when all we had to contend with were late subway trains," Lia said. "Sometimes I wish we had never moved to New Orleans."

Elliot took Lia's hand and kissed her knuckles. "Life *was* simpler, but it was not as good. Moving to NOLA gave our relationship the new start it needed. I don't regret that one bit."

Lia forced a smile onto her face. "I don't regret that either, love."

"I don't think we can argue with the genealogy Leslie put together for you. The historical records support either a huge coincidence that everyone in your blood line died on their fifty-first birthday, or the fact that this curse is real," Marissa said. "I tend to believe this is no coincidence."

"Phoebe is most likely right. If you had stayed in New York, some oddball accident may have taken you out on your fifty-first birthday, and we would have never been the wiser for it—and, we wouldn't have had a chance to prevent it," Julie pointed out. "I know this is no fun to live through, but we *do* have a chance to stop it. We just need to figure out how."

Lia looked at her digital watch. "Today is Wednesday and my birthday is next Wednesday. We have seven days. That's not much time when we are starting with little to no information that makes sense."

Julie took both Elliot and Lia's hands. "But we have one another, and we have Phoebe and Leslie. And we have Marie and Queen Thibodeaux to help as well. I have faith in *us*. We can beat this, Lia. I know we can."

***

"Welcome, my brothers and sisters. I would like to introduce you to Phoebe Frost. Some of you may know of her through her reputation as a medium in the voodoo community. Phoebe and I have asked you here to seek your help. We have an urgent matter to deal with—a matter of life and death.

"Lia Purvis is one of the people responsible for releasing the souls of our departed brothers and sisters. The ones who fell victim to the vile wickedness of the evil one. The ones she tortured, mutilated and killed in the attic of her home at eleven forty Rue Royale in the eighteen-thirties—back when our beautiful people of color were little more than property and forced to serve the elite at the end of a whip.

"You are all aware of this atrocity that happened in our community so long ago. For many decades, the ghosts of our brothers and sisters walked the halls of that great mansion, seeking for a way to go home to their loved ones. Lia gave them the release they so desperately sought.

"Lia is a direct descendant of the slave woman Celeste Bourdeau, who was killed by this evil mistress. Lia now needs our help.

"The evil one cursed the family of Celeste Bourdeau more than one hundred and eighty years ago. Every one of her descendants has died at the age of fifty and one, for that was the age of her master when Celeste was violated and impregnated with a girl child, who also died at the mistress' hands when she was only eight years old."

A horrified moan rose from the collective as they listened to the atrocities that had happened to little Lia at the hands of the mistress.

"I could go into more detail about the horrific abuse these slaves endured at the hands of the master and mistress, but that would only serve to stoke your anger rather than focus your energy on the task that lies before us.

"Lia Purvis is the last in Celeste's lineage. She is the final descendant in Celeste's line that could fall victim to the curse placed on the family by that evil monster, and she will die within a matter of days, as she turns fifty and one on St. John's Eve."

A chorus of no's rose from the group.

The queen raised her hand to silence the room.

"Last night, I attended a séance with the infamous queen, Marie Laveau. She recommended that we band together, as there is indeed strength in numbers. We need to break this curse. We must also banish the evil one forever. Both of these tasks will be difficult—if they are even possible at all. We have limited time, and the life of Lia Purvis hangs in the balance."

Queen Thibodeaux looked at the assembly. "Please indicate who among you are willing to help."

One by one, every queen and king in the room rose to their feet and raised a fist in solidarity.

Queen Thibodeaux nodded. "We have much to do and much to prepare. We will only have one chance to rid the world of this evil and to save the life of Lia Purvis. We may fail, but we must try.

"We do not know what curse was cast by this evil mistress. We know only that it has affected generations of Lia Purvis' family, and if we do not break it by St. John's Eve, it will claim another victim. We will collectively need to determine what the curse was and how it was cast. That knowledge will improve our chances of breaking it. This effort will require intense research and effort from all of you.

"Phoebe and I will make ourselves available this evening to talk with each of you and to solicit and share ideas. Remember, we have two challenges before us—break the curse that threatens the life of Lia Purvis and banish the evil one forever.

"Our first priority must focus on breaking the curse, for failure to do so will result in the death of Lia Purvis seven days from now. Banishment of the evil one will be our second priority but let me be clear—we must accomplish both.

"Thank you, my brothers and sisters. Please come forward now with your thoughts and ideas."

Chapter 31

Lia walked into the kitchen the next morning to find Julie making eggs Benedict and home fries. She approached her friend and kissed her on the cheek. "I'm going to miss your amazing breakfasts when you and Marissa move," she said.

"C'mere, you." Julie opened her arms and pulled Lia in for a long, warm hug. "We're going to miss you and Elliot, too. This has been an amazing time together."

Lia clung to her friend and fought to hold back tears. She sniffed loudly.

Julie released her and held her at arm's length. "Hey. What's all this about?" she asked.

Lia wiped a tear away. "This curse is always at the back of my mind. You know? The scientific part of my brain wants to just pooh-pooh the whole thing off, but we have seen so much and have lived through so many things in this house that I would have not thought possible before we moved here, that my intuition tells me not to ignore it."

Julie rubbed her arm. "We'll get to the bottom of this, Lia. I refuse to admit defeat before we even try. We all need to be strong."

Lia went into Julie's arms once more. "I know. I'm trying, but it's really hard sometimes."

Lia broke the hug and went to make herself a cup of coffee while Julie returned to stirring the hollandaise sauce for the eggs.

"Maybe working on the house today will help to take your mind off things," Julie said. "I'm glad the four of us decided to take the rest of the week off."

"You're right. Staying busy should help my state of mind— all of ours, in fact. We're on hold until we come up with a plan to break this curse. I'm afraid we'll have to rely on the voodoo community to help us with that."

"That's key here, Lia. I know your first instinct is to look at this clinically, but sometimes you have to suspend disbelief to affect real change. I grew up in the voodoo community. They are a deeply caring and compassionate group of people, and they will do everything they can to help. A good number of them are people of color and the mistress is notorious for what she did to her slaves. The fact that you and Elliot lived through so much and ultimately freed their trapped souls earned you infinite respect and support from the black community."

"Elliot and I were surprised by the number of people who attended Celeste and Little Lia's funerals after we found their bones. It was so long ago that they died."

"They came to respect their memories and their newly found freedom. You became part of the community when you defeated the mistress, Lia. We all did, in fact," Julie said.

Lia sipped her coffee. "It's too bad she didn't remain defeated. I worry about where she is right now."

Julie turned the heat off on the burner and moved the saucepan to the back of the stovetop. "I know. I've been wondering how we are going to banish her if we can't find her," Julie said.

"I don't think we'll have a problem finding her, Jules. My guess is that all the tea in China couldn't keep her away from the St. John's Eve ceremonies. I'm more concerned about the damage she will do between now and then. Elliot is worried she might jump the gun and just kill me before the ceremony, but if she's as evil as it seems she was when she was alive, I can't imagine she wouldn't want to see the curse through to the end."

"I tend to agree with you, Lia, but we still need to be cautious and not venture out alone until this is all over," Julie said.

"I agree."

Just then, the doorbell rang in the first-floor entry.

Lia's head snapped up. "Who could that be so early in the morning?"

"Oh, I invited Phoebe and Leslie to breakfast this morning so we can talk about the meeting with the kings and queens last night," Julie said.

Lia looked down at herself. "Well, I guess I should get out of my pajamas then."

"They aren't going to mind. I still have mine on.

Lia put her coffee cup on the island. "Okay, then. I'll go let them in."

***

Lia scurried down the stairs and opened the ornate front door. Phoebe and Leslie stood on the sidewalk, on the other side of the iron gate. They were both dressed for work—Phoebe in her mystic medium attire and makeup, and Leslie in his riverboat gambler outfit. The eccentric appearance of her friends made her smile.

"You know, I really need to get you a key to this house," Lia said while she unlocked the gate. She let them into the vestibule and hugged each one as they entered. "Good morning. Go on inside while I relock the gate."

Leslie was awestruck the moment he stepped inside. "Oh, my God. I have always wanted to see what this house looks like on the inside. There is such history and notoriety here."

"Unfortunately, the history is not all good. How about we give you a full tour, top to bottom after breakfast?" Lia suggested.

"Really? I would love that," Leslie replied.

"It's a date then. Phoebe, why don't you take Leslie to the kitchen while I go get my lazy wife moving. She was still in bed as of five minutes ago. Julie is there working on one of her fabulous breakfast creations. Phoebs, you know where everything is. Help yourself to coffee."

Lia parted ways with her friends on the second story landing and headed up one more floor to their bedroom. She pushed her bedroom door open and found Elliot still asleep. She tiptoed to the side of the bed and slowly lay down beside her. Propped up on one elbow, she leaned in and placed a light kiss on Elliot's lips.

Elliot smiled, but her eyes remained closed.

Lia kissed her again.

Elliot moaned. "Celeste. I've missed you so much. Kiss me again."

"Celeste?" Lia exclaimed loudly.

Elliot's eyes flew open. "Gotcha!"

Lia picked up a pillow and beat Elliot with it. "You snake!" Lia said.

Elliot grabbed Lia by the waist, pulled her down onto the bed and straddled her with her hands trapped on the bed.

"Snake?" she said. "I'll show you snake." Elliot kissed her long and hard.

"Hmm. I like you as a snake," Lia purred.

"How about I slither inside of you?" Elliot wiggled her eyebrows up and down.

"I would love that, but we have company," Lia said.

"Marissa and Julie are not company. They live here."

"Yes, but Phoebe and Leslie do not. They are in the kitchen with Julie right now."

Elliot sat up. "Phoebe and Leslie are here?"

"Yes. Julie invited them for breakfast to talk about the meeting with the kings and queens," Lia said.

"Okay. Well, I guess that we should get out of bed and join them," Elliot suggested.

Lia smiled. "Yes. That might be a good idea."

***

Marissa had already joined Julie, Phoebe and Leslie in the kitchen by the time Lia and Elliot make an appearance. Elliot made the rounds for hugs and then made herself a coffee.

"Elliot, this is an amazing home," Leslie said excitedly.

"I've promised Leslie a tour after breakfast," Lia said.

"Sure. No problem," Elliot replied. "It's a big house. It'll take some time to go through it. I hope you don't have any appointments this morning."

"None until this afternoon, so I'm free and clear for a thorough tour," Leslie said.

"Julie and I will probably head to the house after breakfast to get started," Marissa said.

Leslie looked at Marissa. "I'm sorry. Am I interfering with plans you already have? We can do the tour later."

"No. It's not a problem," Marissa said. "Julie wants to take a load of stuff when we go this morning, so dealing with that will keep us busy until Lia and Elliot can join us."

"So, the four of you are off from work today?" Phoebe asked.

"We're actually off through the weekend," Lia said. "We thought it might be a good way to keep our minds off things while the kings and queens plan our approach to solving this problem we're facing."

"Speaking of the kings and queens, there was unanimous support from the community at the meeting," Phoebe said. "The energy in the room was amazing."

"Did they have any ideas?" Lia asked.

Julie interrupted Phoebe and Lia. "Okay, before we get too far into this discussion, how about we divide and conquer to get breakfast on the table? The ham and home fries are cooked, and the hollandaise sauce is ready. All I need to do is poach the eggs. Oh, and the English muffins need to be toasted."

"Of course!" Lia said.

"I burn water, so I'll do something harmless like set the table if you point me to the dishes," Leslie said.

"I'll do coffee," Elliot piped in.

"I'll toast the muffins," Phoebe volunteered.

"Let's do an assembly line with Phoebe on muffins and ham slices, Julie on eggs, Marissa on sauce and me on home fries," Lia suggested.

Marissa chuckled. "Lia, you should have been an engineer instead of a research scientist."

***

"Wow, this is an amazing breakfast. Home cooking is a rarity for me. I wasn't kidding when I said I burn water," Leslie said. "Thank you for breakfast, Julie."

"Julie is the reason I'm getting fat," Marissa said.

"Don't put that one on me, Mar!" Julie objected.

Phoebe covered Leslie's hand with her own. "It's a good thing I know how to cook."

"Lia keeps telling Julie she's not going to allow them to move out because she loves her cooking," Elliot said.

"You and Marissa are really good grill masters," Lia commented.

"You're an amazing cook yourself, Lia," Julie said.

"Yeah, yeah, yeah. I now conclude this meeting of the mutual admiration society," Lia declared jokingly.

"So, let's get back to the discussion about the meeting. I know it was just the first one, but were there any good ideas brought up?" Elliot asked.

"Like I said, the support was unanimous. Queen Thibodeaux kicked off the meeting by reminding the assembly of what happened in this house and about how the souls were released. The whole atmosphere felt like one of those wonderful black revival meetings. The queen and I made ourselves available at the end of the meeting to discuss ideas that came out during the meeting."

"Can you share any of them with us?" Lia asked.

"The ideas focused mainly on how to organize," Phoebe replied. "There were at least a dozen queens and kings, as well as several of their followers at the meeting. Queen Thibodeaux made it clear that we needed to accomplish two goals— breaking the curse *and* banishing the mistress, so my guess is that the assembly will be divided in two teams."

"How powerful are these kings and queens?" Elliot asked. "I mean, for the lack of a better word, they are the *lesser* queens and kings, right?"

"Yes. Queen Thibodeaux is widely accepted as the reigning queen, but each of the lesser kings and queens is powerful in their own right and they all have relatively large followings. The sheer numbers of followers makes them even more powerful. Anyway, the queen has called for meetings every day for the next few days to solidify plans and ideas. I suspect the final plan will be executed on St. John's Eve on the Bayou St. John, since there will literally be hundreds of people there, if not a thousand or more."

"Was there any discussion about what curse we might be dealing with?" Marissa asked.

"Not much. The queen challenged the group to research curse types used in the eighteen-thirties in an attempt to narrow it down to the most likely one, but there was very little speculation at the meeting. I'm hopeful that all of us together will be able to identify what curse might have been used. That will be critical to breaking this thing."

Lia inhaled deeply and reached for Phoebe's hand. "I can't thank you enough for all this effort, Phoebe."

Phoebe took both of Lia's hands in hers. "Lia, losing you would be like losing a part of ourselves."

She looked around the kitchen island. "I feel very strongly that all of us are destined to travel through several lifetimes together. We are all part of a whole. Losing any one of us before our time upsets the balance of all our lives. I, for one, am not ready for that fulcrum to shift, and I will do whatever it takes to break this curse and stop the mistress from ever bringing harm to you again."

Try as she might, Lia couldn't stop the tears from flowing down her cheeks. She looked at her friends sitting around the island. "I love everyone so much. How was I so lucky to be blessed with such a wonderful family?"

"We are all blessed to have one another, Lia," Julie said.

"Yes, we are," Lia said.

"Me, too?" Leslie asked.

"You, too, love. You, too," Lia replied.

***

Lia, Elliot, Phoebe and Leslie stood in the foyer facing the central staircase.

"Okay, we'll start on the ground floor," Elliot said. "This is where you came into the house this morning, so you are familiar with the entry way. "To the left is one of four apartments in this house."

The four women walked into what appeared to be a kitchen area, with a larger room filling the front corner of Royal Street and Governor Nichols Street, and a smaller back bedroom with

Ground Floor Layout – Street Level Entry

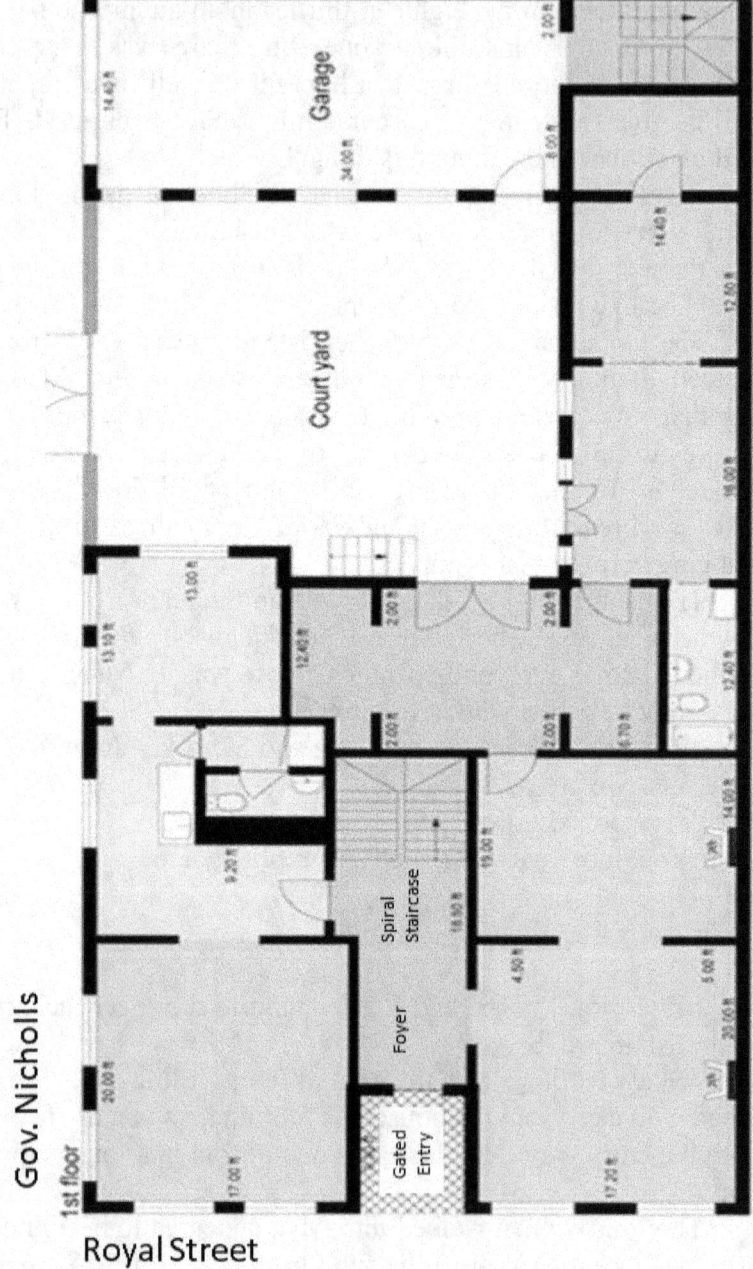

a window that overlooked the courtyard. The bathroom was located behind the kitchen.

"You said there were four apartments in this house?" Leslie asked. "Why so many?"

"The house has changed hands many times during the past one hundred and eighty years. Some of the previous owners turned the property into apartment units. You'll see as we go through the house that there are nine bathrooms and five kitchens, including the kitchen in the main house," Elliot explained.

"What a pity to divide such a grand house into units like that," Leslie remarked.

"I agree, although with more than ten thousand feet of living space, it was probably a profitable move," Lia pointed out.

"I suppose," Leslie said.

"Okay, going back into the foyer, we'll be going to go into the other room that borders Royal Street," Elliot said.

They walked through the foyer and into a room that was as large as the front room of the apartment they had just come from. Marissa and Julie were in this room searching through their belongings for boxes they wished to transport to the Saint Ann Street property that morning.

"Hey, guys," Marissa said.

"Wow, you two have a lot of stuff," Leslie commented.

"This is only half of it. The next room is full, too," Marissa replied. "Can you believe all this fit into a two-bedroom condo in New York City?"

"Let me know when you're ready to move everything. I'd be happy to help," Leslie offered.

Marissa fist-bumped with Leslie. "Thanks. We'll take you up on that."

Julie placed a box on the growing pile they had isolated on one side of the room.

"Be careful not to take too much, love. There's only so much room in the car for this trip," Marissa said.

"Cleaning supplies," Julie said. "Before we take too much more, we need to clean up the residue already there from taking down that wall," Julie replied.

"Okay. Follow me," Elliot said. "Beyond the second room filled with Marissa and Julie's stuff is another foyer that leads both to the courtyard and to the second apartment on this level."

Phoebe froze when they stepped inside the larger room of the second apartment. She grabbed Leslie's arm for support.

"Are you all right, Phoebe?" Leslie said.

Phoebe turned her translucent eyes in his direction. "I feel a heaviness in this part of the house," she said.

Lia approached Phoebe and rubbed her back. "There shouldn't be any more trapped souls in here, Phoebe," she said softly.

"Not trapped. Just residual energy." She opened the French doors to the courtyard and stepped out. She looked up at the building and reached her hand forward. "Come join me."

Leslie, Lia and Elliot did as they were asked and all four stood and looked at the three stories in front of them. There were covered porches on each level that wrapped around to the back of the main house.

"This part of the house is an extension attached to the primary living area. I believe these were slave quarters," Phoebe said. "Look at all three stories. The porches provide access to all three levels without having to go inside the house. This is how the slaves could have moved through the house without being visible to guests."

"Wow, that never occurred to me before," Lia said. "She looked at Phoebe. "The third level is part of our bedroom suite. We always thought it was originally a nursery."

"It may have served as a nursery at some point but judging by the isolated apartments on the other two levels, I would venture to guess that it started out as slave quarters," Phoebe explained.

Elliot and Leslie returned to the lower-level apartment to finish the tour while Lia stayed in the courtyard with Phoebe.

"Are you okay, Phoebs?" Lia asked.

"I'm fine. The residual energy is still intense, even after all these years. There is a lot of painful history in these walls."

Elliot and Leslie joined them in the courtyard.

"We are going to end the tour on the second story, so let's go through the garage and take the back staircase to the third level and work our way down," Elliot suggested.

The women entered the garage through a courtyard door. Before entering the staircase at the back of the room, Elliot pointed to a cement cover under the workbench on the back wall. "This is where we found little Lia's bones."

"No shit?" Leslie exclaimed.

"No shit," Elliot confirmed.

They emerged on their third level porch at the back corner of the property. Elliot stopped in front of a door that was just a few feet away from the back stairway.

Lia pressed herself against the wall facing the doorway. "I'll wait here while you check it out," she said.

Phoebe narrowed her eyes at Lia.

"It's where Celeste was found. It creeps me out," Lia said. "I only go in there when I have to."

"I'm sorry, love. We can skip this if you'd like," Elliot offered.

"No. Go ahead. I'll just wait here," Lia repeated.

Elliot, Leslie and Phoebe entered a small kitchen and through another door into a very large room.

"We believe this is where the female slaves lived," Elliot said. "That wardrobe in the corner is where we found Celeste's bones."

"This is really creepy," Leslie said.

"Yes. Everything about this house in the first three months we lived here was creepy," Elliot explained. "Let's move on."

The trio rejoined Lia outside and moved down the length of the porch to the balcony overlooking the courtyard. Phoebe stood at the railing and closed her eyes. "This is where Chloe appeared to me a while ago."

"That must have been an emotional experience for you," Leslie said.

"It was."

He pointed to a large rectangular area of the courtyard that appeared to have been recently repaired. "What happened there?" he asked.

"That is where the slaves were buried," Lia explained.

3rd Floor Layout – Bedroom Area

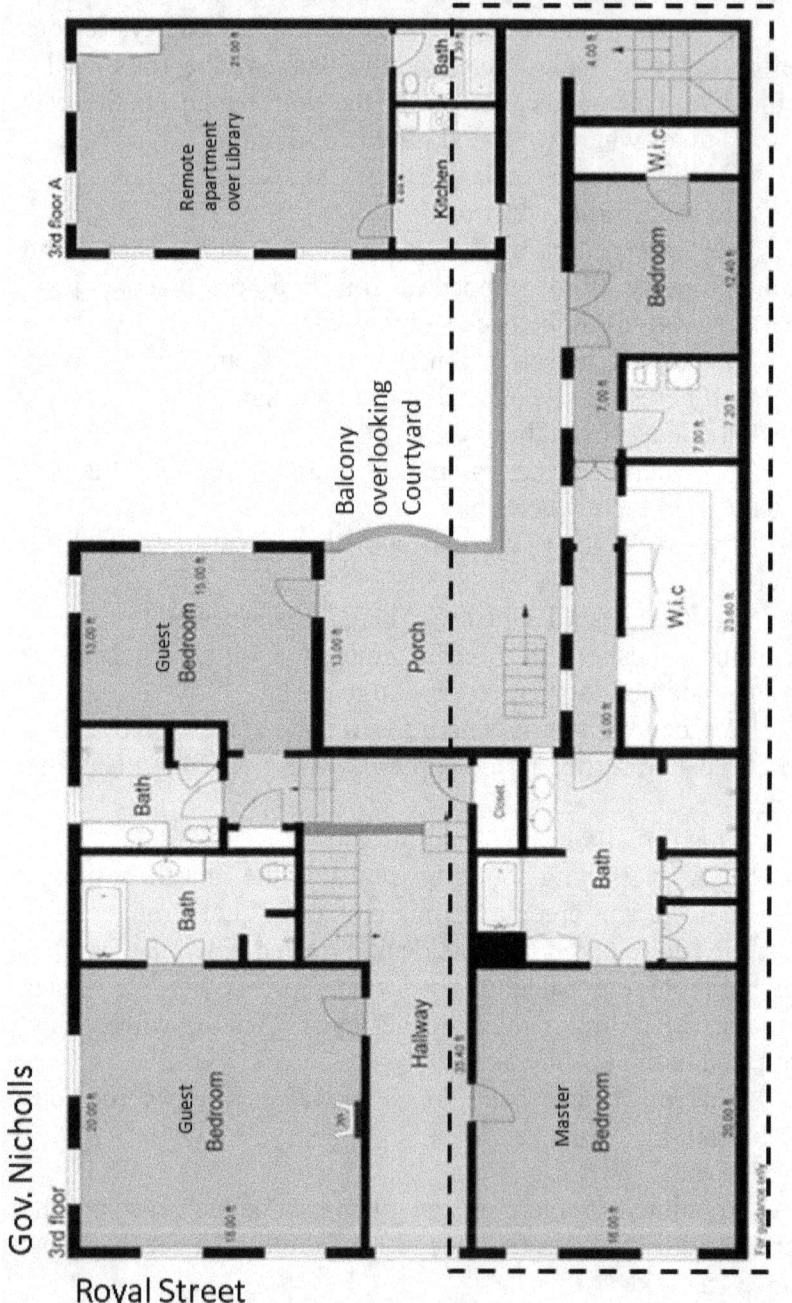

3rd Floor Layout – Prior to 1834 fire

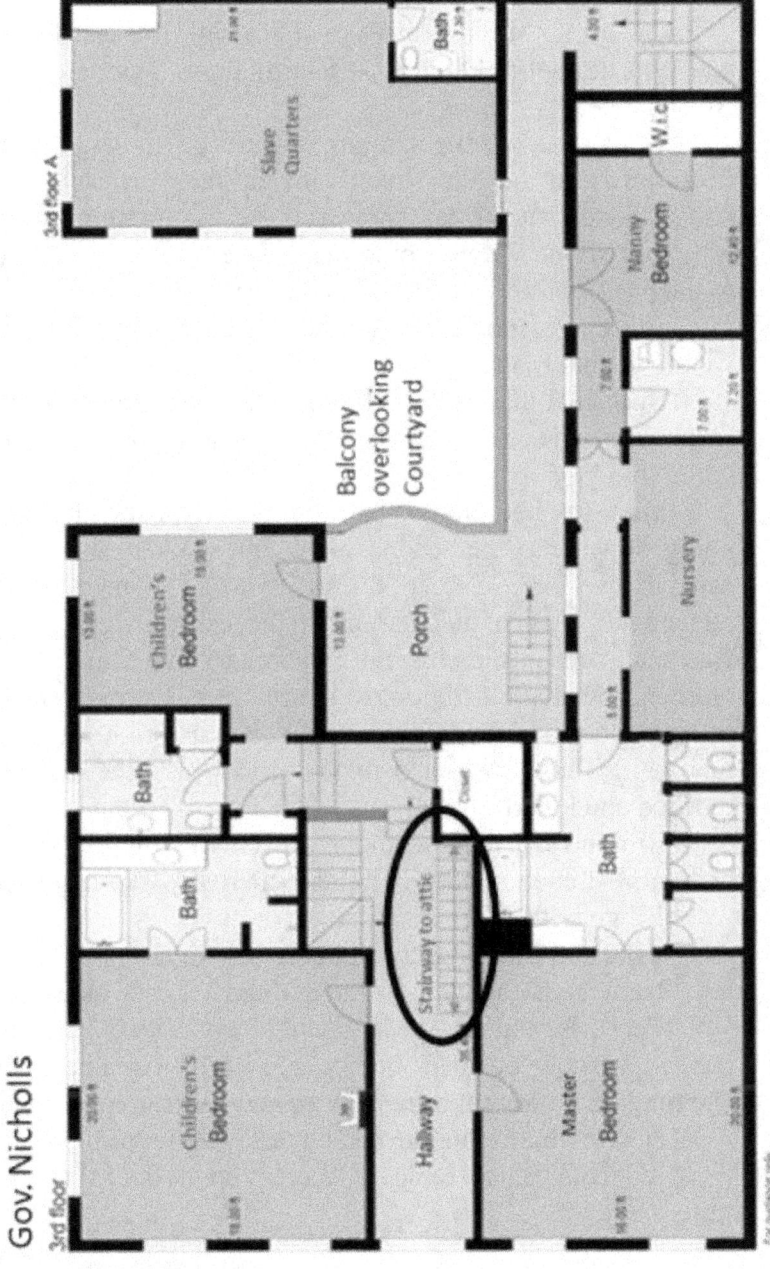

"Jesus," Leslie said.

"This is the doorway to my bedroom," Phoebe said. "It's where I stayed when I was here last."

The group walked through the small courtyard bedroom and into the hall leading to the third floor. They stood facing Royal Street.

"Marissa and Julie's room is there on the right, and our bedroom is on the left. I won't invade their privacy by taking you in there, but we can show you the master suite, which, as Lia pointed out, extends over the apartment below, all the way to the back stairway that leads to the garage."

"Elliot, why don't you tell them about the attic entry before we move on," Lia suggested. "It will save a trip back later."

"Sheesh, I almost forgot about the most important part of this house—the attic—which you'll be happy to hear we are *not* going into."

Elliot stopped in the hallway just opposite the stairway going down into the second level. She looked at the ceiling, causing everyone else to do so as well. "Can you see the rectangular shaped indentation in the ceiling right along this wall that stops at the closet in the corner? We found an old set of blueprints that dated prior to the fire that destroyed this house in eighteen-thirty-four. It showed a staircase right here against this wall. Those stairs led to the attic where the slaves were tortured and killed."

"I'm sorry, I need to move on. I will wait for you in the bedroom," Phoebe said. "The energy here is overwhelming."

"I'll go with you," Lia said.

Leslie and Elliot remained in the hallway.

"Is there another way to get up there?" Leslie asked.

"There is, but it's been boarded up. There's nothing up there right now but bad memories," Elliot explained, "But at one time, there were torture devices and surgical implements."

"How barbaric can one person be?" Leslie said.

"Indeed," Elliot replied. "Let's move on to the master suite."

Elliot led her entourage through the bedroom and bathroom, past a large walk-in closet and finally through another, smaller bedroom, complete with its own bathroom.

"The older blueprints we found indicated this area was the nursery and nanny quarters, but I'm inclined to agree with Phoebe. The original purpose was most likely slave quarters." Lia said.

The group followed Elliot through a door in the smaller bedroom that led to the porch, directly across from the small apartment where Celeste's bones had been found.

"Follow me. We'll go down one more level to the second floor," Elliot said.

"It is amazing to me how large this house is," Leslie commented while they descended the stairs.

"It certainly is large. Too large for us, for sure," Lia said. "But we felt compelled to purchase it. Correction—*I* felt compelled to purchase it," she added. "It wasn't until later that we learned I was a descendant of Celeste."

"Okay. We are now on the second floor. Right in front of us is the library. This room is a real treat, so I'm going to save it for last," Elliot said.

The group walked partway down the porch and stepped into the fourth apartment, complete with a bedroom, living room galley kitchen and bathroom. "This apartment, and the one above the library, are the only two that can only be accessed from the outside," Elliot pointed out. "We are now going back into the kitchen of the main house where we had breakfast this morning."

For the next ten minutes, the friends walked around the kitchen, dining room and both the formal and informal living rooms that made up the primary living areas on the second floor.

"I have learned that it is not unusual for the primary living area to be on the second floor," Leslie said. "I understand that is to avoid heavy damage in the event of a flood."

"Yes, that's what the folks at the Chamber of Commerce said when we found the blueprints," Lia agreed.

2nd Floor Layout – Main Living Area

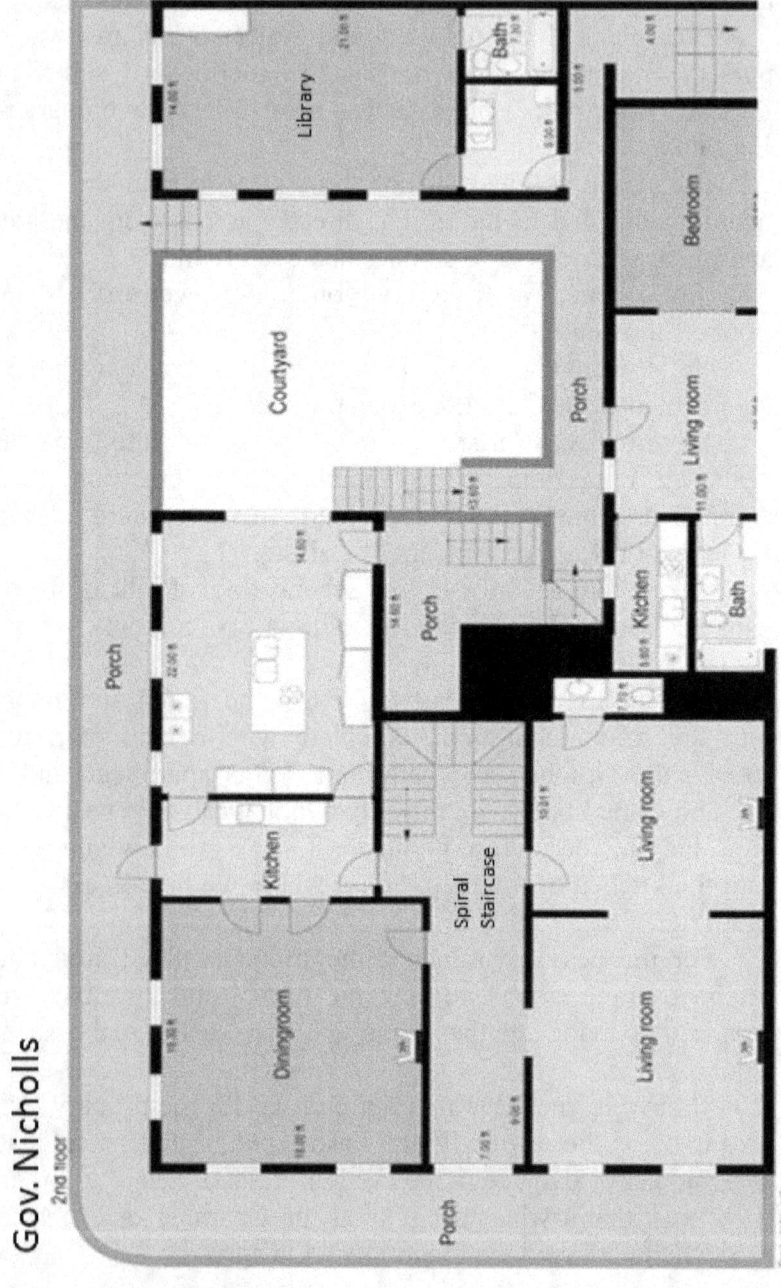

"This house is beautiful," Leslie said. I'm anxious to see the library."

"I'll lead the way on this one," Lia said. "It's my favorite room in the house."

Lia led Elliot and her friends through the kitchen and onto the porch toward the library. She opened the door and let them into a small room currently set up as an office. On the wall opposite the entry door was another door leading into the library. She stepped aside and motioned for Leslie to go before her. "You first," she said.

Leslie reached for the doorknob and pushed it open. His breath caught in his throat as a wonderfully rich and lavish room was revealed. It had high coffered ceilings with ornate medallions and recessed lighting. Mahogany colored wainscoting graced the lower half of the walls while richly textured paper covered the top half. A thick carpet covered the floor and there were bookshelves on all four walls, holding at least a thousand books in a variety of genres. In the center of the far-right wall was a large fireplace with intricately carved molding and a thick, granite mantle.

"I can see why this is your favorite room, Lia," Leslie said. "If this were mine, I would barricade myself in here and never come out. It is truly magical."

Lia and Elliot sat in the wingback chairs strategically positioned on either side of a sofa in front of the fireplace, and watched their friends walk slowly around the room, scan the variety of titles on the shelves.

When Leslie finished scanning the titles, he stood in the middle of the room and admired the fireplace. "I just love old houses—especially large ones. There is such a feeling of history in them," he said. He tilted his head to one side. "I wonder..." He walked directly to the fireplace and felt around the edges of it.

Lia sat forward in her chair. "What is it, Leslie?" she asked.

Phoebe walked up behind Lia's chair and placed her hands on the back of it.

"I did a genealogy for a descendent of a rich New Orleans aristocrat once and they had a fireplace similar to this in their home."

Leslie continued to feel around the edges of the fireplace surround, pulling and pushing on pieces of molding as he went.

"While I was admiring it, quite by accident, I found a..."

He pushed on a piece of molding on the far-left side of the fireplace, and the wainscoting moved behind it. "I found a secret compartment," he finished as the panel swung open.

Their attention was suddenly diverted to the sound of a thump behind Lia.

"Phoebe!" Leslie called out.

Chapter 32

Leslie ran to Phoebe and rolled her onto her back. He lowered his face close to her mouth.

"Is she breathing?" Lia asked.

"Yes. I think she fainted. Elliot, help me carry her to the sofa."

Leslie lifted Phoebe under her arms while Elliot grabbed her feet and they gently laid her on the sofa.

Leslie tapped her on the side of her face. "Phoebe? Phoebe, wake up, sweetie," he said gently.

Phoebe rolled her head from side to side and moaned.

"Lia, go to the kitchen and get a cold cloth," Elliot said.

Lia left the library and ran along the porch toward the kitchen. So focused was she on her task that she didn't notice Marissa and Julie begin to climb into their car in the courtyard.

"Hey! Where's the fire?" Marissa called from below.

Lia stopped abruptly and looked over the railing. "It's Phoebe. In the library. She fainted," Lia called out before she continued toward the kitchen.

"Oh, no!" Julie exclaimed. In a shot, she ran up the porch stairs to the second level with Marissa right on her heels.

Phoebe had regained consciousness by the time Lia returned with a cold cloth. She handed the cloth to Leslie. "Here."

Leslie put the cloth on her forehead. She jumped when the cold material touched her face.

"Relax. Calm down," Leslie said to her in her confused state.

"What happened?" Phoebe asked.

"You fainted," Lia said.

"I did? When?"

"When Leslie found the secret compartment," Elliot replied.

"What secret compartment?" Marissa asked.

Elliot pointed to the fireplace. "There, to the left of the fireplace."

Marissa walked toward it.

"Mar, don't touch it. We don't know what's in there that might have caused Phoebe to faint," Julie said.

"Phoebe has been acting strange all morning," Elliot said.

"Strange, how?" Julie asked.

"She's been acutely affected by the energy in the house—especially when we were near the staircase area to the attic, and when we were in the old slave quarters on the first level. And now, this," Lia explained.

"Maybe I should take her home and put her to bed," Leslie suggested.

"I can do that. Don't you have a meeting this afternoon?" Julie asked.

Leslie glanced at his watch. "It's only eleven. My meeting isn't until two. I have plenty of time to get her home."

"No."

All eyes turned to Phoebe on the sofa.

"What did you say?" Marissa asked.

"I said, no. I'm not going anywhere," Phoebe said.

"But you fainted," Leslie pointed out.

"Occupational hazard," Phoebe replied. "I'm not sick. It was a reaction to that." Phoebe pointed to the open compartment to the left of the fireplace. "Julie, help me up. We need to see what's in that compartment."

Julie helped Phoebe into a sitting position. "Phoebe, are you sure that's wise? Whatever is in there made you pass out. What makes you think it won't happen again?" Julie asked.

"It won't happen again because I'm now aware of it," Phoebe explained. "Being an empath is traumatic enough, but when the shock value is high, it can be overwhelming—even to the point of losing consciousness. The fact that I passed out tells me there's something significant in there."

Phoebe stood and grabbed Leslie's arm to steady herself for a moment of two.

"Are you all right?" Leslie asked.

"I'm fine."

Phoebe walked the few feet between the sofa and the fireplace and stopped in front of the slightly ajar compartment. She looked at the others and slowly opened the door.

The movable panel was the entire height of the wainscoting and approximately sixteen inches wide. It was anchored on the left side by recessed hinges, countersunk in the wooden stud on which they were mounted so that the wainscoting was flush with the next panel beside it. On the right-hand side of the panel, was the same trim that was installed all around the fireplace. To the casual observer, the secret compartment was invisible.

With the panel open, a compartment approximately fifteen inches wide by two feet tall was revealed. It had been constructed between the wall studs, most likely when the library was built. Inside the compartment was a package, wrapped in burlap and tied with string.

The six friends stood in front of the open panel and stared at the package.

"Should we see what's in it?" Marissa asked.

Phoebe stepped forward and touched it. She immediately felt lightheaded and pulled her hand back.

Leslie put his arm around Phoebe to steady her. "Maybe we should leave it alone."

"I'll take it out," Lia said.

"I don't think that's a good idea," Elliot insisted.

"It's okay, Elliot. It's just a package," Lia said.

"Lia..." Elliot said again.

Lia turned to Elliot. "Elliot, I love that you want to protect me, but there are times when we all need to take risks. This is one of those times."

Marissa put her hand on Elliot's shoulder. "It's okay, El. We're all right here to jump in if we need to. Let her do this."

"It seems like I don't have a choice," Elliot said.

Lia reached into the compartment with both hands and grasped the package. The moment she touched it, a surge of emotion ran through her so strong that it immediately caused heart-wrenching sobs to emit from her throat. She dropped to her knees and bent at the waist as the sobs incapacitated her.

"Lia!" Elliot said.

Phoebe stopped her from lunging toward Lia. "Wait! She is not in danger."

Julie dropped to her knees in front of Lia. "Lia, speak to me. What are you feeling?"

Lia turned sad eyes toward Julie and continued to sob. "My heart hurts. There is so much pain here. So much loss." Lia lay on the floor in a fetal position and cried.

"Take the package away from her. Take it away from her!" Elliot shouted.

Leslie looked at Phoebe, who nodded.

Leslie reached for the package, but Lia held on tighter. She held it close to her abdomen. "God, it hurts. I'm sorry. I can't seem to release it. I want to, but it won't come out." Lia doubled again. "So much pain," she said.

Leslie looked at the others. "I don't want to forcibly wrench it out of her. I don't want to hurt her. I need help."

Phoebe looked at Marissa. "I need to you prevent Elliot from jumping in."

"Like hell she will!" Elliot said.

Phoebe walked directly up to Elliot and stopped within inches of her nose.

"Look, Elliot. I'm hoping there is something in that package that will help us with the curse. If we have to damage it to get it away from her and end up rendering it useless, it will be on your head. Can you live with that? I promise you, we will not hurt her."

Elliot struggled with herself for several moments before she turned her back on Phoebe and walked several feet away. "Do it," she said, without looking back.

Phoebe knelt in front of Lia. "Lia, I need you to help us release whatever hold this has on you. Julie and I are going to pry your fingers open and Leslie will take it away. If you can help us, it will make this easier on everyone. We don't want to hurt you."

Lia's forehead creased and she nodded at Phoebe.

"Julie, I don't know what's preventing Lia from releasing it, but if we are able to loosen her grip enough for Leslie to take it, there may be a sudden and total release, so be prepared to immediately let go of her as soon as you feel the resistance end. Otherwise, we could hurt her."

"All right. I understand," Julie replied.

"Are we ready?"

Julie and Leslie both nodded.

"Lia?" Phoebe asked.

"I'm ready. Don't worry about me. What I'm feeling right now is far worse than anything you might do to stop this," Lia said. "Take it out. Take it out now."

"Okay. Let's begin."

"God damn it!" Lia swore as they struggled to pry her fingers open. "Mother fucking son of a bitch, get it out!" she screamed.

At one point, she involuntarily kicked out as they attempted to wrestle it from her. Unexpectedly, Elliot rushed and held her legs. Phoebe glanced at her over her shoulder and nodded. All the while, Leslie maintained a light grip.

It took a full ten minutes to pry her hands open wide enough for the package to slip through them. Phoebe and Julie immediately released their hold on her and she became still.

Elliot gathered Lia in her arms. "Are you okay? Are you hurt?" she asked.

"Elliot, I'm okay. I'm just glad it's done." Lia turned to Phoebe and Julie. "I'm so sorry. I would never speak like that under normal circumstances."

Marissa knelt in front of her. "Admit it, Lia. It felt good to swear like a sailor. You were always so strait-laced and goodie-two-shoes when we were kids. I was always the one getting my mouth washed out with soap."

Lia reached for Marissa's hand. "I didn't have to swear when we were kids. You swore enough for both of us."

Phoebe reached down and offered a hand up to first Lia and then Elliot. "Thanks for the help," she said to Elliot.

"You're welcome. I'm sorry I was such a jerk," Elliot said.

"You weren't a jerk. You were being a protective spouse. I would expect no less," Phoebe said.

She turned to Lia. "Tell me what happened."

"As soon as I touched the package, I felt something inside me that was trying to get out. I tried to let go of it, but it wouldn't move. There was such anguish associated with the *knowledge* that it wouldn't move. When all of you were trying to take it away from me, it felt like you were reaching in and pulling my insides out," she explained.

Phoebe frowned. "It sounds like you're describing childbirth."

"I've never had a child. How would I know what childbirth feels like?" Lia said.

Phoebe rubbed her arms. "Well, I'm glad you're okay. I hope we didn't hurt you too much."

"I'm fine, Phoebs. Really, I am. I just don't understand why I had such a reaction to it."

"What you were feeling was most likely an event from the life of whoever put that package in the compartment. As Queen Thibodeaux said, as a child of St. John's Eve, you have the gifts of empathy and persuasion. Those gifts are yet uncultivated. I can easily understand why you would not be able to control your empathic powers yet."

"So, something like this may happen again?" Lia asked.

"It is quite possible, but now you are aware, and you can shield yourself so as to not get lost in the emotions of others."

"That sounds more like a curse than a gift," Lia said.

"Yes. Sometimes it can feel that way. Empathic gifts become more acute once the gifted are aware of them. The more your awareness increases, the more empathy you will feel for those around you, so it becomes necessary to shield yourself or it can quickly overwhelm you," Phoebe said.

"Teach me how to shield myself," Lia said.

"It's quite simple. We can do this together before we see what is in this package. Give me your hands," Phoebe said.

Lia trustingly placed her hands inside Phoebe's.

"Now, close your eyes and focus on a pink or white light completely surrounding your body. Imagine this light is an impenetrable shield that allows positive energy in but keeps negative energy out. This shield is like body armor, preventing negative energy, emitted by people or by objects, from overwhelming your empathic gifts. Can you see the light?"

Lia nodded. "Yes, I can."

"Do you feel the light? Do you feel its protection?"

Again, Lia nodded. "Yes."

"Good. Open your eyes."

Lia opened her eyes and looked at the anticipation on the faces of those around her.

"How do you feel?" Phoebe asked.

"Calm. Confident," Lia replied.

"Any time you are in a stressful situation, or around difficult people, you can invoke or strengthen this shield by repeating this exercise. Do you understand?"

"I understand."

"Good. Now, let's see what's in that package."

***

Leslie put the package on the coffee table in front of the sofa and then looked at Phoebe. Phoebe, Lia and Julie sat side by side on the couch while Leslie, Marissa and Elliot knelt on the floor around the table.

"We know that Lia and I have adverse reactions to touching this thing, so one of you will need to open it," Phoebe said.

"Leslie has already touched it with no issues," Elliot pointed out.

"Elliot is right," Leslie said. "I don't mind opening it."

Leslie carefully untied the twine holding the package together and pulled back the overlapping flaps of burlap. There was another package inside of it, as well as a piece of paper folded on itself three times and sealed with wax.

"What the hell?" Elliot said.

"Save the document for later. I want to see what's in that package," Marissa said.

Leslie picked up the paper and put it aside. He then carefully untied the twine on the new package. He looked at his friends and then unfolded the new layer of burlap.

Everyone around the table forcibly threw themselves backward when the content was revealed.

"Oh, my God!" Lia exclaimed.

"Jesus Christ!" Marissa yelled.

"Holy shit!" Elliot exclaimed. "Tell me that isn't what it looks like!"

There on the table, was an object that resembled a very small body wrapped in canvas.

Julie covered her mouth with her hand. "Poor little thing," she said. She reached for the package.

"Don't touch it!" Marissa shouted.

Julie looked at her wife. "Mar, it's just a baby." Tears rolled down her cheeks.

"It's a *dead* baby, Jules," Marissa pointed out.

"I'm sorry, Mar, but I need to." Julie lifted the small body and cradled it gently in the crook of her arm. "It's so tiny," she whispered through her tears. She put her hand on the child's chest and suddenly frowned. She looked at her friends. "Something is wrong."

"Of course, something is wrong! You're holding a dead baby!" Marissa said.

"No. You don't understand. Look!" Julie pressed two fingers into the baby's chest. Her fingers sunk deep into the material.

"What the fuck?" Elliot exclaimed. "I'm not a doctor, but if that baby has been dead for as long as I think it has, it shouldn't be squishy."

"Give it to me," Marissa said.

"What?" Julie asked.

"Give me the baby. We need to get to the bottom of this."

Julie handed the small bundle to Marissa, who put it down on the table and stripped away the cloth surrounding it.

"What insanity is this?" Elliot asked when all the material had been stripped away.

"It's a doll," Lia said.

"A voodoo doll?" Leslie asked.

Phoebe reached for the doll.

"Phoebe, should you be touching it? I mean, you had a reaction earlier," Leslie said.

"Lia and I have shielded. We should both be able to touch it without consequence. If the shield fails, I promise to release it, okay?"

Leslie nodded.

Phoebe tentatively picked the doll up and examined it closely after she was confident that her shield was holding. "This appears to be a child's toy. Look, it has clothing, and what looks like real shoes that might fit a newborn baby. Voodoo dolls seldom wear clothing."

"May I see it?" Lia asked.

"Lia, please be careful," Elliot said.

"I will. I promise."

Phoebe handed the doll to Lia who studied it carefully. "This is real blonde hair," she said. "And if I'm not mistaken, this material that the hair is attached to that looks like dried leather, is really human scalp."

"Lia, are you telling me that someone removed a scalp from a human being and put it on this doll?" Julie asked incredulously.

"That is exactly what I'm saying, and judging by how soft the hair is, I'm guessing it is from a human baby."

"Get out of Dodge! Who the hell would do something like that?" Marissa exclaimed.

Lia put the doll back on the table and unbuttoned its shirt. When the last button was released, she opened the shirt wide. There, sewn to the doll's abdomen, was a three-inch piece of umbilical cord, dried as hard as leather.

Julie got up and ran to the bathroom in the corner of the library.

"I'd better go see if she's all right," Marissa said when retching sounds reverberated through the door.

Leslie shook his head. "I have the same question Marissa has. Who would do something like this?"

"Well, there's one way to find out." Elliot reached for the paper that was packaged with the doll. She looked at the wax seal. The initials DL were stamped into it. She turned it around so everyone could see it. "The mistress," she said.

Marissa walked Julie back to the sofa and then knelt on the floor beside her.

"I'm sorry," Julie said to the group.

"There's no reason to be sorry," Lia said. "You've done nothing wrong."

"We waited until you came back to read what's on this paper," Elliot said. "I think we've pretty much concluded that it was written by the mistress, considering the wax seal has DL stamped into it."

"Just when I thought she couldn't be more evil, we find this," Julie said, indicating the doll on the table.

Phoebe reached for Julie's hand. "Let's reserve judgment until after we read what's on that paper," she said.

Julie sobbed anew. "I hope the baby was already dead when she did this. God only knows what she did with the child's body."

"This might explain the skeleton of a small baby they exhumed from the courtyard," Lia said softly. If that child was among the dead, its soul has also been released."

"Open the paper, Elliot. Read it to us," Phoebe said.

Elliot slipped her finger under the seal and shattered the brittle wax into several small pieces. She unfolded the paper and quickly scanned it before reading it to the group. The muscles in her jaw flexed as she absorbed what she was reading.

Elliot cleared her voice and then looked at the group.

"There are several dated entries. The first one is from December fourteenth, eighteen twenty-six."

My child. We finished your nursery today. It is beautiful. Your father hired only the best craftsmen. You will be known as his first-born. The other one will remain in the shadows. She does not deserve his love.

February second, eighteen twenty-seven – I nearly died when you arrived today. Your father delivered you. He said you were an angel baby. You are indeed an angel. You never even cried when you were born. Not one tear. Even when he spanked your little bum. You were such a good boy. That girl cried all day and night when she came. I could hear her all the way from the slave quarters.

March ninth, eighteen twenty-seven – Your father tried to take you away from me today, but I would not let you go. You still have not suckled at my breast. You are always too tired to nurse and choose to sleep instead. That girl child walked today. One day you will be bigger and stronger than she. She will never be as good as you.

May sixth, eighteen twenty-seven – Your father bathed you today and when he brought you back to me, he had dressed you in new clothes, new shoes, and he even brushed your golden hair. You are such a handsome boy. The girl is a monster. She will be trouble. I will deal with her.

June third, eighteen twenty-seven – My dear boy. Your father is trying to convince me to give you up. I will never do that. I fear he will send you away, so I have found a safe place where he will never find you. I am sending this note with you so you will know your mother loves you, and that one day, we will be together again.

Elliot put the letter on the table. "That's all there is. The entries stopped abruptly."

"The child was born after little Lia," Leslie said. "From the information in the genealogy, Lia was about a year older than that boy."

Lia looked at each of her friends. "The child was stillborn and yet she was allowed to keep him for four months. What kind of monsters lived in this house?"

Julie wiped the tears from her eyes and picked up the doll. "This is the work of the master. He scalped his son's dead body and had it sewn onto this doll, all to appease the delusions of a mad woman."

"And little Lia bore the brunt of this child's death," Phoebe said. "She lived, and the boy died. *That* was her sin. That is why every generation after her has been punished."

Chapter 33

Leslie rewrapped the doll and the letter in the outermost layer of burlap and handed it to Elliot.

"I think I'll put this right back where we found it," Elliot said. If we need it, we'll know where it is. In the meantime, I don't want to give that evil bitch any reason to want entrance into this house."

"That is probably wise," Phoebe said. "Of course, this means we now have something that not only belonged to the mistress but is *part* of the mistress. It may be useful later. I will discuss this with Queen Thibodeaux."

"What do you mean by it being part of her?" Marissa asked.

"I assume she gave birth to the stillborn child, and if the scalp that was sewn onto the doll really came from that child, there will be shared DNA in it from both the mistress and the master," Phoebe explained. "This is important because curses and spells that are cast using some physical part of the intended victim are the strongest and most difficult to break."

"Are you suggesting this doll can be used in the banishment spell?" Lia asked.

"That is certainly a possibility."

Leslie looked at his watch. "Well, ladies, as much as I'm enjoying this time with you, I have an appointment to keep in about a half hour, so I'm afraid I must go."

Marissa looked at Lia and Elliot. "Are you two still up to working on the house this afternoon?"

They both nodded.

"Okay." She looked at Leslie. "We'll most likely be at the house until after dark. If you're in the mood for getting covered in construction debris, feel free to join us," Marissa said.

Leslie smiled. "I'd like that. I must say that spending time with you gals is anything but boring. I haven't enjoyed myself this much in a very long time."

"Well, hang on to your boots. If you're in it for the long haul with Miss Phoebe, this will become a way of life," Julie joked.

Phoebe pushed her arm. "Jules! Don't put him on the spot like that."

"Oh, I don't mind that at all," Leslie said. "I'm fond of long hauls if the company is right."

"Speaking of which, could I bother you to haul me to the shop on your way to work?" Phoebe asked.

"Absolutely."

Phoebe turned to her friends. "I'm going to contact the queen as soon as I get to the shop. If I'm lucky, she'll see me this afternoon. I will discuss our new discovery with her and see if she has any updates from the others."

"Do you want me to come with you, Phoebe?" Julie asked.

"No, I think I can cover it. You *can* do something else for me though."

"Anything," Julie said.

"Drop me a text later today with dinner preferences for all of you. I think Indian is in order again if that's okay with everyone else," Phoebe said. "There is another meeting tonight with the kings and queens that I will need to attend, so I'm thinking five-ish."

"Have I told you yet that I love you?" Lia joked.

Phoebe grinned. "If I'd known it would be that easy, I would've offered sooner!"

"Hey!" Elliot and Leslie said together.

***

Phoebe's eyes adjusted to the darkened environment of Queen Thibodeaux's home as she waited for the queen to join her.

"Are you sure there is nothing I can do to help?" Phoebe called out.

"No, child. The tea is almost ready. You are Bettina's guest. Relax," the queen replied.

A moment later, the sound of jingling bracelets signaled the queen's imminent arrival with the tea service. She set it down on the table between them and poured two cups. She handed one to Phoebe. "Here you go, dear." She picked up her own cup and sat back in her chair.

Phoebe sipped her tea. "Oh, this is good. Is it ginger?" she asked.

"Yes. Ginger with a teaspoon of honey."

"It's very good. Thank you."

"You're welcome."

"Have you received any feedback from the kings and queens after the meeting?" Phoebe asked.

"Yes. I've had several calls with suggestions about which curse might have been used one hundred and eighty years ago. I've asked them to consolidate their inputs for discussion at this evening's meeting. Will you be there?"

"Absolutely. Should anyone else go as well, like maybe Lia and Elliot?" Phoebe asked.

"I suspect tonight's meeting will be more brainstorming, so probably not, but once the plan starts to form, then, yes. I think Lia and Elliot should understand in detail what may or may not happen when we attempt to break this curse."

Phoebe sighed.

"I feel your fear, child," the queen said.

Phoebe nodded. "I know there are no guarantees, but what do you think our chances of success are?" she asked.

"The question will be whether the reversal spell will be a close enough inverse of the original spell to be effective. I don't believe we need to know the *exact* spell that was used, but we do need to understand the exact *intent* of the spell, and how it was cast."

"How could we possibly know that, Queen Thibodeaux? Is there some protocol or standard process used when casting a death curse?"

"A reputable practitioner will indeed follow protocol. My fear is that anyone willing to cast a death spell may be less than reputable."

"Marie said the mistress came to her first, but she turned her away."

"I'm not surprised. Marie was a caring and loving individual. She could be shrewd at times—there is no doubt of that, but she was always kind. I can't imagine her agreeing to cast such a heartless spell on generation after generation of innocents. The good Lord only knows why anyone would do such a thing."

"Queen Thibodeaux, I believe I know why the mistress cast such a spell. That is the other reason I asked to see you today."

The queen leaned forward in her seat. "Pray tell, child."

Phoebe put her teacup on the table. "I mentioned earlier about Lia and Elliot giving us a tour of the house this morning."

"Yes."

"During the tour, Leslie was admiring the ornate molding around the fireplace in their library, when he triggered a secret compartment to open."

"Oh, my!" The queen's eyes were wide with anticipation.

"It contained a package wrapped in burlap. Inside the package was a letter, and another, smaller package, also wrapped in burlap. When we unwrapped the smaller package, we found an object that was shaped like the mummified remains of a human baby. It was wrapped in canvas."

The queen's hand flew to her mouth, and she gasped. "Did you unwrap that one as well?"

"We did, and what we found inside startled and horrified us. In fact, Julie felt sick when she realized the implication of what we were looking at. She had to leave the room for a moment."

"Was it a human child?" the queen asked.

"No. It was a fully dressed doll, but the scalp and hair of a human child had been sewed onto it, as well as a piece of umbilical cord. But that's not the worst of it. The letter that had been wrapped in the package with the doll indicated that a boy baby had been stillborn to the mistress nearly a year after Celeste gave birth to the child, Lia. The letter was written by a madwoman. She clung to the baby for four months after its stillborn death—not understanding that the child was dead. Finally, she hid the child in the fireplace compartment, along with the letter that was written for him to read when they were together again."

The queen was speechless for several minutes.

Phoebe reached for her hand. "I don't know if understanding the reason for this curse will help us to break it, but I believe the impetus was because *her* son died, but Celeste's daughter lived."

"Where is this doll now?" the queen asked.

"We returned it to its hiding place in the fireplace compartment."

"I must see it. I will be able to visit Lia and Elliot in their home tomorrow morning if that is convenient for them."

"I suspect they would welcome your visit with open arms. I will tell them," Phoebe said.

"Very good. The meeting tonight will be at eight o'clock. I will see you there, then."

Both women stood to say their goodbyes. As Phoebe turned to leave, she stopped and looked at the queen.

"Queen Thibodeaux, may I ask you a question outside of this problem we're dealing with?"

"Of course, child. What is on your mind?"

"I have noticed of late that I'm struggling with my empathic gifts."

"How so?"

"Sensory inputs are beginning to overwhelm me. For example, several times while Lia and Elliot led us through the house this morning, I felt faint or emotionally overwhelmed—especially when we were in areas of the house with exceptionally high energy. I had to increase my shield in order to touch the doll we found in the fireplace."

"It is not uncommon for residual energy to linger when something traumatic has occurred. People with empathic abilities as well developed as yours are, will always be sensitive to it," the queen said.

"Yes, and before the souls of the slaves were released, it was extremely difficult for me to be in their home, but I have been there since the ascension of souls, and I have even spent the night there, but at those times, I did not experience what I did this morning."

The queen tilted her head to one side. "Has something changed in your life between then and now?"

Phoebe's brow creased and she thought about what changes had taken place in her life the past week or so. Her eyes flew open when it came to her.

"My sister appeared to me through Celeste a little more than a week ago. She made it clear that I was wasting my life by closing my heart to love."

"Your sister?"

"Yes. Her name was Chloe. We were identical twins. We were in a terrible automobile crash in our early twenties. I survived, but she did not. My boyfriend was driving recklessly, and I lost the one person who understood me more than anyone else. I vowed never to make myself vulnerable again. And then, along came Leslie."

The queen smiled. "I thought as much. I see the way he looks at you. It appears he has pierced your shield, my dear."

"Are you saying my relationship with Leslie is a distraction?" Phoebe asked.

"That is a good way to put it. Mind you, I'm not implying in any way that it's a bad thing, but it would explain why things affect you differently since your relationship with him began. Being in love gives you a completely new perspective on life and on the things around you. Opening your heart in some ways makes you more vulnerable, but it can also increase your sensitivity to your surroundings. I recommend you take note of when you feel unusually sensitive, and then learn to build a new shield to filter it out but be careful not to filter out what you feel for Leslie in the process. Love that is true needs no filters."

***

Phoebe went directly home from meeting with the queen and changed into more casual clothes. She then removed her makeup and brushed out her long hair. Since she was appearing at the meeting tonight as Lia's friend and not Phoebe the mystic, she didn't feel that she had to appear in character.

She checked her watch and noted that it was nearly four o'clock. "Time to order dinner," she said aloud.

As if on cue, her phone rang.

"Hey, Julie! You're just in time. So, is Indian food okay with everyone? It's only been about a week since we've had it last."

"Indian food is perfect. I have a list. Do you have something to write with?" Julie asked.

Phoebe grabbed a piece of paper and wrote down each person's order. "Okay. I will call Leslie to see what he wants, and then I'll phone it into the restaurant. It should be ready for me to pick up in about a half-hour or so."

"Awesome. Oh! Wait a minute, Mar is calling to me."

Phoebe could hear muffled voices in the background while she waited for Julie to come back on the line. Finally, she returned.

"Sorry about that," Julie said. "Mar just said Randy called. It seems that Susan is pulling a double shift, so he volunteered to help. Do you mind picking something up for him as well?"

Phoebe fell silent for several moments.

"Phoebs? Did I lose you?" Julie asked.

"No. No, I'm still here. Look, I need you to do me a favor to verify something. If Randy gets there before we do, and he knocks on the door, open it, but don't tell him to come in. Just walk away into the other room."

"What? Why?" Julie asked. "That'll be awkward."

"Hold your phone to your ear like you're talking with your mom or something. That should alleviate some of the weirdness. Then, after he steps into the house, tell him the others are in the back room working, but don't say that until he steps into the house. Okay?" Phoebe instructed.

"I want to know why I need to do this," Julie said.

"Jules, trust me. I'll tell you when I get there. Now give me Randy's order so I can call this in."

***

Marissa and Elliot were doing their best to screw sheet rock pieces into the gaps left open by removing the wall, when Randy walked into the room carrying two six-packs of beer.

Elliot climbed down from the ladder and hugged her friend. "You are a man after my own heart, and that's saying a lot, considering I prefer women." She accepted a cold beer from him.

"Well, that makes two of us. I like women, too," Randy replied.

"I'll take one of those, too," Marissa said. She looked around. "Where's Julie?"

"She was on the phone with her mom when she answered the door. I heard her tell her mom she had to help Lia paint the back bedroom," Randy said.

"She and her mom can spend hours on the phone," Marissa complained. "I mean, I could understand it when we lived in New York City and her mom was here, but now she can see her any time she likes, but still, their phone calls take forever!"

"I'm a 'hello—what do you want—goodbye' kind of girl," Elliot said.

"Me, too," Marissa agreed.

Randy looked at the sheetrock patches they had already hung. "It looks like you two need some help," he said.

"You got that right," Elliot agreed.

Randy picked up the next piece of sheetrock and held it in place while Marissa screwed it in. "You know that celebration coming up next week—St. John's Eve?" he asked.

"I'm aware of it. That's Lia's birthday," Elliot said. She'll be fifty-one."

Randy looked startled. "Really?"

"Yes. I'm hoping we have reason to celebrate it," Elliot replied.

"Why wouldn't you?" Randy asked.

"If that mistress bitch has her way, there won't be much reason to celebrate," Elliot explained. "I, for one, intend to do everything in my power to stop her."

"Likewise," Marissa added.

They cannot stop me.

Randy frowned. "Are you going to the celebration?" he asked.

"I'm not sure. It all depends on whether we can break the curse," Elliot said. "Part of me feels like we should be wrapping her in a cocoon of protection rather than exposing her to hordes of people."

"Curse?" Randy asked.

"Yes. The mistress had a curse put on every person born in Celeste's direct lineage," Marissa said. "All but one of them died on their fifty-first birthdays, and the one who didn't, died in childbirth, otherwise, I'm sure she wouldn't have lived past fifty-one either."

"Why would she do something like that?" Randy asked.

"To punish her husband who forced Celeste into his bed? To punish Celeste because she bore him a healthy daughter while she gave birth to a stillborn son? Because she's an evil, insane madwoman?" Elliot said. "Take your pick."

They know about my boy!

***

Phoebe and Leslie arrived at Saint Ann Street nearly forty-five minutes later with two bags of Indian food and two bottles of wine. Julie met them on the sidewalk.

"Is Randy here?" Phoebe asked.

"Yes. He's in the back room with the girls."

"And..."

"I did as you asked and opened the door without saying a word to him. He just stood on the stoop until he had my attention. Phoebs, he wouldn't step foot inside until I verbally said the words, 'come in'. The mistress is inside him, isn't she? Why else would he have trouble getting into the shop, and now our house?"

"That's exactly what I was worried about, Julie. I've been suspicious since he couldn't come into the shop, but he acted so normal when he was there that I gave him the benefit of the doubt. Where is Lia?" Pheobe asked.

"She's painting the back bedroom. What do we do, Phoebe?"

"Let's get this food into the house. The first thing we need to do is be sure Lia is not alone with him for even a split second. In the meantime, we need to play it cool and to keep the conversation neutral in front of Randy. Okay?"

"Got it."

They brought the food into the house and put it on the dining table that was still set up in the living room from the séance with Queen Thibodeaux.

Phoebe went directly to the back room where Lia was painting. She pushed the door open and peeked inside. "Hey there!" She walked into the room and looked around. "Wow, this looks amazing."

"I'm not much good with a hammer, but I love to paint," Lia said. "Is Julie with you? She abandoned me here."

"She's in the living room unpacking the food. Look, Lia, I think we have a situation brewing and I want you to be aware of it."

Lia put her brush down and turned toward Phoebe. "What is it, Phoebe?"

"I have reason to believe the mistress might have jumped into Randy."

"What? How?"

"I don't know how, or from whom. What I *do* know is that he couldn't come into my shop yesterday—and he couldn't step into this house this evening without being verbally invited in."

"Jesus, Phoebe. What should we do? I mean, Randy is here right now."

"Yes, I know. We need to be sure that you are not alone with him, even for a second. I hope to God I'm wrong, but my intuition is telling me otherwise."

"Will the mistress have the power to hurt any of us just by being in the same room with her?" Lia asked.

"No. She has no power on her own. She gets her power from the people she possesses."

Lia grabbed Phoebe's arm. "Oh, my God, Phoebs. Randy has a gun!"

"Yes, he does. Let's just hope he doesn't have it on him right now."

"What are we going to do? I mean, he's already here. Should we ask him to leave?" Lia asked.

"If he is indeed possessed, I don't want the mistress to realize we know about it, so we need to act as normal as we can. In fact, we can even feed him misleading information to throw him off the track."

"Like what?" Lia asked.

"I don't know. I'm guessing the council will suggest we do the curse reversal at the St. John's Eve celebration, simply because the number of followers will be large and their collective energy will enhance the power of any spell or curse, but I don't want the mistress to know that we'll be there."

"Do the rest of the girls know about this?" Lia asked.

"Julie and Leslie know, and Julie has a plan to get Marissa and Elliot alone to tell them."

Phoebe pulled a gris-gris bag and a medallion out of her pocket. "Before we go into the living room, I want to enhance the aura of protection around you. Put this bag in your pocket, and I want you to wear this talisman—especially around Randy."

Lia looked at the necklace. "Will this protect me from the curse," she asked.

"Unfortunately, no. The curse is generational and self-fulfilling. It is designed to happen with or without the mistress' involvement, but it should protect you from Randy—for now at least."

Lia shoved the gris-gris bag into her pocket and allowed Phoebe to put the talisman around her neck.

"Now, remember, we need to act as normal as possible around him. Okay? And avoid talking about anything that might let the mistress know we're aware she has possessed Randy."

Lia nodded.

***

"How do you know she had a stillborn son?" Randy asked

"Because we found him," Marissa said.

Kill them!

Randy grabbed his head. "Damn!"

Elliot reached for Randy's arm. "Are you okay, dude?"

"Yeah. I will be. Just a flash headache all of a sudden. Damn! That came out of nowhere."

"Maybe some food will help," Phoebe said from the doorway.

All eyes turned toward her. "Thank God. I'm starved!" Marissa declared.

"Well come on, then. The girls and Leslie are setting the table. Let's eat while it's still hot."

Marissa, Elliot and Randy followed Phoebe into the living room.

"I love Indian food," Randy said. "The spices are so aromatic." He pulled out a chair and sat down.

"Oh, Mar and El, come take a look at the room Lia painted before you sit down," Julie said.

"Really, Jules? Can't it wait until after dinner?" Marissa whined.

"It'll only take a minute. Humor me."

"All right, all right." Marissa said. Marissa and Elliot dutifully followed Julie down the hall to the bedroom while the rest of their friends sat around the table.

"Close the door," Julie said once they were all in the room.

Marissa frowned. "Why?"

"Please, don't argue with me, Mar. This is important."

Marissa closed the door. "Okay, what is this all about?"

"Phoebe and I think the mistress has possessed Randy."

"What? Why would you think that?" Elliot said.

"He was unable to open the door of the shop yesterday, and tonight when he got here, he wouldn't step through the doorway until I verbally invited him in. Is that absolute proof? No. But, at this point, I don't think we should take any chances," Julie explained.

"Damn! We just told him—I mean her—about the doll we found this morning, and that we planned to fight the curse," Marissa said.

Elliot ran to the door. "Lia's out there with him!"

"Elliot, stop! Phoebe has given Lia a couple of articles to protect her. And besides, Phoebe and Leslie are with her."

"I want to get back out there, Julie," Elliot said.

"Okay, but please act natural around him. We don't know for sure that he's possessed, but if he is, we don't want the mistress to know what our plans are to fight this thing. She doesn't need any incentive to come up with a backup plan if we are able to break the curse."

"*If* we're able to break the curse? There can be no *if*, Jules. We *have* to break that curse," Elliot said.

"We will certainly try, El. We will certainly try. Oh, and for God's sake, don't let him touch you. We don't need that bitch jumping into any of us."

***

Randy sat directly across the table from Lia.

She looks like Celeste. Did you put your hands on my son, whore?

"How is Susan, Randy?" Lia asked.

"Huh?" Randy snapped back to consciousness.

"I said, how is Susan? We really enjoyed her company at dinner last week," Lia repeated.

"Oh, I'm sorry. I must have zoned out there," Randy said. "Susan is good. She enjoyed meeting all of you."

"So, Randy, you mentioned the St. John's Eve celebration while we were working. This is the first time we'll be here for it. Do you have any suggestions for us?" Elliot asked.

"Sweetie, I'm not sure we're going to be here," Lia said. "We talked about turning it into a long birthday weekend for me and flying back to New York City for a visit." Lia raised her eyebrows at Elliot and nudged her under the table.

"Jesus! You're right. What was I thinking? We did talk about that, didn't we?"

"Can we go with you? It would be nice to visit the old haunts again," Marissa said. She turned her head so that Randy couldn't see her face and winked at Lia and Elliot.

Lia nudged Elliot's shoulder. "You didn't ask them already? I thought we agreed you would talk to Mar about it."

"Sorry! I guess I had a brain fart." Elliot leaned toward Marissa. "Hey, Mar, how would you and Julie like to join us in New York City for Lia's birthday celebration?"

Marissa grinned. "We wouldn't miss it!"

"But, Mar, what about the..." Julie abruptly stopped when Marissa kicked her gently under the table.

"What about what?" Marissa asked pointedly.

"Ah, what about the shop. I mean, a few days is short notice for Phoebe," Julie recovered quickly.

"Don't worry about the shop, Julie. I think I can survive on my own for a while. I don't blame you from wanting to get out of Dodge when the St. John's Eve celebration is happening. It can be pretty crazy around here during that time."

This complicates things. You need to stop them from leaving. I want her here on St. John's Eve. I want her here for the fifty and one. I want to be here to see the last of that whore's family die.

***

Marissa sat back after they had finished eating and patted her stomach. "Ugh! Why did you let me eat so much, Jules?"

"Don't blame *me* for you making a pig of yourself," Julie said.

"Now I don't feel like working for the rest of the evening," Marissa replied.

Elliot looked at her watch. "Well, it's six-forty-five already. Maybe we should call it quits for the night."

Phoebe jumped to her feet. "It's six-forty-five already? I hate to run, but I have a meeting in fifteen minutes."

"Another mystic reading or séance?" Julie asked.

"Yes. It's for a new client, so I need to make a good impression by being on time."

"Leave your dishes. We'll take care of them," Lia insisted.

"Are you sure?" Phoebe asked.

"Absolutely. That's our rule—you cooked, we clean," Elliot said.

"But I didn't cook. I just picked up," Phoebe pointed out.

"Same church, different pew," Marissa said. "Now go before you're late for your very important meeting."

"I should probably go as well," Randy said. "Susan will be out of work by seven."

"Again, we'll take care of the dishes. Go pick up your lady," Lia said.

"What the fuck!" Elliot said as soon as Randy was out of earshot.

"That story about New York City was quick thinking, Lia," Phoebe said. "I hope he bought it. It will be to our advantage if the mistress thinks you will not be at the celebration next Wednesday night."

"You need to get going, Phoebe," Julie said. "Be sure to tell the kings and queens about the doll we found."

"I will." Phoebe turned to Leslie. "Do you mind dropping me off at the council meeting?"

"Not at all," he said. He looked at Marissa. "I'll come back to give you a hand cleaning up if you'd like. It will help to pass the time before I go back to get Phoebe."

"Sure. I appreciate the help."

Lia watched Phoebe and Leslie pull away from the curb. "Oh, the tangled web we weave," she said softly.

Chapter 34

Elliot awoke the next morning to an empty bed. She noticed that the T-shirt Lia had worn to bed was draped across the chair in the corner of the bedroom.

She's probably gone for her morning run, she thought. *I really wish she'd put that off until we break this damned curse.*

She climbed out of bed and slipped on a pair of lounge pants before taking care of morning bathroom needs. She then went to the kitchen in search of coffee. Julie was sitting at the kitchen island in front of a laptop when she entered.

"Good morning, Jules," Elliot said.

"'Morning, Elliot."

Elliot made herself coffee and then peeked over Julie's shoulder at the computer screen. "Death Curses and Banishment Spells," Elliot read from the screen.

"I'm researching spells that might have been used in the eighteen-hundreds," Julie explained. "I'm sure the kings and queens are doing their own research, but I figured it couldn't hurt."

Elliot leaned in and kissed Julie on the cheek.

"What was that for?" Julie asked.

"For being such a good friend. I don't know how I'd be coping with this if the two of you weren't here to support us."

Julie swiveled her stool around to face Elliot. "You and Lia are more than friends to us, El. You are our family."

Elliot walked into the circle of Julie's arms for a warm hug.

"Hey! Are you hitting on my wife?" Marissa teased from the doorway.

"You snooze, you lose," Elliot said. "I was just thanking Jules for all the support the two of you have given us for the past several months."

"You can't do enough for family," Marissa said.

"That's what I said," Julie piped in.

"Does anyone know if Lia went for a run?" Elliot asked.

"I don't think so," Julie said. "About an hour ago she made herself a coffee and then headed out that door in the direction of the library."

"The library? I hope she doesn't touch that doll again," Elliot said.

"She'll learn to harness her empathic abilities with time, but I agree with you. Until she does, she needs to be careful about what she jumps into, or at the very least, needs to surround herself with effective shielding like she did yesterday," Julie commented.

Elliot walked toward the kitchen door. "I think I'll go check on her." Elliot walked down the length of the second story deck to the library and opened the door. There was no one inside. "Lia?" Elliot called out with no response forthcoming.

Elliot closed the door and looked around.

Julie said she was heading toward the library. I wonder if she's in the office.

She walked to the corner of the porch and stopped in front of the office door. She knocked lightly.

"Come in," a soft voice said from inside.

Elliot pushed the door open and looked in. Lia was sitting in front of the computer, typing furiously.

"Julie said you had headed this way. What are you doing?" Elliot asked.

"I'm writing my last will and testament," Lia said.

"You're what? Lia, is that really necessary?"

"I think it is." She stopped typing and looked at her wife. "Elliot, I know you don't want to think about this, but there is a very real possibility that I have less than a week to live."

"Don't say that, Lia."

"I *have* to say that. It can't be a coincidence that everyone in my family died on their fifty-first birthdays, Elliot. I hope to God that we can prevent it from happening to me, but we might fail, no matter how hard we try."

"Then write one up for me as well, because if you die, I don't want to go on without you," Elliot said stubbornly.

"Oh, for God's sake, Elliot. Do you hear yourself? We've had this conversation already. Even without the curse, there is a good chance one of us will die before the other. We both have to deal with that possibility."

Lia's phone suddenly rang. Phoebe's name appeared on the screen.

"Good morning, Phoebe," Lia said.

"Good morning. I was wondering if you're up to having a visitor around nine this morning," Phoebe said.

"Phoebe, you're not a visitor—you're family," Lia said.

"I love you too, Lia, but I was referring to Queen Thibodeaux. She wants to come to your house to see the doll and to talk about some of the plans the kings and queens are proposing."

Lia glanced at her watch. "That's about an hour from now. Sure. Nine o'clock would be fine. Is there something I should prepare?"

"She's a tea drinker," Phoebe said.

"Tea. Okay. I think we can manage that. We'll see you at nine, then."

***

Randy attended the crossover meeting the next morning to see if there were any follow-up items he needed to address on his shift. Susan sat beside him, as she was also there to touch base with her off-shift counterpart.

The night shift supervisor stood up to speak. "It was a relatively quiet night with the exception of a few zombie sightings," he said.

Several of the officers in the room chuckled.

"It's early for the zombies to come out, isn't it?" one officer asked. "I mean, St. John's Eve isn't for another five days."

"I hear the zombies self-medicate for several days ahead," another officer said.

Randy turned around to face the room. "I did some reading on it and it seems they ingest poison from puffer fish to affect that dead-like appearance, oh, and the voodoo community calls them revenants, not zombies."

"They must be out of their freaking minds," yet another officer said.

"I believe the substance they are ingesting is toxic and possibly illegal," Randy added.

"What we need to do is find their supplier. Sooner or later, someone is going to die from doing that shit and then we'll have to answer to the mayor for it," the supervisor replied.

"I think their dealers are called bokors," Randy said. "I'd be happy to track a few down if anyone has any leads I can work with."

One of the officers from the back of the room spoke up. "I might have some information for you, Randy, but just a word of warning—these guys deal in some powerful voodoo shit, so be careful."

"Thanks, man. I'll catch you after the meeting," Randy replied.

***

The front doorbell rang at the Royal Street house at exactly nine o'clock.

"I got it," Elliot said. She ran down the stairs and grabbed the key to the entry gate that hung on a hook just inside the vestibule. Phoebe and Queen Thibodeaux were standing on the sidewalk, on the other side of the gate.

"Good morning," Elliot said as she unlocked the gate. "Come in."

Queen Thibodeaux grabbed Phoebe's arm as soon as she stepped into the vestibule.

"Are you all right?" Phoebe asked the queen.

"I understand what you mean by energy," the queen said. "This home has seen much sorrow, and much joy. The energy I feel right now is one of renewal."

"Yes. It can be overwhelming—much more so when the souls were still trapped here," Phoebe said.

The queen looked at Elliot. "One day, I will return and ask for a full tour of your lovely home, but right now we have work to do. We have a soul of our own to save. I would like to see the effigy you found in your library."

"Of course." Elliot offered her arm to the queen and ascended the stairs to the second story with her.

Elliot led the queen through the butler's pantry and into the kitchen where Lia had just prepared a tea service. When they entered the kitchen, the queen walked directly to Lia and kissed her on both cheeks.

"Thank you," Lia said. "I've prepared tea."

"Excellent," the queen said.

"The library is across the courtyard. Marissa and Julie are there waiting for us," Elliot said. She once again offered her arm to the queen, and they made their way across the porch.

The queen paused and looked around the library. "So much history and knowledge here," she said. "Do you read?"

"We love to read," Lia said. "Unfortunately, life has been quite unsettled since the day we moved into this house, so we've had little time to get acquainted with these treasures." She put the tea service down on the coffee table in front of the sofa and poured six cups.

"Perhaps soon, you will be able to enjoy this room more," the queen said.

Lia looked directly into her eyes. "I sincerely hope you are right."

The queen sat on the sofa, with Lia beside her. She sipped her tea and then addressed the room. "I would like to see the effigy."

"I'll get it," Marissa said. She walked to the fireplace and felt around for the panel that Leslie had found the day before. She located it easily and pulled the door open. She then stepped aside for the queen to see before she removed the package.

"I have seen compartments like this in several homes," the queen said. "Please, bring the package to me."

Marissa removed the package and placed it on the table in front of the queen.

The queen laid her hands on the package and closed her eyes. "There is much sorrow here. Loss. Pain. Grief. Madness." She opened her eyes and untied the twine holding the burlap wrapping together. Finally, she folded back the burlap to reveal the doll and the letter.

"This effigy is the work of evil minds. The mind that created it and the mind that nurtured it. She picked up the letter and read it twice. "She was quite mad," the queen said. "And everyone in the lineage of Celeste Bourdeau paid the price for her madness."

"Everyone except Lia," Elliot said.

"Everyone except Lia, *so far*," the queen replied. "It is up to us to end this curse before Lia falls victim to it as well. And it is up to us to banish the mistress forever. This effigy may be useful in those efforts."

"Phoebe explained to us that curses which use objects that are *part* of the victim are the strongest and most difficult to break," Lia said.

"That is true," the queen replied.

"I understand how a curse might be effective against a single victim, but how is it that my entire family line has been affected when most of us weren't even born yet when it was placed? What could have possibly been used that belonged to my mother, or grandmother—or even me for that matter?" Lia asked.

Queen Thibodeaux took Lia's hand in her own. "A curse is like a recipe, child. It has ingredients and instructions. We call the ingredients taglocks. Taglocks act as anchors that form a bond between the curse and the cursed. Phoebe was correct. The more personal in nature these taglocks are, the stronger the curse will be.

"Cursing a taglock relies on a concept called sympathetic magic. Sympathetic magic assumes that any action, or curse you place on a taglock will also apply to the person the taglock belongs to."

"But, if the mistress cursed Celeste with something that was part of her, then why didn't the curse end with her death?" Lia asked.

The queen nodded. "That is a very good question. The fact that the curse has affected Celeste's entire lineage probably means she didn't curse Celeste. It probably means she cursed

Celeste's children, and all future generations of children to come."

"But how? How could she do that?" Lia persisted.

"By using taglocks that would be shared by her entire lineage."

"Holy shit!" Elliot exclaimed. "Holy shit! I think I know what she used!"

"What is it? Elliot, please tell us," Lia said.

"I'll do better than that. I'll show you. I'll be right back."

Elliot raced out of the room and ran as fast as she could up the stairs to the third level porch, entering the house through the courtyard bedroom. She returned not five minutes after she left and placed an object on the table in front of the queen.

"Oh, my God, Elliot, you're right!" Julie exclaimed when she saw what Elliot had retrieved.

"Yes," Phoebe said. "Yes. That has to be it."

Lia slammed her hand down on top of the object. "No! Dey be my babies. Dey be mine!" she yelled.

The queen looked questioningly at the group. "The box contains the DNA thread we are looking for—a lock of hair from Ethan and a tooth from little Lia. They were Celeste's children," Julie explained. "We found this box mortared into the foundation of Marie Laveau's homestead."

The queen turned sympathetic eyes in Celeste's direction and covered her hand with her own. "Yes, Celeste," she said. "They are your babies, and they were unjustly used to punish all your descendants for crimes they did not commit. This is your chance to release the souls of your loved ones."

Celeste looked at each person in the room, ending with Elliot. Tears rolled down her cheeks. "El-ee-ot?" she said.

Elliot knelt before her and took her face between her hands. "Your Lia would want you to do this. Ethan would want it, too. It's okay, Celeste. Let them help. It is a chance to save my Lia's life—your granddaughter. Please let them help." Try as she might, Elliot couldn't stop the tears from rolling down her own cheeks.

Celeste looked at the queen and removed her hand from the box. "Save my granddaughter, Lia. Save her, my queen."

***

Lia and Elliot walked with Phoebe and Queen Thibodeaux to Phoebe's car.

The queen hugged them before she got into the car. "We have more hope now than we did when I arrived. We still need to find the right curse—or one close to it—to reverse the one cast so many years ago, but now we have the objects that have bound the curse to generations of your family. The task before us is still daunting, and we may not know how effective it will be until we execute it, but there is indeed more hope."

Lia held her close. "Thank you for everything you're doing, Queen Thibodeaux."

The queen held her at arm's length. "Don't you think it's about time you called me Bettina?" she said.

Lia grinned through her tears. "Thank you, Bettina. Thank you so much."

"You are welcome, child. I will meet with the council tonight to discuss this new discovery. Keep the box and the effigy safe. We may need them."

"We will," Elliot promised.

***

From an unmarked car parked on the opposite corner of the intersection between Royal Street and Governor Nichols, Randy watched Phoebe and an unknown woman enter a vehicle and drive away.

They must not leave before the fifty and one. She is the last one. This must not fail.

Chapter 35

Lia turned to Elliot after Phoebe and Bettina drove away. "I so want this to be over, Elliot. We haven't had a moment's peace since we came to New Orleans."

Elliot pulled Lia into her arms. "You and me, too, love. We have been in survival mode for far too long." She kissed her on the side of the head.

Lia looked into Elliot's eyes. "Part of me is feeling hopeful, but the other part is afraid. I have so many hopes for our future, but it's difficult to visualize and plan when the possibility looms that it will all end in a matter of days."

"Lia, I know you think I'm being overprotective, but I really don't want you to be alone for even a moment until this is behind us. Whether you are at work or home, or shopping, or even at Mar and Julie's, I want you to surround yourself with people you trust to keep you safe. In fact, I think we should arrange to take next week off as vacation—both of us. That way, I can be with you, and who knows, maybe that trip to New York City for a birthday weekend might actually be possible if things work out."

"*If* things work out. The uncertainty of it all scares me," Lia said.

"Yeah, it scares me, too," Elliot replied. "What do you say we go inside and see if the girls still want to work on their house? It might be a good way to take our minds off things."

Lia and Elliot entered the lower level of their home and heard noises coming from the storage rooms to the right of the entrance. They went to investigate.

"Hey, you," Lia said.

Marissa looked up from the box she had been rummaging through. "Hi. Jules and I thought we'd pack up a few more things to take to the house this afternoon."

"Are you still interested in working on the house today? We could use some serious distraction," Elliot said.

"Absolutely. We're trying to find all of the office related stuff since the back bedroom has been painted and is ready to be furnished."

"If I remember right, all the boxes marked office are in the other room," Lia said.

"Julie's in there right now looking for them," Marissa said.

"I'll go give her a hand," Lia offered.

Marissa waited for Lia to leave the room and then turned to Elliot. "How is she holding up?"

"She's scared, but hopeful," Elliot said.

"And how about you?"

Elliot put her hands on her hips and looked everywhere but at Marissa in her attempt to maintain control of her emotions. She managed pretty well until Marissa opened arms.

"C'mere, you," Marissa said.

Elliot moved quickly into Marissa's embrace and silently sobbed on her shoulder.

Marissa held her in silence for several long moments.

Finally, Elliot stepped back and wiped her eyes. "I'm sorry, Mar," she said.

Marissa put her hand on Elliot's shoulder. "Nothing to be sorry about. If it were Julie instead of Lia in this situation, I would be a total basket case. Give yourself permission to be human, my friend."

Elliot nodded. "Thank you. I needed that."

"Any time."

Elliot looked at the mountain of boxes in the room. "So, what's the plan?"

"I thought we would sort these boxes by room so that we can just transport them as we finish each room. That way we won't have a huge pile of boxes to work around. We can move the actual furniture when everything is ready so that we don't have to rent a truck more than once."

"That's a good idea. So, Julie and Lia are working on the office stuff. What room is next?" Elliot asked.

"I think the plan is to paint the guest bedroom today, so we should look for those boxes."

"Got it!"

***

Two hours later, all of the boxes in the two storage rooms were sorted into seven piles—office, guest bedroom, master bedroom, dining room, living room, kitchen and bathrooms.

The ladies stood back to admire their efforts.

"Now that's a job well done," Marissa said. "Thanks for the help."

"No problem," Elliot replied.

"I think we should load the office stuff into the car and then break for lunch before we head to the house," Lia suggested.

A half-hour later, the four friends sat around the kitchen island enjoying grilled cheese sandwiches and tomato soup.

"This brings back memories of my childhood," Lia said. "This was a lunch staple when I was a kid."

"So, what did you think of the queen's visit this morning?" Marissa asked.

"I hope it revealed the tools we need to beat this thing," Elliot replied. "I mean, finally understanding how Lia's entire family could have been cursed so many years ago was huge. Thank God you found that box mortared into the foundation of your new home."

"I wonder how that box got there?" Marissa mused. "I mean, the mistress didn't live in that house, and I doubt that Marie would have put it there."

"It's been rumored that the mistress stayed with Marie for a while when she came back from Paris. It could have been done then," Julie suggested.

"But don't you think Marie would know if someone was tampering with the foundation on her house?" Elliot asked.

"You would think, so," Lia agreed. "Did Marie travel much? It could have been done when she wasn't home."

"It was also odd that there was dirt inside the box," Marissa said.

"During the séance, didn't Marie say the artifacts had to be buried with dirt from the graveyard?" Elliot asked.

"Yes, she did say that," Julie replied. "Maybe the dirt inside the box was symbolic of it being buried."

"That would make sense," Lia said. "I would also assume that sealing it inside the foundation of the house would assure it would never be dug up, so that in itself could also represent a burial—similar to the caskets inside the mortared graves in the cemetery."

"Wow! The comparisons are eerily close. Maybe we should give Phoebe a call and talk to her about it," Julie suggested.

"Maybe we should talk to Marie, since she was the one who described what the typical death spell was in the eighteen thirties," Marissa said.

"I agree. Let's take care of these dishes and then head there with the office stuff. I'll call Phoebe once we get there," Julie said.

"Before we leave, we should pack enough clothes for the weekend in the event we work late and decide to stay," Lia suggested.

"I agree. I'll also grab towels for everyone, and the box of bathroom toiletries," Julie added.

"I think we should add wine to that list," Elliot said. "Lots of wine."

***

Julie hung up her phone and slipped it into her back pocket. "Phoebe will be there after she closes the shop. I told her about our discussion this morning and to come prepared to speak to Marie. I also told her to come in work clothes if she was up to helping."

"Great. Did you tell her to invite Leslie?" Marissa asked.

"Actually, I didn't think of that. I just assumed she would. I mean, he's part of our group now," Julie said. "Maybe I should call her back and make that clear."

"That's a good idea. Also, tell them to bring extra clothes if they think they'll stay."

"Beep, beep, coming through!" Elliot exclaimed.

Marissa and Julie cleared the way for Elliot to carry in a box of office supplies that was obviously heavy.

"Do you want some help with that?" Marissa offered.

"Nope, just clear a path so I can get it to the back room without having to stop."

Several trips later, all of the boxes had been unloaded from the car, carried into the back bedroom and stacked against the wall so they were not in the way of Lia and Elliot's air mattress if they chose to stay.

"Mar, the next time we move, let's hire a company to do it for us," Julie said once the last box was stacked.

Marissa wrapped her arms around Julie's waist and pulled her close. "I'm hoping this will be our forever home and we won't *have* to move again," she said.

Julie smiled and kissed her on the lips. "You are so cute. Have I told you today that I love you?"

"I believe you have, but I never tire of hearing it," Marissa replied before she released her wife. "So, what do you say we go see if that sheetrock mud we put up yesterday is ready to sand?" she said to Elliot.

"Lead the way," Elliot replied.

"And we can start painting the guest bedroom," Lia suggested.

***

Phoebe turned the knob and pushed open the door to the vestibule.

"Shouldn't you knock first?" Leslie suggested.

"No. They gave me a key, so I assume it's okay for me to just walk in," Phoebe said.

They walked through the small vestibule and into the living room. It was empty.

"Hello?" she called out.

"Maybe they're not here," Leslie said.

"Their cars are out front, and I hear music, so I assume they're here."

They dropped the air mattress, pillows and their bags in the living room and walked down the hallway to the bedrooms. The music became louder as they walked. They stopped in the doorway of the first bedroom. Lia and Julie were inside, dancing wildly to very loud music as they ran their paint rollers up and down the walls.

Phoebe grinned at Leslie, and then proceeded to dance her way into the room. When she was close enough to Lia, she hip bumped her.

"Ahhh!" Lia screamed, swung around, and effectively ran her roller down Julie's face and shoulder.

"Oh, my God!" Julie exclaimed, barely missing Lia with her own roller.

Phoebe doubled with laughter.

"You scared the shit out of me!" Lia exclaimed. She looked at the cream-colored stripe down Julie's face and she, too, laughed herself to tears.

"Not funny, you shit heads!" Julie said.

"Ah, yes, it is," Leslie reversed the camera on his phone and showed it to Julie. "See for yourself."

Julie looked at her reflection in the camera and completely lost it.

By the time the three women gained control of their laughter, they were all sitting on the floor and each one of them had streaks of paint on their skin and clothing.

"What's going on?" Elliot called as she and Marissa walked down the hall. "You guys were making such a racket, we had to come investigate."

They stopped in the doorway and stood there with their mouths open.

"I thought you were supposed to paint the walls, not each other," Marissa said.

Phoebe, Lia and Julie all rolled on the floor again as another round of laughter made it impossible for them to remain upright.

***

"The pizza is here," Elliot called out after she tipped the delivery boy. She carried the two large pies to the table and then retrieved paper plates and napkins from the kitchen cabinet.

Lia, Phoebe and Julie emerged from the hallway into the kitchen. "Great timing, love. We just finished painting the guestroom." She stopped short when she saw Elliot. "Okay, hand me the plates and napkins and then go outside to brush the dust off yourself. You're a mess," she said.

Elliot walked toward the front door, just as Leslie and Marissa emerged from the dining room. "Follow me, you two. No food for us until we lose some of this sheetrock dust."

While Julie waited for her turn to wash the paint from her face and arms, she walked to the front windows and looked out to see how the girls were doing. "Look at these fools," she exclaimed.

Phoebe and Lia quickly joined her.

"I can't believe they're doing that right on the sidewalk," Phoebe said.

All three of them had taken of their T-shirts and shorts and were shaking the dust out of them and swatting one another.

"Jesus. They're going to get themselves arrested," Lia said. She made a move toward the door.

"No. Let them be," Julie said. They're all wearing boxers and sports bras. If they were men, they'd be out there bare-chested, and no one would even blink an eye."

"You know, you're right," Lia said.

The front door opened and all three marched in, carrying their clothes. Their hair stuck out in all directions from brushing the dust out of it.

"Go throw those on the floor of the master and come back to wash the dust from your face and arms," Lia said. "You look like kabuki dancers."

"Yes, Mommy," Elliot teased. She collected the clothes from Marissa and Leslie and brought them to the other room.

***

"Could you reach me another slice, love?" Elliot asked. "Thank you."

"So, Julie, you said you wanted to talk to Marie about the curse," Phoebe said.

"Yes. We were talking about similarities between how Marie described the most common death curse, and the box that we found in the foundation," Julie explained.

"Such as?"

"Well, we thought the dirt inside the box was symbolic of a burial, and the fact that the whole box was encased in cement was similar to it being entombed, like the caskets in the cemetery," Julie said.

"That does make sense," Phoebe replied.

"We want to talk to Marie about the symbolism and maybe ask her if she recalls any more details about curses like the one that might have been cast on my family," Lia said.

"We're hoping we can learn something new that might help the kings and queens break this thing," Elliot added.

"I feel like I'm doing nothing to help myself, Phoebe. I can't just sit back and let others figure out how to save me. I need to do something." Lia's voice choked with emotion.

Phoebe reached for her hand. "We have nothing to lose by trying, sweetie. We'll do it right after dinner."

***

The six friends sat around the table while holding hands. A pentagram was drawn in black salt on the tablecloth, and a lit candle was positioned at each corner of the star as well as in the center of the figure. The aroma of rosemary and sage filled the air while a thin pillar of smoke rose from a bowl of burning incense.

Phoebe called forth the spirit of Marie Laveau, who came willingly and addressed the group around the table.

"Marie feel sorrow in your hearts," she said. "Why dat be?"

"Marie, we are running out of time to save Lia. She will reach the fifty and one in four short days. We asked you here to help us find a solution," Julie said.

"I say dat I be here if you need me. What can I do?"

"Queen Thibodeaux explained to us that a curse is like a recipe with ingredients and instructions. Marie, we believe we have the ingredients. We have a tooth from Celeste's daughter, and a lock of hair from her son. We believe they are the things the mistress used to curse my entire bloodline," Lia explained.

"Where you get dat tooth and hair?" Marie asked.

"We found them inside a box that was mortared into the foundation of your home," Julie said.

"You found dem in my home," Marie said, rather than asked.

"Yes. We extracted the box from inside the foundation and when we opened it, we found a travel document that belonged to the mistress, a list of her slaves written on parchment, and two packages—one containing a tooth and another containing a lock of hair. They had Ethan and Lia's names written on them," Julie said.

"Don't you see, Marie, those two items contain the DNA shared by everyone in Celeste's lineage," Lia explained. "They represent the common link between every member of my family that died because of this curse. I carry some of that DNA inside of me."

"What be DNA?" Marie asked.

"DNA provides genetic markers to determine relationships between things. It is what each generation passes down to the next. It is the main ingredient that Queen Thibodeaux said was necessary for this curse to work," Lia said.

"Dis box you find in my home—what else be in da box?" Marie asked.

"Like I said, it contained a travel document, a list of her slaves, and the two packages containing the tooth and hair," Julie said.

"Oh, and dirt," Marissa added. "Don't forget the dirt."

"That's right," Lia said. "The box was filled with dirt, as well."

Marie leaned forward. "Dis box be da curse. Da dirt come from da cemetery. Dis box contain da energy of da evil one. Da box need be destroyed, but it need be done right or Lia die still."

Elliot looked at Lia and squeezed her hand. She turned to address Marie. "Are you saying we can break the curse simply by destroying this box?" she asked.

"Noting dat simple, El-ee-ot. If it be done wrong, da curse not be stopped."

"So how do we do it right?" Elliot demanded.

"Elliot, please calm down," Lia said softly.

"No, I won't calm down. Lia, this might be the only chance we get to stop this thing," Elliot said angrily.

"Marie not be offended, child," Marie said to Lia. "I knows love when I sees it. I be angry, too if I be El-ee-ot, but if we be successful, we need to be calm and plan dis ting carefully. Dat box you find change everything."

"Please tell us what to do, Marie," Julie encouraged.

***

After the séance ended, the six friends sat around the table, still holding hands, and tried to hold back the flood of tears that ran down each of their cheeks.

"We're going to beat this, Lia. I can feel it," Elliot said.

Lia looked at her friends. "My heart is so full of love right now. What have I done to deserve all of you?"

"You don't need to do anything to earn our love and support, Lia," Marissa said. "The others see in you what I've known since we were kids. Tell me you wouldn't be here in the same way for every one of us."

"You know I would."

"You're damned right you would."

"This calls for a celebration," Julie said. "I say we go get some champagne and other spirits of our choice. *Laissez les bons temps rouler*!"

"What?" Elliot exclaimed.

"Let the good times roll!" Julie said

"I'm in!" Elliot replied.

"I'll go on a booze run if you'd like," Leslie volunteered.

"I'll go with you," Elliot said.

"Count me in. I want to stop at your place, El, and pick up my stereo system. I want something more powerful than a cell phone to blast our music from."

"Maybe while they're gone, we can get the bedrooms set up," Lia suggested. "Hopefully your room won't smell too much like paint by the time we head to bed tonight, Phoebe."

"I don't mind the smell of fresh paint," Phoebe said. "It smells so clean and new."

"I'm sure I've got some major cleaning to do in the master before I can set that room up. I imagine there's sheetrock dust on everything in there," Julie said.

"In that case, we should all start in there and then once it's clean enough, we can split up and take care of our own rooms," Phoebe suggested.

***

Elliot popped the cork on a bottle of champagne and emptied it into six paper cups. The six friends stood in a circle in the center of the living room.

"A toast," Elliot said. "To Marie Laveau—the best damned voodoo queen this city has ever seen!"

"To Marie Laveau," they all chanted.

"I'm feeling such hope in my heart," Elliot said.

"I feel it, too," Lia added.

"I think we all do," Marissa replied.

"We certainly have reason to hope, but we still have a lot of work ahead of us, and like Marie said, we need to get this right. She may have given us the tools we need to move forward, but we need to use those tools correctly to succeed," Phoebe pointed out.

"You are right, Phoebs," Julie said. "But tonight, I think we have reason to celebrate."

"Yes, we do," Phoebe agreed.

"How about some music?" Marissa asked.

"I can help you set up your system," Leslie offered. He stepped out of the circle and looked around the room. "It might be best if we move the table to that far wall near the outlets and put the stereo system on it," he suggested.

"Good idea," Marissa replied.

"Shit, Mar, did you think to grab your music?" Elliot asked.

Marissa took her phone out of her pocket. "No need to. This thing connects to the stereo through bluetooth. I have thousands of songs in here."

"Awesome!" Elliot replied.

"I call her Inspector Gadget," Julie said. "She's always got to have the latest technology. I swear she could break into the Pentagon's computers if she put her mind to it."

"Okay, while they're doing that, let's see what else Elliot brought back with her," Lia said.

Lia picked up the large duffle bag Elliot had dropped on the floor and opened it. "Ooo! This is going to be a fun night!" she said.

"What have you got in there?" Phoebe asked.

"Monopoly, Uno, Clue...and Twister!" Lia said as she removed each game and handed them to Phoebe.

"Twister? We need to save that one for last—after we've had enough libations not to feel it when we throw our backs out!" Julie chuckled.

The girls' attention was suddenly diverted to the very loud blast of music coming from the stereo.

"Whoo hoo!" Julie shouted. She climbed to her feet and immediately began dancing on her own in the middle of the floor. It did not take long for Marissa to come up behind her and gyrate against her backside.

Elliot approached Lia and reached her hand down. "Come," she said.

Lia's eyebrows raised high on her forehead. "You want me to do *that*?"

Elliot looked at Marissa and Julie, who were actively engaged in foreplay in the middle of the living room. "Why not? Live a little," she replied.

"Ooo, bad choice of words, love," Lia pointed out.

Elliot pulled her to her feet. "Okay then, live a *lot*." Elliot led her to the middle of the room where they melded into one another in a little foreplay of their own.

Leslie joined Phoebe on the floor and leaned in close to her. "I don't know about you, but this is making me hot," he whispered.

"Is that what I'm feeling? I thought it was a hot flash," Phoebe joked.

"Can I interest you in sex on the dance floor?" he asked.

"I can think of better places to have sex, but for now, the dance floor will do."

***

At one point, Elliot and Lia left the dance floor and set out a spread of chips, dips, olives, pickles and cheeses that Elliot had purchased when they went after the drinks. They spread them out on various paper plates that were easily accessible by the three couples when they moved onto board games, which they played while sitting on the floor in a circle.

"For the next several hours, they played Monopoly and then Clue, while consuming their snacks and drinks. By the time they opted to play Twister, they were all relatively tipsy.

"Okay, who wants to be the spinner?" Elliot asked.

"I'll do it," Lia said. "The last thing I want to do is kill myself by falling down...not when we're this close to beating that evil bitch."

"That's probably a good idea," Marissa said. "Everyone take your places."

Lia spun the dial and called out, "Right hand yellow."

With so many players on the mat, it didn't take very many spins for all five bodies to become entangled.

Lia spun again. "Left foot green!"

"You're fucking kidding me," Elliot said as she contorted herself into an unnatural position.

"Right foot red!" Lia called out.

Everyone on the mat looked for an open red dot to move their right foot to, and in the process, Marissa bumped Elliot, who fell into Julie, who toppled Leslie, who fell directly on top of Phoebe, pinning her to the floor in a very compromising position.

"Hello there!" Leslie said when he found himself nose to nose with Phoebe and his knee pressed deeply between her legs. Unfortunately, or maybe fortunately for him, Julie was lying on top of his legs, so he couldn't move.

"Sorry, but I'm trapped here," he said to Phoebe.

"I'm not sorry. Kiss me," she said.

No one had paid much attention to the lovers entwined on the floor until one by one, they climbed off one another and stood.

Elliot walked to them and nudged Leslie's hip with her toe. "Get a room!" she said.

Leslie rolled off Phoebe and looked up at Elliot. "Jealous?" he asked.

"You're damn right I am," Elliot replied. "How about another drink to cool off?"

"Sure," Leslie said.

"Phoebs"?

She looked at Elliot. "Wine cooler please."

Elliot passed drinks out to everyone, and they sat around the Twister mat to enjoy more of their snacks.

Julie looked at her watch. "Jesus, it's nearly one in the morning."

"This has been such a fun evening," Phoebe said. "I hate to see it end."

"It doesn't have to end yet. Tomorrow is Saturday. There's no huge rush to get up early," Marissa pointed out.

"What *are* the plans for tomorrow?" Lia asked.

"Well, I think we need to talk to the queen about the information Marie gave us," Phoebe said.

"That is definitely a priority," Elliot agreed.

"I'd like to see if we can finish most of the painting and maybe get our stuff moved in on Sunday, if that's not too much to ask everyone," Marissa said.

"That is totally doable," Lia said. "I'm in."

"I think the appliances are being delivered tomorrow, too, Mar," Julie commented.

"Yes, they are. It'll be nice to have a refrigerator and stove," Marissa replied.

"I don't have anything pressing through the weekend if you need the help," Leslie added.

Julie tilted her head. "I'm sorry. We just assumed you and Phoebs were a package deal."

Leslie grinned. "Now that's one package I don't mind being under wraps with."

Phoebe bumped his shoulder. "You are such a guy!"

"Thank you for the compliment," he said.

Fleetwood Mac's "Tusk" suddenly played on the stereo.

Elliot jumped to her feet. "I love this song!" she exclaimed. She moved to the strong drumbeat that reverberated throughout the song.

Before long, all six friends were back in the middle of the floor moving their bodies to the tempo of the beat. Somewhere in the middle of the song, they drifted into pairs and clung to one another while the steady rhythm vibrated through their bodies.

The pounding of drums was heard in the distance long after the song ended. The stereo had suddenly stopped, yet the drums continued to beat in hypnotic cadence as they fell into a ceremonial trance.

One by one, each couple left the dance floor and drifted away. Each one carried the hypnotic trance with them, lost in one another, only to meld their bodies, hearts and souls long into the night.

Sometime later, six pristine, white feathers appeared on the dance floor—flitting round on some unseen current of air—and finally settled into the shape of a heart.

Chapter 36

Julie stepped into the living room the next morning and stopped short when she saw the six white feathers in the middle of the floor, laid out in the shape of a heart.

"Oh, wow! Marie must have been watching us last night," she said under her breath.

"Were you just talking to yourself?"

Julie turned to see Marissa behind her. "I'm sorry. Did I wake you when I got out of bed?" Julie asked.

"No. I had to pee, but I noticed you were gone, so I thought I'd come look for you," Marissa said.

"Look." Julie pointed to the floor.

"Ah, Marie has been here."

"Yes. This is an encouraging sign. Don't touch it. I want the others to see it," Julie said. Julie turned around and walked into Marissa's embrace. "I'm thinking about a run to the bakery. How does fresh brewed coffee sound to you?"

"I will forever be your sex slave for a cup of coffee," Marissa said.

"You are already my sex slave," Julie pointed out.

"Oh, yeah. Okay then, for a cup of coffee, I will massage your back for one hour."

"You're on! I need to get dressed."

Lia walked into the living room just as Julie disappeared into the master bedroom. She kissed Marissa on the cheek. "Good morning, Mar. What do we have here?"

"Julie says pristine white feathers are Marie's calling cards. It means good luck or something like that. We found them here this morning."

"They're beautiful." Lia looked around. "We didn't do a very good job cleaning up before we went to bed."

"I don't think any of us were in the shape, or in the mood, to do housework after all that booze and dirty dancing. No problem. I'll take care of it while you and Julie do a bakery run," Marissa said.

"You read my mind. I was about to ask her if she wanted to go with me," Lia replied. "Where is she?"

"She's getting dressed. Oh, and there is no question that someone would go with you. Elliot would break my neck if I allowed you to go alone."

***

Phoebe opened her eyes the next morning and was startled to see Leslie hovering above her. She jumped.

"Jesus, Leslie. You scared me!"

"Sorry. I was about to kiss you awake."

Phoebe grinned. "Now I wish I was still asleep."

Leslie placed a gentle kiss on Phoebe's lips and then continued to look at her with a huge smile on his face.

Phoebe narrowed her eyes. "What?" she asked.

"I was just wondering where you learned to do what you did last night. It was amazing."

"You liked it then?" Phoebe asked.

"God, yes. If I didn't expect the others to descend on us any minute, I would ask you to do it again. Where did you learn to do that?"

"Julie."

"Julie? Are you serious? Does Marissa know?"

Phoebe's eyes flew open. "Wait! You don't think…"

"What do you expect me to think? You said your best friend taught you how to make my eyes roll into the back of my head."

Phoebe grinned again. "They did, didn't they?"

"Hell, yes! So, does Marissa know?"

"I suspect she's used that technique on Marissa, so, yes—I assume she knows."

Leslie frowned. "You are being intentionally coy, so let me ask it out right—have you and Julie had sex?"

Phoebe laughed. "Heavens, no! She's not my type. She just gave me a few pointers."

"You have a type?" Leslie asked.

"Yes—tall, dark, fluid..."

Leslie rolled on top of her. "You are such a tease."

"Is it working?"

"You're damned right it is." He kissed her passionately.

Phoebe turned her head to the side so he could have access to her neck. "God, that feels good, but I think you're right about the girls. I hear them stirring in the other room."

Leslie lifted his head and looked into her eyes. "Did she give you other pointers, too?"

"Ah huh!"

"We will definitely continue this conversation tonight," he said.

"I'm counting on it."

***

Marissa and Elliot had showered and dressed for the day by the time Julie and Lia returned from the bakery with donuts, beignets and coffee.

Julie put the bags of pastries on the table. "Where are Phoebe and Leslie?" she asked.

"I believe they are in the shower. I recommend you stay away from that part of the house for now," Marissa said.

Lia raised her eyebrows. "Really?"

"Oh, yeah. Who would have thought Phoebe was a screamer," Elliot said.

"Be nice, you two. Don't you dare tease. I'm happy for them," Julie scolded.

Lia walked up to Elliot and traced her jaw with her index finger. "I remember someone else in this shower earlier this week."

Elliot turned five shades of red. "Okay. I get the point."

Julie and Marissa smiled at one another.

"I smell coffee!"

Four heads turned to the hallway to the bedrooms. Leslie and Phoebe emerged, freshly showered.

"You're just in time," Julie said. We have donuts and beignets."

"Awesome. I'm starving." Phoebe stopped short when she saw the feathers on the floor. "Oh, my. What have we here?"

"A gift from Marie, perhaps?" Julie suggested.

Phoebe squatted down beside the feathers. "The number of feathers and how they're laid out is intentional. It symbolizes our heart—all of us, collectively. It means, if we listen to our intuition and to what our hearts are telling us, we will be successful in the end. It represents a fresh sense of hope for the future."

Phoebe stood and looked at her friends. "They are also a sign of protection."

"Protection?" Elliot said. "Could they protect Lia from this curse?"

"Maybe not from the curse, but they may be useful during the spell to break the curse." Phoebe collected the feathers from the floor. "I'm going to put these with my things and then I'm coming back for some of those donuts."

Leslie watched Phoebe walk toward the bedrooms and then took Julie aside. "Thank you," he said softly.

"For what?" Julie asked.

Leslie whispered something Julie's ear.

Julie grinned. "Any time."

Leslie hugged her and then helped himself to breakfast.

Marissa sidled up to Julie. "What was that all about?" she asked.

"He was just thanking me for some advice I gave to Phoebe."

"Advice?" Marissa asked.

"The butterfly."

"You didn't!" Marissa exclaimed.

"I did."

"Jesus! No wonder they were so loud!"

"So, what's on the agenda for today?" Elliot asked as Phoebe returned from the bedroom.

"Well, like we agreed, we need to meet with Queen Thibodeaux to discuss the information Marie gave us," Phoebe said.

"Do all of us need to go? Someone has to stay here for the appliance delivery," Marissa said.

"Julie and I should go—and you as well, Lia, if you want to," Phoebe suggested.

"Absolutely," Lia replied.

"We can stay here and work in the master," Marissa suggested. "I think the sheetrock mud is dry enough to sand and paint."

"Count me in," Leslie said. "I'm not too bad with a paint brush."

"Be sure the doors to the bedrooms and bathrooms are closed before you sand. In fact, close the door to the dining room as well. You can open the windows and back door in the master for ventilation. We don't need sheetrock dust on everything again," Julie said.

"And don't forget to wear your masks," Lia added.

"We should be back in a couple of hours," Phoebe called over her shoulder as they left.

Marissa and Elliot stood there with their hands on their hips until their wives were out of earshot.

"Sheesh! It's a good thing we have them here to tell us how to do our jobs!" Elliot said.

"You got that right!" Marissa quipped.

***

Queen Thibodeaux greeted her guests with hugs. "Please, have a seat," she said. "I'm excited to hear what Queen Laveau revealed to you."

"As I said on the phone, we had a séance with her and we told her about the box we found in her foundation," Phoebe began.

"So, she was unaware it was there," the queen said.

"It appears she had no idea the mistress had it mortared into her foundation," Lia said.

"We think she buried it in the foundation to simulate burying it within a tomb in the graveyard," Julie explained. "I mean, the dirt inside of it most likely came from the graveyard and mortaring it into the foundation is similar to encasing it in a concrete tomb."

"Yes, the symbolism is very clear," the queen remarked. "I can only assume the mistress had this burial done while Marie was on one of her many trips."

"That would explain why Marie was unaware of it," Lia reasoned.

"Bettina, Marie said the box containing the tooth and hair *is* the curse. I assume she meant it was used in *casting* the curse, so it would make sense that it would be key in reversing it as well," Phoebe said.

"Yes. If the artifacts in that box were truly the ones used to curse generations of Celeste's family, then they are a critical ingredient in the recipe to resolve this problem. Did she give you any idea what curse might have been used?"

"She said the person casting the curse would have used an effigy, or articles from the person they were attempting to curse," Phoebe began.

"The tooth and hair make sense because they contain the DNA that would be inside all descendants," Lia interjected.

"The person casting the curse would then construct a container to put the articles in and would cover them in dirt from the graveyard, inside the box. They would do this while visualizing the victim with intense hatred in their heart. They would then light a black candle and bury the container in a more permanent location while intensely focusing on the death and destruction of their victim or victims while chanting a death curse." Phoebe paused to allow the queen to absorb the information they had given her.

After a brief pause, the queen replied. "I believe your assumption that this particular box was used in the curse is a good one. The procedure you describe is also typical of a death curse. Did Queen Laveau provide any clues as to what the chant might be?"

"Yes, and no," Julie said. "She wasn't there when it was cast, so she couldn't give us the exact curse, but she did give us the details of what a curse like this one *might* have included."

"Well, don't keep an old woman waiting, girl. What did she say?" the queen urged.

Phoebe pulled a piece of paper out of her bag and handed it to Queen Thibodeaux. She read it aloud.

I curse these articles.
I curse the bearer.
I curse all who come forth from the bearer.

They have inflicted pain on my mind and on my heart.
They have taken from me what was rightfully mine.
They must forfeit their lives through all generations.
They must die painful and undignified deaths.
They must burn forever in the fires of hell.

I bury these articles in ground contaminated by death.
May they spend eternity writhing in pain and anguish for
their sins against me.
May this curse not stop until each descendant pays for their
sins with death, at the age of fifty and one.

Queen Thibodeaux lowered the paper into her lap and looked at the girls. "We must use these words, but we must repeat this curse in reverse. We must repeat it with love in our hearts instead of hatred. We must simulate birth rather than death."

"Marie said the box needs to be destroyed in order to lift the curse. I'm afraid Celeste may not allow that," Lia said.

"Then it will be up to us to convince her otherwise," the queen replied. "May I keep this chant to share with the Council?"

"Yes, please do," Phoebe insisted."

"Very well. I will meet with them tonight."

"I hope it works so we can put this behind us," Lia said.

"Keep in mind child that breaking the curse is only half of what we need to do. We need to banish her as well," the queen pointed out. "We must do both, and we must do them correctly, or we will fail."

Phoebe, Lia and Julie stood and prepared to leave.

"Oh, one more thing, Bettina—Marie also said that Lia has to be the one to break the curse and banish the mistress. At the very least, she needs to be an active participant," Phoebe said.

"Yes, I remember Marie's words," the queen replied. "She said that the good in Lia's heart must kill the hatred in the evil one. Lia's powers will be essential in our attempts to lift this curse."

Phoebe reached into her bag. "We also found these on the living room floor this morning. There are six of them, and they were laid out to form a heart."

Queen Thibodeaux took the white feathers from Phoebe. Tears filled her eyes when she looked at the women before her. "Queen Laveau has blessed you all. The six of you are destined to travel as one through many lifetimes. These feathers are a symbol of hope and protection, not only for Lia, but for all of you. We will use these in the ceremony on St. John's Eve. They will provide an added measure of protection for Lia as we attempt to lift this curse."

"I thought as much," Phoebe said. "Should I leave them with you?"

"Yes, please. I will pass them on to the council. In fact, we should all meet with the council tomorrow. We have many plans to carry out and the council may need your help. At the very least, you need to be informed about what to expect on St. John's Eve."

Lia spontaneously hugged Queen Thibodeaux. "Thank you for everything you are doing," she said through a voice choked with emotion.

"Whether you realize it or not, child, you are a gift to all of us. We will do everything in our power to help you survive this horrible curse." Queen Thibodeaux kissed her on the temple and then released her.

The queen stopped them once more as they prepared to leave. "Oh, Phoebe."

"Yes?" Phoebe asked.

"We could use Queen Laveau's help on St. John's Eve if she is so inclined. She was a very powerful woman in her time and adding her talent and powers to this effort will only help."

Phoebe smiled. "I will certainly request her presence."

***

Leslie, Marissa and Elliot had finished painting the master bedroom by the time the girls returned to Saint Ann Street.

"Oh, my God! This looks amazing!" Julie said. "You can't even tell where the wall was."

"That's the point," Marissa said. "Do you like the color?"

"I love it," Julie replied.

"All we have left in here is the baseboard trim where we took the wall down, and some urethane on the floor. If we get that done today, we could move furniture in as early as tomorrow night," Marissa said.

Julie threw her arms around Marissa. "I'm so glad I have a butch wife." She kissed her soundly.

"Hey, what about *this* butch?" Elliot said.

"And this one!" Leslie added.

Julie kissed both of her friends on the cheek and gave them each a warm hug. "I don't know what we'd do without such great friends." She turned to Lia and Phoebe. "You guys, too," she said, and then proceeded to hug and kiss them as well.

"So, Jules, the appliances haven't arrived yet. Do you want to paint the kitchen, living room and dining room?" Lia asked. "Because if you do, we need to paint where the refrigerator and stove go before they are delivered. That means, pronto!"

"Yikes! You're right!" Julie said.

"Okay then, let's divide and conquer. Mar and Elliot, you two start on the dining room. I'll do the kitchen, and Phoebs and Julie, you two tackle the living room. I think we can get all three rooms done by the end of the day if we put our minds to it," Lia said.

As planned, Lia managed to paint behind the stove and refrigerator long before the deliverymen arrived. With a concerted effort, the rest of the rooms were also finished as the sun set on the horizon. The very last thing was a shiny coat of urethane on the floor of the master bedroom.

The six friends collapsed on the living room floor.

"Wow! That has got to be a marathon effort," Lia said.

"I'll say," Marissa replied. "I think tomorrow, we install the baseboard trim and then start moving boxes and furniture in." She looked around at her exhausted friends. "I totally understand if any of you want to opt out tomorrow. We've already asked a lot of you this weekend."

"You're kidding, right?" Phoebe said. "Do you think we've done all this work just so you and Julie can get the first look at it finished? No way, girlfriend. I'm not missing the reveal. I'll be moving boxes and furniture right along with you tomorrow."

"Me, too," Lia said.

"Ditto," Elliot remarked.

"I'm with Phoebs," Leslie replied. "Package deal—remember?"

Marissa struggled to keep the tears from her eyes. "You guys!" she said. "How is it that we are so blessed?"

Lia walked up to Marissa and kissed her on the cheek. "You're just lucky that way," she said. "Now, how about we get some dinner? The beast is growling."

***

During dinner, the friends decided to stay the night at Lia and Elliot's home to escape the smell of new paint and urethane. Upon rising on Sunday morning, they ate breakfast and then immediately began transporting boxes and smaller pieces of furniture to the new house.

Around midday, Elliot, Leslie and Marissa visited the local rental facility and acquired a truck large enough to accommodate the bulkier furniture such as the couch, living room chairs, mattresses, rugs and dressers. During this time, Phoebe, Lia, and Julie unpacked the boxes they had already transported and did their best to find appropriate places for everything inside them.

The six friends worked all day and managed to transform the empty house into a warm and welcoming home. The one room they did not set up was the office. Marissa insisted that it was low on the priority list and that she would tackle it on her own the following few days.

At the end of the day, they all met in the living room and relaxed on the furniture they had just moved into the house.

"Wow. I can't believe we got it all here in one day. You even managed to hang the television. Now all we need to do is get the cable and internet installed," Julie said. She looked at Marissa. "Mar, we still have a mess to clean in the basement of Lia and El's place, too. I believe there may be a few odds and ends still there."

"Duly noted," Marissa said. "We also need to pack our clothes and toiletries that are still there."

"There's no rush," Lia said.

"How about Jules and I take everyone to the lobster place for a thank you dinner?" Marissa suggested.

***

After dinner, Marissa and Julie followed Lia and Elliot home and spent the next two hours packing up the clothes and accessories that had accumulated in their bedroom during the few months they had spent as houseguests.

While they packed, Lia went through the pantry and refrigerator and put together a care package to get them through a day or two in their new home until they had a chance to stock their own cupboards.

It was ten before Marissa and Julie departed for their new home. The send-off was sad, yet bittersweet, and it left all four women emotionally vulnerable.

Elliot and Lia clung to one another on the sidewalk in front of their home and waved to their friends as they drove away.

Lia wept.

"It's okay, love," Elliot said. "They're less than a mile away. It's not like it was when we were here, and they were still in New York."

"I know, but it feels like a piece of my heart just drove away."

"A piece of your heart *did* just drive away, but it's just a short distance away. We'll see them again soon, I'm sure."

Lia turned in Elliot's arms so that they were face to face. "We are so blessed, Elliot. Growing up an only child, I never felt this close to another human being. They are my sisters. Phoebe and Leslie feel like siblings, too. Queen Thibodeaux said the six of us are destined to travel through many lifetimes together. Maybe that's why I feel this connection to them. Maybe we have *always* been connected."

"Maybe," Elliot replied. "Why don't we go inside and snuggle into bed. We have a busy day tomorrow."

A lone figure, tucked into a doorway diagonally across the intersection, watched four women exit the gated entryway. Two of them carried boxes and suitcases that they placed in the trunk of the car. Affectionate hugs were exchanged and two of them entered the car and drove away, leaving the remaining two embraced on the sidewalk. After a few moments, they entered the house and locked the gate behind them.

Soon. It will all be finished soon, and the last descendant of that whore will be dead. They plan to fight me, but they cannot if they are not here. Their plan to leave was a lie. There is much to do to prevent them from being victorious. I need to focus on stopping them.

The man rubbed his forehead and rested the back of his head against the wall.

This one is fighting me. I must find a more suitable and powerful host. One that will help me finish this once and for all. One that will assure the last of that whore's progeny dies the death she deserves. One that will assure my rightful place in the dark sphere of influence.

Chapter 37

Randy paced back and forth in front of Susan's desk on Monday morning.

"Hey, what's up with you?" Susan asked. "You're pacing like a caged animal."

Randy stopped and rubbed his forehead. "The Chief called an eight o'clock meeting with just me this morning and I don't know why." He stopped pacing and grabbed both sides of his head. "This damned headache won't let up."

Susan reached into her desk and pulled out a bottle. "Here. Take these. They contain acetaminophen and caffeine. Hopefully they'll help."

"Thanks." Randy took two of the tablets and retrieved a cup of water from the water cooler. He stood again in front of Susan's desk. "I hope I'm not being reprimanded for something."

"Don't invite trouble, Randy. Maybe it's something good," Susan said.

"Maybe." He glanced at this watch. The time was seven-fifty-nine. "Okay. Here goes nothing. Wish me luck."

Randy knocked on the chief's door.

"Come in," came the response.

He pushed the door open and stepped inside. "You wanted to see me, Chief?"

"Yes. Please close the door and have a seat," the chief replied.

Randy sat before the chief and nervously clenched his hands.

"Relax, Officer Rocque. You're not here for a reprimand. Quite the opposite, in fact."

"Sir?" Randy said.

"I was in the crossover meeting last week when you volunteered to investigate the zombie sightings."

"Revenants, sir. They are called revenants."

"Yes, and the fact that you had taken the time to research that little bit of information shows me that you have proactively taken the initiative on this problem."

The chief sat back in his chair. "Rocque, I have been reviewing your file and was quite pleased to see several citations and recognitions for your outstanding service and specifically for your investigative skills."

"Thank you, sir," Randy said humbly.

"Officer Rocque, I would like to recommend you for detective training—that is, if you're interested."

Randy's eyebrows rose high onto this forehead. "I...I don't know what to say. Yes, of course, I'm interested. Thank you, sir."

The chief leaned forward and opened the folder on this desk. He signed the paper on top of the stack and handed it to Randy. "Excellent. I'm assigning you to Detective Williams, effective immediately. With St. John's Eve just two days away, you and Williams need to find the underlying cause of this zombie escalation. There were several more sightings this weekend."

Both the chief and Randy rose and shook hands. "Good luck on this assignment, Rocque. It should go a long way toward you successfully passing the detective's exam. Oh, and you'll need to go home and change your clothes. Standard uniform for a detective is suit and tie."

"Thank you, sir. I appreciate the opportunity, Chief. I won't let you down."

Excellent. This may be my opportunity for a more suitable host. I will help you to find the bokors.

***

The first thing Elliot noticed when she woke up on Monday morning was that she was alone. She felt around Lia's side of the bed and noted it was cold.

She's been up for a while, Elliot thought.

She picked up her phone from the bedside table and looked at the time. Seven-thirty-seven.

Elliot got out of bed and reached for her robe hanging on the rack between the two front windows of their bedroom. She stepped into the hall and stopped to listen. It was eerily quiet...quieter than it had been in months.

That's right. Marissa and Julie aren't here anymore. I wonder where Lia is.

Elliot moved to the central staircase and descended one level to the main living area. A short walk through the butler's pantry put her in the kitchen, where she noticed that the door to the courtyard was open. As she approached the open door, she saw Lia standing on the deck, leaning on the railing. She pushed the screen door open and stepped out, allowing the screen door to shut by itself to announce her presence and to avoid scaring Lia.

Elliot stood beside Lia and kissed her on the cheek. "Good morning, my love," she said.

"Good morning," Lia replied without looking at her.

"How long have you been up?"

"For a couple of hours. I couldn't sleep."

Elliot rubbed her back. "Wanna talk about it?"

"I don't know what to say, Elliot. All I can think about is that I may only have two days to live. There are so many things I still want to do with my life. There is so much more living I want to do with you, and now...well, now, none of that may be possible."

"I'm not ready to give up, Lia, and you shouldn't give up either. She hasn't won yet," Elliot said firmly.

Lia looked at Elliot. "That is easy for you to say."

Elliot took Lia by the shoulders and firmly turned her around. "Look, Lia, you are not the only one who is scared here. You are not the only one whose entire life could change in a heartbeat in two days. God knows, I would trade places with you in an instant if I could, but I can't. What I *do* know is that I refuse to play victim. I choose to have faith in our friends and in the community that has stepped up to support us. Don't you dare give up, do you hear me? Don't you dare give up!" A steady stream of tears flowed down Elliot's face as she finished her declaration.

Lia rested her palm on the side of Elliot's face. "I'm sorry. I have been so wrapped up in my own fear that I've neglected to consider how you must be feeling right now."

"Promise me you won't give up, Lia. Promise me," Elliot insisted. "I can't do this...no, I can't do *life* without you."

"I promise."

Just then, Elliot's phone rang. She dug it out of the pocket of her robe and answered it.

"Yeah."

"Elliot? Elliot, this is Julie. Are you crying?"

"I'm sorry, Jules. We're just dealing with some heavy shit right now."

"Sweetie, I know. I so wish I could make all of this go away. Know that Mar and I are here for both of you."

"I know." Julie's expression of love and support only made her cry harder.

"Give me the phone," Lia said.

Elliot handed the phone to her while she tried to compose herself.

"Good morning, love," Lia said.

"Lia! Are you two okay? Elliot sounds like she's a wreck," Julie said.

"I'm afraid that's my fault. I was feeling sorry for myself and Elliot made me see what a fool I've been for wasting precious time on self-pity."

"I can't blame you for that, Lia. There is so much riding on these next two days. That's why I'm calling. Queen Thibodeaux wants to see us all as a group this morning to share the council's plans on how we are going to fight this thing. Can the two of you be ready by nine o'clock? Mar and I will pick you up."

Lia pulled the phone away from her ear and looked at the time displayed on the screen. "Sure. It's seven-fifty now. That should give us enough time to shower and dress before you get here."

"Okay. We'll see you soon then. Oh, and Lia, we are going to do everything we can to beat this. I promise," Julie said.

"We'll see you soon. Bye," Lia replied.

***

"How do I look?" Randy asked Susan.

"Incredibly handsome and professional, Detective Rocque," she replied.

"I'm not a detective yet," he corrected her.

"But you are on your way to being one. You look very nice in a suit."

"Thank you. I guess I'll need to invest in a few more if this will become my daily uniform."

Shut up and get on with finding the bokors. We are wasting precious time. There are only two days left.

Randy shook his head.

"Are you okay?" Susan asked.

"I don't know where these headaches are coming from. One minute I'm fine and the next, I get this shooting pain in my temples."

"Maybe you should get it checked out," Susan suggested.

"Maybe later. Right now, I need to do a little research on bokors. I got a tip from one of the guys in the crossover meeting."

Randy sat down at the desk assigned to him by Detective Williams and began searching the internet, as well as the internal files the department kept on people of interest.

"Holy shit!" Randy exclaimed when he found a particularly interesting article. He picked up the phone and called Detective Williams' cell. "Reg, do you have a minute? I found some information on bokors that you've just gotta hear."

"Yes, I have a couple of minutes. Where are you?" Reg Williams asked.

"I'm in the bullpen."

"Okay. I'll be there in a jiff."

"Have a seat," Randy said when Detective Williams approached his desk. "Listen to this: Bokors have the power to create and control revenants. The process includes using a mixture of mystical herbs, human remains, animal and insect parts and neurotoxins from puffer fish to create a cocktail of potentially toxic substances. When ingested, it causes the victim to become immobile within one to five hours and reduces their heartbeat and respiratory functions to a minimum. The overall effect is that of death, although the victim is still fully aware of their surroundings, but unable to express themselves. It is customary to actually bury the victim alive and then to exhume their body within a day before they can asphyxiate.

"Once the victim is exhumed, the bokor performs a voodoo rite whereby they capture their soul, and place it in a clay jar, which is hidden in a location known only to the bokor. A day or two later, the bokor administers a hallucinogenic mixture to the victim and revives them enough for physical mobility, but not to full awareness. In this state, the revenant is submissive. They cannot speak, nor do they have any memory or personality. This submissive condition makes them easy to control and open to suggestions and commands by the bokor. The revenants remain in a zombie-like state either until they are awakened, or until the bokor dies."

"Are you telling me they actually bury these people alive?" Detective Williams exclaimed.

"That's what the research says, although I can't imagine that practice is still carried out today. I mean, just waiting for a day before doing the soul-capturing ceremony would produce the same result without the residual psychological affect from being buried live."

"Jesus! What a barbaric practice."

"That's exactly why we need to find these bokors," Randy said. "I'm actually more concerned about the fact that they have control of the revenants. I mean, if they are really as easy to control as this article suggests, the bokors can make them do anything they want—including commit crimes."

"The revenants should be relatively easy to spot. They are zombies after all," Detective Williams said.

"Some people call them zombies, but don't confuse them with the how zombies are represented on television. They are not really dead, and their flesh is not rotting like the television versions. Oh, and they don't go around eating people either.

They are real, live people who are drugged. Other than the fact that they have blank looks on their faces and they don't interact with others, they look as normal as you and me. They could easily blend into a crowd," Randy explained.

"We need to find these bokors and stop them before they can create more revenants," Detective Williams reasoned.

"Judging by the reports we have coming in, it may already be too late. St. John's Eve is just two days away. According to this article, creating revenants is a multi-day process, so it may have already started. I think the most we can hope for is to contain any malicious activities that might occur."

"Have you located any of these bokors?" Detective Williams asked.

"I have a lead on a few of them that I plan to check out this morning," Randy replied.

"Do you need me to go with you?"

"You can come if you'd like, but I think I can handle this alone."

"All right then. Get back to me as soon as you have something," Detective Williams instructed.

***

Randy noticed a significant increase in activity around the city as he drove to the locations provided to him by his contact from the crossover meeting. This was not surprising to him, considering a major religious holiday was just two days away. Pop-up vendors lined the streets, selling everything from voodoo dolls to gris-gris bags, to ceremonial masks and costumes. He also noted that a very large bonfire was already under construction on Bayou St. John.

St. John's Eve was almost as big as Mardi Gras to the city of New Orleans, and it attracted visitors from all around the world. In the voodoo religion, it is believed that the barrier between the worlds of the living and dead were especially porous on certain days of the year and that spiritual powers were especially strong. St. John's Eve was one of those days. The ceremonies carried out on that night by the local voodoo and Christian communities were nothing short of magical and involved all manner of mystery, magic, voodoo, sorcery and witchcraft.

Randy struck out at the first two locations he visited. No one responded to his knock, nor to him announcing himself as representing the New Orleans police department. His luck changed at the third location he visited.

Randy knocked on the door of a well-kept building in the French Quarter and waited patiently for a response. Within a minute, the door swung open, and a man dressed in a traditional dashiki tunic stood before him.

This is the one. Touch him.

"How may I help you?" the man said in a rich Haitian accent.

Randy showed the man his badge. "My name is Randy Rocque and I represent the investigative unit of the New Orleans police department. Is a Mr. Ricardo Gedeon here?"

"I'm Ricardo Gedeon," the man said.

"Mr. Gedeon, I'm here to discuss a rash of revenant sightings that have been reported the past few days."

"I know nothing of these reports," the man said.

"I was given your name by a colleague as someone who would be considered a bokor."

"What would a white boy like you know of bokors?" Gedeon asked.

"I beg your pardon, sir, but I happen to be the descendent of an African American who was actually a police officer in this city many years ago, so the color of my skin, or yours for that matter, is irrelevant. Look, I have actually done significant research on bokors, Mr. Gedeon. Are you, or are you not a bokor?" Randy asked.

"I'm a practitioner of voodoo, as are many others who live in this city. I'm not aware that it is a crime to practice voodoo."

"No one is accusing you of committing a crime, Mr. Gedeon. I'm here to follow up on revenant sightings, and it is a well-known fact that revenants are created and controlled by bokors. It is also a known fact that revenants are created through the ingestion of illegal and potentially lethal substances. I have it on good authority that you are a bokor, which gives me reason to suspect you may be connected to these revenant sightings, or that you might have some of these illegal substances in your possession. Now, if you have nothing to hide, then you should not object to me taking a look around inside. I could come back with a warrant if necessary."

Ricardo Gedeon stared directly at Randy for several long moments and then stepped aside. "Please, come in," he said.

Randy spent the next twenty minutes looking around Gedeon's tidy home. Randy did not expect to find evidence of illegal substances, as he suspected illicit practices would be held elsewhere, but he noted with interest that Mr. Gedeon's manner remained calm and unconcerned as he went from room to room and looked inside dressers, closets and cabinets along the way.

Ricardo Gedeon folded his arms across his chest at the end of Randy's inspection. "I trust you are satisfied that there is nothing incriminating here," he said.

"I think I have seen everything I need to see for now," Randy replied. "I will let you know if my superiors wish to visit this in more depth." Randy walked to the front door and turned to address Mr. Gedeon once more before leaving. "One more thing, Mr. Gedeon. Do you plan to attend the St. John's Eve celebrations?"

"Absolutely. I attend every year. As an active practitioner of voodoo, I wouldn't miss it," Mr. Gedeon replied.

Randy nodded and extended his hand. "I thought as much. It was nice to meet you, Mr. Gedeon and I appreciate your cooperation. I will be in touch if we need additional information."

"Of course," Gedeon said as he released Randy's hand.

Ricardo Gedeon stood in the window next to his front door and pulled the curtain aside. He watched as the detective climbed into his car and drove away.

You will do as I instruct.

"Yes, mistress," Gedeon said aloud.

You will allow me to control the revenants, and you will assist me in the destruction of my enemies.

"I will do as you ask, mistress."

***

Lia, Elliot, Julie and Phoebe met with the Council of Kings and Queens in a basement room of St. Louis Cathedral at nine. Bettina Thibodeaux was among them.

"Welcome," Queen Thibodeaux said. "We chose this holy place to protect us from the forces of black magic that cursed your family, Lia. We should be able to speak freely, and plan without fear of disclosure here."

Bettina indicated the assembled group with a sweep of her arm.

"Before you, are all the active queens and kings in New Orleans. Some of them are well acquainted with the events that happened in your home more than one hundred and eighty years ago, and we agree that this curse must be stopped before it can claim you, Lia—its final victim. We have much work to do to prepare for the events of St. John's Eve, just two days hence. Do you have any questions for the group before we begin?"

Lia raised her hand. "Do you think we can stop the curse?"

"We will do everything in our power to reverse it," one of the queens said.

"The artifacts and the box you found in Marie Laveau's home will give us the tools we need for success," another queen called out.

"And the doll effigy found in your home, Ms. Purvis, will be a valuable tool in our attempt to banish the evil one forever," one of the kings added.

"There are many things that need to come together before we can even consider lifting the curse," Bettina said. "We have essentially broken the group into two factions. One has been focused on how to break the curse, and the other on how to banish the mistress. Although the group has worked separately on these two challenges, all of us will come together to participate in both events."

"I have a question," Elliot said. "St. John's Eve is two days away. Why do we have to wait until the last moment to break this curse? Can't it be done at any time? What if we fail and run out of time to try again?"

"Those are all good questions, Elliot," Queen Thibodeaux said. "To answer the first two questions, we need the collective power of all the kings and queens in this room, combined with the power of all their followers, focused all at once on breaking the curse. We will have our best chance for success at the celebration on Wednesday night. There will be hundreds of followers there to add to the collective power. Your concerns about not getting a second chance are valid, however, our risk will best be minimized by strength in numbers." The queen looked around the room once more. "So, if there are no more questions, we'll get started."

***

Later that afternoon, Randy paid a visit to Phoebe's shop. He parked his car out front and walked into the shop and to the back of the store where both Phoebe and Julie stood, waiting on customers. Their eyes opened wide when they realized he had just walked in without having to be invited.

"Randy!" Julie said once her customer had walked away. "You're here! I mean...you're in the shop!"

"Of course, I'm in the shop. Is that a problem?" Randy replied.

"But the door didn't stick," Julie said.

"That's because she is no longer inside him," Phoebe interjected.

"Huh? What are you talking about?" Randy asked.

"Randy, give me your hand," Phoebe said.

He extended his hand toward her. "Julie, give me that vial to the left of the register."

Julie handed the vial to her, and she proceeded to pour it into his hand.

Randy narrowed his eyes. "That's holy water, isn't it?"

"Yes," Phoebe said."

"What the hell? Do you think I'm possessed or something?" he asked.

"You were, but it appears she has jumped," Phoebe replied.

"She?" Randy asked.

"The mistress."

Randy wiped his hand on a paper towel Julie had handed to him. "No way!" he exclaimed.

"Yes. Do you recall having a problem opening the door when you came here...and not being able to step into Julie and Marissa's house without permission?" Phoebe asked.

"Yeah, so what?"

"You couldn't do either of those things because the properties were protected with spells that prevent evil entities from entering without permission."

"The flash headaches you've had the past few days are also a sign of possession," Julie added.

"Like I said, it appears she has jumped," Phoebe said.

"Well, I'll be," Randy said. "I hope I didn't do anything to hurt anyone."

"Probably not. So, you came in here like you were on a mission. Is there something you need?" Phoebe asked.

"Oh, yeah. I came by for information this morning, but the shop was closed. I did some more research on revenants and I was wondering what could be used to contain them. We had several reports of zombie-like creatures causing mischief this weekend, and I suspect we'll see several more of them at the St. John's Eve celebration on Wednesday. I need a way to immobilize them without harming them."

"So, you're going to be there?" Julie asked.

"Yes. I volunteered to cover the event."

"That's good to know," Julie added.

"So, what can we do to stop them, that isn't harmful to them?" Randy asked again.

"Salt," Phoebe said.

***

Elliot and Lia arrived home on Monday evening after spending most of the day with the Council of Kings and Queens. They discussed the details of what to expect from the moment they arrived on site, until the final banishment ceremony was carried out after the curse was broken. The entire process was expected to take more than five hours to complete.

They were given a series of meditation exercises to practice throughout the following day to mentally prepare themselves for the intense ceremonies they would be engaging in. To further ensure Lia's safety, they were also instructed not to leave their home while they waited for the fifty and one to arrive on Wednesday.

Lia and Elliot spent the entire day on Tuesday, making love and sleeping on and off throughout the day. They took no phone calls and they left their room only for meals. Otherwise, they did the one thing they wanted to do if it was truly to be their last day together—they spent it totally wrapped up in one another's love.

Chapter 38

Elliot stayed awake all of Tuesday night, monitoring Lia as she slept. She had no idea how this curse would work itself out and her biggest fear was that Lia would die in her sleep. Several times throughout the night, she checked to see that Lia was still breathing. She spent the entire night alternating between crying and reliving all of the details of the past twenty-two years she had spent with the one person who completed her. Along with the good times, she recalled all of the times she was self-absorbed and chided herself for wasting those precious moments. She vowed to make Lia the focal point of her life if they managed to survive this day.

Around seven on Wednesday morning, Lia opened her eyes and found herself wrapped in Elliot's arms. She looked up and saw such intense love and raw emotion on Elliot's face that it nearly broke her heart. She closed her eyes again and burrowed into Elliot's shoulder, lest Elliot see the tears in her own eyes. She stayed that way for several minutes.

"Lia?" Elliot said softly.

Lia looked up once more and smiled in an attempt to make light of things. "Well, I'm still here!" she joked.

"Yes, you are. I stood guard all night," Elliot confessed.

Lia traced the side of Elliot's face with her fingertip. "I'm sorry, love."

"I'm not. We have seventeen hours to go, and I need to warn you that I will be hovering as much as I can for every second of it."

"What time do we need to be at the bayou?" Lia asked.

"Queen Thibodeaux said the ceremonies will begin this evening," Elliot said. "She asked that we be there around eight for the cleansing ceremony. Until then, we are staying right here in this house. I don't want to risk you being exposed to anyone who might harm you."

"Normally, I would chastise you for being overprotective, but I'm going to give you a pass on this one. Thank you for loving me, Elliot."

"Don't thank me for something I can't help, Lia. You are the air that I breathe. I can't live without you. This is as much about my survival as it is yours."

"Well, let's hope we can pull off a miracle today and then we won't have to worry about that for many more years to come."

"We have the whole day ahead of us before we have to leave. How would you like to spend that time?" Elliot asked.

"I want to spend it with you...and I want to speak to Celeste. We still need her permission to use the box in the curse reversal."

"How do you propose we do that?"

"You and I should go to the room where you found her remains and try to summon her," Lia suggested.

"But, Lia, that room scares you."

"Dying scares me more."

Elliot nodded. "We should do that soon. Marissa and Julie will be collecting the box and the doll when they come for dinner, but first, let's get some breakfast into us."

"Yes. I could use a cup of coffee," Lia said.

"Anything for my birthday girl," Elliot replied.

"Let's not celebrate my birthday until tomorrow, okay?" Lia suggested.

"I like your optimism. Tomorrow it is."

***

Lia and Elliot sat on the floor facing one another in the room above the library. The box containing the hair and tooth was on the floor between them. Lia reached her hands toward Elliot and closed her eyes.

"Celeste, please come to us. We have something important to discuss with you. We need your blessing and your support to break this curse that threatens to end my life today," Lia said. "Please, Celeste, please come to us."

"Celeste be here, child. What you need?"

Elliot had tears in her eyes before she even spoke. "Celeste, thank you for coming to us. Please allow Lia to be part of this discussion."

"Lia be here wid us. She know what we say. I speak for her."

Celeste looked off in the distance for a moment, and then refocused her gaze on Elliot. "Lia say we need da box to break da curse. She say da box be destroyed. Dat be true, El-ee-ot?"

"I'm afraid it is true, Celeste. In order to break the curse, the items that were used to cast it in the first place have to be destroyed. Lia's tooth and Ethan's hair are those items. They contain the footprint that was passed down through every generation after them. *That* is what made it possible for the mistress to kill every single person in your lineage, Celeste. Every single person, except Lia. She may die before the end of the day if we are not able to break this curse."

Celeste cried. "Dat is all dat be left of my babies," she said.

"No, Celeste. Lia is your baby as well. She is all that is left, and she will be gone too if we can't stop this curse," Elliot explained.

Celeste frowned. "Lia say she understand if I don't give dem up. She be willing to die so I can keep dem, El-ee-ot." Celeste shook her head. "Celeste not let her do dat. Lia need to live. You be right. She my baby, too. Take da box, El-ee-ot. Take da box and save Lia. Save my baby."

Tears rolled freely down both Elliot and Celeste's faces. Elliot reached forward and took Celeste into her arms. "Thank you, Celeste. Thank you for helping to save Lia. We both love you very much."

"Celeste love you, too."

"Elliot?" Lia whispered softly.

Elliot broke the embrace and held Lia at arm's length. "We have Celeste's blessing."

"Yes, we do." Lia looked around the room. "Elliot, after this is done, I want to do something special with this room in honor of Celeste."

"What did you have in mind?"

"I don't know. Maybe an art gallery with works depicting what her people...what *my* people lived through. I need to think about it, but I want to do something to honor their sacrifice."

***

Marissa and Julie pulled their car to a stop in front of the Royal Street home and shut off the ignition. Julie had been crying on the entire drive from their house.

Marissa rubbed Julie's arm. "Jules, you need to get a hold of yourself. This isn't going to do Lia any good."

"I'm sorry, Mar, but the thought of losing her today is too much for my heart to bear."

Marissa inhaled deeply to control her own emotions. "I know. I'm struggling with that as well, but we need to transmit confidence to them. Giving in is giving up."

Julie blew her nose. "I know. Give me a minute to compose myself."

A few moments later, Marissa and Julie exited their car and let themselves in through the gated entry.

"Hey there! We're here!" Marissa called out.

"We're in the kitchen," they heard Lia call back.

Julie took a deep breath. "I can do this," she said.

She took Marissa's hand and together, they ascended the stairs and made their way to the kitchen. The moment they stepped into the room, Julie lost it again and ran to Lia's arms.

Lia held her close. "It's okay, Julie. It will be okay. I have faith in our friends. We're going to beat this."

Julie finally regained control of her emotions and broke out of Lia's embrace. "Some friend I am. I should be comforting you, not the other way around."

"I wouldn't want you any other way. Now how about you work some of your kitchen magic and help me make dinner?" Lia said.

***

"We got Celeste's permission to use the box—even if it ends up being destroyed," Elliot said. "We did a mini séance with her this morning."

"That's good news," Marissa said.

"So, Julie, what exactly will happen at this ceremony tonight?" Lia asked.

"Well, like Bettina said, we will focus first on a ceremony to break the curse, and if we're successful, we'll move on to the banishment spell," Julie explained.

"Don't we need the mistress there for that?" Elliot asked.

"Not if we have an effigy. We will use the baby doll we found in the fireplace compartment," Julie said. "Oh! Speaking of the mistress, we don't think she's inside Randy anymore."

"How do you know?" Lia asked.

"Because he walked right into the shop this morning without having to be invited in, not to mention, Phoebe poured holy water into his hand with no adverse reaction. She has obviously jumped again, but Randy has no idea into whom."

"Well, that's not good," Elliot said. "We have no idea who to be wary of now."

"You're right about that," Marissa added.

"We can't worry about that right now. Our first priority is to get this curse lifted. All of our energy has to focus on that," Julie said. "If we fail, then nothing else matters."

Julie's sobering statement cast a deafening silence over the group. Julie sobbed anew. "I'm sorry. I shouldn't have said that."

Lia placed her hand on Julie's arm. "No. No, you are right to say it. We need to stay focused. One step at a time."

Elliot looked at her watch. "We need to go. It's nearly seven-thirty."

Chapter 39

Marissa held Elliot back when they handed Lia to the queens to prepare for the baptism and cleansing ceremonies.

"Let go of my arm, Mar. I need to be with her," Elliot insisted.

"They will keep her safe, Elliot. You'll be able to see her most of the time from a distance, and when you can't see her, know that Julie and Phoebe are with her. We need to stay out of their way."

"I can't lose her, Mar."

"None of us can, Elliot. That's why we need to do our part to make their jobs as easy as possible."

"I'll try, Mar, but I see she's in danger, all bets are off, and I'm going in."

"Fair enough," Marissa said. "Hey, did you wish Lia a happy birthday this morning?"

"I tried, but she didn't want to hear it. She said we would celebrate her birthday tomorrow," Elliot replied.

"I like that she's looking beyond today, Elliot. That's important for all of us to do."

"I know, but it's really hard, Mar."

Marissa wrapped her arm around Elliot's shoulder. "That it is, my friend. That it is."

***

Julie led Lia into a large tent where a tub of warm water sat in the middle of the room. Candles cast a soft glow on everything in the tent. All of the queens stood on both sides of the tub, with Marie Laveau, hosted by Phoebe, on one end and Queen Thibodeaux on the other end.

Marie approached her. "Lia, dis be da head washing ceremony. It be a voodoo baptism. It be done to cleanse da heart and mind so you be open to use your power in da other ceremonies."

Lia took a step back. "Baptism?" she said.

"Yes, child," Marie replied. "You not be happy wid dat?"

Lia turned to Julie. "Julie, you know how I feel about organized religion."

"This isn't that type of baptism, Lia. It is not affiliated with any religion at all. The word baptism is used here to represent a cleansing. In the voodoo sense, it clears away bad juju and bad energy, but it does not bind you to any religion or belief system," Julie explained.

"Okay. I'm good with that."

Julie nodded as a sign they could continue.

Two of the queens placed a board across the tub containing three white candles, a citrus-based cologne water, incense, white flowers, perfume, a comb, a white cup and a white hair scarf. The three candles were lit, and the sound of drumming began in the background. Another queen lit the incense, and yet another poured the cologne water into the tub and stirred it around with her hand. Marie grabbed a handful of white flower petals and threw them into the water.

Bettina took Lia's hand and positioned her at the foot of the tub. "Remove your clothing, child, and send your most fervent wish to the Mother Goddess in the form of a prayer."

Lia cast a doubtful glance at Julie.

"It's all right," Julie said. "Lose yourself in this ritual, Lia. It will help you to release your power. Trust me. I won't allow anything to happen to you."

Lia nodded and removed her clothing. She then closed her eyes and filled her mind with thoughts of living a long life, filled with love and surrounded by Elliot and her family of choice. She then offered this wish to the universe with a promise to always do her best to be loving, caring and supportive of all those around her. When she was finished, she looked at Bettina. "I'm ready," she said.

Bettina offered her hand to Lia and assisted her in stepping into the tub. As she stood in the water, Bettina took the white cup from the tray and poured seven full cups of the water onto

Lia's head. When she was finished, she returned the cup to the tray and motioned for Lia to recline in the water. "Relax, child. Meditate, or pray for thirty minutes," Bettina said.

Julie knelt on the floor beside the tub and stood guard while the queens sat in nearby chairs. After a half-hour had passed, Lia was instructed to exit the tub and to wrap the white headscarf around her hair. She then stood once more, naked and vulnerable, to allow the air to dry her skin. When she was sufficiently dry, the queens dressed her in flowing white robes and slippers for her feet. The six pristine white feathers that Marie Laveau had left for them had been sewn around the neckline of the robe.

***

"Mar, I'm going in there. It's been more than an hour."

"Calm down, Elliot. Julie is with her. If something was wrong, she would have come to tell us," Marissa reasoned.

Just then, the flap to the tent opened and Lia emerged, escorted by Marie Laveau on her right and Bettina Thibodeaux on her left. Elliot was mesmerized.

"Oh, my God. She's beautiful," she said so only Marissa could hear.

"She looks like she's glowing," Marissa added.

Elliot moved forward with the intention of taking Lia into her arms, but she was stopped by Queen Thibodeaux.

"Stop. You cannot touch her. She has been purified, both body and soul, by the cleansing ritual. She must stay as such until our work here is done."

"What? You're telling me I can't touch my wife?" Elliot said.

"That is exactly what I'm telling you," Bettina said.

"Elliot, please do as she says. I don't want to jeopardize any part of this ritual," Lia pleaded with her from a distance.

Marissa took Elliot's arm. "Come on, El. Lia's right."

"We have one hour before the ceremony begins. Please escort Lia to the throne platform," Bettina said.

In a formal procession, the queens escorted Lia to a large, raised platform, upon which were three throne-like chairs. Lia sat in the middle one, while Marie and Bettina sat on either side of her. Several other chairs were positioned on both sides of the thrones for the kings, queens, and honored guests. Elliot, Marissa and Julie were escorted to these seats. Elliot had a clear view of Lia from her vantage point.

Lia looked across the bayou to see hundreds of followers gathered around, engaging in what looked like a party. Most had drinks in their hands, and several of them were dancing and singing to the rhythm of drumming in the distance. Nearly all of them were dressed in costumes and sported colorful face paintings reminiscent of Mardi Gras.

A very large bonfire had been started in the middle of the field, and it illuminated the entire bayou. Lia noted several vendors selling food and artifacts around the periphery of the field. The entire event felt like a celebration. She hoped that in the end, it would be a celebration of life and not of death.

Marie leaned in toward Lia so she could be heard above the din. "Child, feel da energy. Open your heart and mind to da power. You have da gifts."

"I'm afraid, Marie," Lia said.

"Dat be normal, child. We be here to protect you. Trust da spirits of your ancestors. Trust your power."

Lia's attention was suddenly drawn to Queen Thibodeaux, who stood and walked to the front of the dais. She raised her hands to the sides and the crowd became silent.

"Brothers and sisters, we gather here on this holy day to celebrate the cleansing of souls and the renewal of life. This year, we also gather to break a curse that will take the life of one of our sisters by the stroke of midnight if it cannot be stopped. This curse was placed by one of the darkest and most evil souls that has ever lived in our great city. Five generations have succumbed to this curse, and we are here tonight to stop it from destroying the sixth generation and all those who love her. We need the collective power of all believers to put an end to this curse tonight and then to banish the evil one forever. Will you join us in this fight?"

A deafening roar erupted from the crowd.

Queen Thibodeaux turned to Lia and extended her hand toward her. Lia rose to her feet and joined the queen at the front of the platform. The crowd became even louder.

The queen addressed the crowd once more. "Brothers and sisters, we will begin in one hour. Please prepare your hearts and minds to participate in this monumental task."

Queen Thibodeaux nodded in Lia's direction and they both returned to their seats. The queen looked at Lia. "How are you feeling, child?"

Lia placed her hand on her throat. "I'm so nervous I can't even swallow. Is it possible to get some water?"

"Of course, dear."

***

Elliot's leg bounced up and down with nervous energy. "Mar, it's ten o'clock. Is she seriously not going to start the curse reversal for another hour? What if we don't have time to complete it before midnight?"

"I know, El. I've been thinking the same thing, but we've got to trust they know what they're doing," Marissa replied.

"I want so much just to gather Lia into my arms and protect her until midnight. I'm not sure I can make it through two more hours of this."

"Imagine how Lia feels," Marisa said.

Elliot looked at her friend. She had no response as she absorbed the impact of Marissa's words.

***

Randy roamed through the crowd while keeping an eye on potential rabble-rousers. He had volunteered to cover the celebration in the hope of learning more about the revenant situation and the bokors who controlled them. So far, he had seen little evidence of zombie-like partygoers.

His attention was drawn to the stage when an older woman, dressed in traditional African clothing, stood and addressed the crowd. He could feel the energy of the crowd increase as she spoke of eliminating some evil influence that had cursed someone among them. His eyes nearly popped out of his head when he saw Lia join her on the stage.

What the fuck? Lia shouldn't be up there. What if some lunatic with a gun is in this crowd?

Randy suddenly felt a hand on his shoulder. He immediately went to the weapon on his hip as he swung around.

"Leslie! You scared the shit out of me!" he exclaimed.

"I'm sorry. I guess I should have announced myself. I sure hope this ceremony works," Leslie said.

"What the hell is going on here?" Randy asked.

Leslie frowned. "What do you mean?"

"We have no idea who the mistress might have jumped into. Lia shouldn't be out in the open like this."

"Elliot feels the same way, but the queen insisted on following protocol," Leslie said. "She is surrounded by all of the kings and queens up there on that stage, and Elliot is up there, too. It will take an army to get to her if Elliot has anything to say about it."

Randy looked at his watch. "It's nearly ten-thirty. If something is going to happen on her fifty-first birthday, it will need to be soon. I'm going to do my best to hover nearby and keep my eyes open for anyone suspicious."

"I'd be happy to help," Leslie said.

Randy put his hand on Leslie's shoulder. "Do what you can, but don't put yourself in danger. My biggest concern right now is someone with a gun, so keep your eyes open."

***

Ricardo Gedeon stood just a few feet away from the raised platform and watched Queen Thibodeaux make her announcement.

They will fail. They cannot defeat the curse. I will have my revenge on that whore who took everything from me.

"But mistress, what if they are successful? What then?" he whispered under his breath as though he was talking to a confidante.

Then you must kill her. She must die an agonizing and terrifying death. Do you understand?

"I understand, mistress."

He watched the queen and Lia return to their seats on the platform and exchange a few words between them. He noted Lia's body language and her expressions as she spoke to the queen.

"I know what to do," he whispered to himself.

***

At exactly eleven o'clock, Queen Thibodeaux ordered that a path be cleared between the dais and a circular area in the middle of the field that had been sectioned off within a storm fence. The circle was nearly fifty feet in diameter, with a small stage in the middle of it. A fire ring was set up near the front of the stage. In it, was wood that had been saturated with gasoline and lit on fire.

The procession of kings and queens, as well as the honored guests, escorted Lia to this area. Once inside the circle, Lia ascended the stairs and stood in the middle of the platform, while the kings, queens and honored guests positioned themselves on all four sides to act as guards against any potential threat. Elliot, Marissa and Julie stood as close as possible to the stairs so they could be the first to reach Lia if something went horribly wrong. A powerful spotlight was mounted just behind the stage and it cast a column of light straight into the sky behind Lia. The followers filled in all available space around the fenced-in circle.

Queen Laveau and Queen Thibodeaux ascended the stairs to the platform and stood, one on each side of Lia. Marie handed the box to her containing the artifacts removed from the foundation of her home.

Queen Thibodeaux walked to the center of the stage and held her hands high to silence the crowds.

"The time has come to end the curse, and to save our sister, Lia. Focus your hearts and minds on the task at hand. Send all your energy forward. We must not fail, for the consequences are death, and the unleashing of unimaginable evil. Come together as one, brothers and sisters, with love and determination in your hearts to cancel the hatred that gave this curse its power. Channel the strength of your ancestors and unite!"

The crowd roared while Queen Thibodeaux and Queen Laveau left the stage and joined the circle of kings and queens surrounding the platform.

The kings and queens turned around to face the stage and joined hands. Queen Thibodeaux led the chant. The kings and queens, as well as the crowd around them repeated each line.

I lift this curse on the heads of innocents,
So wrongly punished for the sins of others.
I end the wrongful deaths of generations
Condemned simply for being born.

The evil one has taken what was not rightfully hers.
She has taken the lives of innocents.
She has tortured and killed so many of our own.
And through this curse, she has taken the lives
Of generations who did not deserve to die.
They have died painful and undignified deaths.
The deaths must stop here.
The deaths must stop now.

Queen Thibodeaux paused and nodded at Lia.

Lia stepped forward and stood behind the burning fire ring.

"This box contains artifacts belonging to two innocent children," she said. "Children, whose lives were cut short by the evil mistress who tortured and killed their parents. Children, whose lives were profoundly affected by the black and evil heart that killed generations of their descendants. They were my people...my family, and now, she comes for me. Please help me to stop her before the stroke of midnight, for if not, she will win, and her evil will know no bounds."

Lia raised the box she was holding high into the air, and in a loud and clear voice, she continued the chant, allowing the crowd to repeat after her.

I offer these artifacts to the higher power
In hope of breaking the dreadful curse
That took the lives of my family.
I call on our ancestors to lend their power
To end this curse forever.
To end the killing.
To end the death of innocents.
I ask this with love in my heart.
I ask this with hope that I will see another day.
May love and hope overrule hatred,
And end this curse forever,
On this—the day I become fifty and one.

Lia opened the box and reached inside to remove the artifacts and the documents, which she dropped one by one into the fire ring. Finally, she emptied the graveyard dirt onto the stage and then placed the box into the fire as well. A cloud of sparks rose above it and the air crackled with the sound of burning wood. She turned to the crowd once more.

"I have placed the artifacts of the innocent children into the fire, along with two documents that belonged to the evil one responsible for this curse. It is with high hopes that with your support, and by destroying the artifacts, it will break the hold she had on my people. May their spirits forever be free, and may I live to see another day."

Lia stepped back and watched the box burn just as the clock tower in a nearby church chimed the countdown to midnight. The entire assembly fell silent.

Elliot watched helplessly from her position on the ground. She held her breath and squeezed Marissa and Julie's hands tightly as the clock tower chimed...six, seven, eight.

As the clock continued to chime, a surge of fire, nearly as tall as Lia, rose from the fire ring. Lia stumbled several feet back as chaos erupted around her.

***

Do something!

As the clock counted down, Ricardo Gedeon raised his hands out to his sides. "Revenants! Kill her!" he shouted.

At his command, several dozen revenants pushed their way through the crowds and broke down the storm fence. The bystanders were generally afraid of the zombie-like beings and backed away from them as fast as they could. Unfortunately, this served only to clear a path for them to descend on Lia. A few were brave enough to intervene, but their efforts were largely ineffective. Most of them continued toward the stage at a steady pace, with one sole purpose—to kill Lia Purvis.

***

The kings and queens valiantly attempted to stop the revenants from ascending the steps, however, in a drug-induced state, the revenants were single-mindedly determined not to allow anything in their path to stop them, and soon the kings and queens were lying on the ground after being violently pushed away.

***

Elliot was momentarily immobilized by fear and confusion as the revenants approached the stairs. From her vantage point, she couldn't tell if Lia had survived the stroke of midnight. She had somehow lost contact with Marissa and Julie, so she was on her own to fight her way through the crowd of revenants that seemed to be closing in on the stage. She stood in their way, but she was no match against the horde of creatures.

"Lia!" she called after she had been shoved aside and thrown to the ground.

***

Lia stood in the middle of the stage and looked around wildly. Everything seemed to be moving in slow motion. A flood of bodies flowed onto the stage from the stairs—each with a blank look in their eyes and determination in their strides. She realized she had nowhere to go as the revenants closed in around her.

Lia suddenly felt light-headed and fought to maintain consciousness.

Am I dying? she thought. *Did we not break the curse after all?*

She grabbed her head in an attempt to maintain control of her consciousness.

Dey will kill you if you don't stop dem! A voice in her head said.

Within moments, they were on top of her, grabbing for her clothing and her hair. All she could do was to protect her head by crossing her arms in front of her face. She felt like she was on the edge of losing the contents of her stomach as well as her consciousness.

Suddenly, she heard the voice again, and this time, she recognized it as Celeste. *Use your gifts, child.*

"My gifts?" Lia whispered. Lia closed her eyes and summoned all the strength and energy she could muster. When she felt like she would burst at the seams, she opened her eyes and raised her arms out to the sides. "Stop!" she screamed.

All movement ceased, and to Lia, it seemed as though time stood still. A pain shot through her head, so intense that she could barely keep her eyes open. She felt lightheaded and unsteady on her feet, but she was conscious enough to see the crowd of revenants standing within inches of her—close enough to feel their breath on her skin. There were dozens of them—just waiting and staring at her with vacant eyes.

Her head nearly fell onto her shoulders as she struggled to remain upright. "Sleep," she said softly.

Like dominoes, the revenants fell in concentric rings around her.

Lia's vision became cloudy and her hearing impaired, and on the stroke of twelve, she crumbled on top of the bodies surrounding her.

***

Elliot fought her way to the stairs. Fear tore at her heart when she saw the revenants move toward the stage while pushing aside all those who stood in their way. She grabbed the arm of one revenant who had reached the bottom of the stairs.

"No! Stay away from her, you son of a bitch!"

Elliot slammed into the railing on the stairs when the revenant powerfully shook her off and continued to move forward. She fell onto the stairs and was nearly trampled as she strove to catch her breath and regain her footing.

Elliot soon realized that the fastest way to reach Lia was to simply move with the flow of revenants rather than trying to get ahead of them. They seemed oblivious to her presence unless she tried to detain them. The roar of the crowd around them was deafening and she knew Lia couldn't possibly hear her repeatedly call her name above the din.

Elliot was unable to see Lia behind the sea of mindless bodies. All she could do was move forward in unison with them and hope she could reach Lia before they could kill her. She had no idea how she would fight them off, but she knew she would die trying.

She stopped moving when the revenants crumpled around her.

What the hell is happening? God, please let her be okay, she begged silently.

One by one, the revenants fell to the stage, and she could finally see the vision before her. Lia stood in the center of the stage with the bright spotlight shining upward, right behind her. Her arms were outstretched, and her head was tilted back as though looking into the heavens.

"You're alive! Lia, you're alive!" Elliot shouted and then continued to move toward her.

Lia turned her gaze toward Elliot as the clock struck twelve. Just as Elliot reached her, her eyes rolled back into her head, and she collapsed into Elliot's arms.

***

Queen Thibodeaux gathered the kings and queens together. Some had to be helped up from the ground after being attacked by the revenants. "Quickly! We must gather near the bonfire while the energy is still high."

"Lia need our help," Marie said.

"If we don't banish the evil one, she will never stop haunting Lia, dead or alive. We must do this, and we must do this quickly," Bettina said.

The entire assembly of kings and queens stood hand in hand in front of the bonfire while the sounds of the crowd raged behind them. Several of them glanced over their shoulders while Bettina attempted to organize the group.

"I know you are concerned about Lia, but we must focus on the task before us," Queen Thibodeaux said.

Once she had their attention, she began.

Bettina walked toward the bonfire and stood holding the package with the baby doll and documents found in the fireplace compartment in Lia and Elliot's home. She held the package high above her head.

"We call on the higher power to banish forever, the soul of the evil one who has wreaked havoc on your children for so long. While she walked the earth, she tortured and killed your children, and in death, she has cursed six generations of innocents, taking life after life. Together with my brothers and sisters, we are here to lend our hearts and voices to this plea.

May her soul be banished into nothingness.
May her powers be removed.
May her evil be rendered harmless to those living and
dead.
May there be no redemption for her wicked soul.
May she never return to haunt nor harm another being.
So be it in the name of our lord.

Queen Thibodeaux threw the package into the fire, and watched it burn to ash.

An explosion of light and fire erupted from the bonfire, shooting flames and dark smoke high into the air.

At that moment, Phoebe, as Marie, crumpled and fell unconscious to the ground.

***

Just after the stroke of midnight, Randy rushed Ricardo Gedeon and tackled him to the ground. He turned him, straddled his legs and grabbed the front of his shirt.

"What have you done? What have you done?" Randy shouted into his face.

"Go to hell," Gedeon said.

Randy landed a punch on his jaw. "There's more where that came from if you don't tell me what you did!"

Before Gedeon could reply, his body convulsed violently enough to throw Randy off. He seized for a moment or two and then went limp as a dark mist rose from his chest and dissolved into the air.

Randy quickly climbed to his feet and rolled Gedeon onto his stomach so he could cuff his hands behind him. He pulled him to his feet and once again, grasped two handfuls of his shirt. "Last chance. Tell me what you did to her."

***

"Lia, speak to me." Elliot shook her. "Lia, please open your eyes."

Elliot felt for a pulse but found none. "No! Don't you dare leave me!" she shouted. She lowered her cheek to Lia's mouth and felt no air coming from her lungs.

Elliot rolled one of the revenants out of the way and placed Lia on her back. "She's not breathing!" Elliot yelled. "Somebody help me! She's not breathing! Somebody please help me!"

Randy was the first one to reach her.

"Randy, she's not breathing, and I can't find a pulse," Elliot said frantically.

Randy immediately called for an ambulance as Elliot began CPR.

"Come on, Lia. Breathe, damn it! Breathe!" Elliot shouted while she compressed Lia's chest and breathed for her.

With the revenants incapacitated, the crowd congregated on the small stage and offered their support to Elliot and Randy in their effort to revive Lia. There were so many people on the stage that they crowded Randy and Elliot and inhibited their efforts.

Randy stood and addressed the crowd. "Please back up. We need room to work here."

Before Randy could say another word, the stage beneath them moved.

"Shit!" Randy screamed. "Off the stage! Get off the stage," he yelled.

"What's happening, Randy?" Elliot screamed while she continued compressions.

"The stage is collapsing. Get off the stage!" He shouted again to the crowd—to no avail as the stage disintegrated beneath them.

Epilogue

"All right, everyone. You know the drill. Hold hands and don't open your eyes until we've made contact." Phoebe looked at all of her friends sitting around the table in Julie and Marisa's dining room. "We've all been through some pretty traumatic experiences the past few weeks. This is our chance for closure."

Phoebe closed her eyes.

"We call forth, all those who have succumbed to the curse of the evil one throughout the many generations in the family of Lia Purvis. We seek closure, and we seek confirmation that our actions were rightfully just in the midst of all that has been lost. Please grace us with your presence."

Randy's chin suddenly dropped to his chest. He lifted his head and looked around the table. "Who you all be?" he asked.

"Let me ask you the same question. What is your name?" Phoebe replied.

"I be Ethan Roberts."

"Welcome, Ethan. If Leslie got your genealogy correct, you are Lia's great-great-great grandfather," Phoebe said.

"Yes. Dat be true."

"Ethan, does mama know you be here?"

All heads turned to Susan. Leslie's eyes were a big as saucers as he continued to hold her hand.

"Lia Bourdeau?" Phoebe asked.

"Dat be me." She looked at Elliot. "El-ee-ot. I's remembers you."

Elliot smiled. "Nice to see you again, Miss Thing."

Phoebe looked around the table. "Are there others who would like to come forward?" she asked.

Leslie's head dropped back. "My name is Charles. I be Lia's great-great granddaddy. Can I ask why you called us here?"

"We will get to that in a moment, Charles," Phoebe said. "Anyone else?"

Julie's, Marissa's and Elliot's heads all fell back at the same time. Marisa was the first to respond. "I'm James Robert, Lia's great-grandfather."

"I'm Maria Roberts, Lia's grandmother. Hi, Daddy," she said to James. These words were spoken through Elliot's voice.

Phoebe looked at Julie. "And you are?" she asked.

"I'm Liz—Lia's mother."

"Mama?" Lia said. "Mama, is that really you?"

"Yes, sweetling. It's really me."

"Mama, I miss you and Daddy so much," Lia said with a voice heavy with emotion.

"We miss you, too, sweetheart. We have been watching you these past several years, and we are so very proud of you."

"What is this all about?" Charles asked again.

"We've called you all here to understand how you died. Some of you may be aware that we have recently expelled the evil that started your chain of deaths—beginning with you, Lia," Phoebe said.

"Da mistress have a black heart. She never like me. She treat mama and papa bad. Real bad. She kilt dem, and she kilt me."

Lia leaned forward. "Yes, Lia. We know. Sweetheart, I'm so sorry for what she put you through—for what she put all of you through."

"I didn't know da woman," Ethan said.

"No, you didn't. Your grandmother sent you away when you were just a baby to save you from her." Lia looked around the table. "None of you knew her except Lia, but she affected each and every one of you and your families as well."

"How she do dat?" Ethan asked.

"She put a curse on our family, Ethan. A curse designed to kill everyone in the direct line of Celeste Bordeau."

"What demon do dat?" Ethan asked.

"Demon is a good description. You see, Celeste and Lia were slaves in the mistress' home, and she treated them poorly, along with dozens of other slaves. The master of the house took Celeste and she bore him a child. That child is you, Lia. The mistress resented your birth and cast a spell on the entire family for it. That curse doomed each of us to die on our fifty-first birthdays."

"Da master force himself on me!"

Lia's attention suddenly swung to Phoebe. "Celeste?" she said.

"I be here, child." Celeste looked around the table and wept.

"Mama, don't cry," little Lia said.

"I's can't help it, child. All my babies be here. Dey all be here."

Lia's eyes filled with tears. "Celeste, look around you. Your entire family is here."

"Yes, dey all be here. I's don't know how I thank you," Celeste said.

"No thanks necessary, Celeste. It all started with you. None of us would be here today without you. My only regret is that all your lives were cut so short. The mistress intended that each death would look like an accident, but the fact that they all occurred on your fifty-first birthdays cannot be explained by coincidence."

"Won't no accident," James said.

"I'm sorry, James," What did you say?" Lia asked.

"Won't no accident. I was pushed off that building."

"The man who robbed me could have taken my money and ran, but he chose to kill me instead," Maria said. "That was no accident either."

"I was stabbed. That ain't nothin' I could do by accident," Charles added.

"I be poisoned. Dat be no accident either," Ethan added.

"But sweetheart," Liz said. "You turned fifty-one nearly two weeks ago. How did you escape?"

"Mama, I was lucky enough to be surrounded by the most amazing wife and friends a girl could ever ask for. I wouldn't be here today if it wasn't for them. My friend Leslie is a genealogist. He discovered that all of you died at age fifty-one. Phoebe is a mystic and medium. Between her and Julie, they worked with the voodoo queens and kings to break the curse and banish the mistress. Marissa provided the strength we all needed to get through this. And Elliot...well, Elliot is my heart. I would die without her.

"So many things had to come together at just the right time. I believe that everything happened just to get us to this point. I truly believe the universe conspired to bring Elliot and me to New Orleans so we could rid the world of the mistress' evil heart, and so that we could be here today with all of you."

"You done good, girl," James said.

"We's all free now," Ethan said.

"Sweetheart, it's time to put all of this behind you and live your life to the fullest. You have so much life ahead of you. Know that I love you and I'll be watching out for you. Dad is watching you, too," Liz added.

"Thank you, Mama."

"I go now, girl," Charles informed her. "I'm proud to be your kin."

One by one, the goodbyes were made and soon, the eight friends returned to themselves. For several more minutes, they continued to hold hands in an unending circle of love and support.

"I don't know how to thank all of you for making that possible," Lia said.

"Today would not have been possible at all if it wasn't for everyone in this room," Elliot added. "We could be holding a funeral service instead of a celebration of Lia's family."

"We all had a part to play," Phoebe said. "In the end, the curse has been broken and the mistress banished forever. I wish Marie could have been here to celebrate with us today, but the banishment took a lot out of her. It takes a huge amount of energy for a spirt to manifest on our plane, and the fact that she possessed me for nearly an entire day significantly depleted her. It will take time for her to recover."

"Is that why you fainted after the queen banished the mistress?" Leslie asked. "That scared the bejesus out of me! I couldn't get to you fast enough."

Phoebe squeezed Leslie's hand. "Yes. Thank you for being my protector, love."

"Randy, how did you know Lia wasn't really dead?" Marissa asked.

"At the celebration, I ran into the bokor I had encountered a couple of days earlier and let's just say I was able to convince him to cooperate. It turns out that he had someone slip a mixture into Lia's water that contains the same neurotoxin used to create the revenants. It slows the heart rate and respiration down to the point that it simulates death."

"How did you know he was the one responsible?" Julie asked.

"I saw him summoning the revenants just before they attacked Lia."

"Why on earth would he slip something like that into her water?" Julie asked.

"I'm thinking it was an insurance policy," Randy said.

"What do you mean by that?" Phoebe asked.

"When I went into the shop, and you said you believed the mistress had jumped from me to someone else. It got me thinking about who that might have been. He seemed like the logical choice, both because I had just seen him earlier that day, and by choosing him, the mistress gained access to a whole army of revenants that could be used if you had been successful in breaking the curse—which it turns out, you were."

"Plan B," Elliot said.

"Yes," Randy replied. "If the revenants failed to kill her, Lia would have actually been declared dead because of the neurotoxins. She might have been embalmed when she was still alive, or she might have been cremated. Either way, the mistress would win."

"Jesus, Randy. You're giving me the creeps," Leslie said.

"This could have turned out so much worse," Phoebe added. "It was quick thinking to give Lia the salt, Randy."

"I only did what you told me to do," Randy replied.

"I thought we were all goners when the stage collapsed," Elliot said.

"I'm guessing that is how Lia would have died if we had failed to break the curse," Marissa added.

"I agree with you, Marissa," Randy said. "I found out that the bokor I arrested for spiking Lia's water with zombie-juice also owns the construction company that built the stage. I don't think it was an accident that it collapsed—even if it *was* after midnight."

"I'm thankful that we survived with only minor injuries," Lia said.

"The revenants sort of cushioned our fall," Elliot said. "But at least no one was killed."

"Well, I think things turned out just the way they were supposed to," Julie said. "We have all survived and we are together. It doesn't get any better than that."

Lia stood. "This calls for a celebration...a celebration of life, love and friendship, and finally, a celebration of my fifty-first birthday. I'm looking forward to celebrating my fifty and one instead of dreading it. What do you say we order up some pizza, make a run for wine and spirits, and spend the night dancing, playing games and celebrating life?"

"I will agree to that on one condition," Julie said.

"And that is?"

"If we play Twister, I get to be the spinner!"

THE END

Photo Credit: Song of Myself Photography

See Karen's author page at www.karendbadger.com

About the Author

Karen D. Badger is the award-winning author of eighteen novels, all of which have been released by Badger Bliss Books, which Karen co-owns with her wife Barbara Sawyer, aka Bliss.

Born and raised in Vermont, Karen is the second of five children raised by a fiercely independent mother, who remains one of her best friends. Karen earned her B.A. in 1978 in Theater and in Elementary Education, and in 1994, earned a B.S. in mathematics. In addition to her novels, Karen is the author of more than two dozen technical papers and journal articles on photomask manufacturing, which she has published and has presented at numerous semiconductor industry conferences. She is also the holder of several technical patents. Karen is currently in her forty-third year as a principal member of the technical staff with a prominent semiconductor manufacturer in Vermont.

Karen and her wife, Barb, a retired Lt. Colonel, U.S. Air Force, live in the beautiful state of Vermont. They spend their spare time with family as well as doing home improvement projects on both their homes in Vermont and New Mexico. They enjoy camping, kayaking, motorcycling and singing karaoke.

Please take a moment to visit Karen's author website at www.karendbadger.com, or the Badger Bliss Books website at www.badgerblissbooks.com. Also like us on Facebook!

Karen Badger is part of iReadIndies, a collective of self-published, independent authors of women loving women (WLW) literature. Please visit our website at *iReadIndies.com* for more information and to find links to the books published by all our authors!

TITLES BY KAREN D. BADGER
Published by: Badger Bliss Books
www.badgerblissbooks.com

In order of Publication Date:

On A Wing and A Prayer
Published Sept, 2005, ISBN 13: 978-1-945761-01-0

Yesterday Once More
Published July, 2008, ISBN 13: 978-1-945761-02-7
2009 Golden Crown Literary Society Award - Speculative Fiction

In A Family Way – Book One of the Commitment Series
Published March, 2010, ISBN 13: 978-1-945761-05-8

Unchained Memories – Book Two of the Commitment Series
Published Oct, 2011, ISBN 13: 978-1-945761-06-5

Happy Campers - Book Three of the Commitment Series
Published Sept, 2013, ISBN 13: 978-1-945761-07-2

The Blue Feather
Published July, 2014, ISBN 13: 978-1-945761-04-1

Collective Identity – Book Four of the Commitment Series
Published January, 2015, ISBN 13: 978-1-945761-08-9

All My Tomorrows – Sequel to Yesterday Once More
Published May, 2015, ISBN 13: 978-1-945761-03-4

Sweet Angel – Book Five of the Commitment Series
Published June, 2015, ISBN 13: 978-1-945761-09-6

Relative-ly Speaking – Book Six of the Commitment Series
Published March, 2016, ISBN 13: 978-1-945761-10-2

1140 Rue Royale
Published Sept, 2016, ISBN 13: 978-1-945761-00-3
2017 Golden Crown Literary Society Award – Paranormal Fiction

Tailspin- Book Seven of the Commitment Series
Published December, 2017, ISBN 13: 978-1-945761-22-5

Flashpoint – Book Eight of the Commitment Series
Published December, 2018, ISBN 13: 978-1-945761-24-9

Over The Crescent Moon
Published June, 2019, ISBN 13: 978-1-945761-26-3
2019 LesFic Bard Award – Historical and Action/Adventure

In the Blink of an Eye – A Young Adult Novel – Book Nine of the Commitment Series
Published December, 2019, ISBN 13: 978-1-945761-28-7
2019 LesFic Bard Award Finalist – Young Adult

A Shadow in Love
Published January, 2021, ISBN 13: 978-1-945761-32-4

Udder Nonsense – Book Ten of the Commitment Series
Published June, 2021, ISBN 13: 978-1-945761-34-8

The Fifty and One – The Continuation of 1140 Rue Royale
Published August, 2021, ISBN 13: 978-1-945761-36-2

www.ingramcontent.com/pod-product-compliance
Lightning Source LLC
Chambersburg PA
CBHW051436260626
47162CB00001B/123